KAMA PUKA

The Isle of Delights

A Novel by
Aimen Klimmeron

Translated by
Katherine Chapman & János Untener

Strategic Book Publishing and Rights Co.

Strategic Book Publishing and Rights Co.
12620 FM 1960, Suite A4-507
Houston TX 77065
www.sbpra.com

ISBN: 978-1-62212-208-0

...to the Eternal Master

Contents

FIRST PART   7

1. A prophecy   9
2. Lion cub   20
3. Roses and thorns   29
4. Sonata   48
5. Carina Dahl   63
6. Realithéâtre   80
7. Danse macabre   101
8. La Gitanilla   134
9. Love Art   162
10. "Escucha tu corazón!"   183

SECOND PART   205

11. The seed matters   207
12. To be a woman…   224
13. Lessons   242
14. Power of the snake   259
15. Gifts   276
16. Kaula   288
17. Dream and reality   311
18. Play   331
19. LIFE with capital letters   340
20. Triangle in the circle   350

Contents

21. Message from the past   357

22. An old acquaintance…   364

23. Behind the black door   371

24. Roots deepening in the past   380

25 Chakra Puja   387

26. "As above, so below…"   393

27. Together   401

FIRST PART

"Of the book of God
Thou art a copying,
A mirror, wherein showed
The beauty of the King.
All God ever wrought
Dwelleth not apart;
All thou hast ever sought,
Find it in thy heart."

Rumi

1. A prophecy

I cried my presence into the world in the February of 1967. On a starless, foggy night. My father, Thorwald Falkenberg, a descendant of noble ancestors, leapt for joy in the corridor of the maternity ward when he was told the Almighty had presented him with a boy. Had he been a God-fearing man, he would have certainly pleased the barrel-bellied priest of Amiralitetskyrkam with a substantial donation, but my father was an incurable atheist. He just kept shouting: VICTORY!!! VIC-TOR-YYY! After three unsuccessful attempts – that had resulted in three daughters – a son at last! In his mind's eye he already saw me on the command bridge of a military cruiser, wearing a decorated uniform, proudly throwing out my chest under the weight of medals and roaring spirited commands.

Yes, my father was a military man. A man of resolution with a fighting spirit. He served in the navy and beat the drums of the Karlskrona unit's orchestra with unparalleled patriotic self-sacrifice. He "played the kettledrum and the brass triangle as well as other percussion instruments," he used to boast. This activity of his proved to be of invaluable benefit to me since he was able to give full vent to his mildly aggressive, combative nature while bashing his drums. So he never beat me. I was grateful for this favour of Fate, especially when I thought about the boy next door. His father was a tailor, an admirable and just man. As he had nothing to beat during his work, he set about his son every day. And his wife too, on special occasions. Driven by manly courage, he paid no heed to the Swedish government's decree prohibiting physical punishment of its underage subjects – a law that incurred serious penalties if violated. With similar bravery, he ignored the threats of his wife, who was under the spell of feminism, an 'epidemic' that was growing to national dimensions in that period.

That was when I came to the conclusion that politicians were hopeless. My experience strengthened my conviction that it would be much more effective if, instead of these laws that were flouted by everybody, there were courses teaching percussion instruments for all those parents whose work did not allow them to live out their latent aggressive tendencies.

My father was determined to mould me into a soldier by hook or by crook. I was only about five when he dragged me through the military forts of the city for the first time. He told me stories about great battles and glorious victories with an almost religious awe. I remember standing at the rail of the watchtower with torrents of historical data flooding past me, but little of it actually reaching my ears. I gazed at the sea – there was a stunning view from up there. It was a completely different feeling watching this vast expanse of water from up there than from a child's view at sea level. A flock of swans was swimming about not far from the shore. I kept wondering why they had to float around in that icy water. Poor creatures... Who made them to do that? I felt a deep compassion for them. My short life's most bitter moments came into my mind, when in the mornings my father tore the warm blanket off me, ripping me out of my sweet dreams, made me do exercises and then forced me to wash myself from head to toe in stone cold water. I was less than five years old, but I already felt intense repugnance towards waking up early and cold water. "The tower was built in 1857 for the troops in charge of the harbour's defence..." Snippets of my father's words burst into my consciousness from somewhere far, far away.

Although the mute and mossy stones that stood as memorial to glorious battles of the past did awaken a kind of mystical feeling in me, it was not enough to rouse the soldierly spirit of my ancestors – as should have happened according to my father's expectations. Neither the darkly oiled cannons nor the brightly polished swords in the Naval Museum left me impressed. Only the long military tunnel appealed to me that once, long ago, had been a traffic channel between the harbour and the train station. I loved it – in summertime you could ride from one end all the way to the other on a pedalled truck!

A few years later, during the Jules Verne period of my childhood, I studied with different eyes and with greater interest the fully equipped ship museum, the Jarramas. Its hand-mast reached for the heavens loftily even after its retirement. Nevertheless, even back then it was travelling, the open air and the endless skies of the sea that lured me most, not the perspective of naval battles.

When my father took me on my first journey of discovery, I was certainly too immature for that kind of initiation. In those days I was only interested in girls, oh yes, and musical instruments. I loved every moment of the orchestra's rehearsals Dad took me to. While the musicians smoked or played cards in the corridor during breaks, I had the chance to blow into the trumpet, ride in the saddle of the double bass lying on the ground, or hide in the huge funnel of the tuba. That was my favourite. Once the ancient tuba player saw me and, with a mischievous smile creeping under his moustache, he sneaked over and growled into it. I tried to jump out in my alarm, but changed my mind. I noticed that sound waves entwining and encircling my body filled me with a pleasant tingling feeling. From that moment onwards the tuba game rose to the top of the list of my innocent joys of life, overtaking ice creams and roller-skating. I loved that buzzing feeling – and the other one that overran me when, after the break, the conductor's baton swung upwards and its waves set the band in motion. I used to lie down under the piano, my eyes closing unconsciously. Soon I would feel my body floating on the surface of a silently heaving sea. It was similar to the thrill I experienced in the tuba. Yet it was different somehow: tender and enchanting. Waves swept me away to bright, dizzy heights, sometimes dropping me slowly into swirling depths.

I loved music. In this the apple did not fall far from the tree – but we were miles apart in every other respect. For example, while he honoured order and iron discipline, every bone in my body and soul rejected them. Unfortunately my father was the commander at home. To my great distress all my toys had be arranged in perfect military order on the shelves at all times, pencils in their boxes, shoes polished bright and standing to attention in the hall.

Sometimes, defying paternal pressure, I left the room in artistic disarray giving my spirit some malicious satisfaction. This caused real pain to my father. On those occasions, stifling his anger, but still in a trembling voice, he presented the necessity of keeping order and discipline as the most sacred of all moral requirements.

"My dear son, I cannot understand how on earth you can live in this mess. How can you even breathe in this veritable Babel? Shirts crumpled under the chair, one sock on the table, the other on the bookshelf. And it looks as if you used a pitchfork to throw the books onto the shelf. If I move one, all the others will pour down. Your pencils are strewn all over the floor, the desktop is covered in glue, and what is this?! Leftovers of yesterday's chicken on a plate in the middle of your bed! How many times do I have to tell you WE-DO-NOT-EAT in the bedroom?" He became more and more wound up. "Look what a disgusting mess you live in! Look around yourself! You see? DO YOU LIKE IT?!"

I looked around me, saw, and, to be honest, I liked it... The mess radiated a kind of intimacy – it was *my* mess. It meant a kind of order to me. I just could not imagine why on earth he was so upset about it. Why was order solely associated with books tightly arranged on the shelves, clothes in the wardrobe, pencils in boxes and plates in the kitchen? Why couldn't you we arrange things some other way? I was disheartened by my father's taste with its straight lines and impersonal military precision, but at such times I did not resist. I lowered my head repentantly and simulated deep contrition while listening to the second act of his stormy lecture. One that went along familiar lines and sounded something like this:

"I've explained it to you so many times. When on earth will you understand there is no peaceful and well-balanced life without order and discipline? Things need to be carefully calculated, well planned and properly executed. This is the only way to avoid unpleasant surprises."

(And pleasant ones too, I thought to myself.) "Just imagine what would happen if cars on the streets and people and all the other vehicles went whichever way they pleased without rules and regulations?"

Well, that certainly would be terrible, I agreed, remembering how much I liked walking across the road when the lights were red. And it would be so much fun to slalom between honking cars to the other side of the road!

"Or the planets. What would happen if they wandered erratically without any system or rule? Can you imagine the Earth venturing close to the Sun just because it feels like it? Do you have any idea what would happen then?"

I nodded.

"You see? Life is exactly the same. People need rules to follow their own path without any disturbance. That is why rules and discipline exist. Do you understand at last, son?"

I understood. It was he who did not understand that this was different than "cars, people and all the other vehicles". Yet I could not find words to explain it. That was his religion, and he believed in it blindly.

My poor father. He really only meant it for the good, but his methods were horrible. He was totally unable to play. Maybe if he'd tried to teach me order in a playful manner, he might have had some luck. But this way, instead of liking it, I started to hate it even more. Mum was different. She was pure in spirit, affectionate, intuitive and fairly quiet. She believed in God and dreams. Although she never raised her voice to show what she wanted like my father did, she still always managed to guide things according to her own intuition.

In spite of all their arguments – or maybe because of all their arguments – they were very attached to each other. My father's headstrong, masculine character impressed my mother's sensitive feminine ways, and at the same time it provided a pillar to her flighty imagination. She often scolded my father for his obstinacy but her rebukes were only the visible manifestations of a secret loving duel. There was never any real anger or hurtful intention in them.

Seemingly it was my mother who gave in during their discussions about religion. My father categorically refused to let her "fill the children's heads with superstitious mumbo jumbo" but life had the eccentricity to prove my mother right.

One time my father's unit was commanded on drill. Though it was not mandatory for the musicians my father started to prepare feverishly a week before. Every day he went on and on about the preparations, his cheeks flushed with excitement every time he talked about it. He washed his kit bag, and his clothes were ready three days before departure. He was like a child waiting for Father Christmas – he even counted down the days in his excitement. Two days before he left Mum had a bizarre dream. We were sitting at breakfast when she let it out. Her face was white as a sheet, and her quavering voice revealed her deep agitation. She was struggling to find the right words.

"I don't really know how to tell you... I know you don't believe in these things... but last night I had a very strange dream."

"Dinner must have sat heavily on your stomach," chimed in my father with a wide smile, but Mum was not in a joking mood. She continued resolutely.

"You were riding a big black horse and you were wearing a long white robe. You were facing me, but your eyes were closed. I spoke to you but got no response. Then the horse turned around and started to walk away. It wasn't trotting. It was rather floating or flying in the air. You got further and further away. I cried out after you desperately, but you didn't look back. I didn't see your face again. I broke into sobs and heard a choir of angels singing. I woke up and my pillow was wet with tears. It was such a relief to see you breathing near me and that I could hug you. But I still could not calm down. I felt a strange pain in my heart."

"Don't worry, it will pass," he caressed her cheeks trying to soothe her.

"I don't want you to go on the drill. You don't even have to be there."

"You're talking nonsense, Anelie."

"I knew you wouldn't take me seriously. Just this one time, could you do that for me? You know I never ask you to do anything."

"Ask for anything else, my dear Anelie, and I will do it. But not this. I can't just give this up."

Mum spoke no more, but her silence troubled me more than her words. The next day she hugged the love of her life long and passionately before he left. Her eyes filled with tears.

"Promise me you'll really take care of yourself," she whispered.

"Of course I will. I always do."

"And take this with you," she added in a fading voice and slipped something into his palm.

"What is that?" A tiny golden cross shone in my father's hand.

"Please do not deny me that too," said my mother below her breath but in a tone that made me shiver from head to toe.

"All right then, just for you. You know I don't believe in these superstitions."

I saw my father two days later. He was lying in the emergency room of the military hospital. His right leg was in plaster from toe to upper leg, and he was cursing bitterly.

"To hell with all those inept, half-arsed people! Now I will be bedridden for months and, on top of it all, I missed the drill. Damn it." He did not want to tell us exactly what had happened.

Eventually a colleague of his revealed the scene to us.

"So, we were busy loading crates onto the ship. We were passing them to each other. The sergeant was in the boat below us supervising. Then the soldier standing beside the rail grabbed a crate clumsily, and it fell right back into the boat. Our blood froze at the sight. If the sergeant hadn't jumped back so quickly, the crate would certainly have crushed his skull. So that's why only his thigh bone is broken."

The story really troubled me – and my sisters who were also listening in stunned silence. Only Mum was happy and grateful to the Heavens. Bones will always heal – but her other half was alive.

"You see, son," lectured my father later when he was able to walk with crutches, "this is what I keep telling you: the most important thing in life is to do your work precisely and with full attention. That way you can avoid unpleasant surprises."

That was the only thing he concluded from the incident. My questions remained unanswered though. My father would have never admitted it openly that Mum's dream had anything to do with his accident but, from that moment on, some part of his steel conviction seemed to have shattered. He paid more attention to her opinion and had no more objections when she took us to church at times.

❖

There was another member of my large family who played an important role, not only in my childhood, but also in the following years: my maternal grandfather, Marten Lindenholm. Our first significant encounter took place when I was four months old. After lengthy arguments Mum at last won my father's consent to baptize me. After my first visit to church, my mother laid tables for the guests assembling in my honour in our little garden. She put me on a blanket and freed me of my nappy "so the sun will shine upon the tummy of my little bear". I threw my arms and legs in the air, kicking and babbling in delight – I was sincerely devoted to nudism from my early years. Then I suddenly became silent and stopped kicking. Everybody looked at me stunned that my little soldier was pointed in a direction rather unusual at such an early age. Then they watched the colourless ray of the distilled mother's milk flying into my face in a perfect arch. They stared perplexed until the last drops reached their destination.

Then my grandfather ran over to me, grabbed me, smacked a big kiss on my belly button then he lifted me up triumphantly and cried out in joy:

"I am telling you, when this chap grows up he will be a legendary fuc..."

"Shut up you old goat! That's the only thing you ever think about!" My grandmother rebuked him and anxiously took me out of his hands.

"You will see," my grandfather murmured to himself, and withdrew to enjoy the company of a pint.

From that moment on he enclosed me in his heart, and I won the place of 'best grandson'. When Mum fettered me in my nappy and laid me back into my barred cot, my grandfather started to grumble again.

"How can you keep that child in this ugly prison? Soon his Grandpa will carve him a real crib, one befitting Marten Lindenholm's grandson."

He did not seem to mind the fact that my all sisters had grown up behind the very same bars. He had different plans for me.

It took a mere three days for the crib to be ready. With its graceful arches it seemed like a Viking ship and he even carved an authentic decoration on its prow: a mermaid with wondering eyes, long hair and plump breasts. She was naked, of course. Mermaids are just like this. Always naked.

❖

My grandfather was a fisherman through and through; he worshipped freedom and the sea and was passionate about his work, though it got harder and harder every day to make a living from it. He and my grandma lived in a little hamlet near the sea. He had a strong aversion to the city. Not even Grandma's persistent supplications could convince him to choose a more fashionable trade. And he was a master of all trades, a born handyman. There was nothing he could not turn his hand to – from making boats and building houses to turning wood and repairing washing machines. They often invited him to work at the shipbuilding yard and offered him a decent salary, but he was just not interested. The sea attracted him like the light of tornado lamps attracts moths. That is where he felt at home, in the empire of the whistling wind where life and death encounter each other, dancing atop high waves lashed into fury. Now and then he took me with him. I can still recall him standing in the rocking boat singing at the top of his voice. His shirt unbuttoned down to his navel flapping wildly in the wind, the coppery light of the setting sun glittering on the sweat drops making their way through the silvery hair of his chest. His voice broke through the roar of the sea and rose to towering heights like a wild invocation to our ancestors' pagan gods whom he believed in.

His longing for freedom grew to paroxysmal dimensions in other aspects of his life too. He had a boundless sexual appetite that young brides and attractive widows of local fishing villages could take delight in for periods varying in length – each according to their own merit. After these amorous excursions, he made love to my grandmother even more passionately time and again, disarming in advance all possible protest on her part. Though Grandma knew very well where he had passed his time, she never reproached him. Or, to be more precise, she had made an attempt once in her younger days, like every decent and jealous young woman should. She formulated a few questions regarding the nocturnal absence of her spouse and she even attempted to make some biting remarks about certain women with whom my grandfather had presumably had spent merry times. The response came in the form of a tremendous slap in the face, followed by a few choice words.

"Do not be stingy, woman. There is plenty. Enough and more to spare!"

With that momentum he grabbed her and did not let her leave the conjugal bed till noon. My young grandmother's cries of joy drowned out the pigs' squealing in hunger, and the indignant cackling of the hens still locked in their coop.

With this incident my grandfather considered the matter resolved – and my grandmother soon learned that caustic remarks could bring more trouble than gain. She accepted her fate. Now and then she did cry a little on lonely nights, but in the mornings she always awaited the love of her life with clean clothes and a hot bath.

Grandpa had a secret the neighbouring dames talked about with lewd excitement in whispering voices: he made love without ever "finishing it". Rumour said no women could ever "discharge Marten Lindenholm's cannon". Even the wildest women became weary in his unrestrained embrace. That is why they yearned for him and loved him. But none of them could possess him. He never gave them the chance. He stayed loyal to my grandmother until her death – at least according to his interpretation of loyalty.

In an intimate moment he let drop a few words about his secret. I was accompanying him home from the pub but, as he did not feel like going in the house, we sat down on the roadside in front of the house. He began to tell a story. In his bachelor years he had been a seaman on a commercial ship. One time their ship was held up for ten days in Bombay. It was there he met a mysterious Indian woman who, though she was kind of a prostitute, never once accepted any money from him. She taught him a secret trick, and said something like: "If you want to have a long life, and to hold women in your arms till the day of your death, then you must not lose your masculine vigour – no matter how passionate your embrace."

That is all Grandpa said back then. I was inexperienced and, although I couldn't really understand what he was talking about, I had the suspicion great secrets were at hand. I found his whole personality a wonderful and alluring mystery.

My parents were not so keen on me spending time with my grandfather. Maybe they were afraid the old man would "ruin" me – though in my younger days no words were spoken about his amorous adventures. He told wonderful tales and manufactured all kinds of fantastic toys. Later he taught me to fish and ride the wildest waves in a boat.

These were the finest moments of my childhood. After my father's military discipline, I felt the closeness of Grandpa's spirit like someone freed from prison might enjoy the sunshine. He began to talk about his adventures only later when he felt the time was ripe. I was twelve and curious about everything, including love. According to my mother I was too young for it – maybe she was right. My grandfather's stories roused my passions to dangerous heights – burning longings, which still had to wait a long time to be fulfilled. I spent many a torturous night on my bed hot with lonesome desire. Grandpa was a wise man, however: like a good farmer he sowed the seeds when the ground was still soft to accept them. The pain caused by cracking the husk of seeds did not interest him, or maybe he just knew it was natural.

After the death of my grandmother he abandoned his infamous habits overnight. Losing his partner seemed to cut him off from a kind of secret source of energy. This energy had nothing to do with sexual prowess though. That something came from a much deeper level, and deep down in his soul something had broken for good. Maybe that was when he truly understood at last what grandmother had meant to him. He did not become melancholic. He kept his cheerfulness and exuberant joy of life, but he became more of a dreamer. He spoke no more of his adventures but started to tell other kinds of stories. The creative force that until then had fuelled endless lovemaking now started to work on a higher level. His tales were no longer like the traditional ones he had used to cultivate my blooming imagination when I was little. These stories were the sublime products of his uniquely rich erotic fantasy presented to me like celebratory gifts on a golden tray by his sensual and passionately romantic soul.

Like all tales, these too were about love, but they animated the purest and the most selfless forms of love. Although their heroes were human – men and women – these women bore the beauty of the fairies, the sensuality of mermaids and the perfection of goddesses. And the men fought for them with a genuine bravery worthy of heroes, conquered their hearts with boundless tenderness, and loved as only gods can love.

I remember one particular story – not even a tale but rather one of his peculiar convictions. He recounted it many times, always enriching it with extra details. Whenever he talked about these things he was overtaken by a strange awe that gradually gripped me too. We were sitting on the roadside in front of the house the first time he told me.

"Once when I was your age I had an odd dream. I was on a wonderful island. Its shores were guarded by tall palm trees. The winds waved their crowns like a fan. A little bay, glittering in blue light, was bejewelled by flowers of a thousand colours. Beautiful women lived on the island, and they walked completely naked. Belts woven of green leaves and flowers emphasized the curves of their hips. Colourful blooms adorned their long, flowing hair. At times they played in the water, at times they lay on the sands of the beach and pleasured each other with loving caresses. There were also men living on the island. Their skin was golden brown, their bodies like statues. They too were naked and, if they strayed to the shore, they were free to wonder at the divine sight of women playing games of love. If they felt like it, they could join them in their play, any time they wanted, and could take delight with any of them – because these women were always ready for love. If, while searching for sweet fruits, a woman encountered a man on a hidden path in the forest, then she coiled round his body with ecstatic love in the cool shade of lush bushes. Jealousy was unknown on this island. No selfish desire of ownership tormented them. The women never quarrelled over the men. They adored each of them equally, and loved each other with tender feelings.

From time to time, the inhabitants of the island gathered at night around a large fire on the beach, and the men would begin to sing with deep, strong voices. Their songs were accompanied by drums capable of awakening ancient powers. Women swung to entrancing dances that set every sense on fire. Flames dancing with them were projected onto their hot, shimmering bodies. As the drums became silent and the sounds of the songs withdrew to the invisible ether, the men enclosed their strong arms around the women, who were still panting after their feverish dance. Then they adored them with a love most true. There in the starlit temple of the wild, together, around the flaming altar.

Love never tired them since lovemaking was as natural to them as everything around them: like the sun rising from the dark blue waters, like the trees bearing beautiful juicy fruits for the hungry wanderer. If a stranger strayed to the island, the goddesses of love freed him too of the bonds of his clothes. They bathed him, smoothed his body with perfumed oils and adorned him with garlands. They fed him with appetizing fruits then presented him with pleasures most hidden, most delicious. If he wanted to stay on the island with the other men, he was permitted to, but if he wanted to leave they let him go. They knew the embraces they offered had left neither painful yearning nor insatiable thirst in his soul – only pure joy and happiness that can never be lost."

Grandpa breathed heavily for a moment and pulled the collar of his leather jacket tighter around his neck. Light autumn drizzle was falling. The cold damp had crawled under my clothes, and I finally realized I was shivering. My grandfather stared at the large, yellow spot drawn by the kitchen window on the dark ground. His thoughts were far away.

"There must be an island like this, somewhere on Earth. I have always believed there is. That is why I became a sailor. I hoped someday Fate would guide me to find that place: the Island of Delights. Wherever I sailed I peered untiringly towards the horizon. Yet I did not find it anywhere. But there, in the port of Bombay, I felt I was close to it. The woman I met loved me with a love resembling that of the women of my dreams living on the Island of Delights. Her hands caressed me with that kind of tenderness, and I saw the same passionate devotion and infinite warmth glowing in her eyes, her goddess body swaying to the same secret rhythm of love.

At that moment I was certain that, if such a woman exists, then the Island of Delights must exist too. I had only one wish: to find it. After I returned home I met a girl, and with her I discovered another kind of love. She became your grandmother, and then I looked no further. But you... you still have the chance to find it. It does exist somewhere. I feel it. I know it. I am certain."

I did not really believe my grandfather. But his words had stirred in me thrills you only feel when you have the premonition of some great mystery and, for a while, I became that stranger who found the island by chance. Velvety breasts formed like peaches, hips slim as reeds and caressing smiles surrounded me. That was how I saw Woman at the time.

2. Lion cub

I loved tales, (I still do), most of all the stories from the One Thousand and One Nights. Their familiar atmosphere set my imagination alive with mysterious desires. A splendid world of exotic colours, where wealthy kings and sultans possess complete power over the lives of their subjects. Here, frightful genies hold petal-faced noble virgins captive, in the skies there are magic carpets instead of planes and flying horses spread their wings just like the seagulls of the Calanques...

I was not yet four years old when I first entered this strange and cruel world, floating on the waves of my maternal grandfather's deep and tuneful voice. This enigmatic world attracted me more than I can say. A world in which supreme magicians fight magical battles, cloaked in the skins of terrifying wild animals, transformed into poisonous snakes and deadly scorpions, or in the form of blinding bolts of lightning and sparking columns of fire. But perhaps it was the sensual atmosphere of the large, gracious halls filled with scents of myrtle, adorned with red silks and decorated cushions that attracted me most of all. The joyful performance of fountains, the rose-scented baths sunk into colourful marble floors, the precious jewels and large pearls decorating soft divans where gazelle-eyed, silky-skinned young women lounge around, their main occupation being the pursuit of love...

Maybe it was so appealing because I didn't find any average people in this world. Its inhabitants were either filthy-rich caliphs or penniless paupers, good and righteous or bad and loathsome, stunningly beautiful or uglier than the darkest night. There was nothing average, no mediocrity, only the tension between extremes... that is precisely why I loved it.

This world seemed so familiar I was honestly convinced that I belong to it, but, as the result of some evil curse, I had ended up in this noisy concrete forest that stank of petrol. In my heart I hoped that my fiery-eyed savoir, a fair, young man with a golden sword on a jet black horse, would come for me one day to take me back to where the wicked Ifrit had once kidnapped me ... At that time I was sure that the fairy tale world of the Thousand and One Nights actually existed in reality. Whenever I met with veiled Arab women on the street I believed they were undercover envoys led into my path by the benevolent Allah to give me news of my faraway homeland and to encourage me to be patient.

My grandfather had a prosperous gift shop on the Canabière. I loved playing there. The ornamental Arabian saddles, silver sabres, Indian silk saris, Aztec wooden masks, Tibetan bells, shining copper statues of unknown deities and wall hangings depicting mosques with towers or harem scenes... each of these objects spun tales about the existence of my fairy-tale world. I suspected there were concealed caves with fabulous treasures in the nooks and crannies of the cliffs along the shore, and I was convinced that behind If Castle's steep, dark walls a sparkling palace was hiding. That is, until my father took me there. When I saw the bare stone courtyard I burst into tears. Sniffing, I asked my Dad what had happened to the palace, the king and the shimmering court, secretly hoping that some evil magician had made it disappear and that in time it could be conjured up again. But when I found out that no king had ever lived in the castle and it had only ever been a prison where villains were locked up, I felt unspeakable disappointment.

Slowly I realized there was no point looking for my beloved fairy-tale world in my surroundings. It had to be somewhere else. My Grandpa promised me that when I grew up a little he would take me to see the world. Maybe then...

Then later in school they taught me that magicians, genies, flying horses and magic carpets are only in tales ... that meant there was no point me waiting for any saviour because the curse could not be broken and I had to suffer here in this boring, grey and coarse world until the end of my life...

Life is, of course, never as tragic as it seems after a disappointment. I quickly accepted my fate and, no sooner than I had, I busied myself with the question of how to make *this* world more colourful and exciting. I was convinced that I am capable of achieving this aim and planned that when I grow up I will be a queen, or at least have a similar status. I consciously prepared for this duty using the only method available to me: play.

It was as though my playmates intuitively perceived my secret desires; they always conferred the leading role upon me. It seemed totally natural to me to take the lead in whichever group of children I found myself.

What's more, I was filled with pride that they accepted and listened to me; they did what I asked them to; and obeyed me, even when they didn't actually agree with me!

I was nine years old when I really experienced the taste of power for the first time. My parents had just bought a new house. It was lovelier and more spacious than the old one. Mum set about decorating it with great enthusiasm and according to her aristocratic tastes. For a good while Dad just wandered from room to room talking in a nostalgic tone about "our small family nest", to which he attached many fond memories.

The change definitely affected me positively. The new place provided both new playmates and new adventures. The neighbour's daughter, Veronique, made friends with me on our first meeting. She shared her most intimate secrets and dreams, all having one central figure: the deep brown-eyed, attractive Alain. She was the one who took me to the Castle – the playground for the local children.

The Castle was a half-finished house in the next street and construction had been abandoned a couple of years before, probably due to financial difficulties. It was the ideal setting for all sorts of games. The first time I was there I took part in a commando game that Luc, the leader of the gang, had made up. I got the role of the female spy and I had to be in love with the commander of the enemy camp who was, of course, Luc himself.

It was about a week later when the unfortunate incident happened. We were in the middle of enacting aerial warfare – we were sat between the branches of fruit trees, bombarding the others' planes with green apples – when the owner appeared on the battlefield. He gasped and gaped as he weighed up the damage caused by the long-standing war. Unfortunately he recovered his voice and burst into a volley of curses and threats banning all of us useless urchins from his property. We had suffered a serious defeat and the event went down in the annals of our group's history as the "Great Plane Crash".

Three rows of barbed wire appeared above the fence the next day, along with a huge lock on the gate and an enormous, black and bloodthirsty wild animal in the garden whose terrifying bark nipped in the bud any thoughts of going there. We had to go to the playground to swing and play in the sand pit with the little kids. It was a pathetic and untenable situation. I pondered what to do for days because I just couldn't accept that we had lost something that we considered as rightfully ours.

Then I suddenly had a brilliant idea. What if I tame the beast? The thought filled me with excitement. I already saw myself riding on the back of the Black Beast, proud and dignified as I trotted around the garden in front of the frightened gang members jostling for the best view and looking on in wonder from the upstairs windows.

The majestic figure of the lion-taming Lady Cleopatra, dressed in sparkling clothes, appeared before me. I had seen her in the circus when I was five. She was standing on the back of an enormous lion as they paraded around the ring to the beat of the audience's enthusiastic applause. I was enchanted by her gaze, and her voice emanated magical powers with which she managed to bring the three beasts to do all sorts of breath-taking stunts. She even forced the rebellious, growling lion to jump through a ring of fire. But it was probably the infinite courage and the calm self-confidence when she put her head into the gaping jaws of the huge creature that captivated me completely.

I still remember the excitement, the exhilaration that took hold of me at that time. At the end of the show I said to my Dad:

"Dad, I already know …"

"What, my sweet?"

"When I grow up … I will be a lion tamer."

Dad started to laugh and squatted down beside me.

"And a ballet dancer … and a queen too, eh?"

"No… only a lion tamer."

I was not to be so very wrong … but I had no idea it would cost me years of efforts to tame the lion inside me.

"Dad, you know what?" I grabbed his thick black beard. "Let's pretend you're the lion and I want to tame you."

"Here and now?"

"Yes, now."

"I don't know who is going to be able to tame you, you unruly little lion cub," he said, pinching my cheek playfully before going down onto all fours. I jumped onto his back, tugged his tie and proudly started to crack the whip. Then quite unexpectedly his beautiful baritone voice roared so terrifyingly that those standing near us jumped aside in alarm. Then, when they saw this strange pair, they broke into laughter. My father, in his best suit and white shirt, was crawling around on all fours on the dusty ground with me in my bright red dress, my head held proud, as I sat on his back with great dignity, just like the fearless and enchanting Lady Cleopatra. The crowd parted for us and we regally made our way to the exit under the spotlight of the laughing onlookers. My Dad was that crazy. And he loved me so crazily too.

That experience left me restless for weeks and I kept bugging my Dad about how people tame lions. He explained that the power of the lion tamers lies in their boundless courage and self-control. If beasts feel – even for a second – that fear has gripped the person or that they have become unsure, the animal immediately pounces and rips them apart.

When I had the idea of taming the black beast, I remembered my father's words and felt that I was in possession of the great secret: I mustn't be afraid! If that glitteringly clothed woman could do it, then I would also succeed.

I didn't tell anyone of my plan; I wanted to carry it out alone.

I went to the first meeting with great determination. I waited by the wire fence under a tall, slim olive tree. The beast sensed my presence. It raced towards me with a bloodcurdling bark and slammed into the wire fence with terrific force. It was as though the fence fell into bits like some delicate cobweb. As it gnashed its fangs, biting and snapping at the thin steel threads my instincts screamed desperately: Escape! But the steel wires resisted the assault, and I the temptation to flee. I merely took one step back – a really tiny step – and then turned to face him. I forced calm into my shaking body. I stood rooted to the spot for a while, drilling my gaze into his large brown eyes... then I started to speak to him. I talked and talked in a calm voice until finally he went quiet. We stood motionless for a while, each fixing the other's gaze, but as soon as I tried to move the wild assault started afresh. I had to start again from the beginning – with great patience and even more self control. From time to time he went quiet, but the moment he saw me move, he immediately attacked again.

And so it went on for a long time. Days.

On the third day he sat down at the foot of the wire fence and for the first time he let me move... but he kept his eyes on me. I could change position a little but the moment I tried to approach the fence, he started to growl, baring and gnashing his stunning white teeth again.

We slowly approached one another like two lovers who first meet as deadly enemies and the smouldering hate in their eyes is gradually transformed by the fiery desire to annihilate each other into passionate love.

I wanted to defeat him, to conquer him and to force him to obey me. I wanted him to submit to be as gentle as a lamb but he proudly and powerfully resisted all pressure.

On that third day, when he had allowed me to move, I knelt down in front of him and started to observe him. Not with the aggressive, snake charmer's eye I had used up until then. I just ... watched him. With my gaze I stroked his jet-black, shining shaggy coat, his attentive ears and his enormous, strong jaw... what a beautiful animal he was! As I looked at him with wonder, I felt his power entering me and travelling through my whole body. I felt ever stronger, ever more courageous. Amazement gradually, almost unnoticed, became gentle, soft affection.

On the fourth day he allowed me to touch the wire netting with my hands.

On the fifth day I was able to stroke his wet and sniffing nose.

And on the sixth day he ate from my hand the slices of salami I had sneaked out of the house.

From then on, whenever I appeared in our meeting place, under the whispering leaves of the olive tree, he raced over towards me. But he no longer snarled. He jumped up with his tail wagging and the joy of meeting again shining in his deep brown, velvet eyes.

I thought the time for the premiere of the great show had come.

It was Sunday afternoon. The seventh day. The whole gang climbed up the long ladder from Alain's garden into one of the upstairs windows. The terrifying gnashing of my shaggy coated friend's teeth accompanied the noise of him crashing into the front door. They all begged me and tried to dissuade me from my crazy plan. Now, maybe it was the wild attack that made my instincts shudder afresh, maybe it was the others' anxiety, or the thought that there wouldn't be the protective net between us... I don't know... but I started to be afraid. Fear slid in, furtively, like a snake, and gripped my stomach, yet, I knew there was no return.

Alain accompanied me down the steps. I opened the door a smidgeon during one of the pauses in the siege. Our eyes met. He immediately stopped barking and started to wag his bushy tail. I stepped out warily. Alain closed the door behind me. Fourteen tousled heads were pressed to the two upstairs windows; fourteen pairs of startled eyes watched me, the small girl who appeared so delicate, so vulnerable next to that huge beast.

It was over in a second. Terrified screams came from upstairs as the large animal leapt at me. I fell backwards under his enormous weight. He was obviously shocked at what he had done as he immediately looked at me guiltily, and started to lick my face and arms gently. After my initial shock I recovered my senses, picked myself up and wiped the wet traces of my passionate admirer's expression of emotion from my face. Then, in a forgiving voice I started to tell him off:

"You ungrateful beast! Bad boy! You should be ashamed of yourself! Is that the way you treat a friend, jumping up and knocking me to the floor? Tut, tut, tut. And look, you've even scratched my elbow. It's bleeding. See?"

He did see it and it was as though he understood. He stopped jumping. He just stood still and shook his head. Whining and whimpering came from his throat as he looked up at me with that look that only dogs have, when they are desperate to be stroked by their beloved master.

I bent down, hugged his thick, shaggy neck and looked up to the upstairs windows. The others, who were just starting to pull themselves together, waved furiously.

"Come down to the garden carefully, one by one," I shouted up to them in a light and confident voice.

Quarter of an hour passed before the door opened in trepidation. Alain stepped out and came towards us nervously. He stopped at a respectable distance and started the procedure of getting to know the beast from there. A few moments later Luc also dared to come out, then Veronique, and then the rest, one after the other.

Within a few days the whole gang made friends with him. The great black beast proved to be an excellent playmate and thus we decided to make him an honorary a member of the gang.

Since I was the one to recapture the Castle from the enemy, I thought it was fairly natural that from then on I would lead the gang, but Luc didn't want to step down from his role as chief. A serious feud developed between us. In the end we had to organize a leadership vote – democratically with a secret ballot.

I won with a landslide and, with the generosity of the victor, I immediately appointed Luc as my highest commander. He didn't accept the offer ... he couldn't. To this day the picture of him, with that defiant, dark look, voice shaking from emotion, appears before me as he announced, "Thank you, but no thank you. I don't want any part in it ... and I'm not going to play with you any more!"

I felt genuinely sorry for Luc, but there was nothing I could do. The stronger had to win and I was the stronger. The others felt it too.

I set about completing my task without delay and we created a residence fit for a queen within those unplastered brick walls, and named it the Golden Palace. We made strict laws that everyone was bound to keep. Any infringements of the rules were to be punished in the way I chose. My highly trained bodyguards carried out my wishes on every occasion. Within a short time I had become the omnipotent mistress of the Golden Palace.

Of course, I quickly realized that ruling was by no means as easy as it was seductive. I had to learn to accept the opinions of the others too but still rule as I saw best at the same time. I also realized that my "subjects" could be divided into various categories, and I had to deal differently with each category in order to get my way.

First of all there were the "Yes, that's right"s and the "Correct"s. They accepted everything and never put forward an independent opinion. They carried out every task they were given without opposition. I had the fewest problems with them and mainly gave them tasks that required no individual decisions.

And then there were the "Yes, but"s and the "Why like that"s. They always questioned everything, commented on everything, tirelessly coming up with witticisms. Generally they approached things in a positive manner; they just liked to hear the sound of their own voice before they carried out my wish. Occasionally they had innovative ideas but the best thing about them was that I could create the illusion of democracy in the gang through them as I always allowed them to voice their opinions. I just had to stop them in time otherwise we were only arguing about the game instead of playing it.

The smallest in number were those with truly original and useful ideas, the "What if"s and "We could do it another way"s. They were my favourites. They served as my real advisors and came up with revolutionary thoughts and cool ideas. There were the traitors too, of course. They never voiced their opinions in open discussions but were constantly whispering behind my back, "You know that ...", "Yes, because she...", "It's just her again ..." I had to watch them the most otherwise they would have been able, slowly and slyly, to destroy everything I wanted to build.

The "Impossible"s along with their companions the "I don't want to"s and the "Why me"s also caused any number of problems. I realized after a while that logical principles were totally useless in their case. It was far more successful to employ a different category of methods with them – the "That's how it'll be, no arguments" type. I was the only representative of this category. You can't have more than one in a gang. And that is why Luc had had to go.

When I started to study my birth horoscope many years later, I was amazed just how accurately the astrological analysis fitted the former Laurianne, that strong-willed and proud young girl who had to be the centre of attention, who always had to be valued and praised and who, at the age of nine, already sat with such self-confidence on the throne of the Golden Palace, issuing her orders in a voice that defied all opposition.

I was born under the sign of Leo on 27th July 1974. That is probably what I can thank for my extraordinary willpower, my dynamic sense of purpose, my remarkable organizational ability and my desire for independence. But it was Mars, which had entered Leo in honour of my birth that certainly played a significant role in the development of my inclination to lead, as it stood in conjunction with Leo in the centre of the heavens and looked on as the doctor on duty in the Marseille maternity ward cut my umbilical cord.

My family conditions were in perfect accord with the stars. I was an only child. My parents brought me up with special attention and boundless love. They treated me as an adult from an early age. They didn't force me to do anything and always took my opinion into account in any decisions that affected me. And since they could afford to, they gave me almost everything I asked for. My personality developed early and somehow I always felt more mature than my playmates of a similar age, and so it was pretty natural that they always regarded me as their leader.

In addition to my leadership skills, the planets and stars provided me with many other useful abilities. My Scorpio ascendant blessed me with the desire to penetrate beyond the surface of things. The Moon in Scorpio gave an interest in the occult. Jupiter in Pisces provided a fertile imagination. Venus in Cancer gave romantic sentimentalism. Neptune in Sagittarius lent me an artistic sensitivity, while Pluto in Libra furnished me with the power to reform, and a strange tendency to regard life as a great, adventurous Game …

Well, I have much to thank for my auspicious astral influences … but not everything. Today I know that "the stars provide the opportunity, but they do not compel" and whenever I pick up my birth horoscope the Master pops into my mind who once said to me:

"The constellation of your birth is God's mysterious message to you. It hints at the tasks that await you in life, the powers you have at your disposal to reach your goal and the restrictions you may find yourself up against on your way.

The key to the mystery is that although the birth map shows the positions of the planets, it is actually speaking about you. Because those planets and the stars are all in you, just like the limits and opportunities, and alongside them, the Way and the Goal are also inside you ..."

3. Roses and thorns

My interest towards the opposite sex presented itself early in my childhood. The object of my anatomical studies was the three female specimens I lived with. I was about three years old at the time.

I was extremely surprised when I discovered that the device I have at the juncture of my abdomen and thighs had not been installed on my sisters when they were assembled. Because of this flaw in manufacture, they were in a disadvantageous position when using the chamber pot. They had to drop their knickers and situate themselves above the pot while I could elegantly aim from afar.

The mystery needed clarification.

I have always liked to discover things through personal observation and my own experience. For this reason, asking my parents about this oddity was out of the question. I started to observe them more closely while they were having a wash. I tried to be inconspicuous and made furtive glances while sitting at the kitchen table and making splodges in my painting book. Unfortunately even long hours of observation revealed nothing of note. Except one thing: examining the ritual of their bathing filled me with curious excitement. So I grabbed every chance I could to advance my private anatomical studies.

One time I experienced something curious. Two swellings seemed to appear – like two large wasp stings – on the chest of my sister Sigrid. I remembered having been stung before, but she had two and they were situated symmetrically, at the exact same position from the central line of her body. That surprised me. How could those wasps have calculated the exact location of stings? Still, I mused, nature was full of marvellous mysteries. I fancied that they were twin wasps. Actually, it was rather just an empirical hypothesis. No scientific proof confirmed it. Nevertheless, one thing to support the theory of a wasp sting was the fact she seemed to rub them more while bathing – this was obviously a sign they were itching. A month passed though and the swellings did not subside, in fact they grew ostensibly. I began to doubt my scientific theory regarding the origin of the swellings. Then, when I realized that these swellings fired my imagination far more than the most beautiful wasp sting, I was completely bewildered. Of course, the situation would have been totally different had I been able to examine them more closely, possibly even using information gained through the sense of touch. I felt an urge that was hard to overcome but unfortunately I was not on good terms with the object of my observation. Actually, I can safely say I was always at loggerheads with her.

Already at the dawn of my self-consciousness I had noticed my sisters' aversion towards me. They terrorized me continuously, tortured me in many a resourceful way and, when they had the chance, they beat me. When they did not have a reason, they simply created one, and then justified it to my parents with all kinds of shameful lies. The long and short of it is that they made my life hell, and no parental care was able to protect me. Nevertheless, I continued with my observations in spite of these unfavourable conditions. The bitter antipathy that resided in me because of my sisters' underhand behaviour did not prevent me from further studying their bodies as part of my scientific research. Consequently, when the time of the evening bathing came, I strategically took my place at the kitchen table with my painting books. For a long time they did not pay the least bit of attention to me. They believed they had nothing to fear of the little lad still chewing on the end of his pencil. At least not until I became absorbed in the admiration of my sister Sigrid's breathtakingly curvaceous form – that time it was already more than a mere scientific observation. She noticed me and started to yell infernally: "What are you looking at you little brat? Don't you feel ashamed? Get lost!" Then she struggled into her bathrobe and stormed out of the kitchen.

That was the last time she took off her clothes in front of me. Whenever she wanted to take a bath, she chased me off rudely and ruthlessly. Moreover, she probably told my other two sisters about my early sexual interests, as from that moment on they also stopped allowing me to assist during their cleaning ritual. I felt deeply disappointed that Fate had dealt me this unfair blow.

I did not yet know that life closes one door only to open another.

❖

Not long after I fell in love for the first time. There was a carpenter living in our street and he had a beautiful, rosy-cheeked daughter. Her golden locks fluttered cheekily when, with a sudden and sweet nod, she smiled at someone. Her ianthine gaze made the hearts of many boys leap – although she was only five years old. Lads built her dolls houses and presented her with hearts moulded from red plasticine. And when we had to line up in pairs there was always a stampede around her; we all wanted to hold her hand. She was well aware of her irresistible appeal. She consciously held herself with a charming pride, sharing her grace like a capricious princess, bestowing her favour on whomsoever she fancied at that precise moment.

I never forced my way towards her like the others. I merely yearned for her from afar. In secret I hoped that one day she would notice me, cast a light on me with her little blue lanterns, walk to me and take my hand – and all the other boys would stare at us open-mouthed and jealous as we walked happily side by side. Unfortunately, that was never going to happen. Apparently, she liked the kind of bullocks who were willing to fight for their females. In fact the battle itself was a great pleasure to her. I do not think she even realized that I existed. Or if she did, then she did not consider me worthy of attention. My sulky, protesting behaviour did not seem to soften her heart either. She let me lag behind her on the way home, me with a sad face, she giggling away with three or four companions.

Little Lotta was so cruel! She handed over her handkerchief to Wili in front of my eyes! And he, of course, immediately proceeded to blow his nose into it... with amorous awe.

There was one girl in our group who showed obvious interest in me though. Her ginger-blond face was covered in freckles; her snubbed nose was lovely. Tilda was not exactly my ideal, but we had a good time playing tag and rolling about on the freshly mown lawns. I think she must have witnessed my hopeless yearning because one day when we were playing outside she tried to console me. She took my hand and, with an enigmatic expression on her face, she said:

"Come with me. Let me show you something." Then, without saying any more, she led me behind the hedge. She stood in front of me, pulled down her knickers and pulled up her short flowery dress. At the same time, she kept looking at my face; she was curious about the effect the sight would have on me. It kept me spellbound because I had never seen anything like that before from so close. I knelt to have an even closer look. It titillated me. This was different from what I felt when looking at my sisters. She let me wonder at it for a while, then pulled her pants back up and ran away. The next day I asked her to show it to me again. Tilda agreed with delight. She was glad she had piqued my curiosity so. This time she pulled her knickers down to her ankles, then sat on the ground. I leaned close and touched her with my fingers; I stroked her. Her skin, soft as velvet, was breathtaking. She watched what I was doing for a while and then lay back on the ground, opening her knees to let me admire her nudity to my heart's content. I grabbed a flower and caressed her with it. I was just about to explore that exciting little slit when I realized the kindergarten teacher was looking at us. Her face was scarlet. Our newly discovered game had made us forget the barriers of time. Break was long over, and they had been searching for us everywhere.

"What in the name of God are you doing here? Are you not ashamed of yourself? I do not want to see you like this ever again. Get inside!" The teacher herself tugged up Tilda's knickers.

As a punishment we had to stand in the corner for an hour – naturally two different corners.

I could not understand why on Earth I would be punished for something like that. It was just a game like football or tag, just more exciting for some reason. In the end I came to the conclusion that the kindergarten teacher was angry because we had not gone in on time. I decided to be more careful next time.

The experience had given me courage and self-confidence. So, a few days later, I approached the golden-haired fairy of my dreams:

"Come with me Lotta and I'll show you something," taking her hand with a chivalrous self-confidence. She did not say yes, but her eyes sparkled in curiosity – she was a real woman. She let me push her behind the bushes with some reluctance. Arriving at the secret spot I pulled down my pants to reveal my boyhood in its undisguised pomp. I hoped I would please her the same way Tilda had pleased me, but Lotta just giggled, held her hand in front of her mouth and blinked queerly.

"Just go on and hold it," I encouraged her, but she did not move.

She just went on giggling and blinking even more rapidly. I encouraged her to follow my example and show me hers. I was burning with desire to look at it. I wondered if hers was similar to Tilda's. I was willing to help her pull off her knickers, but she protested vehemently and instructed me that "this is not right" and "mum will beat me if she finds out" and "Jesus would be angry if he knew I was doing these kinds of things". But she did not run away. We just stood there looking at each other. Me, my pants round my ankles, and she, with blushed cheeks and eyes wide open in excitement. She was stunning. She only ran away when the kindergarten teacher called for us to line up.

I yanked up my pants, deeply angry at the mothers who filled their daughters' heads with such nonsense, and then this Jesus – who did not have the faintest idea of what was good and right. But I was secretly happy that not all mothers are the same, and at least my sweet Tilda had not been brought up this way.

Nevertheless my self-revelation had not been completely fruitless. From that moment on my dearest Lotta visibly showed greater interest in me. Though I was still not the only beneficiary of her graces, she did hold my hand sometimes on the way home. I could not imagine what might have roused her interest.

❖

But even these tangible experiences did not bring me any closer to my goal on the journey to solve the mystery of the feminine. In fact, the puzzle became more intricate and more intriguing – like puzzles do. I felt adults possessed some immense secret that they desperately wanted to shroud from us children, and that they were probably protecting us from this only out of solicitous care as it was something inherently "bad".

Consequently, the emerging buds of my attraction towards women were attacked by the parasites of remorse. Slowly and insidiously. As the shoots developed an unpleasant tension started to overpower me. In my first year at school I was in love with three girls at the same time. One captivated me with her hair, one with her eyes, and one with her lips and smile. I can recall those raspberry coloured lips to this very day. I wrote my first love letter to this young lady, though I never actually gave it to her. I found it fifteen years later between the pages of a maths book that had turned yellow with age, written in the chubby letters of a first year. In it I confessed that I loved her more than anything in the world, and that I would like to taste sweet honey off her lips.

❖

As I started to grow, I became clumsier in approaching girls. I was still in love with several girls at the same time but in reality these loves were just flowers sprouting out of the exuberant jungle of my fantasies. Aching and poignantly beautiful just like carnivorous plants, they had little to do with the genuine flowers of love I confused them with. I imagined ecstatic trysts down to the very last detail, but in practice I made not one step towards the objects of my feverish desires. Maybe it was the remorse darkly whirling under the mirror of my consciousness or maybe it was some other unknown and numbing force, but I felt I had to hide my feelings, longings and yearnings, bury them somewhere deep into a dark tomb prison of my subconscious so that no one could ever see them.

However, these desires lived on in the depths. They boiled away continuously, rising to the surface now and then. While the conscious will of my daydreams concealed the objects of these desires as enigmatic beauties, fairies with eyes like almond blossoms, silver hair and velvety bodies, at the inspiration of the bat-winged night they moulded their bodies out of their own ugly nature. They assumed jellied, medusa-like forms that changed shape with my mood. When sexual desires teased me; round buttocks, luscious breasts and beguiling lips floated towards me in a sticky, slimy dream-swamp. However, when fear overpowered me, tentacles grew out of the breasts, embraced me with a tormenting, strangling lust and held me tight. The excruciating and tormenting delight was followed by horror. Groins swirling between skeleton-like thighs would suck me in with overwhelming force, like a lethal swamp. I was frightened to death. I kicked and struggled, suffocating until the last of my strength had evaporated. My last breath broke out of my tormented body like a silent cry; a concentrated power from the bottom of my soul that finally freed me from the hands of this monstrous dream world's damned inhabitants. I woke tired and jaded in my icy sweat and tried desperately not to be seized again by the nightmarish wave. However, together with my vitality, my willpower faded away and a few minutes later I would find myself drifting away in the fog of dreams once again. Fortunately after these agonizing nightmares, the fairy of the night gave me relaxing dreams that made the nightmares sink into oblivion.

These torturous dreams occurred too often. They had basically the same content with but only slight differences. I became a recluse. Girls did not fancy me because of my reticence. I lived in the world of unrequited loves, tormenting desires, and merciless nightmares.

I did have a secret treasure though: an erotic magazine. I paid a sizeable sum to an older boy to procure it. It showed – with close-up shots taken from the most provocative angles – a seemingly inexhaustible number of possibilities of two or more bodies in the act of penetration. This was meant to be the source that helped me understand the great secret of adults, but all I actually got out of it was that it made my sexual desires burn with more pain than before. The naked feminine body, which had already excited me at the early stages of my awakening to consciousness, began to attract me irresistibly. I had no other means to satisfy this interminable curiosity but peeping. I became a master at spying on girls and women undressing. Fate gave me a loyal companion in this endeavour, my great friend Arne Larsson.

I was about twelve when I met him. He was a new student and he tried to woo my secret love right in the first week. I did not even have the guts to approach the pretty-bottomed Klara, not even to borrow a rubber, so Arne's confident demeanour and blatant courting manoeuvres made me utterly dejected. I gave him a dressing down in front of the whole class at the first chance I had, and then we fought. Our hot-headed, hostile sentiments were not destined to last even a day. During break we saw our beloved lady with pointed breasts kissing a sixteen-year-old behind the school building.

That cold shower extinguished our great loves in a second. We shook hands and formed a secret alliance without saying a word. We declared war upon girls, a war of love with a great many battles to fight.

Much of what we did together was aimed at uncovering sexual secrets – and, of course, to get rid of our virginity as soon as possible. In the case of Arne it was even trickier as he was a Virgo. A genuine one. I soon realized his apparent self-confidence was just a mask under which shyness lay. He was intelligent, had an inquisitive mind and wanted to understand and touch everything. He was extremely practical and only believed in the tangible, those things with a taste, a smell or a scent, regarding everything else as foolish illusion. For me, he represented my only connection to the physical world. It was always he who drew me out of my illusory world's swamp; he made me discover the joys of playing pranks and the taste of unforgettable adventures.

When we first met he was much more experienced than me. He had some older friends who had initiated him into the matters of sexuality. He knew perfectly "how it is done" (in theory), he knew the location of the female erogenous zones, and he was fully aware as to how to arouse a woman. In brief, he felt like an authority in the subject. We used every possible occasion we had to peep at naked women, but we still had to manufacture the pleasure for ourselves. Our hands were always faithfully at hand. He was the one who got me into this habit. We spread our seeds generously, wherever we could: we fed the grass on the field, the trees in the forest, the fish in the sea. We blessed every bathroom and every lavatory we used.

Arne organized our peeping sessions with tremendous finesse. One time we spied upon the women working in the canning factory while they were washing. Near the heating centre of the factory were two large shower chambers, one for women and one for men – and there was an air vent on the roof from where we could comfortably survey the whole place. His older friends informed him of this opportunity, and he immediately worked out the strategy. It was a dangerous operation. We executed it after the afternoon shift. Thanks to Arne's precise plan it was successful, and we were able to feast our eyes upon the exciting bodies of naked women. We took turns, as there was only enough space for one at the hole. However, there was a fault in Arne's plan; it failed to calculate in random chance. There was a complication when we began to retire from our post – a huge truck was parked where we had planned to climb down from the roof, and the workers were loading crates of tinned fish for four hours. We ended up shivering with cold above the annoyingly empty bathroom until three in the morning. We started to think the morning would catch us there – and we would be forced to enjoy the showering of those finishing their night shift too.

This operation raised new questions. I did not understand why some bodies were so desirable while others had no appeal to me, or in some cases even repulsed me. What was the secret ingredient that one had and the other lacked? I observed that the truth was about more than just the curves of the bodies. I was to find out the answer to that question during another spying session. One time, Amor generously rewarded our peeping efforts. It was Karin, the friend of Arne's sister. She was having a clandestine affair with an older man. Her parents were opposed because of the age difference so they always had to meet in secret.

One time when we knew she was going to a meeting we decided to follow her. The first time we did not see anything of interest. The lovers met in a weekend cottage and there was no way we could get near without being noticed. Never mind, we thought, this operation was worth some investment. The next day we returned to explore the area. The little lock on the gate was easy to wrench off. We walked around the house with just one room. The windows opened onto the narrow garden but heavy curtains covered them. The door was locked but we were prepared like professional bank-robbers. Arne had brought a bunch of keys so we managed to open the door with one of them. There was nothing inside except for a wide bed covered with grey and red patterned blankets; a brass candlestick with a half-burnt candle. A little vase containing a withered rose sat on the bedside table. Arne went to the bed, folded the blanket and examined the white sheets thoroughly. Then he pointed at a yellowish spot that was remarkably similar to the map of Britain:

"You see that? Real action took place here."

Then he folded the blanket back up and we started our preparations. We drilled two holes in the thin boarding to avoid the nuisance that had happened in the canning factory. Then we removed all our traces, put everything back to its place and locked the door. My friend, who always paid attention to the tiniest details, even greased the hinges of the gate. Arne's sister told us the date of the lovers' next tryst. I felt my heart pounding in my throat, and I could hardly move for excitement when I saw Karin at the end of the street disappearing behind the turquoise gate.

"Come on! Don't just stand there gaping." My friend tugged at my sleeves impatiently. "Here comes the great moment. I want to see everything from beginning to end."

I do not know what was more overpowering, the fear that we might be caught or the excitement that at last the great mystery would open up in front of my eyes. This concealed privilege of the adults that had been calling and cajoling me for such a long time and that had denied itself up until that day. The secret I had been looking for so fervently in erotic stories' dim references and porn magazines reeking of sperm. But all in vain.

Arne practically had to push me in front of him along the dark, deserted road.

The door opened gently without a sound, and a few seconds later our eyes were eagerly scanning the dimness of the candlelit room. They were standing at the door where the bearded man was waiting for her. They were holding each other tightly. Transposed and still, like statues, they remained in this silent embrace for a long, long time. Arne winked at me impatiently, a mute question in his eyes: "What now? No action tonight?" I, however, was no longer impatient because in the motionless air I knew something was happening. Something out of the ordinary that Arne could not see — as it was invisible. But I felt it. Yes. I felt it beyond doubt that some great force was being born out of this moment frozen in time that slowly started to overpower them. And me. This force awakened in me a new and unknown feeling that permeated my body with a blissful sense of being. Joy filled my soul. They finally freed themselves from the embrace. The man took her hand and led her to the bed. By then I could even see that feeling! It was palpable on their rosy cheeks, in their sparkling eyes, and on their thirsty lips stalling the moment of touching the other. It was there in the tender arms of the silver bearded man as he slowly freed her slender figure of the skin-tight clothes. It impregnated all her cells as she received into herself the man she loved. Because this was the unknown feeling: love. They loved each other with an honest and deep love, and in that they became great and radiant. Everything I had read about love in books became eclipsed in the shadow of this enormous feeling. How fake, how miserably ordinary everything that I had thought about love seemed. This was completely different. A true celebration. Like festive moments that are able to lift us out of our selfish small-mindedness to be somebody different for a fleeting moment: to become... beautiful. Because they were beautiful together. As their bodies tuned to each other in the rhythm of the festive dance under the protective light of the candle, I knew it was the most splendid thing I had ever seen. Then and there, for the first time in my life, I had a glimpse of the great mystery of beauty.

I have no idea how much time might have passed until their bodies became silent in motionless satisfaction, but I felt Arne's words suddenly yanking me back to a harsh reality. More than ever before I felt like a stranger in this world.

"Let's go. We have seen everything there was to see."

"Yes. Everything," I responded in a low voice.

We walked home in silence.

We did not discuss what we had just seen as we usually did. In the middle of the great bridge we paused for a second and looked down into the depths. The moon pierced a bright hole in the silent darkness.

"Arne, I felt it. I felt what love is. I want to fall in love."

The moon winked at me from the deep. It heard my words. Or maybe it was just the splash of a fish that broke the mirrored light for a second.

❖

Ylva Ekberg. Sweat and dark heat flicker through my body whenever I pronounce her name. With her Mediterranean beauty, Greek features, and dark auburn hair touching her slim waist, she glowed in that dreary north like the sunshine of an exotic world. Our first fairy-tale meeting is still vividly imprinted in my mind.

It was a weekend. After the long hibernation of the winter, the city dwellers were lured out into nature. My family went to the "Kingdom of Oaks" and we sat near the shore of an ice-cold pond. It was late in the afternoon when I at last managed to get away from the boring obligatory family pastimes. With a little hatchet in my hand I made for the forest to search for odd-shaped roots. I liked these twisted, gnarled roots. They reminded me of stripped skeletons of ancient animals. I had been wandering around for some time when I heard a sonorous voice from afar. I started walking in that direction. As I reached a small clearing, I noticed a girl standing with her back to me. She lifted her hands towards the sky and swayed in the mild, twilight wind like sprouting oak branches in the breeze. The setting sun looked back at her one last time. Its light made her clothes translucent and set her long hair aflame. I hid in the shadow of an ancient oak so as not to alarm this ravishing fairy. She kept singing and slowly began spinning around. Then I saw her face too. I think that was when love struck me. She just kept spinning and spinning, faster and faster as her singing turned into laughter – an ecstatic laughter like thousands of butterflies flying towards the sky. Then she stretched out on the ground. The waist of her dress slipped up revealing the breathtaking curves of her hips and thighs. My heart started to pump an increased amount of blood towards my lower body. Then suddenly she jumped up and started to run. As soon as I regained my senses, I followed her. I tracked her from afar, moving stealthily from tree to tree, silently, with growing excitement. Like a hunter who, intoxicated by his hunt, stalls the moment of releasing the arrow. She reached the shore of a lake. Blue and yellow flowers mottled the green tapestry around it. She knelt down beside the bank and brushed her hair with her hands letting it drop onto her chest. She looked at her image in the curious mirror of the lake. She dipped her hand in the water, filling her palm and lifting it close to her face so she could let the water touch and flow down her gently curving neck, round shoulders, and naked arms. How jealous I was of that water! Then she plucked some flowers – but only the yellow ones, she let the blue ones live – wove them into her hair and looked one last time at her image in the lake, as though she was about to meet her secret lover.

I could stand it no longer. I felt such strength and bravery as princes feel in fairy tales. At least that is what I thought at the time. I stepped out from behind the oak. A dry twig cracked loudly under my shoes. She shivered, raised her head and for a second did not dare turn back.

"Who are you beauty? Maybe the benign fairy of the dark forest?" My voice echoed with surprising force in the twilight silence.

She jumped up and turned to face me.

"Don't be afraid. I won't hurt you," I smiled at her.

For a few moments she sized me up, and then she smiled at me. She accepted my invitation to play.

"I am the princess of wolves. My name is Ylva. And who are you, golden-haired prince?"

"My name is Balder and I am the Prince of the Midnight Sun."

"And what are you doing in my forest?"

"I was hunting alone. Then I saw you in a little clearing bidding farewell to the Sun with your beautiful song. I have been following you since then."

"You play a dangerous game, brave knight. The hunter who is after forbidden prey can easily raise the fury of my people. The other name of the wolves is Death. You should know that."

"Your beauty set my heart on fire. I shall fight ten thousand wolves, alone, if I must."

"Put down your weapon and step closer."

The little axe landed with a soft thud. I stepped close to her. So close I felt her hair exhaling a flowery fragrance.

"I reward your bravery. You may kiss me now."

I looked into her deep emerald eyes and, for a moment, I did feel that the other name of love is Death! A soft curtain fell on the greenish light and a moist, shining slit opened between her lips. I closed my eyes and approached her.

As my lips reached the soft target, she suddenly jerked her head away.

"I have to go now. It is late. My father is waiting for me. The old king of the wolves."

The sun had left us alone for some time and darkness descended between the trees. Ylva reached for my hand.

"Prince of the Midnight Sun, illuminate my way and lead me out of the dark woods."

I had absolutely no idea which way to go. With the self-confidence of a professional bluffer I set out into the dusk. At times, we heard branches cracking and bird-wings touching the whispering foliage nearby. Ylva pressed close to me. I put my protective arms around her. She clung even closer to me. I felt her warm breath on my neck. How I wished that the road would never end! I wished we would lose our way so we would have to dispel the cold of the night by nestling up close. But some odd instinct led me in the right direction, and after a while I could discern the light of a campfire between the trees. As we reached the clearing she released my hand.

"There is my father. He's waiting for me. I'm sure he must be really impatient by now."

I looked towards that direction. I saw a man in a leather jacket standing near a black jeep. He was looking around restlessly.

"I have to go," she said and was on her way.

"Don't! Wait! One last second!" I grabbed her arm. "I must know, who you are, where you live. I must meet you again. Where can I find you?"

"You found me once. You will find me again."

"But, that is crazy! This..."

"As a farewell you may kiss my hand."

My burning lips pressed on the hand she presented playfully to me. With an elegant motion she withdrew her hand and started on her way. She did not hurry, nor did she look back. She walked slowly, and gracefully. A real queen... of the wolves.

I watched her heart-stricken and tried to hold her back with my gaze. I hoped she would turn back one last time, to bid farewell, but she did not. The doors of the car slammed painfully, and the engine roared. I was only able to move when the two red dots of the lights had been engulfed by the darkness.

I could hardly wait for the first break on Monday to tell Arne about my amazing adventure. My voice quavered with excitement. He listened with an incredulous grimace on his face and said with an annoying calmness:

"You must have been knocked out by the after-lunch sluggishness. You exposed your stuffed belly to the sun and snored through the afternoon. Gullible lads slumbering on the banks of rivers are visited by these kinds of fairies, obviously, in their sleep."

"Please don't take me for an idiot!" I protested with obvious agitation in my voice. "Anyway, I have this flower here. I filched it out of her hair when we were in the clearing. Here you are. Look at it. See?"

"Yes, I see that it is a flower. A withered yellow flower. Nothing more." He held it in his hand pondering, smelled it a few times and looked at me.

"All right then, let's assume that it was not a dream. When are you going to introduce her to me?"

"That is exactly the problem. I don't know how to search for her, where to find her. I don't know where she lives. I don't know which school she goes to. She didn't want to reveal anything about herself. She said I would find her."

"You're bonkers! How the hell could you let her go without even asking for her telephone number? That's goddamn typical. What were you thinking? You just burn the flower and suddenly she'll appear next to you out of nothing?"

"Don't mock me. I've got enough on my mind."

Noticing my sincere desperation, my friend and his sensitive nature decided to strike me on my back so strongly that I almost fell over.

"Heads up! We are going to search for that fairy of yours even if we have to go to the back of beyond and wear a hole in seventy-seven boots on the way."

Arne did not believe in coincidences. He was a man of action. By the next day he had a plan ready, and we started our search methodically. We surveyed all the schools in the city, one by one. We had precise notes about which class finished when. Then, based on our elaborate schedule, we waited in front of the schools to watch all the pupils coming out. Although we had to skip some of our classes for this, Arne was ready to make any sacrifice – probably not for me but rather for the sake of the adventure. After three weeks we had exhausted all our options. Arne's plan was proving fruitless this time. Obviously it was not his plan he doubted but me.

"Are you sure you will recognize her if you see her?"

"Absolutely positive."

"Then she must have been swallowed up by the ground."

"What if she does not even live in this town" the ominous thought struck me.

"What if it was just one of your obsessive dreams after all?"

Since we had no idea what to do next, we gave up the search. However, I still hoped I would meet her by chance. Fate proved me right this time. Arne was with me when the beautiful fairy of my heart appeared on the horizon. She was walking with her father on the other side of the street. I was so excited I couldn't even breathe. Gesticulating vehemently, I tried to inform my dumbfounded friend that at last I had found the lady we had been searching for for a month. By the time he had understood and we had manoeuvred to the other side of the busy road, they had already got into the car and driven away. I felt all my strength leaving me. It was all over. But for Arne the whole adventure had just started. He flagged down a cab, shoved me into the back seat and, in a tragic tone emphasizing the gravity of the situation, instructed the driver:

"Follow that jeep, but please make sure we don't lose it as lives are at stake."

The driver looked at us incredulously, but stepped on the gas anyway.

The jeep pulled up at a villa. We presumed they must live there. We kept the house under observation while we racked our brains for a plan. A little later an upstairs window opened, and Ylva looked out for a moment. Instinctively I started to wave, but in vain. She did not notice me.

"Hmm. So that is her room then," concluded Arne with the confidence of a crime investigator. "I have a revolutionary idea. We'll come back in the evening, and you play Romeo and Juliet, the balcony scene, as directed by

Arne Larsson. You see the pine tree there? You climb up and knock on her window with a long stick. She will stick out her charming face eventually. Though you won't be able to kiss her, you will at least be able to talk to her. After all, a romantic gesture like that is more captivating than simply knocking on the door like a postman. Believe me, I know what women want."

I believed him so at bedtime there we were hanging around the villa again. We waited until all the lights went out. Then I shinned up the tree and knocked on her window. Not long after I saw Ylva's puzzled face illuminated by the milky light of a street lamp. At first she had no idea where the knocking was coming from. She only noticed me after I whistled softly.

"Well, well. The Prince of the Midnight Sun – in the form of a midnight owl."

I did not want to hear the overtones of mockery in her voice. The same way I refused to notice that her expression lacked any sign of joy when she accepted my invitation. The only thing I was conscious of was that two days later – for the first time in my life – I would have a date with a girl. And she was the most beautiful girl I had ever seen.

Forty-two hours – I was counting as I was walking home – forty-two hours to go, and then...

My impatient anticipation transformed those forty-two hours into two thousand five hundred and twenty sweetly aching minutes. And the very last minutes of the wait, as I was pacing up and down on Ulrica Pia, made me feel the mystery of the endless nature of time.

At exactly 6 o'clock the bells in the ornate wooden belfry of Amiralitetskyrkam started to toll. The three-hundred-year-old smile on the painted face of Matts Rosenbom's statue seemed annoyingly contemptuous. Although Ylva was only one minute late. She was to add only one more interminable minute to my wait, and then there she was, standing in front of me. Her emerald eyes penetrated my body like tiny arrows.

"Where are we going?" The very dumb question spilled out of my confused lips.

"Wherever you want."

"Then let's go to the forest, to the bank of the little lake, to pick yellow flowers."

I intended it as a joke to fix my previous blunder, but she did not smile.

"Let's have a walk on the beach," she suggested. Her voice struck me as cool as the evening wind.

As we strolled along we talked about everything except for our encounter in the forest. I wanted to embrace her, to kiss her, or at least to touch her hand. But something kept me back. And that something came from her.

Around sunset, when the icy shell around her began to melt, she had "to go". And this was the only thing that resembled our adventure in the forest. I asked for another meeting and decided that the next time I would be more daring. We were walking under the coastal trees as night fell. That darkness came as an ally, and I sneaked my hand around her waist. Meanwhile I was mainly talking any nonsense that popped into my mind. My arm slowly slipped upwards till my index finger reached that fine curve where the exciting mound of her breast began. There it came to a halt and dared go no further.

I accompanied her home that night. In front of the gate I kissed her goodbye – on her lips following Arne's advice. It was a marvellous night. The wind brought an intoxicating haze of perfume on my way home. A little group of roses was in full bloom in the garden of a villa. I stopped and inhaled their inebriating scent with closed eyes. The next moment I vaulted lightly over the high fence. The huge dog next door started to bark gruffly. I threw myself into achieving my aim. The roses fought for their lives passionately. Their steely thorns pierced my fingers, gouged under my nails, and ploughed the surface of my hand, drawing blood. But I could not care less about pain. By the time the neighbour came out, drawn by the continuous barking, I was already back on the street. A few minutes later I was standing under the Ylva's window once again. One by one, I snapped the thorns off the roses and climbed back up the tree. I used my laces to fasten the bouquet to the stick I had left among the branches during my first visit. Then I knocked gently on her window.

Ylva was truly surprised and delighted by the flowers. She buried her face between the velvety petals and with a deep sigh she breathed in their scent. And then suddenly she turned to me.

"But where are the thorns?"

"I tore them off," I answered with vain satisfaction "so they wouldn't prick you."

"Oh, that's a pity. Roses need their thorns. That's what makes them lovely. They wither without their thorns, and soon die."

The next day Arne sneeringly looked at my hand ornamented with the tattoos of a love sacrifice.

"Who would have thought such a fiery wild cat dwelled in that fairy body!"

"It's not what you think. It was just the roses."

"So you have already given her flowers. Then you are hopelessly lost, man."

"I am in love. So much in love that I could fly."

"I know, I know," he slapped me on the back, but I sensed ridicule in his manner. "You gave yourself away yesterday, in astronomy. Remember?

No, of course not. You don't remember a thing. When Pleiades called you to write the solution to the homework on the board, and you walked out with glazed eyes, literature exercise book in your hand, and then with perfectly formed letters you started to write your essay "Description of an Acquaintance". And to top it all it started like this: "Her eyes like stars of pearl shine under the tent of her sweet-scented, silken hair". Then I suspected something bad was up. I saw the whole class fall about laughing – and even Pleiades made a huge effort not to crack up when he asked, "So to which constellation do these stars belong to?" And you still had not the faintest clue what was going on. That was the moment I knew Balder Falkenberg was done for. But never mind. It can happen with beginners. And tell me, did you at least reach under her skirt?"

"You can't just do that right on the first date," I defended. "She's not like that. She's different. She hardly let me touch her breast."

"Then there must be some problem here."

"Why would there be a problem?" I asked surprised.

"Because she seemed "like that" to me, not "different" at all. I smell a rat here."

My friend Arne, who was more experienced than me at the time, felt that there was a problem. Had I paid a little more attention to Ylva, I would have realized it too. But I was inexperienced and pathetically naive. I presented her with a mountain of love letters and flowers. I waited for her after school and walked her home. At times, I succeeded in convincing her to come with me to the cinema or to Hoglands Park. She was pleased by my romantic adoration, and my unconditional attachment flattered her coquettish heart. When I wanted to kiss her, she let me, but her lips stayed closed. When I touched her breast, she gently pushed away my hand. I was only allowed to caress her hair. But that was no longer enough for me. I madly desired the whole of her. I wanted her to look at me the way Karin looked at the silver-bearded man in that candlelit room: with rosy cheeks and glittering eyes. At least once.

Of course, I knew that it was harder to win the heart of certain girls. That is why I was so persistent and patient. But somewhere deep inside me the anguish and pain started to sprout. Then these buds grew until they were choking, venomous tendrils that slowly wound around my heart. I felt the pain but I did not want to acknowledge it. I neglected it like a coward neglects his mild toothache, ignoring the fact that there will be a time when he will be screaming with pain, and he will find himself in the hands of the dentist anyway.

Finally, my turn to scream came.

It happened during a birthday party. I was dancing with Ylva, and I was the happiest man in the world. I embraced her longingly – but could not see her exchanging secret glances with a boy leaning against the door. I pressed her to me more and more passionately, and at times I also felt her drawing me closer. After our third dance she freed herself from my embrace. A new, unknown light was shining on her face. She smiled at me, excused herself for a minute and started walking towards the toilet. I waited for her with great anticipation but to no avail. She did not come back for ages so, suspecting the worst, I went to search for her. I knocked on the toilet door but it was empty. I continued to search the rooms with growing anxiety. She was nowhere to be found. As I stepped out into the garden an icy current crippled me. My eyes ran down the white gravel path and stopped when they reached Ylva's red dress. There she was lying on a bench in Mikhael's lap – and they were necking wildly, oblivious to all around them. I staggered closer. They did not even notice me although I was standing in the centre of the path for ages. I was just transfixed. As if I had been struck by lightning. I did not feel anything except for emptiness. Ylva's opening thighs were illuminated by the dim, amber light of the garden lantern. Mikhael's vehemently grasping fingers brought forth lustful sighs from her trembling body.

Murderous anger, smouldering desire and waves of desperate inertia overcame me. The last turned out to be the strongest. Silent sobs racked my body, and I ran away. I left that damned garden. I would have left the whole cruel world had I had the courage. But I did not have enough, so I just rebelled. And obviously I attacked the one who had made it all happen.

I waited for her on Monday after school at the exit and, without saying hello, I let loose all my soul's bitter anger. It is said that love and pain make one a poet. Yes, inspiration flooded me completely. The most extraordinary metaphors and other poetic expressions poured out of my trembling lips. My muse did not even have the chance to speak. Words streamed out of me like bloody pus from an abscess. However, I was not the only one to be inspired. With a few choice words she then began to draw a portrait of me, the "inexperienced, gullible dummy who doesn't even know how to kiss, who can only use his tongue to lick ice cream, who had only seen a female sexual organ (well, she chose a shorter word for this) in a picture..." After we had both exhausted our artistic duties, we bade each other farewell. Forever.

She called me three days later. She apologized for her "atrocious behaviour" and, for the first time during our short but adventurous time together, it was she who suggested a date...

Like a phoenix rising up from its ashes, hope reawakened in me. Fresh perfume of flowers filled the air again and merry birds were chirping between the branches. The evening breeze started to sing its love song to the sea again. She invited me up to her place. She was at home alone. Her parents were out of town. I brought her a large bouquet of yellow roses, complete with outfit of thorns. Though she took them carefully they still pierced her fingers as she arranged them in a black ceramic vase. She was wearing the same flimsy green dress she had had on when we first met in the forest. Her freshly washed hair had the same fragrance of flowers.

She took my hand and led me up to her bedroom. She turned on a little red lamp, then sat in my lap and hugged me. My body started to shake in excitement. As our lips touched I felt a warm tide rushing through my body, and Ylva's fine little tongue breaking a trail between my surprised lips. My hands, bewildered by desire started grabbing her breasts, then her thighs, then with a tentative motion slipped up till they reached a place I had been dreaming about for so long. Ylva did not resist. Nor did she push away my hand or close her knees. She fumbled with the zip of my trousers. I eagerly sucked in her breath which smelt of honey while one of my fingers was searching for the desired aperture... once found it immersed in it inquiringly. First, she turned her head away, then slowly pushed me away and started to cry silently. My hand slipped out from between her inert thighs. What could have happened? What wrong had I committed? What mistake? Now that I was only one step away from the fulfilment of my most fervent desire, now that the goddess of my dreams opened up to me at last, and I could have been the first to be accepted into her untouched place. Ylva was still a virgin. Virgo Intacta.

"Don't be angry at me. Please don't. I cannot do it, not with you," she whispered, sniffing. "I wanted to... I really did. But my body... my body does not like it... it closes at your touch. I cannot force it. I cannot love you, Bald, however strongly I want it. I cannot love you." Then she burst into sobs and sank her head into a pillow.

Her words bestrewed with salt the deep wound of my soul. The gruesome pain blunted my senses. Disconsolate, I rushed away. I do not remember tottering down the stairs, nor going out onto the street, but I do remember my last drops of energy being concentrated into one last outburst as I slammed my fists into a tree trunk. Blood streamed down my hands. Then the night overtook everything. Not the dark that soothes and regenerates, but a deaf and blind emptiness. The great nihil that sets its axe to the root of all life.

I haunted an empty and godforsaken world like the living dead. Arne tried everything to animate me, but all his attempts fell flat. My mother's desperation, my sisters' malicious mocking, and my father's rugged encouragement all proved ineffective. My parents' last resort was to send me to the county to my grandfather. They hoped this would help me. The trained eyes of the old man noticed the source of my ache, but he did not pretend sympathy like the others. He remained annoyingly cheerful. In fact, he added irony to his exuberantly radiating high spirits.

"Well, well, I see the plague broke out in the city and took all the pretty girls. None were left for my dear grandson."

It was different from my sisters' mockery, and something moved in me. I felt antipathy towards my grandfather's conceited behaviour combined with an eagerness to prove the legitimacy of my sorrow and the tragic weight of my situation. That is exactly what he wanted. Like a good doctor who starts the treatment at the true source of the disease, not where the patient feels the pain.

A wish to prove the realness of my pain mixed with sickly self-pity vibrated in my voice as I told him the story of my suffering. The expression on his face became serious as he listened. He stopped mocking me and did not interrupt me – he let me spill out all the tormenting bitterness. Then he said:

"Love, is that what you said? It isn't real love, son. Just an illusion. Your own desires clothed an attractive disguise on the first person who resembles the ideal you have in your heart. It was not even that poor girl that attracted you but the fairy garments in which you clothed her. Love which is false can only lead to disillusionment and suffering. Real love is different. You will see it when you find it. Real love is the joyful connection of two souls. Real love is always mutual. This love does not lack suffering either, as its fire burns the cinders of its own soul – and this too brings pain. But this pain does at least have a meaning. It heals, purifies and gives strength. But the pain of illusory love is a meaningless and pointless self-torment. It embitters the soul, wearing out life and stealing your vitality, and makes you weak and vulnerable."

Grandfather was lost in his thoughts for a few seconds. He continued after a deep sigh:

"If only you knew how many people suffer like a donkey because of their own illusions. How many of them think that they have found real love! Make sure you don't increase their number. Don't give up your search for the genuine."

Although my mind had become clear enough to understand the meaning of my grandfather's words that did little to alleviate my pain. I still had a long way to go from understanding to accomplishing.

"Tomorrow we're gonna wake up early," he continued in a calm and low voice. "We'll go out to catch some fish. You can shout all your sorrow into the wind of daybreak – like I used to. The wind will take the pain back to where it came from and return with happiness. Joy and sorrow come from the same spring, you know. The wind knows that secret spring."

4. Sonata

I was convinced that love only exists in tales, just like magic mirrors and flying carpets. So I didn't fall in love for a long time. Who could I have fallen for anyway? On the streets of Marseille I saw not one worthy prince, handsome knight or dragon killing poor wanderer.

Not long after I had woken up from the One Thousand and One Nights to find myself in the 'real' world, Mum started my sexual education.

At the age of seven I already knew exactly how boys' bodies differ from girls' and I was also aware that "Mums and Dads can do something together that produces us, the children, nine months later". My parents answered my every question openly and never tried to confuse me with stories of the stork. We watched the erotic scenes together with such ease and naturalness as though we were watching innocent children's films. There was however a significant disadvantage to this free-thinking, modern upbringing. By treating sexuality with equal naturalness to eating, excreting and other basic functions the sexual act lost all its attractive mystery and uplifting romantic beauty for me and so somehow I didn't manage to feel the erotica in it. My parents were often naked in front of me and they had no inhibitions at home. I often had a bath with Dad or Mum, sometimes with both so I got used to the naturalness of bodies touching. It felt nice to soap my father's muscly brown chest and strong arms or Mum's soft but still interestingly hard breasts. But I didn't feel any eroticism in this; it was rather one of the many expressions of love.

❖

One day something happened that made me aware that nudity was not so natural to everyone as it was in our family. A few months after the memorable election when I had become the omnipotent queen of the Golden Palace I came up with a new game. I gathered the girls and suggested that we prepare a ballet performance in secret. I had been attending ballet lessons for two years and so I felt perfectly prepared for the task. The girls absolutely loved the idea and we planned that when the piece was ready we would organize a proper premiere to which we would invite the boys and the parents. We took an oath to keep the idea to ourselves, just for the element of surprise.

I decided the upper floor of the palace would be the rehearsal room and we banned the boys during our practices. They were happy about it, as at last they were free of the girls for a while and could play a real boys' game: war. I started teaching with great enthusiasm. The ballet teacher role suited me perfectly. I put on Miss Giselle's authoritative and determined allure and called out the commands loudly: "ATTENTION!... NOW DEMI-PLIÉ... one, two, three, four... GRAND-PLIÉ, two, three, four... GO LOWER, JEANNE!... five, six, sev'n, eight... LIFT YOUR ARMS SLOWLY!... one, two, three, four... RELAX YOUR WRIST, VÉRONIQUE! BEND YOUR ELBOW, CLAIRE! STRAIGHT KNEES, MICHELLE – oh, what wooden legs, my goodness! – DON'T STARE AT THE FLOOR, MARIE JO!... LOOK AHEAD!... YOU TOO, YVONNE... AND SMILE, GIRLS, WE'RE NOT AT A FUNERAL! ... DON'T WORRY IF IT HURTS, KEEP SMILING! Yes, that's it."

The attempts at smiling were just pained and twisted grimaces, but that's the way it is at the start. I looked on with proud satisfaction as they suffered, sweated and struggled for breath.

A heated debate developed after the rehearsal. What dance clothes should we wear at the premiere? In the end I cut the Gordian knot with a novel idea: "Let's dance naked!" My suggestion was met with general astonishment and so, to add weight to my words, I said that I had seen a ballet performance on TV where they were dancing naked ... and it was fantastic. This, of course, was not true, but the theory worked and, with some exceptions, they thought it was a fun idea.

In fact I had seen a performance in which the dancers were actually in a close-fitting, skin-coloured costume that perfectly imitated nakedness. But why imitate nudity? Wouldn't it just be so much easier and more stunning if they really were dancing naked?

We tried out the new costume the very next day. At the start some of them didn't want to undress but, when they saw just how good the braver ones felt without clothes, they wanted to join in too. When the sun peeped in at the top of the wall half an hour later, it delighted in the sight of nine naked little girls dancing and panting.

We had an absolutely amazing time. Better than ever. Now we had a real shared secret, the girls' secret. And it was so exciting!

But the Creator didn't make girls to keep secrets. A few days later the parents found out and the scandal broke. The neighbourhood parents' council met and questioned my Mum in detail as to "why she didn't pay more attention to her sweet little girl's perverse tendencies", letting her know that they wouldn't let their children play with me any more because "I'll ruin them". My parents promised that they would see to me and that nothing similar would happen in the future. Of course, they had no intention of punishing me. Poor Mum couldn't even find a proper reason to tell me off. She was used to the naturalness of nakedness. So, in the end, Dad held a brief lecture as to the unwritten laws of society. He explained that people were different, had diverse ideas about sexuality and that it was best if we respect others' feeling and thoughts and try not to scandalize them. That meant not to undress just anywhere, and particularly not in front of those that are bothered by nudity.

The family never talked about the incident again but my parents thought it wouldn't hurt if my sex education was supplemented with a little religious input. They picked my maternal grandmother for the task. A passionate churchgoer and ardent Catholic, she was the one who had taught me to pray and took me to church sometimes. This time though she probably received more definite instructions from my parents regarding my initiation into spiritual matters.

From then on I spent a month with my grandparents every summer in a picturesque small village at the foot of the St Baume Mountains where my grandfather had bought a lsizeable farm after his retirement. On the land stood an attractive whitewashed villa with dark brown doors and window frames, and a high tile roof. The two sides of the main drive were decorated by hundreds of flowers in every shade imaginable: the splendid empire of my grandmother. A wide grassy area stretched out from it that my grandfather cut to a short, English style from time to time.

There was a large orchard behind the house and a long stable – the residence of my grandfather's pets. Horse racing, in spite of the fact that it was money thrown out of the window, was his passion. He placed huge bets and always lost. But he had money to lose. He owned one of the most successful bank chains in Marseille. Actually he had extraordinary business acumen but the goddess Fortuna never favoured him in his gambling exploits. After his retirement my Uncle Frédérick took over the management of the business interests. So Grandfather went into town for the occasional important meeting, but spent most of his time in this little paradise.

I absolutely adored this place. I grew to love the dogs, the horses, the smell of fresh manure, the taste of warm cow's milk, the roses' evening fragrance and the feel of dewy grass on my bare feet. I started to recognize the flowers: the large, white hibiscus, the begonias, the crown imperials, the yellow mimosas with their furry flowers dangling on the long stems, the small slipper orchids, the amaryllis splendid in the whole rainbow of colours, and the large flame lily that stretched her large reddish fire tongues towards the sun with such proud dignity. She was my favourite. I told her tales about the city, my friends, the Golden Palace and I had the feeling that she told me stories too, about another world: the world of One Thousand and One Nights, the one that I had thought had been lost forever. Whenever I sat in front of her and took her velvety petal chalice in my hand I felt that she also belonged to this other world somehow. That was why I loved her so much.

Grandmother took me to church every morning. I was forced to sit silently among the toothless old ladies dressed in clothes that smelt of funerals and listen to the flat-faced priest's hollow-sounding sermon about "some other kind of kingdom into which only those who attend church regularly are allowed". Meanwhile the sun would be shining, the birds singing to their hearts' content, and Blanche would be whinnying impatiently in the stable – she could hardly wait to carry me on her back.

Time dragged interminably in that cold, gloomy church smelling of mothballs. Now and again stunning large green and blue flies would fly in through the window. They circled for a while in the air before landing on the red necks of old men snoozing. The sound of them being swatted broke the monotonous boredom of the murmured prayer. Once a sparrow flew in, that was really exciting. Everyone woke up... unfortunately it too was seized by devotion after a while. It landed on the head of the Virgin Mary and sat there for the rest of the mass.

At night my grandmother would read biblical stories to me. I loved them because they were like fairy tales. They told of kings, great battles, beautiful orchards, snakes and love...

When Grandmother thought the time was right she started to speak about sin. She also talked about Satan, who is always waiting to tempt people, leading us onto the path of sin. We, however, are helpless to resist because, since the time a woman called Eve gave an apple to her faithful partner, we have all been sinners at the mercy of Satan's evil malice. Well, this is at least kind of how I understood it at the time.

When Grandmother talked about these things, the wrinkles on her thin, birdlike face smoothed out and a peculiar light illuminated her eyes, particularly when she spoke of the worst sin of them all: lust. With a sparkling look and a practically lascivious enjoyment she painted a detailed picture of it. Gloating overtones were barely hidden in her voice whenever she sketched out the "terrible passions" with which Hell awaits "wrongdoers who succumb to Satan's underhand temptations and dare to taste bodily pleasures without the protection of the sacred bonds of marriage". My grandmother's words blasted into the moonlit silence, just like the trumpets of the Last Judgment. They stirred disquieting waves in me and engraved themselves deep into my soul. It was as though the room was filled with suffocating sulphurous fumes and the hellish stink of flesh being grilled alive. I felt I heard the desperate moans from bodies piled on top of one another and saw a twisting male goat with eyes burning blood red in front of me. An intangible terror rising from extremely deep within took hold of me. Until then I had never known this type of fear. The sort of horror we might feel on a dark night when a flapping bat wing brushes our cheek.

Grandmother taught me devotedly and she enthusiastically instilled in me a sense of sin. And, surprisingly, along with fear and guilt, desire also awoke in me. The desire to know, to taste and experience that "sin". What before had seemed natural all of a sudden became exhilarating, mysterious and incredibly attractive. Until then the erotic scenes in films had left me completely cold, but now, even the sight of the stallion mounting the mare – that the stable boy showed me – filled me with an unusual and turbulent excitement.

My poor grandmother wanted to deter me from sin but she actually managed to awaken my desire for it. By the peculiar irony of Fate, it was in her house that one year later I first savoured the unforgettable taste of the forbidden fruit...

❖

It all started one Sunday in July. As usual Grandmother took me to church. But this time she also managed to drag Grandfather along too, although he was even more bored of this "entertainment for old people" than I was. On Sundays the atmosphere was different from the other days of the week as the church was full and many of the young people also came. They sat up in the gallery next to the organ. Grandmother did not allow me to stray from her side. I had to sit there with her, among the adults.

I glanced longingly up at the cheerful group sitting in the gallery. Unexpectedly my wandering gaze met with a pair of eyes that were observing me intensely. A subtle shiver ran through my body when I realized that the boy was looking at me. I quickly turned my head and looked up into nothing but I couldn't ignore this pair of eyes shining with a strange light. After a while I stole a glance and took a better look. Short, dark blond hair, handsome face, a boy about seventeen... All of a sudden he turned towards me again and caught my eye. A satisfied smile appeared at the corner of his mouth. I was irritated that he had noticed my interest, but I held his gaze because I didn't want to give him more cause for satisfaction by bashfully turning my head like someone caught in a prank. Self-confidence and curiosity mingled in the bluish but fiery light of his gaze, and something else that I didn't yet recognize. And that "something else" was the strongest. It made me shiver from the first moments and then started to flood me with an unknown heat as we watched each other. A silent battle had begun, who could hold out longer...

I gave in first but only because I was afraid that Grandmother would notice. Not once did I look in his direction for the rest of the mass, despite being incredibly curious with a new feeling that had been lit inside me. There was something exciting in this opposition ...As I was swept towards the door with the crowd at the end of the mass I felt a strong squeeze of my left hand. It was him! He winked at me, pressed a piece of paper into my palm and then disappeared without a word. I was terribly curious about its content but was only able read it when I got back to my room. In the top half of a page ripped from the prayer book and written in pencil with large scribbled letters was the message:

I'll be waiting for you at Three Willows today at five.

R.

Now, just wait a second! How dare you order me to a meeting without at least asking my opinion? I had definitely no intention of going... but I couldn't free myself from the memory of his piercing look either. Well, he was the first boy to look at me like that. I tried to discover the meaning of the strange glint that shone in his eyes. The way he looked at me... It filled me with such a good feeling... it was pleasant... and exciting. He definitely liked me... because... he looked at me with wonder. But what was that disturbing new feeling that had so ensnared me? Might it be...? No, it can't be... I pushed the thought away. Love exists only in books... and in films... But why he was eyeing me so... brazenly?

I was the first to arrive at the appointed place, although I had been late on purpose. What if he won't even come? What if he just wanted to mock at me? Those village rascals are capable of anything ... and there was something roguish in his look, I had already noticed that in the church. What should I do now? I'll wait for one more minute, then leave.

The Three Willows was actually a spring at the edge of the village. It was surrounded by three willow trees that created a fairly regular equilateral triangle. I loved to visit this place, it seemed somewhat mythical to me. But what is this noise? A galloping horseman was approaching on the path. My goodness! It's him! Total and hopeless confusion. I had already planned well in advance how to give him a roasting for his ill breeding. Now suddenly all thoughts scrambled in my head.

"Do you like riding?" he asked smiling as he came to a halt next to me.

He could have said sorry for being late, or at least greeted me I thought, but aloud I said:

"Y-yes... I love it."

"Would you like to ride with me?" he asked as he jumped off the horse.

Then, without even waiting for an answer, he helped me up into the saddle and jumped in front of me.

"Hold onto me tightly," he said over his shoulder and tugged at the reins.

The horse started to trot and then to gallop. My hair flying freely tickled my bare shoulder pleasantly.

"I'VE WANTED TO MEET YOU FOR AGES!" my knight shouted back in a confident voice. "YOU ARE THE ONLY REASON I WENT TO CHURCH. I NEVER GO NORMALLY! IT'S INCREDIBLY BORING! DO YOU LIKE GOING TO CHURCH?"

"NO!" – I shouted into the wind. "BUT MY GRANDMOTHER ALWAYS DRAGS ME WITH HER!"

"I'M ROGER! ROGER CHAUVIN!"

"I'M LAURIANNE..."

"I KNOW! AND I ALSO KNOW THAT YOU LIVE IN MARSEILLE ... AND THAT YOUR FATHER IS THE DIRECTOR OF A PRINTERS ... AND THAT YOU'LL BE FOURTEEN NEXT WEEK!"

"HOW DO YOU KNOW ALL THAT?!"

"I MADE INQUIRIES! PEOPLE KNOW EVERYTHING HERE IN THE VILLAGE!"

We galloped the length of the forest, the trees flashing past us at great speed. I hugged Roger's waist tightly and for a second I felt I never wanted to let go again. When we arrived back at the spring after an exhausting gallop he lifted me off the horse as though I was nothing less than his bride to be. He was in no hurry to let go of my waist, but neither did he hold me for too long, keeping me in his arms just long enough for me to feel their strength. Then we drank from the spring, scooping up water in our palms to wash our flushed faces.

And we chatted for a while, or rather he spoke. He told me everything about himself. At least everything he thought may pique the interest of a fourteen year old city girl... that he practiced martial arts, that he was planning to enter the military academy after secondary school... When I wanted to leave he suggested that he took me home on horseback but I refused. I didn't want my grandmother to see us together. I sang the whole way back, thinking about our next meeting with a bubbling excitement.

Those clandestine meetings had a unique flavour. Like forbidden fruit generally does. Roger knew the area well and always took me to interesting places, planning routes with some kind of a surprise in store for me. He proved inventive in this. With amazing ability he shinnied up the smooth tree trunk to bring me bird eggs from the tip of the branch and, when I told him off for stealing the eggs, he climbed back up without a word and p`laced them back in the nest. He caught fish in the stream with his bare hands and, when the sheepdog came lunging aggressively towards us, he sent it back just with his look.

With his clear sense of purpose, his courage and his attractive, muscly figure he won my favour. The fire that burnt in his eyes, the power that radiated from his movements, and the way he stole glances at my body thoroughly moved me. I felt I was gradually losing my self-confidence and imagined superiority. I realised his conquering me was inevitable. There was a strange ambiguity in the feeling; I didn't want to surrender to him, but there was still an exciting joy that filled me every moment when I allowed him one step closer to me.

The proud and wild lassie, who thought that love was only born of a writer's fantasy, fell deeply in love. Nothing else interested me any more, but to be with Roger as much as possible. I was no longer as watchful and careful as I had been at the beginning and I risked far more. Love gave me a new kind of crazy power. I believed I was capable of fighting anyone for it. Come what may!

Well, my grandparents found out. The villagers saw us together and betrayed us. The family scandal broke out... a more serious one than I could have ever imagined. Grandmother was red with fury. She looked awful. Her voice trembled with anger when she chastened me:

"Laurianne, my dear, have you totally lost your pretty little head! How on earth could you even look at such a good-for-nothing charlatan as that ruffian Chauvin, that forsaken bastard? He's already turned the heads of all the ignorant lasses in the village. But those aren't good enough for him any longer. That insolent wretch has his eye on nice girls now! He's just after your fortune. I know. I know his kind well. His father was a drunken crook who drank until he dropped, and his mother was the local prostitute, while they still looked at her. Now not even the lowest of low needs her. And now this upstart has his eye on my granddaughter. But you... how could you... with him?! I'm certain he's in league with Satan. I'm sure he put a spell on you! There's no other explanation, that you... Laurianne Lamy... I hope he didn't dishonour you, because if he did, then... then... I'll kill him!"

Words, like spit, spattered from her lips accustomed to prayer. It was disgusting. I didn't even find them worthy of a reply.

After that I was strictly banned from having any contact with Roger at all and I was not allowed out of the garden without a chaperone. The stable boy was entrusted with my strict supervision. He took me for a walk sometimes. Other than that I huddled in my room the whole day. I only went to church because Roger was always sitting there so at least we were able to exchange the odd glance. But that only served to increase my loneliness making it even more unbearable.

There was one advantage to my grounding: I discovered Grandfather's library and started to read. I searched for those novels telling of love because that was the only thing I was interested in, and I recognized myself in every love story. Now I knew that every story was true! I knew that love exists! I read the parts about love making at least ten times until I knew them all by heart. And in my thoughts I gave myself to Roger many times. We met in large marble halls lined with silk cushions that had a joyful fountain playing in the centre and baths filled with rose-scented warm water. Pure gold jewels and large pearls adorned my body, and I wore nothing but that jewels … This is how Roger enveloped me in his strong arms and made me his, time and again, on the generous divan draped in red silks.

❖

One afternoon the stable boy knocked on my bedroom door and invited me for a walk. The horses were already saddled in the yard. Poor Blanche. In my grief I had even forgotten about her. She whinnied with joy when she saw me. I hugged her beautiful muscly neck and, as I buried my face in her coat a little, I felt just how much she loved me.

When I jumped into the saddle she moulded to me as though we two had always been just one body. Instinctively I set off in the direction of Three Willows. From afar I could see a figure sitting by the spring, leaning back against one of the trees. When he saw me he jumped to his feet. I thought I recognized Roger's elastic movements. Yes, it is him! Blanche felt just how fast my heart was beating, and quickened her step. I pulled on the reins and looked at my bodyguard. Smiling he waved that I should go on without fear.

"But you're not going to tell on me, are you?"

"I'll be as silent as the grave."

I gave my horse free rein. She reared up onto two legs when I yanked the reins as we reached the willow tree. I wanted to jump straight onto his neck from the saddle, but I had second thoughts.

"Would you like to ride with me?" I asked, forcing a smiling calm over myself.

Roger appeared behind me with one single extraordinary leap. Blanche's knees creaked with the surprise.

"Hold onto me tightly," I shouted over my shoulder and slapped the horse's hindquarters.

Roger squeezed me so tight that my breath stopped. Hungry lips pressed to my neck. A pleasant shiver ran through my body. Then he started to hug me ardently, covering my neck, my shoulders and my arms in hot kisses. His breath scorched my ears as Blanche galloped on madly. My breasts flattened in surprise under his large, strong palms; heat coursed through me. I felt all my power drain out of my limbs. Now I only felt his strength in his arms that held me so tightly. Blanche slowed and came to a stop. Stunned I leaned back and happily gave myself over to Roger's thirsty kisses. When our lips finally parted after a long time he lifted his head to the heavens and let out a great shout. It was almost frightening: "I LOVE YOU!!!" And then again: "I LOVE YOU!!!" It shook the leaves on the trees, and the birds stopped singing for a moment.

Trotting slowly we returned to the spring. Roger lifted me down from the horse and enclosed me in his arms. He wouldn't let me go. We stayed like this for a long time. It had already gone quite dark. The stable boy's whistle awoke us from our sweet intoxication. He motioned that we should go.

"Will you come again?"

"I'll be here tomorrow night. Wait for me, my love!"

That night I tossed and turned without falling into a dream. During the day I didn't know where to put myself and feverishly awaited the evening.

Our second meeting was not so passionate, rather romantic and tender. We walked hand in hand in the forest, drank spring water from each other's palm and promised eternal fidelity to one another in the temple of the Three Willows. The moon was already shining palely in the eastern sky. She was our witness... and the sun which looked back with one last loving glance to his heavenly partner before giving over the space to her.

The stable boy took me for a walk every day. Later I found out that Roger had paid a considerable sum for the first meeting but after that the boy brought me of his own free will, out of the goodness of his heart. A type of complicit friendship developed between the three of us.

But then one day he announced he didn't dare take the risk any longer. He said plainly that he was afraid because, if my Grandmother suspected something, then that 'was the end of him'. But that which has started cannot be stopped. Roger came up with an even more daring plan. At night, when everyone was sleeping, he stole into my room. I've no idea how he did it but out of the blue there he was, standing at the window and softly, like a tiger, he jumped next to my bed. My breath stopped. I could hardly utter a word.

"You've gone completely bonkers! If Grandfather catches you, he'll set the dogs on you!"

"Yes, I have gone completely bonkers. You've made me crazy and I can't bear another day without you..."

They were crazy nights. The knowledge that my grandparents were sleeping in the room below, the power of fear made the forbidden fruit so much sweeter.

There inside, in the intimacy of my room, different kinds of feelings and desires were born than out in the natural environment: hotter and more demanding. Inside there was a bed, my bed, in which I had given myself to him on countless occasions – even if only in my imagination. And it was dark, practically demanding nakedness. I submitted to these demands and I submitted to Roger too, allowing him to peel my clothes off me, his hand to touch that place where no man's hand had yet touched. But I stopped there. I didn't let him go further. He asked in vain. He persuaded and pleaded, begged and beseeched... I was an impenetrable castle. Even though my body was shaking, burning and writhing from its own demands, a kind of coldness ruled in me, and I felt that however strong desire might be it would never triumph over me.

For a long time I believed the fear and guilt that Grandmother had burnt into me over the years stopped me giving my virginity to Roger. But, no, there was something else. Something rooted in my own nature. The fact that I was the stronger unconsciously filled me with exciting pleasure. Stronger than Roger and stronger than my own instincts. I was proud to be able to keep my inner beast under control.

❖

The summer flew by. Soon we had to say our goodbyes. We made a pact that we would write to each other and meet as soon as possible. And we did write often, at the start. Long letters full of heated memories and burning desires, but the meeting never happened. Roger didn't come to see me.

As autumn passed our letters became less frequent, and shorter and shorter, just like the winter days... and ever cooler too. Unable to stretch this far into the future the heat of summer memories could no longer keep our correspondence warm. Then winter passed too, and spring arrived. The days started to become warmer, and finally Roger came. Excitedly I awaited the meeting, but I was afraid of it at the same time.

We met at the railway station. I waved to him from afar, but we did not rush into one another's arms, nor did we leap to hug each other tears flowing down our cheeks. He approached me calmly and somewhat stiffly, kissed me and hugged me. There was something strange in the kiss and something odd in the hug.

We walked towards the sea. We held hands and talked. All the while Roger watched my face, his eyes boring into me. I was looking for the same Roger I had got to know the summer before, the lad I had been carrying in my heart ever since. But I didn't find him. The person who was walking alongside me holding my hand resembled him, but wasn't him. That awe was missing from his look, the glowing desire that had so stirred me had become much less intense and, I think, less honest too.

Suddenly we ran out of things to say. The silence was embarrassing because the wordless feeling of togetherness was also missing. It was an empty, frightening and painful silence.

I desperately searched for something to say, just in case there was something I hadn't said, or a question I hadn't yet aired. But apparently we had already said everything to each other... We sat on a rocky outcrop and watched the sea. Then Roger turned me towards him and kissed me. Fragments of memories stirred in me – wild galloping and passionate nights, but I didn't feel that same feeling any more. I don't think he did either… So we didn't force it any longer.

"We've changed, Laurie," he said quietly.

"Yes, I think we have…"

"Last summer was so beautiful…" Roger sighed deeply and then unexpectedly hugged me tightly.

That felt good. Really good. There was something calming in it, something relaxing, like in a friend's hug.

"Let's go. I'm sure they're waiting for you at home."

"Where will you go?"

"One of my aunts lives in the city so I'll sleep at hers and then go back to Montpellier tomorrow."

He accompanied me to our house and then we said goodbye.

"Well, I'll… erm… visit you."

"That'll be good…" But I knew he wouldn't visit me again.

Sobs constricted my throat, but I only let my tears flow when I reached my room.

Well, so that is the great and famous love! It leaves with summer and cannot renew with the spring when everything in nature rejuvenates. I had denied the existence of love for so long and, just when I was most convinced that it didn't exist, Life just threw it around my neck, sweeping me along with it… and when I was finally able to proclaim to the world: "Yes! Love does exist, not only in tales, because I, Laurianne, am in love!" it was taken away from me. I don't need this kind of love any more!

My bedroom door opened quietly. Mum came in and sat down beside me, hugged my head to her breast and started to rock me – just as she had when I was a baby. Silent sobs racked my body. When, finally, I had calmed down a little she turned me to look at her:

"Where were you this afternoon?" she asked in a warm and comforting voice.

I told her everything: Roger, the spring, the evening walks, the exhilarating nights… I was afraid she'd be angry and would reject me, but there was no way I could stop the flood of words. They just poured out, overflowing… then a peaceful calm remained after them… there inside. Mum didn't push me away. She didn't tell me off. All she asked was:

"Did you sleep with him?"

And I was so glad to be able to tell her, "No, I didn't give myself to him completely."

Relieved, she sighed, "You did the right thing." And then she continued,

"You see, first love is like that. Like the pine branch it cracks, burns bright and soon turns to ashes. And you are… so young still, such a child!"

"Is there another kind of love?" The words burst out from me involuntarily.

"Yes, there is. That's real love. That's different. It burns like the eternal flame: evenly. And it never goes out."

"And how do you know that this kind of love exists?"

"I know… and you will also know"

"Do you love Dad that way?"

Mum just looked and smiled. Then she took my hand and led me into the living room. She sat down at the piano. Her fingers touched the keys lightly and she started to play. The painfully sweet chords of Beethoven's Moonlight sonata rose from between the strings and filled the room. My mother's fingers wandered across the keys as though they were stroking them, not even touching them. It seemed she was able to bring the instrument to give sound merely with her radiating soul. As she gave herself over to the magical joy of playing, her body started to move in subtle and graceful waves. I watched as her eyes slowly closed, a secret radiance spread over her face and her lips opened in a barely perceptible smile. Then I realized that it wasn't actually her lips that were smiling but something was happening inside, deep inside. A mysterious state, a marvellous feeling had awakened in her soul, and it was this that was drawing the invisible smile on her ecstatic face. As the delicate sounds of light rain falling grew into the wild torrents of mountain streams so did the movement of my mother's slim body change as if strong wind were whipping the willow trees into a dance. The soft smile blazed into glowing passion on her opening lips.

I had never seen her like this before…

Though the vibrations of the final chord that dissolved everything around us had long been absorbed into the ether, Mum's hands still hadn't left the keys. It was as though she wanted to make eternal that expansive feeling born within her. As though her soul could not leave that other world where her joyful and free flying was not limited by anything.

Then she opened her eyes. She had returned to me.

"Mum, you're so amazingly beautiful when you play the piano!"

"When I play this piece," she replied and her face went slightly flushed. "Because this is what I had been playing when I got to know the man that you now call Dad."

Mum started to laugh as she searched among her memories.

"It was such a funny situation. I always laugh whenever I think of it. Your grandfather was an influential public figure at the time, you know. He was present at every important gathering, reception and party and one time he took me with him to one of these glittering occasions. Every single member of the city elite was there and I had to play the piano after the ceremonial dinner. Your Grandfather wanted it – he was so very proud of me. I played the Moonlight sonata and, when I finished the piece, I noticed that a tall, dark and handsome young man was standing next to me on the small stage. As our eyes met, he smiled. He had the same smile as those children who are always up to something. He took the microphone into his hands and asked the 'honoured guests' for permission to sing a song, as a present for his bride-to-be. Then he started to sing. He sang in Italian, a romantic love song. He had a beautifully resounding strong voice. Everyone listened with pleasure. Even the piano strings replied to him... and a subtle vibration began in me too. The way he sang the song so seriously, putting his whole heart into it was so seductive that I almost started to envy his fiancée. He received rapturous applause, and then a couple of people shouted out:

"But Niccolo, you didn't tell us you were getting married!" "Who's your bride-to-be, Niccolo?" "Introduce us to your bride, too!" A little unnerved he scratched his shaggy black mop, and then answered: "The only problem is, I don't know her name yet..." Tumultuous laughter broke out in the room. He turned to me as if looking for help. I didn't understand what was happening. Then he came over to me, led me by the hand to the microphone and asked me to introduce myself to the guests. Suddenly I was so confused that I didn't know what I was called. When he saw that I was in trouble, he introduced himself first and then kissed my hand. After that I somehow managed to mumble my name too and then, in front of all the guests, he solemnly asked for my hand. Everyone was rolling about laughing. The mayor wiped his tears with his handkerchief – and your Grandfather smiled uncomfortably and blinked a lot. He did not know what to make of the whole comedy.

"And you? What did you do?"

"Me? I laughed along with the others for a little while and then said "Yes" to him."

"Just like that? Straight away? But you didn't even know him!"

"I did know him. Enough as was necessary. Anyway, you feel these things from the first moment."

"And then what happened?"

"Exactly a year later to the day, we got married and we lived happily ever after..."

I thought a lot about the story after I went to bed and I suppose I got a glimpse about the kind of love Mum was talking about. And the radiance I saw on her face while she was playing said more than her words. But it was only later that I came to understand the nature of this radiance. On a special occasion.

My parents were celebrating their wedding anniversary. Mum had made a delicious dinner and set the table in the dining room. Dad brought a huge bunch of stunning flowers. A candle burned in the centre of the table, and we all drank champagne. Mum was dressed in her favourite dark blue evening dress, her hair was gathered up in a splendid knot. A new amethyst pendant shone on her breast. She had just received it from Dad. Ecstatic light upon her face. My father's large, admiring eyes were glued to her the whole time. He even forgot to eat at times.

After dinner I asked Mum to allow me to clean up the kitchen. She agreed and they went to their bedroom. I cleared the table, washed up and cleaned the dining room and the kitchen. Before I went to bed I wanted to wish them good night. As I reached their bedroom door I hesitated... strange and disturbing sounds were coming from within... I heard Dad's heavy breathing and Mum's moaning voice that sometimes changed into a little whimpering giggle, sometimes increasing into a shriek. The realization hit me like a bolt of lightning: they were making love! I pressed my ears to the door. Sometimes the noises quietened before breaking through once again with renewed force. It was all rather unexpected. I knew that men and women made love with each other, but the possibility that this was also true of my parents... Well, it hadn't really crossed my mind.

I peeped in through the keyhole. The gentle light of the small reading lamp made my Mum's bare body shine. It was as if she was sitting at the piano – she was supporting herself on her two hands on Dad's broad chest and her body was moving the same wonderfully undulating dance. The same mysterious light shone from her face as when she had been playing the piano... only that she was even more beautiful now, more passionate and even more radiant...

I went to the salon. My hands excitedly fumbled among the records. And then I found it! I pushed up the volume to the maximum on the record player and the amorous nostalgic sounds of Beethoven's Moonlight sonata triumphantly took possession of the whole house.

5. Carina Dahl

My father caught the first glimpse of my musical skills when he saw me riding merrily in the saddle of the double bass and fishing for imaginary goldfish with the bow between the shabby chairs of the auditorium. A few years later when he heard me humming faultlessly the main and secondary themes of rather difficult musical pieces he came to the valid decision that an expert's hands were needed to nurse my emerging talent. The bony-fingered hands, covered with a network of purple veins he chose for this purpose belonged to Aunt Selma, a distant relative of ours. As during band rehearsals my father had seen me loitering mostly around the piano, he came to the logical conclusion that we were perfectly matched. At that time there certainly was a secret attraction between the two of us. Probably because the piano was the only instrument from which I could lure out acceptable sounds. I did my best to blow the trumpets, trombones, and horns till I was red in the face, but hardly any noises – other than grotesque burps – emerged from their gleaming funnels. The flute just hissed like an old snake, the clarinet quacked like a suffocating drake and the fiddle was only willing to sound notes ranging between a frightened asthmatic mouse and a croaky tomcat suffering from tonsillitis. But the piano – that was different. It responded to my hands with the same fine and ringing notes as those brought alive by the touch of the wide-bottomed pianist. The lowest notes could mimic the roar of the sea while the highest rang like brilliant raindrops falling on the leaves of the vine under my window.

Under the tutelage of the grey-haired and severe Aunt Selma I quickly had to realize that playing the piano is in no way the same as freely and joyfully hitting the key but actually an extremely unpleasant and tiring art. I soon started to regret that I had bowed down to my father's will so easily.

My father had chosen me a teacher according to his own taste: Aunt Selma was just as strict, authoritative and stiff as him. She even shared his lack of playfulness – her chronic spinster syndrome made it even more unbearable. I suffered through many hours of boring and exhausting practice listening to Aunt Selma's shrieking instructions. That ugly composer named Czerny made me the angriest. It seemed his only reason for writing sheet music full of scribbles was to provide piano teachers a chance to torment their students. Aunt Selma had another instrument of torture in her toolkit: scales practice. The worst part was when – in spite of all my efforts to do it correctly – I made a mistake, and she mercilessly screeched: "FROM THE BEGINNING"! Then I would sit there hopeless, like one who just received his death sentence, and I had to draw strength from my soul's hidden reserves to start again.

I had to restart after every mistake. That was her way of teaching me to concentrate completely on playing. My mind rebelled against it desperately; it cherished only the free flight of inspiration and unconstrained imagination. It took a lot of time for my old tutor to close the restless wonder bird of my spirit in the cage of treble and bass clef lines. The bird still managed to fly out occasionally. At times, when Aunt Selma left me alone and went to the kitchen, a moment of absentmindedness would descend over me and my fingers would start to play something completely different from that written on the sheet music. At first I only improvised to the theme of the piece, but the ecstasy of creation captivated me in seconds. I forgot where I was and what I had been doing. The shabby, brown wardrobe, the lumpy settee, the little window covered with thick lace curtain, and the musty smell of the apartment along with the kitchen and Aunt Selma herself were absorbed in the ether that was now only filled by sounds that shone like a colourful magnetic field.

Daydreaming like this could never last for long – only until the unknown notes reached Aunt Selma's ears and she rushed back from the kitchen. She slammed down the piano lid with such force I hardly had time to draw back my startled hands. She relentlessly chopped down every sapling of my creative tendency. She was convinced that everybody can tickle the ivories but that the true virtuoso has to, above all, play with perfect exactitude what the maestro had written. Aunt Selma's drastic methods turned out to be effective. Within four years my ability to focus developed enormously and I was able to play even the tougher pieces correctly. But I never grew fond of the piano. We lived together like patient spouses in a lousy marriage. I accepted it. I put up with my fate and I overlooked the fact that, under my hands, it started to grow old, the odd ivory pieces chipping off its yellowish white denture. Though I tried to be an attentive and devoted spouse, I lacked the inspiring force of a loving affection. And, like all bad marriages this too lasted till I found real love – for this is how I would define my first encounter with the cello: love at first hearing.

I was around twelve when Stockholm's Royal Philharmonic gave a concert in our town. A remarkably talented Austrian cellist played Haydn's cello concerto in D major. My heart started to beat rapidly when I heard the expansive arcs of melody and virtuoso cello scales in the first movement. Then as the second movement's silently dreaming and sorrowfully delicate parts burst forth from the young cellist's instrument, my obscure wish crystallized in one definite thought: "I want to learn to play the cello!" These tones, so similar to my inner world, left vibrations that echoed in me for days.

I was still under the spell of the experience when I categorically stated to my father that I would no longer learn the piano and that only one thing in the world interested me: the cello!

This odd enthusiasm even managed to touch my father, and he discussed the matter with a retired cellist colleague of his. Mr. Helmer was delighted to accept the job. I liked the old man. He had a much more sensitive and refined soul than Aunt Selma. He retained his youthful, romantic passions though he was well over sixty-five. His favourite of all the aesthetic categories was, without doubt, the tragic. The only problem was that he lacked any pedagogical talent – he was a natural born performer. He played through the musical pieces I had to learn with a soul-stirring tenderness, but he just could not explain clearly how I should play it. In contrast with Aunt Selma, who deconstructed everything to its base and made me practice it note by note, he only kept repeating: "Don't you feel it? Listen to me! I'll show you one more time." He played the piece for the fourth time and added, "This is how you do it. Make the instrument cry so the audience will have their hearts broken over it." I felt my own heart break because I did hear the difference. I just had no idea what I should do to "make the instrument cry". Nor did he manage to explain that to me. He showed me for the seventh time, but as I replayed the same empty sounding passages he lost his temper and exploded, "How can someone be such an insensitive ass? I don't get why someone like that would touch a musical instrument. You'd better go to the shipyard to forge screws. Music should be played from the soul. And I have told you a thousand times; what you hold in your hand is not a saw but a bow – so hold it properly." The problem was he had not even mentioned how to hold the bow. When he noticed my despair after these streams of abuse he tried to console me. "Don't worry, it will be fine. I started out just like you. You know, son, music is like love: it requires great sacrifice, you have to suffer for it, and for the soul it means the greatest delight and darkest agony at the same time... Music and Love...!"

Speaking about this subject he was always emotional. You could see him choking down sobs, especially if he had been drinking – unfortunately that was his other shortcoming: he drank a lot. He had buried his wife ten years earlier; she had died of cancer. They had loved each other immensely and he spoke of her often. He could not forgive Fate for her early death. Since that time he had stopped laughing, he did not even smile, and drank more and more. Yet I liked the old man, and I think he grew fond of me too. He also sensed our souls' resemblance. I began to feel sorry for him. Occasionally, while playing pieces that had overtones of sorrow, he made me stop. Trying to suppress his tears he asked me not to play it any more...

#yaml

and with a shaking hand he poured himself another glass. I often tried to console him and advised him to forget the past and be happy with what he had in the present but he just waved his hand saying, "You cannot understand it son…" I did understand it perfectly. The disappointment caused by Ylva Ekberg had left me wounded, with a pain so agonizing I felt like drinking with him…

My experience with Ylva had a striking influence on me that also had its impact on my musical development. It stirred up great depths in me, and these depths enriched my inner moods. Maybe it was exactly this infernal suffering that liberated in me the boundless power which transformed my sterile practice into live music. I began to understand what my old teacher required from me, to discover that every musical piece has its own soul that comes alive only when it meets the performer's soul. "That is it, son! Perfect! I told you it would work one day!" That was the first time I saw Mr. Helmer happy. "Don't worry about missing a few notes. You will correct it in time, but do make sure you play from the heart. That will touch other's hearts too. Music needs to animate you, to stir up the very depths of your being, to burn through the soul, cleansing it of every last bit of dirt and dross."

After that conversation he treated me as an equal, even though he had no idea that the infernal fires raging because of Ylva were already incinerating the "dirt and dross" in me. I did not speak to him about my pain. He might not even have been able to hear it because of his own grief.

He drank more and more, and was as drunk as a skunk during our lessons increasingly often. I had to ask my father to search for another cello tutor because Mr. Helmer was not reliable any more. I sincerely regretted leaving him behind. He awakened many wonderful impressions in me, and I had been given the chance to observe many secrets of playing music. My performances were to bear the mark of his passionate and romantic style for a long time.

❖

My father remembered that a newly arrived colleague's wife was a cellist. Before they moved to Karlskrona she had played with the Stockholm Philharmonic Orchestra. My father picked her as Mr. Helmer's successor.

We went to see her together. My first impression of Carina Dahl was of an impressive woman. She was twenty-six at that time. Her majestic physique radiated a mysterious strength and commanded respect; her brown eyes and big breasts emanated motherly cordiality.

Generous arched eyebrows, long dark eyelashes, curvy lips, and well-defined nose… All this endowed her face with an oriental charm. Her hips, widening to support a thin waist, swayed delicately under her white dress at each step. Her thick black hair was gathered up in a knot leaving the gentle sweep of her neck adorned with light blue pearls visible.

My father was completely charmed by her and kept blushing like a teen in love. He was only able to stutter in his embarrassment until Carina melted the ice with her humorous remarks. Then she started questioning me – who had taught me, what kinds of pieces I had learned, how I had practiced – meanwhile looking deeply into my eyes. I had the feeling she was not paying the slightest attention to my answers but was penetrating right into my soul with her eyes to figure out the answers she deemed interesting.

All the way home my father could not stop enthusing over Carina, loud in his praise of her teaching skills, attention, fortitude, intelligence and culture. He did not realize – or maybe just did not want to admit – that Carina had enchanted him with something else. As for me, well, I sensed a yet unknown femininity surrounding her. When we got home he enthusiastically announced to my mother that he had found an extraordinary teacher for his son. While he was talking you could see a gentle smile hiding behind mother's lips. Her intuitive spirit sensed the real nature of what was making my father's eyes gleam.

I also kept thinking about Carina after our first meeting. She did not exactly fit my taste at the time – so I did not judge her to be attractive. Although her femininity bursting with earthly vitality was far from my ethereal fairy ideal, her irresistible attraction gripped me.

That night it took me ages to fall asleep. The figure of Carina Dahl in her brilliant white dress surfaced incessantly from the dark sea of my memories. Until that day the minutes before I fell asleep had been haunted by Ylva Ekberg's elusive phantom. God, how I had clung to that image! How much I had wished and desired the tormenting pain it caused! I only realized my desperate and mad addiction to it when Carina Dahl's sensually curving buxom charms emerged and replaced the pain with an elemental force. My mind adhered to its self-tormenting ideal, its bitterly burning yet mysteriously sweet nourishment, like a child clings to his toys. Ylva Ekberg's phantom fought for its survival desperately but there was no doubt which would succumb. Carina's enigmatic radiance kindled my instincts that cried out for bodily pleasures. I desired her, and she gave herself to me the very first night. She visited me in my dream.

I was holding hands with Ylva. We were walking on a clearing of silky grass surrounded by a dark verdant forest. At the centre of the clearing was a pond shining, bright as silver. I wanted us to bathe in the pond together, naked, but she resisted. With a sudden move I embraced her and pressed her body to me. I wanted to kiss her but she ducked away, struggling desperately like an animal sensing its death. My arms embraced her with a steely grip. Her body quivered as though the most vehement currents of joy had just passed through it. I ripped off her clothes violently. The little pink nipples of her white bosoms glinted from below the ragged shreds of her clothes. I hurled myself at them eagerly, but she pushed me away with such an immense strength that I fell backwards, and she fled. Eerie forces nailed me to the ground; I could not move. As I looked up to the sky I saw a large white cloud. Its beauty kept me spellbound. Its radiating peace calmed my jangled nerves. The wind that rolled the cloud through the ocean of the sky first outlined large breasts, then a slender waist and curvaceous hips, until a fabulous beauty unfolded from the boundless blue. The face that emerged from the long, black wavy hair was the Sun itself. "Close your eyes," whispered a powerful but velvety voice. This voice came both from the sky and the ground at the same time, from between the treetops and the grass. Or it did not even come from anywhere; it was everywhere around me. It was as though I was inside the sound that was undulating around me, thrilling me, like the cool water of the evening lake. My eyes closed involuntarily. "Wait for me... I am coming to you", the mysterious tone kept vibrating in my cells. Soft hands touched my forehead. As I slowly opened my eyes Carina Dahl's kneeling figure emerged in front of me. I suddenly looked up at the sky. It was ravishingly blue and deep like an ocean, no longer rippled with clouds and the sun had also disappeared. It descended to the ground with Carina. She reached for my hands, pulled them towards her and placed them on her oyster-shell breasts, where her snow-white velvet skin shone from under the low neckline of her dress. I got on my knees, my hands slipped downwards. At the touch of my fingers her clothes vanished as though a magician had made them disappear, and an altar of pleasures was revealed in front of my marvelling eyes. She bent backwards, opened her arms and with a radiant look motioned silently for me to enter her embrace. My body burned in desire to touch her nakedness. I leaned over her quivering, but was not welcomed by the hot, flexible feminine body that I so desired – her being was now an ethereal splendour and I sank into it as though into fragrant warm water. The fire in me disassembled me into billions of cells with one big bang, and I dissolved in that shining liquid – melted and diffused in the infinite and impersonal bliss.

When I woke up the next moment, the recognition that I was alone between the rigid walls of my room came like a thunderbolt. I desperately tried to recall Carina's wondrously shimmering figure and the indescribable delight her embrace brought forth. As images of the dream came back and became more pronounced, the feeling too became more and more alive. I savoured it till sleep overcame me again. In the morning I woke up fresh and beaming. I felt bursting with energy and was unusually happy. Carina was expecting me at five in the afternoon. I pushed the bell five minutes before five with a shaking hand. I had mixed feelings and thoughts: there was the hope that I would satisfy her professional expectations, the desire to access her feminine mystery, and the happy excitement she had presented me in my nocturnal experience.

Carina's round, smiling face appeared at the door. She was wearing a flimsy pink bathrobe without a belt. She was holding it together with her hand; as though she had just flung it on to hide her nudity. She led me to the spacious lounge where we had talked the first time. Then she excused herself for a few minutes. As she started to leave, her freshly washed, joyously wavy hair left an intoxicating cloud of scent. She stopped near the door and reached for a tray on a small table. For a fleeting second her beautiful breasts appeared as she let go of her robe. An electric shock went through my body. In my embarrassment I turned away, but she did not get flustered. Before leaving the room, she smiled back at me. For a moment it crossed my mind that she had been waiting for me in that negligee on purpose. I brushed off the idea, laid my instrument on the floor, and sank back into the leather armchair.

It was a pleasant room. Its huge windows let in the light in abundance. The afternoon sun sat with joyful sparkle on the leaves of the branched figs, fleshy aloes and lissom Japanese roses. A mahogany coloured upright piano with a wide stool upholstered in crimson reigned over the space. The bookshelves lining the walls were groaning with books. A wide oil painting hanging behind the armchair grabbed my attention: it depicted a naked woman lying on a luxurious four-poster bed, playing a mandolin-like instrument with a long neck. Her enigmatic smile, her faraway look reflected an otherworldly expression. I was engaged in figuring out its secret when Carina stepped back into the room. She was wearing a flowing black skirt and a lilac silky blouse. Her hair was gathered at the back with a simple oval-shaped ebony clip.

She sat in front of me on the generous piano stool and looked at me from head to toe.

"How did you sleep last night?"

I shuddered. When I heard her question I was just looking at the curving forms drawing her blouse, remembering the dream when these curves were revealed in front of me. Her question was like the morning alarm of the clock that drags you from sweet dreams into reality.

"Me? Pretty well, thank you," my voice quivered hardly noticeably. "And you, Miss...?"

"Me too, thanks. Do call me Carina. I am not as old as I may look."

I heard coquettish overtones in her voice that made me feel awkward.

"No, no, you do not seem old," I stuttered. "In fact you... well..." I was unable to find the words to finish the sentence.

She looked at me pryingly for a moment, then said, "It is important for one to sleep well, and dream well because then you will feel fine all day, full of energy and vigour, eager to work. An artist needs to have passion for life and momentum above all else."

My frequent nightmares came to my mind, and the depression, exhaustion and bad humour that lasted for days after these 'night frights'.

"Have you experienced anything like this?"

"Yes, I did. Last night I had an excellent dream... and..." I did not want to expose myself so I continued in another way, "And now I am ready to..."

"Time will show," she interrupted me. "Now take the instrument into your arms and undress it."

This expression confused me. I laid the cello on my knees and flustering nervously, I tried to undo its case. She paid attention to every movement and looked at me as though I was fumbling with the buttons on her blouse. This made me more confused, and I almost dropped the instrument.

"You don't have to hurry. We have plenty of time. Rushing ruins everything. Don't focus on the result but the way you get there. Undoing can be just as exciting, if you give it time and pay attention."

I felt my cheeks flush with colour. I took off the case of the instrument as though under it Carina's sensual curves were to be found – with a shaking hand, but slowly as she had asked me. Strangely, it calmed me, and I started to enjoy this game. I let the soft material fall to the ground as I would let go a skirt before making love.

"All right. Now hold it gently between your legs," she said.

A barely noticeable smile hid on her lips as she talked. I had no idea whether she was being serious or just teasing me on purpose. Whether it really was a provocative flirtation in her voice or just my mind playing tricks on me and misinterpreting words.

I held the instrument between my legs like a professional; I took the bow and drew a few notes on the cello to check its tuning.

"Not yet... don't touch it. You need to be prepared for it," Carina instructed me, then stood up and placed herself behind me. I looked up over my shoulder, surprised. Gently she put her hands on my shoulder. Her touch made new sensations emerge in me. Calming and stirring at the same time.

"First of all, let's check the posture." She then slipped one hand down to my chest, the other down on my back. "Sit straight, your backbone is like a question mark."

I felt ashamed; my posture really was terrible. I was skinny and tall, maybe too tall for my age, so I always walked with a bent back.

"It is important that your spine be straight, then your actions will also be straight."

I drew myself up as much as I could.

"Don't force it. Be more loose." Meanwhile she started to caress me, making a warm current flood through my body. "Looser, looser. Only a relaxed body can give life to real feelings, and only genuine emotions can give inspiration to music. You know that too."

I felt a mystical force coming from her hand that awakened in me the feeling she had just talked about. She then removed her hand, stood farther away and asked me to play something. I played a virtuoso scale from Brahms's double concerto, with complete surrender and passion to the play as Mr. Helmer had taught me. But Carina had different tastes. "What is this?!" – She stopped me. I was surprised and explained to her that Mr. Helmer had said one had to play with emotion and passion.

"That is true but do not forget that the instrument is itself a sentient being. It has a soul too. Try to listen to what it wants, what pleases it. Touch its soul. Only then will it surrender to you. Only then can you cajole beautiful tones out of it. While you see it as a mere piece of wood that has to endure your capricious passion you will not be an artist. At best you will be a musician. You don't want that, do you?"

She disarmed me completely with her theory. In addition I sensed again the same ambiguity in her words. She talked about the instrument, about music, but something told me her words had a second layer, a deeper meaning. I could only sense it. At the time I did not understand what they hid and what they wanted to reveal. I looked up at her perplexed.

"Get to know it. Caress it. Touch its fine, slender line with your fingers, feel its curves in your palms."

"But it is just a..." piece of wood I almost said, but I only took a deep breath.

"Speaking hinders the feeling. Just act and feel!"

I obeyed reluctantly. I was annoyed I had to caress a piece of wood – it seemed so silly. I thought she was making fun of me and I wanted to stop but that voice, that warm, stirring tone sounded again.

"Do not give up that easily. Caressing needs time to bring forth the feeling."

I continued and tried to treat it as a game. Then suddenly, as my hands slipped upwards on the wider side of the cello, the thought struck me that I was caressing Carina's rounded hips. It made me smile. I let myself enjoy the thought for a few moments. I pulled my hands farther up her slender waist, curves of her chest. I caressed her neck, head, and then slipped my hand down to her belly, where my fingers played on the edge of a sound hole. My middle finger even slipped into the hole...

"Now take the bow," she interrupted. "Caress with that – it likes it."

Needless to say the first notes touched my animated soul like amorous sighs.

This new game enchanted me – like all great discoveries do. The instrument became alive in my hands, turning into a woman with feelings. It responded to my touch with richly shaded tones, and these sounds perfectly mirrored the feelings and thoughts I caressed and touched it with. At times it stirred up great depths in me, its tones were warm and velvety, occasionally imitating light laughter, other times transforming into delightful sighs.

It was then I realized for the first time just how important it is what we think and how we feel when we act. These feelings define the essence of the act. They can completely transform it; make it aesthetic and uplifting, or make it banal and ordinary, or even reducing it to something abominable.

I went on playing with a joyful self-abandonment. My fingers knew what they had to do without my need to control them. I watched Carina. Her smile – the one I had originally interpreted as mockery – faded from her lips. I found her incredibly beautiful and attractive, and I felt I had to tell her this. Deep, softly arching melodic lines, playfully leaping movements, and chords hiding overtones of silent desire talked to her about my feelings.

Carina stood up from the piano, took out her instrument, laid it softly in her lap and started to undress it. I thought she wanted to show me something so I stopped but then silently, almost in a whisper she told me, "Don't stop, please. Not yet. Let's play together."

A new feeling vibrated in her voice. A shiver ran down my spine. Carina's thighs opened with flirtatious obedience under the long, wide skirt. Her knees embraced the instrument gently.

"Close your eyes and continue playing. Somewhere deep inside let the sound, the rhythm and the melody be born."

She spoke no more. The sweetly resonating tones of her instrument took the place of words, and she let herself be carried away in the delight of playing. She moulded herself perfectly to me. At times nestling into my song, as though we were running hand in hand, or rather flying over hills and dales. At other times she raised thrilling tension with playful, stubborn counterpoint, and raced after my impetuous fortissimos, caught and seized me down into softly billowing abysses. Then I felt she gently took the lead. She initiated little games; we chased each other and hid from one another. Provoking words echoed that I had to respond to. Sometimes we hid behind the masquerade of playful debates. She orchestrated carefully and with expertise, but still I was hardly able to follow. It was an arduous task to attune to her mood swings. Her changes were guided by other inner principles, and started on different paths than the familiar ones taking shape in me. I opened my eyes, listened and tried to feel her. I tried to understand that secret language spoken by her body's swiftly undulating movements, by the gentle vibrations of her lips and lashes, by the delicate nuances of the expressions on her face. How beautiful a language it is! Though then I did not yet speak it. I merely had an inkling of its existence. Yet I knew great artists, painters, sculptors must possess it. Only through this can they immortalize on canvas or chisel into stone the spirit's inconceivable states and shaded veins. So magical a language that one who understands it shall grasp a thousand times more from a lip's incline, a wrinkling of the brow and a beckoning look than from countless pages of psychological dissertations. No lies were ever spoken in this language, as even innermost feelings that words leave unsaid and ideas elude are cast upon the telltale mirror of our face; those who listen shall discover. This is a language known not only to great artists but to great lovers too.

This is how my thoughts roamed and rambled while I watched Carina's transfigured face, trying desperately to be a fitting companion. Then, suddenly, she opened her eyes and a smile passed over her face. I felt our dream journey together was nearing its end. We played out our long goodbyes. Neither of us wanted to let the other have the last word. At the end we dissolved our discussion with the fading vibrato of a unison.

"That is all for today," she symbolically put on her disguise of a teacher. Happy as a sandboy I buttoned the instrument into its case, without a word.

"Not bad for a start, you have a pretty good eye for things."

Not bad?! I was extremely proud of my performance and believed I had discovered the great secret of music. I felt like a real artist.

"But don't think too highly of yourself just yet. Our work has just started."

The meaning of her last statement did not sink in straight away. Just like after our meeting in my dream I felt elevated, filled with momentum, strength and determination. I thought all our sessions would be the same but I was quite wrong. Carina proved to be surprisingly severe and made me work hard. I soon realized that the first lesson was a kind of a gift; a little taste of what I would have to accomplish with effort and perseverance; an example of how the relationship between music and performer should look. First of all I had to learn to always perform from the deepest depths of my soul. For this I had to have a presentiment of the state of mind, the feelings, and the atmosphere the composer wanted to convey with his piece. I had to learn to evoke these inner states with all the details of changes in mood and impulses, and finally to let play according to it. It was a hard but beautiful task. Carina often said, "The piece has its own soul, and you have to discover it and bring it to life. This is the performer's aim, not merely to use the notes of the sheet music to express his personal impulses, passion and artistic individuality. When a composition comes to life, it will serve as an ultimate source for the artist's most alluring and offbeat senses – just as for the listener. Always be conscious of what you feel while playing. When it makes your soul shout for joy then you are on the right path, but if not, then stop, or start from the beginning in another way."

She continued to use ambiguous phrases. I was often unsure whether she was speaking about music or love, or both at the same time. As if music and love could amalgamate into one and the same. Maybe she actually wanted to teach me both. Whichever was true, her method of teaching was explicitly erotic, and not only apparent in her figure of speech or intonation. She radiated it through her entire individuality and attitude.

She dressed up prettily for the lessons, and there was a reserved coquetry in all her gestures, expressions and smile; in that she let me admire her shapely legs when she sat in front of me; in that she brushed my neck with her breasts as she leaned over me to show a new technique on the instrument. As if she intended to keep me aroused all the time. She succeeded perfectly. I avidly sought and waited for a position when our bodies could touch for a second. Later she found new ways for these secret touches to happen. We played the piano together, as a way to relax after exhausting lessons. We played four hand pieces, sitting on the crimson-covered stool, close to each other. Our thighs pressed close. In pieces with a larger range, our hands reached over the other's and our bodies pressed close as though in a secret embrace. I felt her hair touching my face; her scent surrounded me like an exhilarating cloud. My blood boiled in my veins. But she just played. Joyfully and abandoned, as though nothing existed around us, and smiled. I could not grasp what her smile might have concealed. Her whole attitude baffled me; it was contradictory yet soul-stirring.

She saw the desire in my eyes. She must have seen it as she spoke that secret language – of the body – that I was just starting to discover. She must have felt my body searching for hers. She did not reject my concealed advances – in fact at times I felt she even responded to them, but so subtly I had the suspicion it was all just my imagination. I fantasized about her for days after our piano practices. Her sensual and tangible figure completely replaced the chimerical image of Ylva Ekberg. My wounds, that had tormented me for long and painful months, healed in a strikingly short period of time. Carina's treatment proved to be effective. I would not say it was love that I felt for her, but her whole being's magnetic force attracted me irresistibly. It was a new kind of feeling. One that I could not categorize. It was more than mere carnal desire – I could already recognize that. But I was not in love with her either.

I was often determined that I would caress her the next time, embrace her in a courageous moment, bend her backwards and, right there on the stool, I would... But I always contented myself with what she gave me: the touches during piano practice, our thighs pressed together, shoulder by shoulder, swaying movements that gave wings to my imagination.

One time we were improvising a four hand and, as my fingers stumbled on the keys whilst seeking the notes to play, my thoughts were somewhere

Kama Pura - The Island of Delights

else again. Carina said, "Be more courageous". Her firm voice shook me up from the dreams, and I concentrated on playing. As I was walking home I kept thinking about Carina's demand "Be more courageous". I began to consider the expression's double meaning. An hour later it became more than obvious.

The next day I discussed the matter with Arne and asked for his opinion. He answered with the confidence of a professional.

"I'm telling you, this woman has a crush on you. You must be a fool not to take advantage of it."

"But she is nine years older than me, and she has a husband, a handsome one" I tried to argue. "Moreover, a beauty like this... with me? Just look at me, no muscles, my back is like a question mark, my nose is too big."

"Women at times have such a ridiculous taste you cannot make head nor tail of it." Arne's explanation was by no means flattering, but he went on without stopping. "My advice is to grope her a bit. You have nothing to lose. Well, maybe, she'll slap you in the face. You can take as much, and there is always the possibility that she'll like it – and then the world is yours. And do not forget what she told you – be courageous."

The next time she received me in a bathrobe as at our first lesson. Her hair was flowing free, wafting a fragrance behind. She led me to the lounge but this time did not go to change. She sat in front of me as she usually did. She leaned back, supporting herself on the piano, and folded her hands. Her splendid breasts sat in the basket of her arms like fruits for a sacred offering. A part of the robe slipped down her crossed legs. The other side shed an enigmatic shadow on the tantalizing line where her two thighs met.

Carina was unusually silent. She neither bantered nor smiled, and I had to perform in front of this marvellous sculpture. My thoughts and feelings whirled wildly. I kept blundering. I was starting a piece for the fourth time when I heard her light melodious voice.

"Come, let's play together!" Then she turned and with one fluid motion, as though she was opening a case hiding precious jewels, she opened up the lid of the piano and started to play. I carefully laid my instrument on the ground. But I did not sit next to Carina. I took my place behind her. This spectacle turned me into stone – I was unable to move. As Carina bent forwards her robe fell open and I could see her stunning breasts. I had butterflies in my stomach, and the blood began to pump wildly in my veins.

"Be more courageous! Be more courageous!" emerged Carina's advice in my thoughts. I put my faltering hands on her naked neck, and then slipped them forward. Her soft skin scorched my hand, and the fire gradually

75

spread through my body. With a sudden but delicate move I seized the two peaks. In her surprise Carina gave a hiss and a soft vibration ran through her body, but she did not stop playing. I started to caress her. Her eyes closed, her head leaned back, her face nestled in my chest – and she continued to play. Melodies concealing silent desires and harmonies calling for amorous nostalgia were born under her fingertips. My hands became more daring and explored the territory with a conqueror's curiosity, finding smooth skin, seeking every curve, contour, and niche voraciously. They avoided just one point, the one secret spot, the most attractive one. Carina was still playing as her breathing became heavier. Passionate motifs found their way into her music. I stood down behind her and pressed her to me tight. I noticed her body tremble slightly. Then the piano fell silent. Only Carina's quiet sighs raised faint waves of energy in the tranquillity that covered us. But for me those sighs meant more than any music of the world.

Carina took my hand and pulled it towards her body's yet untouched area. Smooth labia heaved between my astonished hands. She navigated my fingers as though she was just teaching me to play an unknown instrument. Sounds of mysterious music emerged from her moist lips, and I felt like these sounds flew me on angel wings to unknown worlds.

Desires attacked me with irresistible force. I undid the robe's belt and turned her to face me. She wore her nudity with such maddening calmness – like others wear their fanciest clothes. She was no prude, but neither was she shameless. She did not feel awkward nor did she flaunt her charms. She was just herself. As I was watching her, my eyes wide open in astonishment – I had the feeling that she was flawless. I stepped back involuntarily to see the whole picture in front of me; her body leaning slightly back, her arms spread on the keys of the piano. Her legs stretched out elegantly in peculiar harmony with the background, like a perfectly composed painting, and these mystical lines all converged in one focus point somewhere between her breasts.

Another wave of desire awakened me from my artistic contemplations. I stepped near her body that she was offering submissively, and started to unbutton my trousers. Carina stood up, embraced me and whispered into my ears, "Not yet, Bald. Not now. You need to be prepared for this. In your soul."

This unexpected turn left me stunned. I was at a total loss, and then responded, "I am prepared! I have been preparing for this for seventeen years!" This was the second time I'd knocked on the door of fulfilment without being admitted. For a second I thought I needed to be more insistent. According to Arne, certain women like to be a bit violated.

"Listen to me, Bald. It will be better, you will see. I promise." Her voice was gentle and warm, but I realized she would hold firm. I had to watch with a desperate sigh as she put on her robe again. A wet spot remained on the crimson-covered stool.

"Now come, let's finish the lesson," she said with a smile as though nothing had happened. She was utterly mad, I thought. How could you possibly have a lesson like this? But it was possible. To my great surprise, this time I played the piece without any mistakes.

Before we said goodbye she embraced me, looked into my eyes and said, "When it is time, I will tell you. Trust me," and she kissed me.

❖

Though we met three or four times more Carina did not say a word about what had happened. It seemed she had completely forgotten about it. I was preparing for a solo performance so we kept our nose to the grindstone. She, of course, did not abandon her flirtatious character, but she gave me no opportunity to approach her. We did not even 'play the piano'. That felt terrible because I really was preparing for it. Not only 'in my soul' but theoretically too. One of Arne's experienced friends gave me a blow-by-blow account of what should be done. He trained me thoroughly. I even visited my grandfather. He was sincerely happy that I would be a 'man' soon and gave me several useful pieces of advice, adding that he was awaiting further developments with excitement. To my shame I had nothing to tell him, even two weeks later. I lost my patience and resolved to question Carina after my performance.

For the time being though, these thoughts receded into background because of the preparations and practices.

The day of my performance arrived. I thought I played fairly well and the applause of the audience confirmed my feeling. But I was still very excited to hear Carina's assessment. After the performance she called me out for a little professional consultation. In three or four points she summarized my mistakes, but over all she was content with me – that felt good. Her opinion meant more than anybody else's. After our discussion she added – as though it was just a part of the assessment:

"Come to my place tomorrow at seven. No need to bring your instrument."

The invitation took me by surprise and I was lost for words.

"But..."

"My husband won't be at home," guessed Carina my thought. "He is away. I will be alone. With you. You'll come?"

"I certainly will be there," I said, although some doubt could have been heard in my voice. I could not believe my ears. I dared not believe, not to miss the sweet chance again. Gleeful to the bottom of my heart, I was thinking about the next day as though it had already happened. She neither hugged nor kissed me – my parents were only a few meters away – she simply winked a mischievous wink and off she went, leaving me with escalating excitement and hidden joy.

❖

The next evening when Carina opened the door, I dropped the bouquet of flowers in my astonishment. It was not Carina but a stunning goddess standing in front of me. A ruby Indian sari with golden embroidery covered her proud slender figure. Brilliant hairpins and clips bejewelled her jet-black hair. Her cheeks, slightly rouged, were framed by two curls swinging freely. Her neck, arms and naked ankles were adorned with sparkling gems.

I was speechless. She didn't speak either. She took my hand and led me to her room. Brightly coloured flowers sat in the four corners of the room in vases bearing oriental patterns. The mysterious semi-darkness dissolved the contours of objects, transforming them into something fluid or rather ethereal. I felt I was stepping into a whole new dimension where the laws of the material world no longer governed. I looked around with amazement. In the centre of the room there was a low, unusually wide bed. Colourful, silky materials were draped around the walls. Near one of the walls stood a platform covered with white silk, on it a brass sculpture depicting a dancing god. On the wall above the bed there was a tapestry showing a naked woman tightly embracing a man in meditative posture.

The unfamiliar music and extraordinary fragrances filled me with wonder and deep awe. I handed her the bouquet of flowers. She accepted it with a smile and placed it in front of the dancing god's statue. She led me by the hand to the bed and made me sit. She caressed me gently and slowly started to undress me. All of a sudden I did not know what to do. I forgot everything I had planned. My heart was beating rapidly. I did not even have the slightest idea how to take off the Indian dress she was wearing... I resigned myself into Carina's experienced hands in exultation. She stripped me naked and spoiled me with a thousand caresses. That calmed me somewhat, and my hands began their own journey of discoveries. Carina directed me gently, helping me to peel off that strange dress of hers. Meanwhile my mind had become fully calm and everything Carina had taught me during the cello lessons came into my mind. With slow, restrained caressing I tried to sound the exquisite instrument of her body. And I only succeed when my caresses touched her very soul. The moment she let me in I was overcome with the same emotions as when we had first met in my dream, but this time the blissful dissolution in another mystical dimension became more real and appetizing by our bodies' delightful connection.

Carina was wonderful as she surrendered herself to love. Her refined musical taste brought countless rhythmic tones and variations to life. She transformed from the attentive and experienced leader into the role of a woman submitting to the wish of a man with playful easiness. The devotion she emanated turned the shy and gangling seventeen-year-old youth into a self-confident man – that was exactly what happened. The Balder who had been burning on fire ignited by lustful peeping episodes and crazy desires for years died that night in the magical embrace of Carina. Another Balder was born. It was like an ancient curse had been broken. I could not describe with words that being someone else, but I felt it. I thought it was natural and everybody goes through it when they enter the door of sexual initiation. But neither Arne nor any other friends of mine gave an account of an experience similar to mine. It was many years later that I understood just how important a station in my destiny this moment of grace was.

My grandfather was the first man with whom I shared this experience. He listened to me with attention and gradually increasing interest, then said to me: "This woman who initiated you must have been on the Island of Delights. Only women of that kind can handle the power of love like this."

I could only smile at Grandfather's conclusion. By that time obviously I no longer believed in tales but I did not want to contradict him. He gave a sigh and continued, "Though it would be a waste of time to ask her. She wouldn't reveal her secret. Maybe with time... if she finds you worthy of it."

I did not ask Carina about my grandfather's fantasy island. For me the secret sanctuary of her bedroom meant the real island of delights. I was to be an honoured guest of this wonderful island for exactly one year.

She surprised me with a different adventure at each of our meetings. Carina had a thousand faces and she uncovered them one by one. At times she was childishly playful, at times captivating and passionate. She could be coquettish and elevated but maddeningly sensual; warm and deep like the sound of a cello, but serious and ceremonial like someone driven by religious awe.

That was my happiest and most ecstatic period – and I believed it would stay like that for the rest of my life. But Carina Dahl's role was just to supply me with provisions for a long journey, to start me on a way with dangers and obstacles that would cause suffering I could not yet foresee.

And it was right this way.

6. Realithéâtre

One way to summarize my ballet dance years is 'playing with forces'. That was what movement and dance meant to me.

The first task was to tame my body and bring it into subservience. The tough exercises practiced under the severe command of Miss Giselle, provided the perfect means for this. I was amazed to realize what a lazy and cunning creature the body is; with what awe it worships the sacred pleasures of idleness and lazing around and how desperately it tries to elude any sort of effort. And those devious excuses it came up with to escape the work: tiredness, lack of strength, illness. At the beginning it managed to deceive me too. I often felt sorry for it, spared it and babied it benignly. Out of gratefulness, my body was willing to do increasingly little. It started to rebel at even the slightest requirement of effort and shamelessly demanded its right to sloth.

Luckily Miss Giselle saw through those cheap tricks and did not allow any opportunity for rebellion. When I finally realized this cunning creature merely wanted to make me believe all its reserves of strength had been exhausted and that it could hardly move after ten minutes of practice – when actually it was still fresh and bursting with energy after an hour of intense workout – I no longer showed it any mercy. I discovered its energy resources are practically inexhaustible. I started to enjoy the steaming scent of the glowing body and the pleasant tingling racing through exercised muscles. The charming elixir of strenuous effort gradually turned the stubborn beast into a friendly and wonderful ally.

And so, the second act of 'playing with forces' began. I discovered that dance has a magic power, that I can create and destroy with this power, just like a sorceress who is able to magic a stunning palace out of nothing or turn a beautiful princess into a disgusting toad merely with the wave of the hand. I felt like an enchantress even though when I waved my hand no giant beanstalk grew immediately, and Miss Giselle certainly did not turn into the most stunning sylph. I definitely felt that for every sweep of my arm, every pirouette and every tiny gesture, somewhere in another dimension, in an invisible world, something happens. Something is born and starts to live. I was absolutely positive.

I felt this secret dimension was in actual fact the 'soul-world' in which feelings and thoughts appear dressed as trees, flowers, animals, fairies and giants – just like in fairy tales. And I realized that, with the aid of motion charged with the power of thought and will, I was able to create in this world; I could bring fragrant flowers to life out of thin air and then transform them into a leaping deer or a darting hawk. That did not mean that I had to imitate the movement of the hawk or the deer. These were different types of movement, the laws of which I did not fully understand. I just had a feeling about it, realizing that certain movements allow you to create, others to destroy. And I delighted in experimenting with both.

I created glittering palaces, orchards filled with fruits and fragrant flower gardens. Then, evoking the power of lightning, whirlwinds, great fires, floods and earthquakes, I destroyed them all. And proudly looked over the shattered ruins in the knowledge of my terrifying strength.

I could only play these games at home, when I was alone but I would have dearly loved to try out my magical power on stage, in front of an audience! I was curious as to whether or not I would be able to transform the harpy of hate or the toad of disgust into the fairy of kindness, or the flower of love in people's souls.

Unfortunately though I had no opportunity for such experimentation under the steel hand of Miss Giselle. Although we performed in front of an audience at the end of every year, the moves of Miss Giselle's choreographies were lacking all aspects of magical power. After nearly forty years of ballet the true secrets of dance remained a mystery to her. She was a firm believer in classical ballet, repulsed by any type of innovative experimentation. While for me traditional ballet with its artificially created movements so fixed in a stiff system seemed empty and weak. Of course, they too produced something in the invisible dimension of the soul. All movement infused with power creates something – but these were merely nebulous and confused forms, like fluffy clouds or algae growing in murky waters.

As I grew older and more experienced I often argued with Miss Giselle about the choreography she was preparing. But I was unable to make her understand what I felt and what I had discovered. This other world simply did not exist for her. Or if it did, then it was way too intangible. She did not see why we should bother with it since the audience would not see it anyway. She was only interested in perfectly polished and precisely executed *visible* elements. I explained in vain: "Even if the audience does not see it, just as I do not see it, unconsciously they can still feel the effect of the forms that we dancers are creating in the hidden dimension." She just didn't get it.

This, however was precisely what I perceived as the only true value of dance. Finally I managed to carry out the experiment. Without Miss Giselle's knowledge, of course.

The end of year performance was approaching, and we were preparing an excerpt from Swan Lake. Miss Giselle's choreography seemed particularly simplistic and, luckily, not only to me but also to the others. So it was easy to persuade them to join me in a little innocent mischief. While we diligently studied the moves composed by our enthusiastic teacher, I prepared a different choreography to the same music, one in which the movements were based on my own magical intuition. I arranged a secret meeting and presented my own variation to the others. They were stunned by it, already anticipating the amazing surprise Miss Giselle would have on performance night when she sees a piece of choreography completely unknown to her. Our defiance gave us a kind of impish joy, providing us with extraordinary power and momentum. Everyone made superhuman efforts to perfect all their movements in the new dance, which had turned out to be far more difficult than Miss Giselle's. I was quite nervous at the beginning. Would we be able to do this? Would it be a success? I only relaxed a couple of days before the performance when I saw that the standard of their dancing was fairly acceptable.

There was only one problem. I had been so involved in creating and teaching the group choreography that I had not left any time or energy for my solo part. And I had so wanted to create something excitingly fresh, unique and contemporary! Something that would leave people agape! But inspiration failed me.

An hour before the performance the knots in my stomach forced me to realize that my dance did not exist. Of course, I could still totter around with Miss Giselle's chicken dance, but I really didn't want to resort to that, as I'd promised the girls that my part would be something extra special, and assured them that the only reason I hadn't shown them was because I wanted them to have a surprise too in the performance.

I did a last desperate effort in the dressing room in the hope of a miracle. But, when I looked in the mirror at that ungracious, struggling and worn-out little sparrow facing me, I collapsed into a chair. The next moment Mum came in. It's strange how mums sense when they're needed. Then and there I badly needed her. She was surprised to see me in that pitiable state, so much put down to nerves, as I had never been nervous before a stage performance.

She took me into her arms and spoke in a calm, warm voice. She told the story of a time when I was a little girl. Guests were round and they asked her to play the piano for them. As the first notes sounded I started to dance, perfectly in time with the rhythm of the music. The precision, refinement and radiant power charmed all those present. I had to dance for all our guests from that day on. And I fulfilled their request with great pleasure. I always moved with my eyes closed, allowing myself to be carried along on the waves of the music...

She spoke with a magical quality to her voice. Her arms were around me, her fingers stroked me encouragingly. The feeling travelled through my body and refilled my soul that had dried empty from bitterness. The waves of her loving tenderness were almost painful and they gently opened the dams to my tear ducts. But I did not start to cry. Wordlessly, with one squeeze of the hand, I thanked her for her encouragement... and for the idea I knew might well save me. I will improvise! I will surrender my body and soul to the music as I had to my mother's piano playing so many years earlier, before I knew of Miss Giselle, or ballet, or the need to create.... when I knew nothing but the happy freedom of pure existence.

As I stepped onto the stage the heady joy of returning home permeated my every cell. I heard the imperceptible sound of the breath of the audience as it had become one huge, living being in the dark auditorium. In that even breathing and in the several hundred pairs of watching eyes I sensed a mysterious source of energy and drew from it courage, self-confidence and momentum.

In the group part I danced as though I was flying through infinite space, becoming one with the others. I wasn't actually dancing. I, myself, was the dance – the dance that I had created for the others, that was a part of me for it was born of me. I saw my fellow dancers as multiple me's, as though we were in an enchanted play in a tunnel of mirrors. My solo piece was next. Without thinking I gave myself over to the will of the music. The image of my piano-playing mother was right before my mind's eye: her head bent back a little, eyes closed, happy smile on her opening lips. Then I saw her in my father's arms. The soft waves of her undulating body gradually became a sensual dance.

My creative forces sparked. My movements became inspired gestures. I called a lake with sparkling water to life in the hidden universe of the soul. The moonlight made its mirror-like surface silver, and slim-necked swans drew fine swirls on the glassy plane. I created this landscape for my parents. A fitting venue for their breathtaking love.

It was a stunning success. The audience stood clapping and cheering. My mother wiped her tears, and my father shouted out ecstatically, "Bravo!" "Bravo!" "Bravo!" Miss Giselle clapped, her cheeks flushed. I felt neither the heady feeling of triumph nor proud satisfaction. Only love. An all-embracing out-pouring of love.

When the storm of applause quieted, Miss Giselle came into the dressing room. Feigning anger she inspected the group.

"Who did it?" she asked in an accusatory tone, looking at me all the while.

We just stood there smiling – sometimes at Miss Giselle, sometimes at each other. She couldn't contain herself any longer and burst into tears. As she hugged me, my tears welled up too – I was so grateful to her. After all the performance was the crowning glory of her work.

My parents were waiting by the exit. Mum hugged me and just whispered in my ear, "Thank you…"

My father grabbed me in his arms and danced me down the steps.

Just as we were about to get into the car a tall young man approached us and asked permission to congratulate me:

"Young lady, that was absolutely enchanting," he said. His hand's delicate but masculine grip was pleasant, pleasing me even more than his laudatory words. "You improvise with excellent inspiration," he added, smiling with a twinkle.

His words surprised me as even Miss Giselle had not realized that I was improvising. Embarrassed I thanked him for his appreciation and would have left but I saw he wanted to say something more.

"Please allow me to introduce myself. Antonin Gautier is my name. I am a choreographer but I am also involved in directing. I have an opportunity for you."

"Y-es, could you tell me more?"

There's lots to explain. I would like to meet with you one of these days. Of course, only if your dear parents agree…"

My parents had no objections about our meeting and neither did I, so we arranged the time and place, and then he politely bid us farewell.

We met two days later in a small café in Jean Jaurès Square. He told a few things about himself. He had been born in Marseille, but had gone to Paris to study dance and had even worked under Maurice Béjart. Since his return to Marseille he had gathered a company of talented young artists with whom he thought may be able to put his innovative ideas into practice. They were already working on García Lorca's Blood Wedding. He thought I was perfect for the female lead: the role of the bride.

Appealing offer. I had always had a compelling attraction to lead roles. To be honest, other roles did not really interest me. The only problem was that I still had to go to school. But Antonin assured me the lion's share of the work would be in the summer holidays and that we would plan the performances around me.

Inside I had already accepted the proposal, but I did not say yes to him straight away. I did not wish to give in so easily… I asked for three days thinking time.

It was easy to convince my parents about the rightfulness of my decision. They thought that some theatrical experience would only be advantageous in founding my artistic career. I did have to give up my other holiday plans though, but what was that compared to the new and exciting task lying ahead of me!

Antonin's voice vibrated with barely concealed joy when I told him, after the three days were up, that I would accept his offer.

❖

He introduced me to the group a few days later. And a new chapter in my life started that, with painful lessons, made me discover the laws, dangers, possible failures and the amazing opportunities of stage magic.

Antonin's company, the Cercle d'Ailes, seemed quite united and unique as a whole, yet stunningly varied and striking in its individual components: impatient young actors, dancers bursting with energy, open-minded musicians... Antonin had selected exceptionally talented individuals who also boasted very strong personalities. People with an unconcealed desire 'to be different from the crowd'. They used every possible method to draw attention to themselves. They loathed inflexible rules, social conventions and traditions. Nothing was sacred to them. They were even prepared to spear their own non-conformist convictions on the spit of irony. I hardly need to say just how much this group was to my taste and how surprisingly at home I felt among them.

Antonin had the most difficult task imaginable. He had to forge one unified and tightly knit group from this shining collection of egos bursting with wild and rebellious energy. And he managed to, more or less, in a mysterious way that only he knew, or maybe he himself did not know. He might have recognized the desire to renew and the urge to be different we all shared – and cultivated this as a cohesive force of the team. He set out goals and ideas that were new, striking and rebellious enough to make it worth cooperating to achieve them. The hidden motivation that several outsiders can produce much more powerful eccentricities than a single isolated eccentric actually brought us closer to each other.

When I joined them, I found a group that was already well forged and in no respects resembled a traditional theatre company. It gave the impression of a large and crazy family living in a neo-hippy atmosphere. They spent most of their time together. After rehearsals too. They went out together, on trips together, ate together, slept together and ... made love together. The group's love life in particular seemed unusual and surprising to me and quite hard to figure out how it actually worked. I had the impression that everyone "loves" everyone and that they could sleep with anyone without any inhibitions or moral restraints. A kind of relational *ommun*-ism. Some deeper attention and personal experience made me realize that there were also more or less stable relationships, but still fairly free movement between the couples. This was partly result of the natural expression of their free spirits – sworn to break all the restrictions – and partly Antonin's tireless work. Antonin had his own unique understanding of love and emotions and this is what he tried to instil in the group.

He was convinced that feelings, emotions and desires should be allowed their expression with full freedom and naturalness in the artist's soul, thoughts and actions. He believed any kind of rule, law, habit or

85

tradition that restricted the free flow of emotions, is a fatal enemy of the artistic creative process.

"Artists must learn to love from the whole of their heart when they love, and to hate with the whole of their soul, if they hate," he would say "And they should learn to allow free expression to both their love and their hate. When we have learned in our daily lives and our relationships to be open, free and mercilessly honest, then, and only then, can we also be honest and true on the stage Otherwise our play is merely a lie, and the role is simply a pathetic mask no different from the lifeless and empty costume we put on before we step onto the stage. Unfortunately, people, instead of facing one another fuelled by true emotions, they actually play pathetically weak roles in deceitful masks on the stage of their everyday life.

Actually Antonin was looking for exactly the same as all theatre people do: the genuine in everything that appears on the stage. He did not just want convincing acting but real emotions. His methods were different from others in as much as he allowed freedom of expression for all kinds of emotions in off-stage relationships then attempted to sublimate the energy drawn from those emotions that had been heated to the maximum, into a stage experience. He called this particular endeavour of his: Realithéâtre. To put this into practice he needed a team in which the people knew each other deeply, accepted each other and, as far as possible, loved each other. So he gathered a group of young people who had not yet been spoiled by the black magic of traditional theatrical training or by professional jealousy, artists whose natural instincts and feelings were still pure and ready to be freed.

Antonin, however, had not factored in certain elements. Probably because he wasn't aware of them and no one around had warmed him of their existence. He didn't take into account the fact that moral rules, traditions and social tethers might be unnecessary limits and burdens beyond a certain level of spiritual development, but before that they fulfil the beneficial role of the dam that can prevent the mindless destruction and pointless suffering caused by the flood of emotions. Nor did he consider that Realithéâtre would express its influence in two directions. It's true that the increased emotions of real relationships do help in creating the reality of the stage experience, but it works the other way too: when the actor identifies totally with the role he plays on the stage, it can also bring forth fatal changes in his off stage life and destiny. Antonin wasn't aware that even if his fully dedicated group would attack the bastions of tradition with contemptuous enjoyment, they would be totally at the mercy of the insidious mine field of the collective subconscious. He kept emphasizing that the only core of freedom is love, and that jealousy and the urge to possess the other are fatal enemies of love, affection and all that is good and beautiful. The group believed him and tried to orientate their lives on the stormy waters of relationships according to the compass of these noble ideas. But it was almost in vain. The mines of the subconscious exploded at every step. Jealous hysterical onsets, bitter retreats of resentment and hateful verbal outbursts kept destroying the picture, sweeping the community life into danger again and again. Luckily we talked over each and every one of these situations and, after the fires awakened by violations of fidelity had lived out their outbursts of anger, we would all sing together: "The Show Must Go on!"

Antonin's choice of play was no coincidence either. Lorca's Blood Wedding – in his reading at least – was precisely about dissecting the problem of tense, apparently irreconcilable, contradictions between emotions and the unwritten laws of society. The only way out for the hero – elevated to tragedy by his refusal to compromise – is to accept his own death.

He planned to present Lorca's message to the audience in a combined form of expression. He tried to forge the creative power of the word and the dramatic tension of body-movement into one single powerful language. He wanted to feed both the mind and the soul with aesthetic experience at the same time. The mind through words expressing crystal clear ideas and evocative series of pictures. The soul through the expressiveness of dance and movement touching our deep and ancient roots. And he had found the dance that is closest to the spirit of *Blood Wedding*: flamenco. We were initiated by a young Spanish couple, Pilar and Rodrigo, who had come to our group straight from the heart of Andalusia, from Seville. Rodrigo had a devilish talent for the guitar and Pilar sang breathtakingly in her husky voice. And both of them were superb dancers. They assumed the task to lead our first steps in the discovery of this swirling world of instincts, sometimes painful, sometimes frenzied from emotional-elemental forces. After the delicate artistry of ballet, this dance, bursting with raw power, swept along my soul as if I had arrived in a forest being blown in a wild storm. Terrifying and uplifting at the same time.

Antonin had a strange method among his exercises that he called the "cat game". We crept around on all fours in the mysterious dim room, lit only by one single candle, touching the others with various parts of our bodies, brushing up, rubbing and pressing each other so that we would "get used to the feeling of bodies touching" and "to increase the intimacy between the members of the group". My first cat experience truly astounded me. The combination of moving on all fours, the subdued light and the impersonal touching of bodies awoke elemental forces in me that had been unknown to that point. Sleeping instincts from a distant and misty animal past awakened, deeply sexual, orgiastic creative forces that, if the game went on for too long, were terribly hard to hold in check. They demanded our clothes be taken off, and our bodies screamed for the most intimate touch of another body. A strange buzzing always ran through my body for days after one of these cat games.

One of the rules was you were not allowed to nuzzle up with anyone for too long a time. We had to try the taste of rubbing against everyone in turn. And they were surprisingly varied tastes. If a woman's body touched me it provoked a different feeling than when a man's body came into contact with mine. Certain bodies were less attractive while others stirred deep ripples in me, their touch leaving the desire to continue … One of these was the brown-skinned, hard as steel, muscly body of Louis Moreno.

Destiny, always projecting the future with hidden signs, had brought us together before I had even met the other members of the group. I was on my way to the rehearsal room. The moment I got on the bus a pair of fiery bright eyes met my gaze and travelled down me from head to toe, undressed me and lustfully stroked me. A handsome, dark complexioned young man belonged to those brown, intensely glowing eyes. His wavy hair reached down to his well-formed shoulders. A feminine, delicately arched upper lip with a narrow, dense, black moustache drawn above his strongly defined, fleshy lower lip. His whole being emitted bold and self-confident masculinity that made my chest tighten involuntarily, and ants started to run the length of my spine. I suddenly awoke into the awareness that I am a woman.

His attention followed my every movement like a predator watching his prey. As I was fumbling around with the clip on my bag, taking money out, buying the ticket and then as I chose between the two empty seats… the one closer to him. His look was already tickling the nape of my neck and goose bumps vibrated my spine. Instinctively I turned towards him. Our eyes met and the scorching rays of their meeting made invisible sparks fly around us. We stayed with this silent and exciting tension between us for ages. Until he suddenly stood up and came towards me. He bent down close to me, his lips parted and made space for whispering, brazen sounds:

"Oh, if only you knew how long I've been looking for you! Wherever you go, I'll go with you!"

Incendiary impetus burnt in his voice charming and frightening at the same time. In another situation I would probably have laughed, but now, somehow he had me in his power with his strange radiation. As if I was acting in some play lost in the mists of time, but I had just forgotten the lines of my role.

"You know me from somewhere?" I blurted out in my unease but I already felt that the lines weren't right and I should have said something completely different.

"Know you?" he laughed in a slightly pathetic manner. "What do you mean I know you! That we know each other's names, dates of birth, habits? That is merely the surface! I have known you deep in my soul since the moment I was born! And you must know me too! I know you do!"

The strange lights burning in his eyes made me tense. I seized the chance to direct the conversation into less dangerous waters and asked where he was headed and about him. It turned out we were both going to the same place.

With a good deal of pathos in his voice he shouted out:

"Oh graceful Fate! You who lead the way of ignorant mortals with thy infinite wisdom! Grace and thanks to you!"

I had to laugh in my discomfort. All the passengers turned to look at us but that didn't disturb Louis one bit. He kissed my hand with ceremonial adoration as though he wanted to give his grateful homage to Fate through me.

Louis Moreno was a born actor. He had attended the academy of theatre for a year but then fled. He couldn't stand the education there. Then he had met Antonin whose life visions fitted perfectly with his own nature. The only difference being that he did not differentiate between stage and real life. You could never tell when he was being himself and when he was playing a role. Maybe there was actually no difference between the two. He acted on stage as a man heated by instinctive emotions and he lived his life as a passionate actor.

"This is where we get off," he breathed into my ear, and grabbed my hand.

He only let it go when we arrived at the door to the rehearsal room. When we entered, a platinum blonde, slim, pretty-faced girl leapt round his neck and, after a long and passionate kiss, introduced herself to me as Sylvie. Suddenly and surprisingly too, my stomach clenched. What's that, jealousy? I asked myself in shock. It can't be. I don't even know this guy, and anyway, I hadn't taken any of his words seriously.

Louis and Sylvie had been together for three years. They loved each other with a tender care and passionate ardour. At first sight they looked so different but on closer inspection they turned out to be a well-suited couple. Sylvie's sentimental emotion and mysterious femininity attracted and complemented Louis's fervent, fanciful and fickle nature. I liked Sylvie. She soon became my best friend. This unexpected turn of events created a tricky situation for Louis who wanted to get closer to me at every cost. He never showed his feelings for me in front of Sylvie. In spite of all the principles of freedom that ruled in the Cercle d'Ailes, he wanted to spare her and I think our nicely forming friendship too. But if Sylvie was not there, he grabbed every opportunity to bear into me with the dark rays of his look, to touch my body with his. In the dim light of the corridors, in the protection of the set walls he drew me to him passionately, kissing me with irresistible force. During cat games his conquering hands took shameless possession of my most intimate body parts. And I let him. This secret game was definitely titillating. Actually I often found myself searching for just such occasions under the cover of transparent pretences. It filled me with deeply disturbing and pleasant tension.

In front of the others we kept our distance - Apart from the odd quick flash of the eyes that was meaningful for us. But this freed the space for another of my fervent conquerors, Daniel Turpin. His strategy was to try and sweep me off my feet with a sustained courtship. He was in the unarguably advantageous position of being single when I landed in the group.

Daniel had also flown from a ballet background into the Cercle d'Ailes, just like me. So we had plenty to talk about and share our experiences. And lots of mutual dissatisfaction too that brings people together more strongly than shared desire. Daniel was actually quite a nice guy. The kind of bloke people feel comfortable with. Polite and attentive, generous and witty. And he was always hanging around me with loving attention, which definitely felt good. I accepted his approach. He accompanied me home after rehearsals and, in the dark of the arched gateway, presented me with long kisses, a fitting end to our romantic walks.

After one of the rehearsals that we had finished with an extended cat game I stayed behind with Daniel in the room and we continued our nuzzling.

We gave free expression to our passions that we had brought up in each other during the rehearsal. But we didn't make love. He was pretty surprised when I confessed I was still untouched and that I didn't feel this was the most suitable moment and place for removing this barrier. Actually I was the only one of the girls to be lagging behind. I did feel somehow uncomfortable with it. I decided that I would get the initiation over with at the first suitable moment. And there, in the cat-scented dimness of the rehearsal room, I promised the prima nox privilege to Daniel. But then...

❖

... one afternoon I met Louis on the street "by chance". We hugged each other fervently and passionately like great loves who haven't met for a long time. We were not far from his flat... he asked me to go up to his. I knew what it meant. One part of my being wished it greedily but something in me opposed it. In that ambivalent state I swirled in his arms until his look, burning with unquenchable desire, gradually seared the wooden planks of my resistance to ashes. He started to undress me as soon as we entered the hall. My powerless opposition, just like my responsive cooperation, visibly increased his desire. His breath became faster, his movements ever more impatient. We pressed our heaving bodies together in the total joy of nudity.

He threw me onto the bed and himself on top of me. If he had done what he wanted at the start, at the opening of the flood of the lava, I wouldn't have been able to resist. My body opened for him with uncontrollable instinct. But Louis was no longer in a rush. He wanted to enjoy every delicious moment of the slow approach. When after the first eruption the lava flow quietened a little, the cliffs of my protesting thoughts rose up again. Daniel popped into my mind, to whom I had promised an unforgettable rendezvous that night, and Sylvie, who in her trusting naivety and friendly sharing had confided in me the most intimate secrets of her soul that fluttered around the adored figure of her Louis. I felt I was doing something terribly dirty and low. With silent resistance my body closed with a jerk and words that could not be suppressed burst forth from my throat:

"No! No! No! No, Louis no! I can't do it! …"

I thought in his fiery anger he was going to put me on a spit or even rape me, but to my surprise he gently stroked me and just said:

"You little fool."

Undisguised sadness sat in his deep brown eyes as he looked on while my nudity disappeared behind the cloak of clothes.

"I love you, Laurie," he said quietly, before letting me out of the door.

"I love you too, Louis," echoed my mind, but I didn't say it out loud. I wasn't sure it was true. I just stroked his unruly curls. I stumbled down the stairs. My heart was contracted, my body ravaged and my thoughts swirling. I felt awful and I couldn't understand what was happening. And, to top it all, I was already regretting that I had refused Louis. I had already betrayed Daniel and Sylvie anyway, and now I had deeply hurt Louis too. What should I do? I was in a vicious circle and I just couldn't find the way out. I didn't know any more what was good or bad, what was right or wrong. My affairs were in total confusion, and exasperatingly the solution kept escaping me.

I phoned Daniel and called off our date saying I wasn't feeling well. I sensed bitterness in his surprised silence. He said goodbye with anguished concern. I hated myself for the pitiful lie… but I couldn't have faced him and not one cell of my body, so attuned to Louis, desired to meet Daniel.

❖

Two days later Antonin read out the cast list. I awaited the moment with trepidation. He started with the minor roles and only later came round to the main roles. As he emphasized his words seriously, they echoed between the walls of the room and my skull like a final, unchangeable verdict:

"Bridegroom: Daniel Roubeau... Bridegroom's mother: Pilar Sanches... Bride: Laurianne Lamy... Leonardo, the Bride's secret lover: Louis Moreno... The treacherous Moon: Rodrigo Sanches...

I had thought the casting would be like this but to hear it was still a shock. – and I felt as though I had been caught in the act. I couldn't tell if Antonin actually suspected something about my secret relationship with Louis, or if the casting was simply inspired by his mind focused on the principle of Realithéâtre.

❖

We started the work. The rehearsals were tough. Antonin wanted to heat up all emotions to the maximum and he was never satisfied with the intensity. Once he set Daniel and Louis face to face and demanded they hit each other. At first they punched rather cautiously.

"That's not hitting! It's stroking!" threw in Antonin with the very same hate vibrating in his voice that he was demanding from us. "More! No one ever died from a couple of blows! Harder!"

Daniel gathered all his strength and punched. Louis stumbled and grabbed his burning face and then with a sudden movement hit Daniel full in the face. Daniel fell back, struggled to his feet and his hand tightly clenched went to jump on Louis, murderous intent in his eyes. Suddenly with a light and patronizing movement Antonin was standing between them.

"That's it. That's what I want to see. You have to hate each other. To death. Let that be in your dance and in your words. "And you," he turned to me, "Must love them both. Particularly Leonardo. You love him to death... because that's what it's all about: Love and Death! Actually I'd prefer to have real sex too," growled Antonin, more to himself.

"And real murder as well," added Pilar cynically.

"That too!" Antonin retorted, and at his words the danger bell of fear sounded in me.

❖

At the weekend we went for a trip to the nearby St Baume Mountains. The cool refreshing shade of the leaves was like a paradise lost after the rehearsals in the dusty, suffocating heat of the city that had drained every last ounce of our energy. We played around in the forest all day and fell exhausted into our tents at night. Daniel quickly fell asleep beside me but I could not lose myself in dreamland. Now that I was alone with my thoughts the ghosts of tightly gripping tension again broke through, despite the fact that the hard physical work followed by the healing magic of the forest had enclosed them into the bottle of my deep consciousness for a while. The sight of Louis's eyes blinking with sadness as he had watched me disappearing into Daniel's tent was all I could see.

It was narrow and oppressive in there. I felt like I needed some fresh air. Daniel woke up as I was moving around. I told him that I needed to go out into for a while. He acted as though he understood, stroked me and then turned over onto the other side.

I saw Louis as I stepped out. He was leaning on the stump of a tree and staring at the full moon like a lonely, beaten wolf.

"What are you doing?" My voice rang out softly but still loudly in the silence of the night.

When he saw me involuntary joy illuminated his pale moonlit face, "And you?"

"I couldn't sleep. I had to come out..."

"I haven't been able to sleep for ages. Since I first saw you..." His lips opened in a bitter smile.

With a sudden decision I went over to him, taking his face in my two hands and drawing his adoring lips to me. The kiss was long and powerful, magically dissolving all tension.

"I want to be yours tonight." My voice was not passionate, rather calm and warm. "Come," I whispered to him smiling.

I took his hand and we went into the forest. Not too far, just to a small clearing opening between the trees and bushes. There I opened myself to Louis, and there my body received a man for the first time. I was happy and free, and I felt ecstatic abandonment...

I took the memory of two different feelings with me from the moonlit forest and have treasured them to this day as precious jewels. One is the feeling of the silky grass bathing me with the cool dew of the night, the other the burning caress of Louis's hot tears as they fell like rain onto my face.

With sweet tenderness we hugged each other tightly as we walked back towards the tents. They both were sitting by the smoking ashy remains of the fire. Daniel and Sylvie were waiting for us. As we stepped into the clearing Daniel leapt to his feet.

"You bastard!" His voice sounded like the last gasp of a fatally wounded animal. His hands clenched into fists, his body shaking with anger.

Louis avoided him and went to Sylvie. He went to stroke her ash-coloured hair but she pushed him away.

"Leave me alone," she jumped up in tears and ran into the forest.

Louis looked around with glazed eyes, then slowly followed Sylvie.

Daniel grabbed me roughly, and turned me towards him.

"So you let him screw you, hey?"

"Leave me alone," as I wrestled myself out of his angry grip.

I hid in the tent, pulled the sleeping bag over my head and started to cry. It felt so good to cry!

I didn't know what I was crying for: myself, Sylvie, Daniel, or my lost virginity. I didn't know, but I kept crying until the weight was lifted and sleep took me away.

The next day the forest woke me with the joyfulness and birdsong of dawn. But I no longer felt right here. Quietly I packed up and went home before the others woke up.

❖

It was embarrassing to face Sylvie and Daniel, and even Louis, at the Monday rehearsal but we had to suppress all those feelings that were demanding to bubble up to the surface – for the good of the group and for the sake of the performance. But those suppressed feelings started their destructive work in an invisible dimension, one over which we had no control, and it spread insidiously like a noxious gas poisoning the moods of the others too. Everyone was irritable, impatient and extremely strained. Sometimes it felt like the sublimating effect of the play and the dance were dissolving the tensions, but then the next minute they broke through with renewed force. Antonin watched the turn of events with ill-concealed anxiety. He had started to realize, similar to the magician's apprentice, that he had released powers that did not obey him because he was unable to control or to understand them. He was becoming aware that for a while he had merely been a powerless spectator in the very process that he had initiated.

Antonin had outstanding occult abilities but he was lacking knowledge that would have ensured his power over things. Had it been a simple routine job, things would never have gone so far. But we had been working with nerves stretched to breaking point and had heated our emotions to boiling. We had given ourselves over to our roles identifying totally with them; we had sold our souls to them.

I was constantly nervous, hysterical even aggressive. My attraction to Leonardo-Louis had become almost pathological. I desperately desired him when we were not together but when he tried to come close I rejected him. While he, like a hunted animal, was incapable of communicating with anyone and blamed his withdrawal on my behaviour. I just couldn't get close to him because the passion burning in his eyes frightened me. Daniel and I had become total strangers. A numbing curtain of ice fell between us whenever we got close to each other. And Sylvie was on the verge of a nervous breakdown. I couldn't get through to her.

The worst was that I sensed Antonin's fear! But there was no return – we had already advertised the premiere... The Show Must Go On!

❖

Three days before the premiere Antonin tried a final experiment to see if he could improve the atmosphere, with a method that had been successful on other occasions – the cat game. But in a way we had never done it before, in the pitch black "so we would be able to relax more". The experience was incredible.

Antonin stepped to the light switch and we went down onto all fours. The next moment all familiar colours and shapes were absorbed by the dark. Only sounds remained. Very hushed sounds. The soft touch of palms and the silent shuffle of knees sliding across the rubber floor. I paid attention to the noises with bated breath and sharply tuned hearing as though I had to fend off a sinister danger that was watching. Terror started to grow in me, unnoticed at the start. The fear of the dark stemming from our deepest instincts. The dark in which the mysterious noises slowly transform into the soft steps of wild animal paws and the threatening beating of night birds' wings.

After the noises, the touches came. I shivered involuntarily at the first touch as though the furry body of an animal animated by my imagination had brushed past me. But the next touch was pleasant because even in the darkness, my mind recognized the warmth and the protective breath of a similar creature. We nuzzled and pressed each other as if we had wanted to escape from invisible dangers. Then I noticed the scents – very strange scents that I had never observed before. Now I realized just how much security that small, dimly flickering candle flame had provided at other times, and how unlimited the power of one single point of light is over the densest darkness. But now, with my sense of sight crippled by the total darkness, my other orphaned senses had to latch onto every sign that could project a calming message about the reality which had become invisible. From rubbing up and pressing each other the bodies started to get warmer and warmer – it is a law of physics – and the smells changed too. The heated body has a peculiar scent that the widely opened, trembling nostrils thirstily inhale. This awakens strange thoughts and associations in the mind. In the oven of the heated body the forces of the life instinct are gradually changed to sexual desire and it is not content with merely stroking; it has to taste... Wet lips searched on my neck and my face, and greedy tongues slashed their way through the thicket of my hair, discovering the sensitive creases of my ears. The sounds had also changed. The quiet breaths had sped up into panting and moans. And the feeling of touch… Now there were large naked expanses, also on places in the body where there should have been clothes… Hot thighs and naked bottoms smoothed themselves curiously under my palm. The slipping-sliding hands continuously peeled away my clothes too. The ticklish feel of silky bunches of hair and upright nipples grazed my naked skin.

Increasingly loud heaving breaths mixed with suppressed screams, and my imagination painted enticing pictures of that going on around me. Heat ran right through me and ever larger waves engulfed me. My body was wild in its demands, and I started to feel around, as my mind was overturned by the unstoppable instinctual forces breaking through. I was searching for something, something that would enter me and fill that painfully burning emptiness that had opened up inside me. My hand met with a muscly male chest and quickly slid down the skin wet with sweat… until it found what it was looking for. But it couldn't reach it; the wet opening of another body devoured it… I went on searching. Naked limbs, greedily searching lips, bodies slipping on one another wet with sweat, sexual organs seeking another were everywhere…

Suddenly, like a bolt of lightning, my Grandmother's religion lessons flashed before me, evoking the picture I had seen whenever she had talked of the sin of fornication. That picture seemed to have prophesized with amazing accuracy what was happening around me now. The nails of freezing horror dug into me. I was feeling that suffocating sulphurous stink again, and I thought I saw in the darkness the hairy black goat with glowing eyes and a grin distorted by lascivious satisfaction. An overpowering cry rose in me – a crazed, desperate, soundless cry arising from the greatest depths, the cry of the soul for light…

Someone turned on the light. It cut into my eyes with a sharp pain. As my sight returned it discovered a startling picture. Clothes were lying all over the place. Motionless from surprise, naked and half-naked bodies sprawled on top of one another as though after a battle. Sylvie was standing by the switch, crying. Another girl by the wall looked around, eyes wide open, at the pile of bodies slowly unravelling, disengaging. Then she started to scream hysterically at a girl who was lying in a post-coital embrace, in an intoxicated, stunned stupor on the floor. She saw her partner, kneeling beside the other girl, his sexual organ ready for action and glistening with moisture. Blind with anger, she leapt at him and started to pummel him…

"STOP IT!" At Antonin's sharp exclamation everyone caught their breath for a moment. "Are you incapable of doing anything properly from beginning to end?"

"I'm not going to do this any more…"

"Me neither…"

"Me neither…" The protesting voices rang out.

"Listen to me!" continued Antonin. His voice was surprisingly calm. "Now we're all going to go home. We'll meet again tomorrow morning and talk it all over."

We nodded and wordlessly gathered our scattered clothes. Confused, with a bitter taste in my mouth I left the rehearsal room.

❖

Next morning we were all there. The mood had settled to some extent. Antonin talked about art and about those sacrifices the genuine artist has to make both for his creation and for all those to whom it speaks. He mentioned the difficulties and trials the artist has to face during the creation of truly great works. But he spoke mostly of the group spirit, the need for solidarity in good and in bad, of endurance, and about just how important it is to stick together until the end, until the group has achieved its shared aim...

His words sunk home with the irrefutable weight of the principle. We decided that we would achieve our "shared aim", to hold the premiere, and then we would determine where to go from there.

Preparations went on in silence on the day of the premiere. Like the quiet before a storm. Antonin directed us in a calm, firm tone, trying to enthuse us with encouraging words. A depressed, tense atmosphere ruled, but this was not the usual healthy pre-premiere nerves. It was a strange and inexplicable feeling that emanated one thought only: "If only we could get it over with!"

Finally Antonin announced the start.

Infinite moments full of excruciating tension followed, until I finally heard the first lines on stage:

"Give me my knife, Mother!" Daniel's voice echoed dully above the packed auditorium like the cry of the warning bird in the depths of the forest.

"The knife, the knife… let them all be cursed, including he who invented it! And every gun, and pistol, the smallest blade, spade, fork, may they all be cursed." The French words sounded strange from Pilar's mouth but she pronounced them with such terrifying weight that a chill ran down my spine.

So, the play began. It all seemed like a strange, incomprehensible dream. The scenes beat out in the frantic flamenco rhythm: my meeting with Leonardo, the wedding, the escape, the lovemaking – which could have been called anything but lovemaking. Leonardo-Louis ripped my clothes off with wild power and nearly raped me. I gave my body over to his passion with cold indifference, I only felt sorry for my parents who had to watch all this... And then I heard the woodcutter's voice:

"They contained themselves as long as they could but in the end it is blood that is thicker than water."

"Blood."

"You must follow the road of blood."

"But the trace of blood is absorbed by the earth..."

And then came the final scene.

Leonardo and the Bridegroom drew arms. The music sounded wildly and the dance stepped in a frenetic rhythm. And they attacked each other tirelessly – with the full force of their bodies and the absolute hate of their souls. Even the audience hissed at the dull thuds. This was no longer art, nor was it theatre. It was Daniel and Louis wrestling helplessly among the storm waves of their own sea of passions.

And I was no longer the Bride, but the unfortunate Laurianne, who wanted one thing only – to run in between them and to stop this... this merciless madness. My body moved instinctively but Pilar caught my arm.

"Let it be done" she improvised a line, and with a wise resignation that befitted her character she watched the duel.

And then the knives glinted. The boys lunged at the same time with that realistic masculine thrust they had practiced to the point of nose bleeds in rehearsals. The wild music stopped as if it had been cut.

The audience gasped in horror, and the room sank into silence. The silence of the cemetery at night. Leonardo and the Bridegroom in a twisted embrace, panting and holding to one another. Then their knees buckled and they collapsed to the floor. The mother stepped to the body of her son. She knelt down beside him, closed his eyes and drew a cross on his forehead.

I rushed to Leonardo, fell on his naked chest and hugged him. Pilar's husky, almost singing voice broke the deadly silence.

"Such a small knife, it scarcely sits in the hand.

But still penetrates so quickly,

through the startled flesh,

to reach the point, where

it is silent in the thicket and trembles

enmeshed the dark root of a cry."

I felt wet heat on my shoulder. I looked there in horror. It was blood! Real blood! Louis Moreno's blood! A small red lake glistened on the floor.

Finally the lights went out.

I started to shake him:

"Leonardo! Louis! Louis!..."

I heard the enthusiastic applause of the audience and shouts of "Bravo". Louis supported himself with me and I helped him to his feet. The lights lit up again; Louis hugged me tightly and leaned with his whole weight on my shoulder. A large, red patch was spreading across my white gauze dress.

"The Show Must Go On!" he whispered in my ear and tried to smile.

After we left the stage following the first bow I wanted to take him back to the dressing room. But he wouldn't hear of it. We went back five times to accept the audience's rapturous applause. The mark on my dress got bigger and bigger. When we finally got back behind stage he collapsed. I couldn't hold him. The boys lifted him up and carried him into the dressing room. There was a small cut under his ribs. It wasn't serious, but he had lost a lot of blood.

Daniel, his face deathly pale, stood by him while Antonin and Pilar bandaged his wound.

"I'm sorry, please forgive me, please... I didn't want to..." his voice faltered. He was struggling with his tears. "I know, at the start when we were fighting... I lost my head... but this... I really didn't want this!"

"You were good, Danny... A great partner." Louis wiped some tears from Daniel's face and hugged him. They stayed like that, embracing, for a long while. I joined them, squeezing them tightly, and then Sylvie came, followed by Pilar and the rest.

A throng of reporters was stamping impatiently at the door but Antonin kept them out ruthlessly. The real closing scene still had to be played out and it was ours only. This was genuine "realithéâtre", with real, honest and shockingly powerful emotions, just how Antonin wanted it...

I felt our hugging arms to be like wings covering one another. The name Cercle d'Ailes had thus received a new and secret meaning. That is when I felt that people have to learn to hug in order to be able to fly... I keep wondering whether Antonin had thought about this when he had chosen the name to the company.

We all met up the next day. Some announced that they wanted to quit the group, including Pilar and Rodrigo. They planned to return to Seville. But most of the group stayed. They were determined to continue the work with Antonin and still felt the spirit of "realithéâtre" as theirs. They wanted to build on their newly gained experience in further trials. We all knew that this piece could not be performed again...like this. And it wasn't worth doing it another way.

We felt like irresponsible children who had survived a life-endangering adventure for which, of course, someone had to pay. But we were glad that we had escaped so lightly. And we were relieved that amazingly the tensions between us had disappeared, as if by magic.

Daniel and Louis became friends and remained faithful acting partners.

Sylvie was once again just as nice to me as she had been at the beginning. Actually the shocking experiences fused our friendship even closer.

Louis totally recovered from me but we remained good friends and afterwards spent many a pleasant time together.

The only one I felt no affection for afterwards was Daniel. Something between us had been damaged forever.

Pilar and Rodrigo invited me to Seville, to learn flamenco, and I promised them I would go to visit them at the first opportunity that arose.

I didn't carry on working with the group either, but I met up with Antonin many times. We talked a lot, discussing and losing ourselves in art, theatre and the secrets of the human soul. For some reason I liked him best of all in the group. We were similar in many ways. He was a searching soul like me. He wanted to understand the why's of things and was ready to learn from his mistakes. He never retreated and never accepted compromise. And he had the guts to be wrong. He was convinced that sin can ruin only the weak but that it can serve as a useful learning tool for the strong. We both felt strong.

7. Danse macabre

For a long time I believed in neither God nor the Devil. Or let me be more precise: I could not care less about either of them. Later, during my senior school years, when I became interested in figuring out how this strange world had been manufactured, I definitely denied their existence – with nuclear-energy powered, computer-precise facts based on steel-hard fundamentals inherited from my father. I think this vehement denial was exactly what opened the door in me for both of them. The Devil seized the privilege to be the first to enter.

After senior school my father enrolled me to study cello at Stockholm's Conservatory. My loyal friend Arne Larsson came with me to the capital. He chose the faculty of biology. The anatomy of the human body had always been one of his main interests – especially that of the female body...

We rented an apartment not far from the Royal Philharmonic's concert hall. With no further delay we threw ourselves into the big city life with great enthusiasm. The grim city spread across fourteen islands held the promise of inexhaustible source of adventures. The innumerable historical buildings and architectural riches, the theatre performances, concerts, movies and exhibitions, the cultural programs, and festivals consumed most of our time and energy. Little was left for learning and practice. But we were loyal to our true priorities.

The charm of the novelty lasted about a year. Then we started to get bored of the mundane entertainment. We desired something out of the ordinary, something more exciting and grittier. The metropolis with its inexhaustible possibilities – just like the whirling fog of Stanislav Lem's planet of Solaris – fulfilled our wishes at once: the shadowy gates of the underground opened before us.

The gate that Fate designated for our entrance belonged to the Nightriders Art Club, a gloomy space hiding in a large cellar under a luxury villa in Strandwägen. The villa and the club belonged to a well-to-do philanthropist called Magnus Evans, who was also a kind of spiritual leader of the club. Most of us were young artists, poets, writers, and rock musicians gathering there to socialize, drink, and enjoy lengthy discussions. It was a rather secretive place, maintained mainly for chosen members. One night Arne and I were shown that place by just one such "chosen member", a guy called Jarl. This was the cheapest place to buy beer in the city, and an unlimited quantity of drugs were available for both addicts and occasional users. From time to time, organized sessions were held: poetic geniuses misunderstood by society recited their "poems", photographers displayed their "artworks", and rock bands played their "songs". There was one common feature to all: rebellion against something – against society, laws, the political system, but especially against everything that represented beauty, harmony, order, love, and, of course, against God.

I let myself be engulfed in this world with mixed feelings. It undoubtedly attracted me with its wild non-conformism and shocking eccentricity, but at the same time I found it oppressive and unfamiliar – especially in the beginning. But slowly I got used to it. Habit is a deceitful adviser so before long my anxiety reduced to an imperceptible level and Nightriders became my home.

I belonged to a group intent on draining its cups to the very last drop. Girls frequenting that place were easy, so Arne's insatiable carnal desire had found its paradise. He bedded every girl he could, and almost every girl was up for it. I was also offered this "fresh meat", but the underground allured and chained me down with other kinds of temptations.

❖

One night, Jarl presented me to a wild-looking, husky bloke with a shaggy beard and long hair. Of his mumbled and incoherent words I managed to decipher that he was the solo guitarist of the band Atro-city. When the fact that I was a musician, more precisely a cellist, reached his inebriated mind, I saw his hazy eyes light up. He told me the bass guitarist had just died – "AIDS took him" – and that he saw a worthy successor in me.

"Your mane is long enough – and with a little make-up we can improve your look," he murmured, as he checked me thoroughly, handling me as though I was a horse at a fair.

"But I have never played a guitar."

"No problem. You'll soon get the hang of it."

I was tempted by this chance, as by everything new, so I accepted the 'appointment'.

The music we played turned out to be horrendous. In the beginning my hair stood on end, I felt terrible, I felt sick. Ramborg – that was his name – was right that no musical knowledge was necessary. In fact my education actually put me at a disadvantage. But, with time, I surmounted this disadvantage and the nausea too. The "lyrics" were written by Ramborg, but I doubt it required much intellectual effort. At least three-quarters of the songs were roars, growls, and grunts; the remaining quarter was mostly words joined illogically. Let me mention a few of them as an example: decay, murder, plague, morbid, destruction, nothingness, death... The message of the songs

– because they did have a message and Ramborg was obviously proud of that fact – were founded on the philosophical conviction that "the only and omnipotent lord of the world is Satan, and sooner or later all men will surrender to him", and "the only meaning of life is annihilation and death and its realization should be promoted with every possible means. The most precious human feeling is hatred, and death should come down upon those who preach against that. And, of course, death to the church, and especially to Christ who had earned his befitting punishment with the crucifixion, but we should still ridicule his spirit and all his followers".

I did not believe a word of all this, just as I did not believe in the existence of God. It seemed to me a kind of a game – an exciting and grim game – and I had no idea why they were all so upset with this Jesus Christ, this "innocent fictional hero". After a time I began to wonder what if such character did exist since Ramborg and his kind were showing such mortal hatred towards him.

❖

Our first show took place in the club. All the regulars were there and they had to elbow their way through the hall that proved to be way too small for that large audience. It was a hell of a concert. Everybody was shouting, growling and raging. As I was standing there on the stage a peculiar ecstasy took hold of me. As I looked over the undulating, raging crowd, I felt huge – and powerful. The guitar served as a kind of magical instrument that gave me powers over people. It was a frighteningly exciting and inebriating feeling – one more addictive and dangerous than alcohol.

After the concert Jarl told me that a special person would like to meet me. He introduced me to a twenty-six year old woman who was exceptionally pretty: Sibylla Hultgrens. She really was "special" – eccentric, like almost everybody in the Nightriders – but her haughty elegance and seductive femininity elevated her far above everyone else there. Thick locks of her black hair were gathered up like the leaves and branches of a weeping willow, crowning her head. Pomegranate-shaped breasts screamed for attention from under the metallic lustre of her bra. Her naked thighs were visible between the boots reaching up to her knees and her short leather skirt. Shiny black nails made her fingers seem long and fragile. She wore a necklace made of little skulls and a pentagram carved in a brass disc. Her lips painted black added a slight grimness to her otherwise charming face.

After we were introduced she measured me up thoroughly and said, "You were pretty good up there. Not bad from close to either."

I considered her words of praise and felt honoured. She had me sit next to her. There was another man sitting at the table, but she found it unnecessary to introduce him. Her prying black eyes hung upon me steadily while we were talking. To be more precise, while she was questioning me. She didn't tell much about herself, I only found out that she was a painter, and the ex-partner of Magnus Evans, the patron of Nightriders.

Then I noticed the misty-eyed man sitting next to her putting his hand on her naked thigh and stroking it. Then with a lewd grin on his face he reached deep under her skirt. I realized with a shock that Sibylla was continuing our chat with calmness, as though it was the most natural thing in the world to have someone groping under her skirt while conversing. She even started to move her hip slightly, to and fro, noting my confusion with cool indifference. This strange game went on for a while, until a gentle shiver ran through her body. She closed her eyes. It took just a few moments. She opened them again. With a calm movement she pulled out the man's hand from under her skirt and turned to me.

"Escort me home. I want to show you my paintings." Her voice sounded like a command rather than an invitation. She stood up and motioned to me to follow her. As I was leaving, I heard the man we left alone at the table shouting after us, "You owe me a whisky, man!" awarding his joke with a husky laugh.

We got in a cab. As soon as she had informed the driver about the destination she unbuttoned her long black coat, put my hand on her thigh and asked me to caress her. I obeyed her. I felt dazed. She leaned back, pulled up her skirt and, with a silent nod, indicated where to touch her.

I was worried what would happen if the driver turned back, but nevertheless I took advantage of the opportunity with joy. And I had rarely felt as bad as when I heard the driver saying in a polite tone, "Ma'am, we've arrived".

Sibylla pulled a banknote from her pocket and handed it forward with the words, "Drive on, wherever you feel like."

The driver shook his head and started the car. She put up one of her legs on the seat, clutched my hair with both hands and pulled me towards her. "Now with your tongue!" she ordered me with cold determination.

I set to it with great momentum. Her fingers were in my hair; occasionally she guided me with subtle signs. She was moving her hips the same way she had done at the bar, maybe a bit more passionately. Suddenly I felt her body becoming taut and warm juice dripping on my lips. A little time passed before I concluded from its salty taste what had really happened. A mild aversion ran through me, and I wanted to move away. But she clamped my head to her groin till she was finished. She noticed my grimace and, with irony in her voice, she said, "You never tasted it before?"

"No," I told her surprised.

"Still many things you need to learn... You can stop here," she said to the driver.

Before I closed the door I looked back into the cab. A damp spot shone on the leather upholstery. I wiped my wet neck with my shirtsleeve and peered around.

The district we arrived to was deep in sleep. Only two or three windows were still awake. We went round the back of a building where the curious lights of street lanterns could no longer spy on us. Only the iridescent light of the half-moon outlined the contours of trees. Sibylla picked a dark-coloured car, lay down on it, and opened up her naked lap again.

"Come here, you know what to do," she said in a simple, passionless voice. At last I could satisfy my aching lust inflamed in the extended foreplay. My naked thigh kept knocking against the cold metal; the cool evening breeze gave me goose bumps all over my body.

At the end she merely said, "You were great", hastily wrapping her body in her black coat. "Now we'll go to my place," she said as we got back to the street. "I do want to show you my paintings, if you are still interested."

Her apartment was as odd as she was.

In the hall a large vulture with spread wings fixed its eyes upon those who entered. Its terrifying claws were sunk deep into the shadowy eye sockets of the yellowed skull supporting the bird. I shuddered – I had the feeling it would plunge its beak into my eyes at any moment.

The only furniture in the room we entered was a long, low table draped with dark purple velvet reaching to the ground. Set on the luxurious cloth was an inch-thick black marble slab with a gilt-edged pentagram carved in the centre. It reminded me of a sarcophagus.

Sibylla's murals were all around, covering the walls. The vulture at the entrance now seemed a kind of preparation, a mild warning for what was to come: depressing images painted in dark tones, twitching, entwined figures joining the other. Here and there shapes of the material world would crystallize into something recognizable: naked body parts, animal heads, beaks, reptile tails, and octopus arms. Their size, proportion and the way they melted into each other completely contradicted the laws of nature – a gruesome, apocalyptic vision, unearthly shapes lustfully reaching for the other, like in a dream. Yes! I had seen similar images in my nightmares! Disgusted I tried to tear myself away from that view, but my eyes found no sanctuary. Suffocating images surrounded me on every side as though it was my own tormenting night terrors projected onto the walls.

Then small details attracted my attention that were extremely intricate: a tiny flower painted with vivid colours, a child's face smiling cheerfully, a flamboyant fraction of a rainbow. Like small islands of life, beauty, and hope scattered around in that slowly putrefying maelstrom of shapes and colours.

"You like it?" she asked, watching the surprised look in my face. There was not a trace of an artist's vanity in her voice.

"Yeah, hell of a work"

"Hmm, appropriate remark," she responded with an absorbed look, then suddenly looked into my eyes. "You want to do it again?"

She did not wait for an answer. She took off her clothes, switched off the lamp, turned on a lantern spreading a green light, and stretched herself out on the sarcophagus. Her impeccable figure was brilliant, like driven snow framed by that black marble. I watched her entranced. The body reminiscent of a celestial beauty, and divine purity acted in this depressing atmosphere like the child's smiling face in her mural.

The magic lasted for a moment only, then Sibylla pressed a large dagger in my hand. At the end of its grip two snakes were creeping out of the egg-shaped hilt. They twisted upwards the dagger, coiling around and looking at each other with emerald eyes carved in flattened cobra heads. It was a superb piece of work. I was lost in its details when Sibylla's cold, commanding voice suddenly brought me round. "Caress me with it!"

As I drew the point of the dagger on her skin I had the crazy idea that if I wanted, I could thrust it into her. That snow-white body seemed so defenceless. The feeling was similar to standing on stage: the strength, unrestricted power, the thought that I could destroy life at any moment. I was terrified of this idea and jerked away my head to escape from the sight of the soft skin tempting the glinting metal. I noticed an inscription shining on the wall with golden roundabout letters.

DO WHAT THOU WILT, THAT WILL BE THE WHOLE OF THE LAW

Sibylla went down on all fours and gave the next order, "Push in the handle... and move it."

❖

She always created these strange foreplays with me before opening the gates to her body. She chose the most bizarre places for these games; we had sex in elevators, under staircases, in a truck's trailer, on scaffolding and at a junkyard... but never in a bed.

She preferred places where we were in danger of getting caught. She tested my bravery at every moment, and so I had to overcome my fear and anxiety to be able to have sex with her.

Her favourite place was the graveyard. She adored the scent of decay and the flat stone's thrilling sensation on her naked body. She liked to dance on the graves, decorate her body with faded flowers stolen from the tombs, and even rub her pelvis against the cold marble crosses.

One night we had sex in a freshly dug grave. She said it was the most special experience of her life. That was the only time I saw her happy.

I never saw her laugh, not even smile. She took satisfaction in telling eerie tales about ghosts, and gory murders. Trying to keep me frightened seemed to be one of her perverted pleasures.

For ages I had no idea why I stayed with her for such a long period: two years! I thought it was that maddening, tormenting desire she kept alive in me. She was an expert in this. She was also an expert of emotionless relationships; it was pure, stone-cold sex between us. She consciously tried to eradicate every germ of emotion in herself, and in me too, considering love a 'sickness of the weak'. She had the conviction that one should never fall in love because love makes you pathetic, kills your courage, and forces you to compromise. And it leads to meaningless suffering.

Unfortunately my affair with Ylva supported this infernal logic and I had no other experience to relate to. I was not really in love with Carina. It felt good to be with her, but back then I could not fathom out what she had really meant to me. I visited her occasionally even after I had moved to Stockholm but, as the city's mirage suffused with its alluring new adventures had permeated me, our meetings became rarer, and ceased entirely after I had met Sibylla.

As time passed the memory of Carina's motherly nourishing, warmly embracing figure became clouded by my gruesome adventures with Sibylla. Slowly, almost imperceptibly, I began to identify with her value system and its keywords of "power" and "will".

She possessed enormous energy and unconquerable willpower. She got everything that she wanted – no moral restraints would ever confine her. She acted with frightening self-confidence and never regretted a thing. Many people balanced on the razor-edge of her will. There was only one exception: the patron of the Nightriders, Magnus Evans. Her former partner was still able to dominate her with some secret power.

Atro-city was flourishing. We released our first album – with the resonant title of "Satanic Rejoice" – and started to gain fame. Magnus pumped considerable amounts of money into the band. We gave concerts throughout the country and were successful everywhere, especially after Sibylla began to work on the set and choreography. Together, she and Ramborg came up with most hair-raising ideas, organizing real black Sabbaths and invocations of the devil during our concerts.

Meanwhile, Magnus had bought an ultramodern studio, and we started to work on our second album titled "Ritual Slayings". I neglected my studies and revealed nothing to my parents of what I was really doing. I guess I wanted to protect them.

During one of my holidays I bumped into Carina on the street. She looked at me as though she had just seen a ghost, and, with a worried expression, asked about my life in Stockholm. I told her I was playing in a rock band but I did not want to go into detail. She invited me to her place the next day, to have a talk. I did not show up. I did not dare tell her what I had been doing, or about Sibylla and our grotesque relationship. But I could not lie either, so I decided not to go. I returned to Stockholm without saying goodbye to Carina, but I did take her concerned expression with me. It kept bothering me. Filled with anguish, I started to really think about what I was actually doing. My meeting with Carina awoke a secret inner voice that, with superhuman efforts, I managed to repress for a long period. For the first time it crossed my mind that what I was doing might not be right. However I no longer had a system of values upon which I could establish right and wrong. But thoughts kept running through my head, and I had to admit that it was no longer a game, or if it was, then its weight seemed to be increasingly burdensome.

My friend Arne was not involved in these matters. His interest in women stood firm, and the capital seemed to be an inexhaustible source of 'fresh meat' – even after three years. He kept pressing me, "Come on, mate! Look around you! There are so many lovely chicks in this city! Where did you hide your brain when you chained yourself to that harpy."

That is what he always called her: 'the harpy'.

But 'the harpy' made sure she absorbed all my energy, and squeezed all the juice out of me – not a drop remained for other girls.

❖

One night Arne came home accompanied by two girls. "To have a good time." He introduced them, called me to the kitchen and whispered into my ear: "I have brought Christa Forshman for you. I have been with her a few times – and she is totally charming when she makes love." That was a magical night. After two years of steel hard sex I felt warmth again: the true warmth of the female heart.

Christa Forshman was one of the most peculiar girls I have ever met – I was utterly unable to comprehend her behaviour. She was not at all picky when it came to men; she slept with everybody who desired her, and loved everyone. And she did that with indescribable warmth and complete self-abandonment. I have no idea in which part of her skinny figure and small breasts she could have kept that enormous love she gave everybody with such surprising ease and generosity.

I had known her for a long time, and had often seen her sleeping with two or three people during one party.

I was not attracted by her in the slightest and, had Arne not brought her right into my bed, I would probably never have noticed who she really was. My feelings for her were best described as pity because, though she was immensely generous with everybody, nobody cared for her.

Lots of guys had sex with her but she was nobody's partner. Strangely though, she was happy and cheerful. A kind of otherworldly innocence radiated from her wondering, light-blue eyes that kept her clean even in the abomination that surrounded us. She never felt like she was being used. She truly adored men; she loved to make love and was deeply grateful for all the bits and pieces of attention she received.

With her slight, bony figure she could not offer me great physical pleasures, but the heavenly bliss that glowed on her face during lovemaking touched my heart. Something happened that night. Christa planted a tiny seed of light into my soul sitting right in the pits of hell. A process began that night, though I was not yet conscious of it. I still coveted Sibylla's flexible body and perverted games. I was still raging on stage, inebriated by the yelling of the crowd, and I considered myself the true prince of hell. This was, by the way, my stage name: "Prince of Hell". That was my predecessor's name too, the previous bass guitarist of Atro-city who had died of AIDS. And as my name – Balder – means prince in the language of ancient Normans, Ramborg found it appropriate that I should carry on the name. Back then I knew nothing about the correlation between one's name and destiny.

❖

That was when I became a member of the secret order of Thelema Knights, whose grandmaster was Magnus Evans himself. I was admitted on Sibylla's recommendation. I became a member of that eccentric brotherhood only after its dignitaries had found me eligible after putting me under serious surveillance – without my knowledge.

To this very day I shiver at the memory of saying yes and the feeling that overtook me during that ceremony conducted by Magnus as pontiff. It sounded like the bang of a prison door closing... and this prison was mine. One that I had chosen as my living place when I stepped over the doorstep of the Nightriders. The only difference was that until then the door of my cell had stood open, and I had been free to stay or leave. Now the door closed behind me. By saying yes I willingly became a prisoner. I went through with the initiation, swore eternal loyalty to the order and promised total discretion. There was only one way out of this prison: death. At least that is what they wanted me to believe.

In the beginning I had no idea as to the weight of events. It all seemed like an exciting new adventure. The clandestine meetings, rituals, practices of concentration and meditation led by Sibylla, and the mystery of the occult all combined to draw a curtain in front of the wanly flickering light of my judgment.

But I gradually started to realize that the ideology of the order is utterly religious. A religion of power and will that teaches its followers to always enforce their will upon others, even using violent means if necessary. One that condemns compassion, pity and love as grave weaknesses, and proudly propagates the domination of a few strong over the many weak.

To this very day I can evoke the image of Magnus reading with great seriousness and conviction the declaration by the Egyptian God of this bizarre religion. He was reading from the holy book of the order:

"Pity not the fallen! I never knew them. I am not for them. I console not: I hate the consoled & the consoler. We have nothing with the outcast and the unfit: let them die in their misery. Compassion is the vice of kings: stamp down the wretched & the weak: this is the law of the strong: this is our law and the joy of the world. The kings of the earth shall be Kings for ever: the slaves shall serve.

Worship me with fire & blood; worship me with swords & with spears.

Veil not your vices in virtuous words: these vices are my service; ye do well, & I will reward you here and hereafter."

I could no longer look upon these events as mere adventures, or innocent games.

The Order promised power, wealth, and social recognition to its members and strived for this with all its acts, political and financial manoeuvres. The promise was undoubtedly tempting, but required a high price to pay: to sacrifice my freedom. I felt the loop into which I had voluntarily put my neck getting tighter.

My instinct to escape started to grow. Mostly I blamed Sibylla for my situation and began to avoid contact with her. This was harder than I had thought it would be. Though she let me be and did not force me to see her, my yearning for her body, that aching desire she had ingrained in me escalated to an unbearable pain in her absence. I sought refuge in other girls' arms but even Christa Forshman's restorative warmth could provide relief for no more than a few hours.

One time after we made love Christa said, "Bald, I do not know why but I feel strange when I make love to you. You seem so cold, so far away, like I am with a rock. I see a weird, chilling shadow in your eyes, and when I close mine I see distorted images flashing through like in a nightmare, and I am afraid. I am afraid of you, Bald."

Christa's words made me feel desperate. Had I lost all affection? Was my soul already dead? Had I become a monster from whom people withdraw? If anyone else had said it then... But Christa? She never cared who she gave herself to!

I started to assess the gravity of my situation. I made up my mind to break up with Sibylla for good. She sensed my intentions, guessed my thoughts and disarmed me before I could say a word.

"You are so naive, kiddo! You still think you can break up with me? You are mine now, my captive forever. I bound you with magical chains to me. There is no power in this world that can break the chain. This bond is stronger than anything. Even than death. Be contented as long as you can enjoy my body 'cause if I deny it then you will taste the tortures of Hell."

So that is how we stood. For her body I gave my soul – the bitter realization flashed through my mind. Though I did not really believe her words, a weird sense of alarm still swept through me.

"You should give up all pointless attempts and prepare yourself because within two weeks you will participate in an important and exceptional ritual, with me. Until then, you need to practice meditation every day, and you are not allowed to lie with women. Nor with me or with anyone else."

I was positively happy that I would not have to sleep with Sibylla. And rituals had always awakened my curiosity. So for the time being I made no protest. I faithfully executed my meditation practices and avoided women.

One night Christa knocked on my door. She seemed anxious, and her large blue eyes expressed deep fear.

"O Bald, I'm so happy to see you. I thought something happened to you. I had such a strange dream, I saw you in a clearing in the middle of a dark forest, tied to a high column. Naked women were dancing around you but as they approached you their arms transformed into wings of vultures, scales and claws grew on their legs, their lustful lips turned to beaks. With frightening, wild wing strokes they flew around you, gouged out your eyes, ripped your skin to shreds, and you screamed for help. You shouted my name. It was horrifying."

"You can calm down now. You can see that my eyes and flesh are all right," I said with a forced smile. But my heart was pounding rapidly, and I felt sick to the stomach.

My mother's dream came to my mind, the one she'd had before my father's accident. That event left a deep impression on me, and since that time I had never been able to ignore dreams. There was something in Christa's expression and voice that reminded me of my mother.

"Bald, you are shaking and your hands are like ice, are you ill?"

"No, no, it is just cold here"

"Let's go to the bed and I'll make you warm."

"I can't now Chris, next time OK?" I said as I pushed away her hand caressing my face.

"Why can't you now? You can do it any time. Right now too, I feel it."

"No, Chris, no." I was desperately looking for an excuse.

"O, Bald, hold me please, I really want it, I love you so much."

I noticed an unfamiliar light in her eyes, her cheeks were rosy, and she spoke in an irresistible manner.

"Do not refuse me, please do not. Let me love you. Let me love you just this one time. I know that you don't love me. I know you love someone else. But if you do not want it, I will not ask it any more. Just this time, for a last time, as a farewell."

Words burst forth out of her like boiling lava flows, and they started to melt my ice-cold resolution. I softened, fell into her arms, put my arms around her tiny waist, and let it happen.

She fell asleep in my arms satisfied, but my dreams were chased away by fear. I was afraid of Sibylla, Magnus and the other members of the Thelema Knights. And I was afraid of the unforeseeable consequences.

I did not dare to confess to Sibylla that I had cheated.

The moment I stepped into the frightfully solemn hall of the order's secret meeting place, I was again seized by fear. Sibylla left me alone as she still had to prepare for the ritual.

Ominous music started up when everybody arrived. Sibylla appeared behind the altar standing between one white and one black column, her slim body covered with sky-blue robe adorned with golden motives. With a slow, serene motion she pulled aside the white veil that concealed the ceremonial objects.

Then Magnus stepped forward out of the candlelit dimness. He wore a long white gown and held a lance with black hilt in his hand. First he conferred holy orders on the objects and then took a leather-bound book off a stand: The Book of the Law of the order. He started to read from it with at a high pitch that resonated through the hall.

"Let the Scarlet Woman beware! If pity and compassion and tenderness visit her heart; if she leave my work to toy with old sweetnesses; then shall my vengeance be known. I will slay me her child: I will alienate her heart: I will cast her out from men: as a shrinking and despised harlot shall she crawl through dusk wet streets, and die cold and an-hungered.

But let her raise herself in pride! Let her follow me in my way! Let her work the work of wickedness! Let her kill her heart! Let her be loud and adulterous! Let her be covered with jewels, and rich garments, and let her be shameless before all men!"

Before the ceremony itself started Magnus looked at the participants severely and asked if there was anybody who had not respected the twelve-day chastity.

I felt all strength leaving my body, and my face burning as though everybody was watching me. I did not have the will to keep it a secret. I stood up. Icy glances pierced me from all sides. Murderous fire burned in Sibylla's eyes.

"Leave the hall at once," said Magnus. "We will pronounce your sentence at the next meeting."

With slow, dignified steps and a defiantly raised head I started for the exit.

One of Magnus's bodyguards called for a taxi, escorted me out, and closed the large, barred iron gate behind me.

I regretted revealing what I had done as I was still curious about the ritual. A bold idea struck me. I stopped the cab and got out. I went back and walked around the high concrete fence. The gate and the main walkway were too brightly lit so I did not dare enter that way but then I found what I was looking for: a tall pine tree near the fence. I climbed up nimbly and jumped onto the wall, then down into the courtyard. While I was slinking my way to the building I remembered all those peeping tom and commando games I had played with Arne. It made me smile. Maybe I had not changed that much since... This adventure cheered me up. It would have been good to have my trustworthy and resourceful friend nearby. I was grateful for his tutoring and dearly hoped I would not bring shame on my mentor. I found the upstairs bathroom window open so I climbed up carefully and dropped in. From there it was easy. I knew the building well.

The large hall had a side entrance with a thick velvet curtain on the inside. That place provided a good view of the whole hall. Fortunately there was music playing, otherwise they would definitely have heard my heart beating. Only my curiosity surpassed my excitement. The sight that opened up in front of me compensated for the risk.

Everybody was naked. Jewels sparkled on the women's bodies. Sibylla was lying on the altar, her legs spread. One by one the men approached the altar, knelt, lowered their heads and touched Sibylla's naked groin with their lips.

At the same time, the women processed to Magnus who touched them on certain points of their body with his lance and murmured something. Then every woman removed a jewel and dropped it into a bowl placed in the centre of the hall. Sibylla took the bowl around the hall, and every man – his eyes closed – took out a jewel.

As each woman made her way to the man holding her trinket I realized this was a pairing ritual. Every pair was given a silver cup. Then the copulation started. It was the same emotionless cold sex I was accustomed to with Sibylla. The sight gave me no satisfaction any more.

I could have left then but something kept me there. Not only curiosity – something else too. Maybe it was the surreal image of bodies intertwining in the spotlights provided by the dancing flames of candles. Maybe the paralyzing attraction of screams bursting out in the sexual delirium. In spite of its emotionless nature the picture was captivating, like an ancient Greek tragedy, or like a group of animated statues illustrating a wild orgy. It was an authentic pagan ritual, a celebration of impersonal lust. There was Sibylla, dancing ecstatically on the altar, offering herself to the cruel god of this bizarre religion, drawing cold sacrifices from her marble body with the snake-ornamented dagger. Yes. It was a celebration of the body – but the soul was entirely absent, and that is why its beauty was so bleak, its pleasure so empty. I had once been given the chance to know what it feels like when body and soul celebrate together, playing the merry dance of true love. Suddenly it became clear why I did not want to continue this sort of life any longer. That life with Sibylla, that life as a member of the order was no longer my life. I thirsted after something else. Some other kind of celebration.

Soon I discovered the purpose of the little silver cups: to catch the fluid, fruit of the copulation, trickling out of women's loins. But they could not enjoy this nectar for long. They had to offer the content to their "big brother", a larger, golden bowl ornamented with jewels that Sibylla carried from one couple to the next.

After collecting the levy from everybody she put the bowl on the altar. Magnus poured a cherry-red coloured liquid into it from a crystal jug, and Sibylla stirred it with the dagger. Magnus sketched strange forms above it with his lance muttering spells in some unknown language.

Meanwhile they all sat down forming a large circle – the women sitting to the left of their partners. Then Magnus sent around the bowl, like Christ during the last supper, and all drank from it with reverence. Then they closed their eyes and sank into themselves.

That is all I saw. I could stay no longer. I left the same way I had entered in, determined that, whatever it might take, I would break away from everything of my previous two years. That meant breaking up with Sibylla, with the knights of Thelema, with Atro-city and the Nightriders. I would start a new life.

❖

A few days later Sibylla and Magnus came looking for me in my apartment. They held me to task about my "behaviour not appropriate for a member of the secret brotherhood". I listened to the grave charges in a good-humoured and calm manner, self-confident as I told them about my resolution. Magnus went red with rage and threatened me. He reminded me of the strict rules of the order, the oath I had pledged, and the occult, magical forces with which they could do anything to me. He also reminded me there was only one way to leave the order: death – that I would inflict upon myself willingly in the event the order instructed me to. He also reminded me of the girl who had committed suicide a year earlier. His revelation shocked me. I knew the girl but hadn't a clue she had also been a member of the order. From my shock they concluded they had won the argument and left with a self-assured satisfaction. They promised the order would be willing to forgive me for my momentary lapse of judgment, if I appeared at the next meeting.

I did not go.

The following day Sibylla visited me again, but that time she neither scolded nor threatened me. She simply asked me to go to her place because she was going to prepare a surprise for me. The reason I accepted her invitation was not only because I was curious about her surprise but also because I felt strong enough to resist any temptation. I wanted to prove that to her, and to myself.

She led me to her room, asked me to sit and left me alone. She came back later wearing luxurious, sensual clothes dripping in jewels. She brought the dagger with the snake hilt, a jug of red wine and a silver cup on a tray.

Then she stood up on the marble slab covered table and started to dance. With the expertise of a professional stripper she removed her clothes one by one. Her gaze, like that of a snake charmer, was fixed on me. Her slender waist's circular movements formed invisible spirals of energy that boiled my blood and clouded my mind. She called me with coquettish glances, undulating movements and seducing words... to coil round me, for me to lose myself in her. My mind resisted the temptation fiercely; I did not move. She stepped off the altar, swung towards me, and raised a magical circle around me with her serpentine movements. She touched my body with her icy dagger, traced my neck with it... and with a sudden movement ripped open my shirt. I tried to calm my shaking body, but when the blade reached my groin I pushed her away with incredible power and sprang to my feet. Sibylla fell back against the altar then slowly slipped onto the ground. She gazed at me in surprise.

Words cannot describe what came next. It surpassed my most terrifying nightmares: her eyes became blurred, her face disfigured. Her expressions distorted, as she grinned a dreadful grimace, her body jerking in convulsions, broken rattles bursting out of her mouth. Horror dipped its vulture nails into my soul. What I had thought existed only in horror movies – that I considered to be nothing more than the distraught brainchild of psychotic film directors – was right here in front of my eyes, quivering and shaking in convulsions. Though the face – distorted to a frightening and evil apparition

– still reminded me of Sibylla, it was a different face.

Slowly the twitching and jerking abated, the gargling sounds became comprehensible, and words began to form sentences. But the voice I heard was not Sibylla's – somebody else was talking... through her.

All my senses urged me to escape but some terrific and icy force numbed me, and the wheels of my mind suddenly stopped turning. Commands ran through my nerve paths in chaotic disorder, and my body did not obey my mind. My brain recorded her words unconsciously, like a tape recorder.

"There is no escape for you Balder Falkenberg. You are a dog chained down. The bond is ancient... but then you had a different name; the spell cannot be broken by either cradle or the grave. Your efforts to seek redemption in the affection of sluts like Christa are in vain. You are my prisoner. You gave yourself to me... it's me you worshipped by indulging in pleasures with Sibylla's body, it's me you offered yourself to when spreading your seeds, it's me you fed with your vitality. And you will do the same henceforth till your last breath."

A terrible, diabolical laughter burst from her contorted lips. Then the voice continued, "This is how I want it. I am stronger than anyone, because I know the secret of the blood. The blood... the blood." Her hands, shaking and holding the dagger tensely, pressed the point of the weapon against her thigh. Ruby coloured blood sprang from the cut.

With a sudden movement I jumped over to her and twisted the lethal weapon out of her hands. Unaware of what I was doing, I started to make signs of cross with it over her, mumbling the Lord's Prayer, but I could not finish it, not one time. I heard a spine-chilling shriek, "NOOOO!"

I was petrified and kept repeating in my confusion: "Apage Satanas! Apage Satanas!" – as I had seen in the movies. Her body started to jerk ever more violently, and words became nonsensical again. Then there was dead silence. Her face became calm, and Sibylla woke up with a startled, uncomprehending look. She wiped the blood on her thigh with her fingers. "What has happened? What are you doing with that dagger?"

She remembered nothing at all. Her voice was dull and weak, and she soaked in sweat. "Have we just had sex?"

"No, we have not, and we never will again. Never!"

She said something in a fading tone that sounded like a threat, then collapsed wearily onto the floor. She fell asleep. She did not wake even when I carried her into her bedroom. Her body was limp and heavy like a corpse. I put her to bed and left, carrying the dagger with me.

❖

Real hell was to break loose after that. The experience was burnt with hot iron into my memory. But it was not like a memory, it was the incessant presence of a torturing reality. The terrifying face and twitching body haunted me ceaselessly Her threatening words stuck in my head. I could not eat, I could not sleep. Only complete exhaustion let me sleep like a log at times.

Arne was genuinely worried for me but could not help. I didn't tell him what had happened. Christa did not want to meet me. She said she was afraid of me and she would pray for me.

The worst part of it was that I could not comprehend what was going on. Many a time I replayed the scene in my head trying to make sense out of it, but shadows of unanswered questions kept haunting me. How could her face have become so distorted? What had made her voice unrecognizable? Why did not she remember anything after it was all over? Why could not I finish the Lord's Prayer not even once, when I had always been able to recite it correctly? What was that "ancient bond" she was talking about? And who the hell was talking? Did she change back because I had drawn crosses and cried out Apage Satanas? Did Satan and devils exist? And if so, then God must exist too? Should I start praying? ... but I did not believe in it. Christa's words came into my mind "I will pray for you", and I felt warmth in my heart, the way I used to feel when I was with her. I wondered if she believed in God, though it is strange, religious girls do not usually sleep with every stranger who comes their way. She certainly was so different, so generous.

"I will pray for you."

What if I simply started praying, just for myself? My fingers intertwined spontaneously, and words bursting out of my worn soul began to form themselves into a prayer: "Lord, I do not know whether you exist or not, and where you might be. But if you are somewhere and are listening to me, I ask you one thing, let me be free from this abomination that I got involved in like a stupid ass. Amen."

Except for the Amen I would not say my appeal had taken the form of a prayer, but at least it came from the heart, and I felt relieved. The next moment I was smiling at myself: Oh, Balder Falkenberg, where have you got to? Are you really praying?

Christa came into my mind again. I remembered the first time we made love and the way I felt then. It was similar to my times with Carina. Yes, Carina was wonderful, there must be some secret power she possesses, she knows about many things. She knows more than she had let me know. Her whole being was still an enigma for me. Should I talk to Carina? I could tell her about everything, maybe she could give me an idea. Yes. That is what I would do! I would ask for her help!

The thought made me feel relieved. There still was hope, a last thread to hold on to.

Two days later I met Sibylla on the street but I hardly recognized her. She was leaning against a lamppost, staring hazily ahead. I tried to talk to her but she just mumbled inconsistently — I don't think she even recognized me. She was drugged.

I was really taken aback. Never before had she done anything like that. She had never used drugs. In fact she never even touched alcohol. I put her into a cab and took her home. I stayed with her till the morning to talk to her before she could get high again. She looked miserable even while sober. Her once exuberant life energy and self-confidence was now just a dim reflection of the past, hardly perceptible on her face.

"You broke your oath, for this I will also be... I mean that they, you know, I vouched for you, they will kill me, we are both sentenced to death, do you understand?" she said racked with sobs.

I was not afraid of what she said, but the way she said it. Her whining voice, her gaze staring into nothingness, her deplorable state were quite fearful on top of what she had just said. Since we had met this was the first time I felt something human in her — the fallible and suffering woman. I felt sorry for her.

Then I saw her rummaging in her handbag, she took out a little black box and flipped up its lid. It contained white powder. I knocked it out of her hand and it fell to the ground.

"You won't do this any more," I shouted. "I'll stand by you. I am gonna tie you up if I have to, understand? I don't want you to do this to yourself."

She jumped up and attacked me: "You miserable... You destroyed my life! And now this! My only cure!" Her nails cut deep into the skin of my neck. I was hardly able to wrench her hands off me. Finally I managed to hold her down despite her strength. She was fuming with rage and tried to scratch and bite me, spit in my eye. Then I slapped her as hard as I could. She fell down to the ground and started crying like a child.

"Leave me, leave me alone, I want to be alone, to die alone."

I was so angry I could have screamed. I looked at her for a few moments, then turned around silently and staggered out of the apartment.

Hopelessness and desperation swept through me before long. Sibylla was the reason for it. I felt responsible for her. We had been together for a long time, two years. I wanted to help her somehow.

One night Arne said that at the weekend he would be going to Karlskona and asked whether I wanted to go with him.

"I don't know yet, I may have some business to attend to," I answered.

"Just think about it, I'm sure your parents would be happy to see you. When was the last time you were at home?"

The last time? I thought for a while. I had no idea. Probably at Christmas, three months earlier. I said I would think about it. For two days I struggled to decide. Like it was an important decision, a question of life and death – my life and Sibylla's, of course. In the end I decided to go home and see Carina.

Carina welcomed me with undisguised pleasure.

Without any further polite small talk I told her that I needed help in something I was unable to resolve alone. Signs of worry flashed across her sunny face.

She led me to her bedroom. I was astonished to see that almost everything was exactly as it had been three years earlier. Every piece of furniture, every knick knack and painting in their place, many a silent witness to a life squandered, to a paradise lost. In other circumstances the intimate familiarity of these objects would have recalled fond memories. But now my anguish, like a slowly killing poison seemed to suffocate even my memories. I told her everything. Not only the events and facts but my thoughts and feelings too. As she listened her face became serious. She did not interrupt me. After I had finished silence hung in the room for a long time.

When she did start to talk, her warm and reassuring voice did not hide her somber mood.

"The situation is more serious than I had thought. I concluded from the bits and pieces I heard from Arne that you were walking a dangerous path, and I knew I was unable to help you unless you asked me to. You are involved in something that is hard to escape. But in spite of all your mindless deeds you did not fall from God's grace. You owe Christa Forshman eternal gratitude for preventing you, from participating in that ceremony. Magnus's sperm ritual would have bound you to the order of Thelema Knights with such a powerful magical tie that you would have remained its captive forever. If it had happened I would not be able to help you. And probably no one else. This way we still have hope. Let me work something out and meet me tomorrow evening. By that time I'll have a plan ready."

I struggled with tormenting anxiety as the river of Time slowed down to stagnant water. What had once been inconceivable suspicion was now solidified into certainty by Carina's words.

The next day she chose the mysterious intimacy of her bedroom again as the place for our discussion. I scanned her face desperately, as though the micro-expressions of her face would reveal my very fate any moment. Since she was neither overly cheerful nor excessively care laden, I calmed down a bit.

"Today we need to talk about things of highest importance. I hope you are mature enough to understand them. Anything I am going to say shall stay between us, do you understand?"

"Yes," I answered with growing tension that was at last tinged with some hope.

"This Magnus Evans is an extremely dangerous person. He will probably cause you much trouble. He possesses great powers, and I have figured out how he came to them. With the use of sexual magic he has been able to access the greatest sources of the human psyche, and it seems Sibylla was an exceptional partner in this. I thought that would happen. He was always intrigued by these kinds of things."

"Wait a moment, you know Magnus?"

"Yes, and Sibylla too."

Her face became meditative. She was searching for memories. She continued after a short break: "We started out together, on a way that was dangerous, a way on which failure is inevitable without an experienced guide. Providence saved me just like it saved you. For some reason Magnus was not so lucky. Or he just simply refused the help. We went to the conservatory together. Magnus was living with his parents and the basement there was already used as a secret meeting place for artists. One time Magnus invited an Indian guru, Swami Kamaraja who held a few lectures about Tantra. This is a branch of Indian yoga that uses the human body's most powerful source of energy, sexuality, as the fuel for spiritual development. Everything he said, and even the mystical and enthralling energy he emanated, had a defining influence on us.

After the lectures we started to learn about Tantra. Magnus was the most enthusiastic. He seemed like someone who had just found the meaning of his life. I felt similarly. We formed study groups and collected every book that dealt with Tantra. The problem was that these books often contradicted each other. For a long time we strayed helpless in the labyrinth of ambiguous hints and perplexing allusions. There was one thing we figured out: practicing Tantra needs initiation, and for this we needed an initiated tantric Master.

"So we started to search for this master. Swami Kamaraja was never to be found again. A few of us travelled to India to try our luck. We searched the country far and wide but with no result. We visited many gurus. Most of them had never even heard about Tantra, many of them were against it and some knew even less about it than we did. But it is possible that they just hid the knowledge because they did not find us worthy enough. I think they were right.

Returning to Stockholm we began to experiment with certain rituals. Magnus liked playing leader. But these rituals were mostly unsuccessful. We were not even close to the results the tantric texts promised, although we followed the teachings letter by letter. We must have missed something and we had no idea what it was. So many of us lost interest. Four of us stayed: Magnus, Sibylla, a friend of mine and me.

One time Magnus came to our meeting with a triumphant face, waving a ten-page text in his hands. He showed us the front page proudly;

it said "Yoni Tantra". He explained it was an essential piece about left-handed Tantra and that it contained the secret we had been looking for. His attitude showed his confidence that he held the key to the great secret. I examined it carefully and found many odd practices. For example it mentioned that the greatest power lays in the *yoni tattva* which is the mixture of sperm and menstruation blood dissolved in wine. Those who drink it will find ultimate liberation and unlimited strength. I argued with Magnus many times as I believe that the language of tantric writings is coded and that without a key the uninitiated student will walk on the wrong path. He kept repeating that what he had found was unique, and its value was precisely that its message was not hidden behind dubious allegories and it described everything clearly.

I could not accept this idea. One reason was that the only Tantra teacher we met, Swami Kamaraja, kept emphasizing that a man's ejaculation means an irreplaceable loss of energy, and during tantric intercourse it should never happen. In addition, Yoni Tantra also mentioned that the whole ritual is worthless without a specific mantra – one that a student can only receive from a Master.

Magnus replied that when a student is ready the master finds him and that he would prepare himself with or without me. His attitude was eccentric even then. I believed he was not interested in the spiritual possibilities but was driven by the ideal of unlimited power the Yoni Tantra promised. I knew Sibylla would fall for it easily – she was deeply infatuated with Magnus. Her steadfast devotion towards him made her frail spirit vulnerable to the tyrannical will of Magnus. Our ways parted then. Magnus moved to England with his parents and took Sibylla with him. I did not give up studying Tantra. I tried to live and love by its teachings and prepare myself for the time when the Master would arrive.

I met Magnus three years later in Stockholm. His attitude surprised me and set me wondering what might have happened. He had become secretive and tremendously conceited. He told me he had found what we had been looking for. In England he had joined a clandestine order that initiated him into the mysteries of Tantra. Now, as an initiate, he had returned to Stockholm to establish his own order with himself as the grandmaster. As these things were "highly confidential" he could not share anything further but promised me that if I was curious and when I felt suitably prepared, he would initiate me. I did want to know more, but not from him – his pompousness angered me. On leaving he said that, if I really wanted to know, he had been right all along. He had correctly interpreted the Yoni Tantra; they practiced it with success. In a certain way the result was indisputable. His fortitude, will power and self-confidence had increased ostensibly, and his charismatic look and powerful tone obliged many a strong individual to back down when it came to an argument.

The change in Sibylla was even more shocking. The once weak and fragile chick was now a strong-minded tiger of a woman. With one glance, with her body's sensual radiation she could reduce even the toughest men to mere puppies rubbing up against her leg. She was not as arrogant as Magnus; she wore her feminine superiority with surprising naturalness and did not feel compelled to prove herself all the time. It was she who told me that the secret order they had joined was the English lodge of the Ordo Templi Orientis. She didn't tell me either what this order was involved in, though she did mention that Magnus – who had proved to be an exceptional student and developed rapidly – was not content with the way the order interpreted the Book of the Law written by the OTO founding grandmaster, Aleister Crowley. Magnus judged their operations to be too tempered and too effeminate. After three years he had decided to establish his own order, one where he could use the rules set down by Master Therion as he saw fit. However he had not presented his plan to the order as he did not dare face the consequences of this decision. Excusing himself on personal reasons he moved back to Stockholm. The Swedish capital promised an excellent opportunity to realize his plans. What happened next you know better than me. I moved to Karlskrona with my husband and heard nothing more of the matter until now."

I was stunned to hear everything Carina said. Events connecting in this way left me stunned. Everything that had been so obscure in the past few months started to become clear. I had been feeling around in a dark room for a long time, dangers looming around me, but now the faint candlelight of Carina's words made this darkness disperse. Things were given a solid contour, and at last some light was shed upon the connections between them. I think that was the first time I felt enlightened. I realized that events and things are not sporadic facts – hidden connections weave them into the fabric of a precisely elaborated plan. I had the vision of a large, dust-covered mosaic from which the breeze of understanding keeps sweeping the dust away, so the colourful stones gradually reveal the complete picture and the secret of its essence. And I felt that this was just the beginning. Much dust still needed to be swept off before I would see the whole picture.

"Why is that that you never spoke to me about Tantra?" I asked Carina.

"I am not sure. I guess I was concerned for you."

"But if I had known all about it, then maybe I would have avoided all this trouble. Knowledge would have protected me."

"No knowledge saves the inexperienced. Instead it plunges them into greater dangers. Believe me, I considered my decision for a long time. When I first met you a kind of inexplicable suspicion crept into my mind about the connection of our destinies. I was attracted to you from the first moment. It was not the attraction a woman feels when she sees a man and falls in love with him at first sight. It was something different, a feeling that reaches far back in the tunnel of Time, to many lives before this one."

"How is that?" I asked perplexed. "You believe in reincarnation?"

"Yes, for me it is as real as you are sitting in front of me."

Her statements sounded so persuasive as to make any counter argument seem ridiculous and pointless. I was just listening, bewildered by this woman. I felt as though I was entering the gates of a huge, cosmic mystery.

"I felt it was not the first time we had met. I was convinced it had happened before, and it was connected to Tantra. In your eyes I saw a light that shines only in the eyes of those who had once been initiated into the secrets of Tantra."

"So you mean that I was once..."

"What do you feel when you hear the word TANTRA?"

"I feel like I'm standing on the brink of a whirlwind. It attracts me like all mysteries do."

"Long-forgotten memories show themselves this way. That means I was right. But I also felt something in you that frightened me. You are more similar to Magnus than you may like to think. You are driven by the same wild, sensual desire, by the same childish, irresponsible curiosity and the same mindless resolution. After we first met I was puzzled over what to do with you, how to relate to you. Then I made the decision not to talk to you about Tantra. I was sure that if God wants you to find it then you will, some other way. I see now that I made the correct decision. It was not the right time then. Your insatiable sexual desires might have led to failure without an experienced master. The way it happened to Magnus. There is no way back from these failures. There was a difference however. There is a spiritual purity in you that Magnus lacked. This is what protected you. Had I been an enlightened master maybe I would have initiated you, but I was not. I could not see through the complex network of causes and effects, so I could not take responsibility. It is your life that was at stake. More than your life – your soul. All I could do was to make love to you, and this way pass on as much of this divine energy as you were able to receive. I could do this as I was attracted to you and desired you. The only thing I feared was that you would not be attracted to me. Then I did something I am still not sure was appropriate: I practiced astral love. I first made love to you in your dream as I knew you would not deny me this way. From that moment on it was an exciting game. I provoked you but did not initiate anything. I knew that if it was meant to happen, you also had to want it, feel it and act on it. I was delighted to hear you had never made love before. Then I was sure Fate was presenting me with the privilege of initiating you. I knew that the first time is essential, just like the first step on a path; it is your first step that defines the way you go."

"Judging my current situation, that road goes sideways," I said with unconcealed irony in my voice.

"At this time you cannot see the direction. This is just a section of the road you are treading, a tough section that sooner or later you will surpass."

"I want to overcome it as soon as possible. Please help me with this if you can."

"That is exactly what I am doing. I told you all this so you would understand your situation. That was the first step, and now it is time you act upon it."

"What do I have to do?"

"First of all I am going to teach you about the protective aura. If you use it, the astral being that possesses Sibylla will have little opportunity to harass you. And I also would like you to stay here at home for some time, say two weeks. You need to gather some strength before you go back to Stockholm. Energy waves that your actions set in motion have to calm down, to consume themselves. You cannot stop them now. But beware that you do not set forth negative energy waves again, because then this vicious circle will absorb you deeper, and liberation will be more and more difficult – impossible after a certain point."

"And what about Sibylla? I need to help her. We were lovers for two years and I feel responsible for her. I left her in an awful state."

"I don't want to deceive you, Bald. You are in an awful state yourself. First of all you need to help yourself and for this you need all the energy you have. Remember, you are not responsible for anyone else's actions, only your own. What Sibylla did was of her own free will. No one can remove that burden from her shoulders – except God if He finds her deserving, but now is not your time to help her. You don't have enough strength to pull her out of the swamp that you are both immersed in. If you try, then both of you will drown. Listen to me Bald, and do not take more risks. I know there is nothing worse than to see people fall and realize we cannot lift them up. We have to accept that every man has his own path on which hardships and suffering have just as much a role as success and happiness. We can only help someone if God wants it too. If He wants it, then He will give us a sign. You can be assured of that. But if we try to free from suffering someone who still needs that suffering to learn an important life lesson, we are not acting wisely – even if our acts are driven by good intention. Never forget, pity is a bad adviser. It clouds judgment and persuades you to help when no help can actually assist. It is compassion that shows you the right way. Try to awaken that in yourself. That is all for now. Be careful. One last thing, come to my place on Saturday night. I'm going to prepare a surprise for you."

I replayed the conversation in my head many times, but Carina's advice was still not clear. She spoke of things about which I had not the vaguest idea. I lacked the experience to comprehend them. She was probably trying to prepare me for these very experiences. For some reason I trusted her deeply. Her mere presence meant a kind of protection and support to me.

❖

Her surprise on Saturday was very dear to me. She invited old friends of mine, familiar faces I had almost forgotten. Talking to them and laughing with them truly refreshed my spirit. Suddenly a world became alive I had thought no longer existed.

There was one new person in the group – a gorgeous girl called Linnéa Svenson. Carina introduced her as a friend. Later it turned out that actually Linnéa was Carina's surprise for me. She was about the same age as me and was remarkably similar to my childhood love Ylva Ekberg – only that Ylva's girlish charms had changed into sensually curving lines. Carina knew my taste well. Linnéa aroused my interest from the first. An excitement I had not felt for some time ran through my revived nerve paths. I was relieved to realize she was not indifferent to me either, but that was probably thanks to Carina's setting us up rather than my appearance, which was definitely not so inviting.

"So you are the famous Balder Falkenberg," she said as she granted her hand and charming fingers to me. "Carina has told me a lot about you."

"I hope only good," I smiled.

"No, only the bad things. That is why I was curious about you."

I immersed myself deep in the greenish-blue pool of her eyes and, for a moment, time seemed to stop, a mysterious deepness absorbed me, along with the dancing couples, the clinking of glasses and all the laughter around.

When I recovered my senses I felt as though I was waking up from a long dream during which the world had changed around me. The crystal chandelier scattered fresh cascades of light around the room, tinkling laughter drifted around, and colours became more dazzling. Red was redder, and blue bluer. Even black got new sparkling tones. And Linnéa... Linnéa was beautiful. Her smile became angelic, her naked shoulders appeared pure white. I looked around in surprise. Was anyone else seeing this metamorphosis? I was disappointed to realize everyone else was carrying on as though nothing at all was happening. Only Carina winked at me mischievously. She was the only one to see what had happened. She also knew it was not the world changing but me being reborn. She made no attempt to hide her contentment that everything was going according to her plan.

I did not leave Linnéa for the rest of the night. It was unspeakably good to be with her, to look into her eyes and listen to the melody of her voice. She told me about herself. She had just returned from India where she often went to learn dancing. Her parents lived in Malmö, and she was living with her aunt here in Karlskrona. She spent most of her time on tour and before long she would have to travel to France because she was invited to give a few performances. She told me something else that I was secretly delighted to hear: she did not have a boyfriend.

"I am always on tour you know, and I have to practice a lot," she explained sadly. "And men are too impatient to wait for me."

"Well, I am famous for my infinite patience," I joked.

"You don't look like it," she replied with bell-like laughter.

She was incredibly charming, and she could laugh so brightly I felt I owed eternal gratitude to Carina for that evening. Of course, Linnéa and I met the next day, and the next, and the next. Indeed every day. Linnéa accepted my approaches and that made me truly happy. My life in Stockholm, with all its hideous events, faded to a distant memory. I was overjoyed by the caressing sensation of careless freedom. My love sprouted together with the trees' buds and the first flowers. Spring had arrived in Karlskrona and, after years of winter, in my soul too. We strolled outside all day long and laughed a lot. We laughed at every silly idea, and I realized I had not done that for a very long time. As soon as the sun peeked out from behind the clouds we were out in the fresh air. After nightfall we often went strolling on the beach, listening to the ever renewing symphony of the sea. This is how our feelings deepened and became as boundless as the ocean. We talked a lot, recounting pleasant memories and amusing adventures. We talked about everything except for one thing: our unfolding love. Although we did not mention it, we recognized it, watching as it grew like a baby in his mother's lap. We were delighted about it but neither of us wanted to dress its beautiful naked body with phrases.

We did not think about how long we would stay together, and we did not hurry. It was as though eternity was at our disposal, yet we strived to give each other every minute as though it was the last one. I kissed her for the first time after a week. It was complete fulfilment. That kiss did not give way to burning desires yearning for more physical pleasure. There was neither the taste of nostalgia for the passing moments nor the tempting promises of the future in that kiss. Rather it was the feeling of the infinite presence of the moment, suspended between the planes of time. Of course I still desired to join with her in physical union, but at that moment it was not the most important. I wanted to enjoy to my heart's content the excitement of our slow approach to each other. But time did not stop the way we believed it would. Minutes that seemed countless were all swept away by the March wind. Two weeks flew away, and I knew I could stay no longer. I had to return to Stockholm.

We did not agree how our relationship would go on when we separated. Actually I felt that we did not even separate. Only our bodies ended up further away while our souls stayed together in a dimension outside time and space.

Carina had judged my situation correctly. I did need to charge up on this divine energy to face what was awaiting me in Stockholm. What Carina was unable to give me she presented me through Linnéa. She wanted to give me strength that would serve me as a protective shield in my battle against the dark powers. She knew well what these powers really were. I only suspected them, or maybe just felt them unconsciously.

❖

The first thing I found out when I arrived to Stockholm was that I had been dismissed from university for missing seminars, neglecting exams and my generally antisocial behaviour that was 'bringing shame on the reputation of the conservatory'. At least these were the main reasons set out in the letter of dismissal the dean handed to me, his eyes downcast as if it he were the one who should be ashamed of something. I found out the teaching staff had not met as was customary in such cases. The decision was personally made by the rector of the university and it was final – no chance for an appeal. It was all unexpected, and I suspected Magnus's hand in the case. This was a blow below belt, utterly painful. I was particularly upset for my parents. They trusted me completely and had cherished a desire for my successful musical career. I had no idea how to tell them.

The next day Magnus visited me in my apartment with two other members of the order. Without any delay or explanation he read me the oath I had signed and then reminded me of the punishment I would suffer if I did not abide by it. Then he told me they would welcome me at the next meeting scheduled three days later. Before he left he added, "I thought you would not want to waste any more time on the conservatory. You have another mission to accomplish now. You will be a great star. Fans from all over the world will kneel before you. That certainly is more exciting than scraping some god-awful tune on a cello in a musty room, isn't it?"

Blood rushed to my head, and I clenched my fists. I was on the edge of hitting him but I restrained myself. Hissing through my teeth I told him, "Go to hell, that's what you deserve".

"Yeah sure, I'm gonna wait for you there," he grinned.

As a parting he pinched my face, and they started to make their way out.

"Oh yes, there is something else." He turned back, rummaging in his pockets. Then he handed me a folded piece of paper. "Your lover sends this."

I could hardly read the scribble that said, *"I am waiting for you, I am suffering and you are not with me. Have you forgotten me? Have you forgotten everything? You are the only one who can help me, the only one. I am waiting, hurry please! Sibylla."*

Carina's warning words came to my mind but I could not resist the temptation. I went to meet Sibylla that very evening. It was quite an eerie sight. Sibylla was lying naked on the black marble slab of her altar. Jewels hung on her gaunt body and oily blobs of paints were splattered all around the room. Her dazed eyes sat deep in her hollow face, looking at me.

"So you have come my darling. I have been waiting for a long time."

The word darling astounded me. She never addressed me like that

"I knew you would come," she tried to smile but her face worn by narcotics distorted it to a pitiful smirk. Then she waved her skinny fingers at me. "Come my love, I have already prepared everything. I adorned myself just for you, so I would be beautiful... so you can rejoice and make love... and then we will be happy at last... Do you want to?"

Then she stood up on the table and started to dance. The grotesque movements of her skeleton body composed an abhorrent danse macabre. Nauseated at the sight, I knew I had to escape. It was as though she had sensed it too. She jumped off the table, knelt before me and held my hand tight.

"Do not leave me my love," she said as she started to cry and shrill. "Magnus told me he would kill me if you do not make love to me. I do not want to die, no, no, not now... when I want to love you, when we could be together."

She fell at my feet and cried. She went on crying without dropping a tear.

Then suddenly she fell silent. She released my hand, stood up and climbed back onto the altar.

"I knew you did not love me, you never loved me, I knew it and Magnus also told me so." She started swaying her body again, moaning some bizarre kindergarten melody.

"Sibylla! Sibylla! Stop it!" I rebuked her firmly. But she was not in our world any more. She was somewhere where nobody and nothing could reach her, not Magnus, not the suffering, not me. I left the room quietly. She didn't even notice me leaving. The awful sight stuck in my head. I felt faint.

Sibylla was not drugged. She did not need it any longer. That fog, the strangling hands of madness choked her mind. But even so her behaviour seemed strange. Beyond all the things she said, beyond all that nonsense there was an alarming logic. As if the tender words were the cries for help of a crushed female soul yearning for love that only now, on the brink of madness, were able to surface.

I am not even sure she recognized me. She may have been talking to phantoms haunting her crazed imagination. I was sure about one thing though; she could not have written that letter. It must have been Magnus. He wanted to lure me there to show his destructive power. He had used his former partner for one last thing she was useful for: to serve as a terrifying warning.

This cruelty upset me profoundly. I was more than simply outraged. I saw at last how deep a human being can sink if he plays the games of the Devil. Carina was right. No one could help Sibylla at that point, maybe not even God.

❖

The next day Arne rushed into my room white as a sheet and terror in his eyes.

"You remember Christa Forshman?"

"Yes, of course, why?"

"Yesterday afternoon she committed suicide. It turns out she had AIDS. I guess she did not opt for the slow death."

Everything went dark in front of my eyes. I thought I would fall of the chair. "When was the last time you went with her?" asked Arne.

"About a month ago, and you?"

"Six weeks."

"That means..."

"Yes Bald, we are sentenced to death."

He collapsed on the bed and lay there insipidly. "I think it has already started in me. I have had terrible diarrhoea for three days now, and no medicine is working. Why the hell did I have to sleep with that little bitch? Where was I thinking?"

"It's done, Arne. No use of speaking about her this way, you know that she was..." I did not continue, what could have I said?

Suddenly Linnéa came to my mind, and I thought my heart would break. Now that I had fallen in love at last. Now that there was somebody to love me. Now this, just when I could have started a new life. It couldn't be true!

"Arne, we have to do something, we cannot just wait, twirling our thumbs while we rot to death."

"What Bald, what should we do? You know very well it is incurable. Not even God can help."

His words kept ringing in my head. As though he had proclaimed the death sentence – "Not even God can help". But what if He could? It had worked once,... it was He who inspired me to ask Carina for help. Maybe I should pray again. Though... maybe it had just been a coincidence. Well, who cared, it was all over anyway.

❖

Two days later we went to the funeral. The others were there too, all Christa's former bedmates. We listened to the sermon, each as white as a ghost. That sermon was our funeral oration too.

After the funeral seven of us – comrades in misfortune – walked home, totally out of sorts. Silence settled on us like a black veil. I was searching for something to say but everything seemed meaningless. We walked past a church. One half of the large reddish oak-wood gate was open. Organ music pierced through from the obscure half-light of the inside. I was thinking about going in but dismissed the idea. Ridiculous, the others would definitely laugh at me. But after all, what was being laughed at to somebody already on death row. How vain was I! At last I made up my mind and brought up my suggestion. To my surprise nobody laughed at me. There was not one smile – or even the hint of a smirk. In fact, some of them admitted they had been thinking about it too.

First we looked around to check that none of our acquaintances would see us, and then we silently processed in. There was nobody inside except for a janitor removing the cobwebs with a long broom and an organist who was practicing. Arne, a man of resolution as always, was the first one to kneel down in front of the altar. We followed him, kneeling beside him in a line. From the corner of my eye I saw the janitor stop sweeping, obviously wondering at this rare sight. The organist also stopped in the middle of a movement. As if we had just heard a command, we all folded our hands at once and started to pray. Everybody in his own way.

The organ started to play again. Sounds of a beautiful piece filled with tragically lofty chords echoed between the bald walls. I recognized Johann Sebastian Bach's unique harmonies. The gradually intensifying waves of sounds twined around me and filled the thronging emptiness that I had been feeling inside. A kind of otherworldly silence descended upon me.

The second prayer of my life was just as simple and sincere as the first: "Lord, once you helped me. Now I turn to you a second time. There is only one thing I wish: to know the true love that I have only experienced in fragments until now. If you find me worthy, then I ask you to let me live. Thy will be done, Amen."

I stayed there for a long time after that without moving. Until the organ went silent. I felt magnificent. It was like Linnéa's kiss. I saw the janitor praying, the broom leaning against a pillar. We stood up. My knees were aching. The janitor watched us walking out of the church in single file again. His face was beaming, full of wonder and awe. We stood for a moment in front of the church, and I saw a sparkling something in the others' eyes too: it was a ray of hope.

❖

I was in bed with flu for two days and had a splitting headache and a terrible cough. Arne spent most of his time on the loo taking his temperature every half an hour. We were certain these signs were the heralds of death. I stayed in bed all day while Arne paced up and down the room with a weary look. I had a sudden turn of mind and jumped out of bed. "You know what? I am not going to wait for death here. I want to use the time I have left. I want to enjoy life."

I put on my shoes and walked out to the street in a shirt. The chilly April wind shivered through me, rain beat upon my face and water ran in trickles under my shirt. It was cold but it felt good. I did not have to worry about getting sicker and that made me feel free and careless. I hastened my steps and started to run. My hair bounced in the wind and, despite my situation, I was… happy! Suddenly everything around me seemed so lovely: the wet walls of houses, branches swinging in the wind, passengers taking shelter under their umbrellas, and the flying sculptures in the Carl Milles garden.

I set off towards the Kungstratgarden and by the time I got there it had stopped raining. Beams of sunlight pierced through from behind dissolving clouds, and tiny diamonds sparkled on the fresh leaves of trees and bushes. A blond girl with braided hair was walking a St Bernard dog, or vice versa. Whatever. I caressed them both. I was thinking of Linnéa and was infinitely grateful to the Heavens that I hadn't slept with her. At least she would escape.

❖

I was getting accustomed to the idea of my imminent death. I realized that one can get used to everything, even death. I learned how to live with it, and relished every minute I had left. I planned that when my fever dropped I would go back home, visit my parents, say goodbye to my sisters, Grandfather, Carina and Linnéa.

I gave away all my books, values, and clothes that were in a decent condition. I even gave my cello to a former classmate. Arne did not understand my philanthropy. "I will no longer need them on the other side, let those who stay enjoy it," I argued.

I called Linnéa's aunt to ask about her whereabouts and she told me she had gone to France but she had left a number in case anyone was looking for her. I called that number many times but no one picked it up. In secret I was happy; it would have been so hard to say goodbye to Linnéa.

❖

Arne's diarrhoea was gone, and I felt all right too. We regained the weight we had lost due to fright and our illnesses. One day Arne came home with news that our friends had gone to take a blood test.

"And the results?" I asked.

"They don't know, they have to wait until tomorrow. We should go too, what do you think?"

"I don't know. I won't risk my peace of mind"

But, of course, we also went along the next day to take the test. Before giving our blood, the assistant – one of Arne's close friends – had told us not to worry because the guy who infected Christa had showed up. They had only met a little while before and it seemed Christa did not sleep with anyone else afterwards.

Words cannot describe what I felt at that moment. Probably someone standing on the hangman's platform, the rope already around his neck, feels something similar when he hears he has been pardoned. We hugged and kissed the nurse in our joy, rushed down the stairs and raced through the streets in absolute delight. We had no idea where we were running. We were probably just looking for someone to tell the good news. But who would have understood what had just happened to us? We rushed past people, they looked at us puzzled.

Arne was three steps in front of me. I could hardly keep up with him. He was faster but I was given wings by the promise of a new life. I shouted after him as loud as I could: "Hey Arne, there is God after all!"

Arne stopped and looked at me severely.

"What now? Aren't you happy?" I asked panting.

After a long pause he answered, "You know what I had promised when I was in church? That if I survive I will serve God for the rest of my life."

"Well, my friend, you'd better exchange the women for a cassock," I patted him on the shoulders.

"And what promise did you make?"

"That I will search for true love."

"Lucky as always!" he said slapping me hard on the back. Then he continued with a serious expression, "You know Bald, as I was kneeling in front of the altar, I felt something I had never had before. As I joined my hands, and heard that gracious music, I felt my soul swelling, growing larger and larger, encompassing you guys, the church, the city, the Earth with all its creatures. I felt I had found God. Can you understand it? My only wish was to be able to pass this sensation to others. That was my prayer about, see what I mean?"

"I do Arne. I understand you completely."

We embraced each other, and it felt good like never before.

"For the autumn semester I am going to enrol for theology," Arne said quietly. "I think our roads go separate ways now. What are you going to do with your new life?"

"Like I said, I also made a promise. I am going to see the world and find true love. I am going to France to meet Linnéa, and God knows what comes next."

I was curious what kind of deal the others made with God. We met in a nearby café. They had just found out the results and were celebrating. To my surprise they were only drinking soft drinks – turns out three of them promised never to smoke or drink again if they survived. I wished them a happy new life and said goodbye. I did not want to stay in Stockholm a minute longer. Before leaving, I visited Christa's grave. I spoke as though she was there listening to me, her great spirit freed from her fragile body, floating between the trees and fresh foliage of the graveyard.

I thanked her for everything she had done for me. For the boundless warmth and tender love she had given me when I was in such great need of it. To this day I think of her and wonder. She was like a life-giving beam of light in that dark, corrupt nest of vipers. A green oasis amongst the desert of souls. What she could not give us alive was given to us through her death. How odd that someone needed to die for us to awaken.

8. La Gitanilla

Of all Grandmother's religious stories the parable of the prodigal son made the greatest impression on me, although at the time I understood little of its meaning. And Grandmother even less I think. For her the whole story was nothing more than a warning against ignoring parental advice, against the futile waste of life and against falling into sin, while the positive hero was obviously the good boy who stayed at home. For me the story seemed to convey a completely different message although I was yet unable to grasp it. Actually it wasn't even what I understood that gripped me, but rather that which remained a mystery and I merely sensed; this great and grave truth hidden under the disguise of words, whose complex message was to become clear to me gradually and only with years of experience. Or maybe it worked the other way: it was the story itself, embedded deep in my subconscious that, by secret desires and instinctive impulses, urged me towards those experiences bringing understanding.

To break out from the protection of home; to tear the invisible umbilical cord strengthened by familiarity and the desire for security; to go out into the world as a determined hero, jumping in the waves where the spray is the highest and you are sucked into the vortex with the greatest power; rebelling against things that seem pointless; becoming acquainted with the bitter-tart aftertaste of the sweetly tempting forbidden fruit; being disappointed after the intoxication of false freedom gained through force – the only route towards true freedom – all attracted my thirstily searching consciousness as inevitable stations of a life fully lived. To deny and then accept again, to lose and to find again, to part and to come together, to live out the pain of desperation and the joy of being forgiven, to encounter destruction and know the eternal... each and every one appears in this wonderful story. I once unconsciously shared a spiritual communion with its hero and my pull to the tale lived on in me until the magical creative forces of my hidden desires gave birth to the circumstances that allowed their fulfilment

❖

After I finished grammar school my parents wanted to send me to university, to study law. It was my banker grandfather's obsession, and he had managed to infect my mother too, and, since the disease spread quickly in the family, my father soon aligned himself with them. Grandfather had been through many legal proceedings during his adventurous life and must have been very clear about the undisputable social advantages of the profession. I, however, was interested in the arts. I wanted to dance. I had very little affinity for law, maybe only that I could become outraged at terrible injustices, and I hated lying. My parents knew that, perhaps that is why they found this career suitable for their only daughter. As for me, back then I hadn't the slightest idea that actually the profession has almost nothing to do with truth and justice.

My parents did not oppose my dance career, but they thought that a lawyer's certificate would bring a more secure future for me. The interminable family discussions finally ended with a compromise. I asked for a year off so I could learn flamenco, promising that afterwards they could enrol me wherever they wanted to. Grandfather even agreed to finance my Spanish trip on the condition I kept my word.

That is how I ended up in Seville.

Pilar and Rodrigo were overjoyed at my visit and immediately moved me into one of the two rooms in their small rented flat. We spent the first evening going over intense memories, reliving the adventures of the *Blood Wedding*. Time had smoothed all their roughness and sharp, painful edges. With the distance of the year passed, the events had gained an affectionate nostalgia that made us smile.

On my second day Rodrigo took me to Doña Alicia Benités' dance studio, the place where six years earlier he had become acquainted with flamenco … and Pilar. He told me tales about those times with a touch of melancholy. They no longer went dancing. Pilar was six months pregnant and Rodrigo had to work a lot to be able to provide the suitable conditions for the next generation. But he did dust off his guitar from time to time to play a heart-rending Soleares or an ecstatic Alegría.

I went to the studio four or five times a week, leaving me plenty of time to discover that city so rich in architectural heritage.

Flamenco was like a tailor-made dress for me, much more so than ballet. Of course, I needed some time to get used to my new costume. At the beginning I felt resentful: my airy movements acquired under the direction of Miss Giselle seemed so feeble and delicate. I tried in vain to copy my fellow Andalusian students' movements that radiated such raw energy. I only saw lifeless flapping reflected in the derisory mirror on the wall… Until I realized that it was not the movement, it was all about something else, a distinctive inner state, the "flamenco state". I started to study, discover and feel it. Difficult to put into words, as it was so complex: passion for life, strong dynamics, restrained and fiery erotica, obstinate tenacity, defiance and rebellion against fate. A kind of desperate cry of the marginalized and outcast gypsies as they drowned their century-old sorrows into dance, and mingled it with life joy to make it bearable.

Although she had not been born into a gypsy family, Doña Alicia had managed to identify with the spirit of flamenco perfectly. She was the living proof that disproves the myth that only people "brought by the crow" can really dance flamenco. I loved to watch her dance. When she lifted her arm so purposefully – it was like the waving of the wand – she transformed completely. She really had been possessed by the "spirit of flamenco" that the dancers spoke of. She packed enormous intensity into her dance as though every moment she was holding in check passions increased to the extreme and ready to explode. Her body was like a furnace with terrifying flame burning in it, that, were it let out, would set ablaze all surrounding it. Only a single tongue of fire flicked out from time to time, announcing its destructive power. There really was some kind of devastating force hidden in the dance that had to be kept in the bottle because, were it to be freed, it would first destroy the dancer and then the whole world... There was something of this in Doña Alicia's dance, when I had finally sensed it everything became easier.

Once Rodrigo also came to the studio, he was curious how I was progressing. That was the first time I danced with everyone standing around and watching me. When the music started I glanced at Doña Alicia. I thought about her dance, lit my furnace and summoned the spirit of flamenco. Amazing forces travelled through my body. All of a sudden I felt that I could stir a whirlwind capable of moving mountains with a single sweep of my arm.

The guitars went wild pouring out the ever faster rhythm of the zapateado. As I stirred more and more waves of energy, the ripples of the whirlpools swept everyone with them. My feet struck the floor like a machine gun while the circle accompanied me with contratempo clapping. Elemental energy rising from the depths of my body kept me moving – the sibling of the force of earthquakes and volcanic eruptions. It pervaded me, sweeping me along. A wonderful and terrifying state in which the conscience, pushing out the boundaries of physical existence, brings you to a mysterious world where there is neither matter nor form. Only bodiless desire and pure passion.

I was not the only one surprised by the performance. My virtuoso dance teacher too, along with everyone there. The silence that fell upon us after the vibration of the last chord was broken by the old guitarist with big moustache "Ay-ay! La chica tiene el duende, como una gitanilla!"

They clapped enthusiastically and after that always called me "La Gitanilla". I loved the name, I thought it suited me. I was proud of it too.

❖

One weekend Rodrigo suggested we went to a nearby gypsy village. He thought it would be useful for me to see how "the real flamencos" dance. We stayed with a well-to-do family in their surprisingly clean house that had a real gypsy flavour to the decor. An old friend of Rodrigo's, Diego, lived there with his wife Pepa and his mother – a tall, respectable looking woman of about fifty who everyone called La Faraona.

Rodrigo knew the villagers well. Years before he had come here regularly to learn to dance. As news of our arrival spread around, half the village gathered together with three guitars and a dozen castanets. We hadn't even finished dinner when the fiesta in front of the house was already in full swing. The fiesta for them was the glorious parade of the holy trinity of flamenco: cante, baile and guitarra. We gulped down our last mouthfuls and went out to the yard to join them.

A stunning experience. Rodrigo was right. Their dance differed a lot from what I had seen in the studio. Although Doña Alicia was a believer in " flamenco puro", by comparison her movements seemed somewhat false, too artistic. These gypsies danced with inimitable rawness and poignant abruptness... And they could all dance. From the barefoot wide-eyed kids up to the toothless, old people who held themselves proudly, everyone was dancing... and everyone was smoking.

They stood up in turn to dance. That was the tradition. And in the meantime the others played music, clapped and sang. I have no idea how they decided on the order but one certainly existed, and it was as if everyone sensed exactly when the time had come for them to take the centre of the circle. Rodrigo's turn came deep into the night. I knew I wouldn't escape either, although I had no desire at all to hold a demonstration of their own dance. Then all of a sudden I saw that the circle was empty and that all eyes were fixed on me. There was no way out. I stood in the centre of the circle and waited for that familiar and secret force to possess me. Sparkling eyes and glowing cigarettes enclosed the magical circle for the venue of my spirit-evoking dance. I gave myself over to that mysterious force and, as the tempo of my movements became more heated, the shimmering points around became hypnotically sparking dots of light. An increasingly intoxicating trance state took hold of me...

After one particular turn my eyes met the sparkling pair of another. A young man in a red silk shirt was standing next to me. His arms stiffened into the flamenco pose, his fiery look provoking me to a couple dance. Avoiding touching one another, we started to dance. His movements were distinctly erotic. And involuntarily I answered him with movements filled with a similar emotion. Every sweep of the arm was an imagined embrace and felt like real physical touch. His eyes burned through my clothes, unashamedly and pleasantly stroking me. I felt more and more naked. Not once did we touch each other but I still felt desire filling me. A familiar face flashed into my mind... Louis Moreno! He was the one able to ignite desire in my body from a distance. Few men have the ability, but the red-shirted gipsy guy who challenged me to this strange mating dance certainly possessed a mysterious magnetism. I was never able to resist it. Nor did I want to, I adore this state. So I gave myself over to it and to the game. Our movements tuned into the rhythm of imagined lovemaking. Had it been about physical contact, I would have protested wildly but this way I found the play somehow acceptable, although I felt distinctly that some part of my being was actually making love to him. Our bodies' magnetic fields met and touched, sparking the kind of enjoyment that even physical touch is rarely able to. We sensed each other perfectly with our hidden senses. We also knew when to slow down... and when to stop. Perfectly tense in motion-lessness we looked into each other's eyes. Only our panting broke the silence that had descended on us like an offering to the magical moment. Then the joyful uproar of enthusiastic applause, whistling and complementary shouts embraced us. I could sense that with my dance I had stolen into their hearts forever. Wordlessly my red-shirted partner inclined his head politely and, putting his hand on his heart, thanked me for the experience. Then he melted back into the crowd.

I thought about it for a long time afterwards, trying to figure out what had made this experience so special for me. Maybe it was because my ember-eyed playmate did not want to conquer me. I did not sense in his dance the showy contempt of the male desiring to charm the female. It was only the spontaneous naturalness of the play for its own sake.

On Sunday afternoon our warm-hearted hosts did not want to hear of us leaving. Rodrigo had an excuse: he had to go to work the next day. But I couldn't come up with any acceptable reason as to why I had to rush, so I allowed myself to be persuaded. I didn't have to force myself too much as I felt surprisingly at home in that environment. I was probably starting to feel the effect of the name given me in Seville... I felt I belonged in the community: Como una gitanilla de verdad. And for some reason they also felt I belonged between them.

I planned to stay an extra couple of days but as the next weekend came I still didn't have a great desire to leave. The people had started to interest me and now not only their dance, but also their habits, work, way of thinking and relationships with each other. With something of a sociologist's obsession I began studying their lives. During the day I went out to work with them in the fields, sat listening to the gypsy women gossiping on the banks of the drainage ditches. Although I couldn't understand much of what they said because of gaping holes in my Spanish, it was still an unforgettable experience. Particularly when arguments broke out, and that happened fairly often. My fascination lay not only in the exotic nature of their daily life, it was the radiation of their whole being that seemed so new, so intriguing to me. Some raw instinct instilled destructive enormity into their conflicts but when they were at peace they radiated a kind of primeval harmony, like an ancient forest or a harsh, rocky outcrop. The seemingly irreconcilable tension between their innate desire for freedom and the "civilizing" effects of the modern world provided a touchingly tragic shade to their lives. The memory of paradise lost lived on more strongly in them than in other people, but it was as though ancient curses had swept them even further from it than their white-skinned compatriots, and thus they had become even unhappier. Of the knowledge they had brought from their eastern homeland only distorted, strange beliefs and superstitions had been retained. They believed in fortune telling and the power of curses, and possessed an astonishingly extensive love magic.

I always had to laugh at these, but I restrained myself as I had no desire to offend. I allowed myself a little discussion about such matters only with my host, Diego. During one of these debates he suggested we go to a fortune teller. So we went together to look for Doña Esperanza and I experienced my first divination. Well, even though at that time I didn't believe a word she said and I searched for all sorts of scientific and psychological explanations for those things she outlined correctly, the conversation still left an impression on me. With the greatest precision I noted it into my diary:

7th September 1992.

Today I finally gave in to Diego's prodding and allowed myself to be dragged to the fortune teller. In this area legends about her ability abound. In secret I hoped she wouldn't say anything of note so I'd win the debate.

Doña Esperanza is no different from any of the other gypsy women. Her house is a simple peasant's house, no magic mirror, no crystal ball or magic scribbling on the wall of the room where she received us. Nor was it dimly lit by candlelight as one might think after seeing fortune tellers in films. There were just old-fashioned, light green kitchen units, a crudely carved table covered by a white linen cloth and four stools.

Diego explained that I'd be pleased if she would tell my future and he also disclosed that I didn't believe in the whole caboodle. Doña Esperanza measured me up intently, examining me from head to toe. I didn't even try to guess her age. It's extremely difficult with gypsies and whenever I've tried I've always been a good few years out. There was a sprinkling of grey in her thick black hair but her face was smooth. She could have been a worn-out thirties, or just as easily a well-conserved sixties.

"I only tell people their future if they believe in it," she said with a serious expression, not taking her eyes off me for one moment. "But an extraordinary life path is awaiting the young lady. So I will have a look what the cards say."

She sat down at the table and took a thick deck of cards out of the kitchen drawer. I had to say the Lord's Prayer three times and only then did she set to work. She shuffled the cards, fanned them out in front of me to choose, and then she started to lay them out one by one. She looked at them intently for a long time before saying: "Interesting, very interesting. Strength and power. That is what is written... Happy childhood... You had everything you wanted... Your parents raised you with love and spoiled you in their affection because they couldn't have any other children... And now they're still worrying about you... There's a man here... a powerful and rich man, quite old, with great plans for you but don't believe him as what he wants isn't right... I see a true and beautiful friendship... Money and wealth surround you... But be careful because it can sweep you into great danger... A death changes your life... I see many, many men around you and great dangers."

She went silent for a moment and I waited for her to say the stock "happy marriage" and the "lots of luck" but she didn't say anything of the kind so I asked:

"And what will my family life be like? Husband? Children?"

"There's a young man here who you will meet... an attractive and wealthy man who will love you very much and who will be jealous... There will be a great journey and an important decision. If you choose well, you will find what you're looking for and you'll be happy."

"And will I choose well? Will I be happy? What do the cards say?" I asked a little derisively.

"Every decision is right if it comes from the heart. La mente miente, escucha tu corazón." She didn't want to say any more, and I didn't force her as I saw that she always gave deflective answers to specific questions. I thanked her for the prediction and we left. She didn't accept any money which surprised me. And Rodrigo too.

Yes, it's true she'd described my family circumstances but the rest was just generalizations that can't be proved. It could all be forced onto many a specific event, if the person is naïve enough...

That is what I thought at the time. But the predictions fitted some occurrences in my later life perfectly, and retrospectively I understood exactly what Doña Esperanza was talking about. At that moment I certainly didn't imagine that some of the points of the prediction would refer to the very near future. If I'd paid attention, maybe...

One afternoon an expensive, cherry red car stopped in front of the house. An elegantly dressed woman stepped out of it. My hosts greeted her emotionally and with loud expressions of love. She introduced herself as Estrella. I soon found out that she was the daughter of Faraona who, without the knowledge of her husband, had created her with the help of an "attractive, foreign man" who was passing through. So Estrella was only half gypsy and only half-sister to Diego. She had married a rich man and lived in Seville. She hadn't been home for a year and had brought extravagant gifts for all the family. That wasn't such an easy task as a whole army besieged the house within the blink of an eye. I suspected that the news of present giving had swelled the number of relations. Estrella seemed accustomed to this phenomenon, as she was able to provide everyone with something from the cornucopia of her car which was packed to bursting. Even I had to accept a little silver bracelet, in spite of my protests. She wasn't a person you could refuse... We quickly became friends. She inspired wonder in me from the first moment. She was the kind of woman that makes all men turn their heads on the street, and many women too, I imagine.

Her thick, jet-black hair, height, hazel eyes, strength of character and self-confidence were obviously inherited from her mother but her pale skin, pretty facial features and radiating sensuality – that completed this masterpiece of nature – were probably thanks to her "attractive, foreign" father. In addition she seemed intelligent and, compared to her background, surprisingly cultured. She spoke French quite well, a great relief for me. We were mutually attracted, so she could hardly pull herself away from me to spend some time with her family. At night she slept in my room. Or more correctly I stayed in her room. We talked for ages before we went to sleep. Special emotional threads started to be woven between us, so obvious, I could almost see them shining in the dark. She invited me to live with her in Seville. She had a spacious flat with plenty of room for me too. The offer seemed tempting particularly as Pilar was about to give birth and the tiny nest would become very cramped for four of us.

I accepted her offer and decided that I would go back with her to the city.

❖

The next day, just as we were coming to the end of emotional goodbyes and were about to get into the car, we saw an old lady coming towards us. She was shouting violently and fiercely shaking her fist. The poisonous words were targeting Estrella. She bore the attack without saying a word, defiantly, her head held high. The enraged old woman was moving threateningly and it seemed she was going to attack with her waving nails until she was forced to stop at a safe distance by Estrella's icy look. The woman's eyes flamed with anger and she spat out a torrent of ugly abuse. I couldn't decipher the reason for her agitation but I understood the curses. These belong to the most basic vocabulary of every language, and my enthusiastic flamenco friends had seen to it that I learn them as fast as possible.

Estrella spoke to her for a while in a placating but determined tone as people talk to their dogs that are too enthusiastic about their duties. But the old woman's mouth did not pause for one second. I saw that Estrella losing her temper. She said something forcefully, at which the woman immediately modulated to shrieking. She must have replied something dreadful because Estrella's words suddenly stuck in her throat. She went pale and turned away muttering to me to get into the car. Then Faraona, who had observed the battle with wise calm till then, let rip in her deep smoker's voice. That proved more effective and a stunned silence followed… We didn't await further developments. Estrella threw herself into the car and slammed the door. She didn't even look back at her family who were waving. She looked ahead intently as she drove along the bumpy road. A shadow had fallen across her charming face.

Only when I saw that she started to recover her typical composure I dared to ask what had happened.

"I had an affair with her son, a year ago, when I came home," she said. "He was totally mad for me and wanted me to be his wife. It was pointless trying to explain to him that I couldn't because I already had my own life. He pleaded, cried and implored, and then threatened me. I felt really sorry for him – actually he's a nice guy – but there was nothing I could do. When he realized that he couldn't persuade me he asked me to let him kiss me, just once, as a farewell. I agreed. One kiss became kissing, kissing hugging, and, God knows how it happened, but the flood swept me away. I gave myself to him. I knew it wasn't good. I knew I shouldn't but still… Some irresistible power – as if it was the power of doom – carried me, whirled me towards the unavoidable ending. He kept his promise and never asked anything else from me, but from that moment on he became depressed. He hasn't eaten or slept. He doesn't want to work. He just hangs about like the living dead. His mother accuses me of being a witch. She says I ruined her son with magic, and that I stole his soul."

"And what did he say at the end that made you so sombre?"

"She cursed me. She said 'may death take you just when you most want to live'."

"You don't seriously believe in that nonsense, do you?"

"I don't want to believe in it," sadness and tension lurked in her voice. "But words burning with the force of hate have great power…"

"I think it's all rubbish. You shouldn't take it seriously," I tried to cheer her up. Then I asked what she thought of fortune telling and of Doña Esperanza.

"I've never been to her," she answered.

"You don't believe in fortune telling?"

"I believe Doña Esperanza has the gift. And that's why I've never been to her. I don't want to know my future."

She still could have gone without worrying, I thought. I still wouldn't know anything about my future, if even I believed the things Doña Esperanza had said: "friendship, death, danger, great journey, choice". With hindsight I was sure I'd find something that would explain it. But now? Yes, and the men, the "lots of men". That wouldn't be bad. I like to have a choice…

"I have to tell you something," Estrella interrupted my reverie slowly drifting off into erotic fantasy. "I… earn my money with men."

"You mean you sleep with them for money?" I spluttered, without trying to cover my surprise.

"Yes, I'm a prostitute."

"And the rich man you married?"

"A lie. The disguise I put on when I go to visit my family." She let me chew that particular bite a while before continuing, "If it disturbs you, then you don't have to come with me. You can change your mind."

"No… no, it doesn't bother me… I'm just a little surprised."

"I know I should have told you before but… somehow I couldn't."

I should have been disgusted, as befits a respectable and well-brought-up girl like myself, and I should have refused her offer, disguising my condemnation in some acceptable precept. But that's not the way it happened. Maybe, if I had met the prostitute Estrella first, then my deeply entrenched preconceptions would have made me keep a distance. But Estrella – the person, the amazing woman who had so easily won my tight-fisted wonder – was also able to conjure this "little" flaw into acceptability.

"Actually I live in the apartment alone," she continued. "I never take my clients home. So my work won't affect you."

She said "my work" with such naturalness, like a kindergarten teacher speaking about the joy of working with children. I made her tell me about "her work" for the rest of the journey. She spoke with the enthusiasm of those people who have found their life's meaning. She said she worked alone, that she had her own hunting ground and only hunted the biggest sharks. Generally she had stable clients who spent enormous sums on her and, since there was much competition for her, she could always afford to choose whomever she pleased. She painted such a bright picture of the whole prostitute profession that I almost envied her.

❖

And this is how I moved from the Sanches couple's little family nest to

Aimen Klimmeron

Estrella's stunning luxury apartment decorated in a way which betrayed her family background... and into a totally new world. At the beginning we rarely met. She worked at night and slept during the day. I still attended Doña Alicia's dance studio regularly and, in my free time, continued to discover the city with its seemingly unending chest of sightseeing treasures.

From time to time she took me along with her to gatherings, evening and garden parties her clients invited her to. And so I had the opportunity to become acquainted with the leading figures of the city, or more accurately, the "terrifying sharks", as Estrella called them. She really looked after me, like a lioness her cub, and before she left with a client she always took me home first. She said she had started to become so attached to me that she couldn't go on if something happened to me.

"There are ruthless laws in this world outside the law," she warned more than once. "And the weak who don't understand these laws are certainly condemned to destruction. They have driven out conscience, humanity and forgiveness from this world. The only moral is power, the tool of which is money. You can buy pretty much anything with money: the body, the soul and even death. There's only one thing you cannot buy: love. That is stronger than everything. More powerful than life, more powerful than death. Even than money."

This is how Estrella taught me, sometimes adding with a sigh:

"I can never be in love. Prostitutes are not allowed to fall in love – or that is the end of our business, and so the end of our life." She strongly warned me against sleeping with anyone for money. "It's a dangerous thing, it's like a drug. If you taste it once, it's impossible to free yourself. Like a darkly swirling whirlpool that slowly but surely drags you into the deep... It's too late for me. I'm infected to my very last cell. I couldn't live a proper family life. But you... please take care of yourself."

She received huge amounts of money and spent just as much. She loved throwing money around. And on a free afternoon we would go to the exclusive boutiques on Calle de las Sierpes or to the Corte Inglés department store. She bought everything she desired – often totally pointless things. She also provided me with loads of clothes, jewels and all sorts of little trinkets that she thought would make me happy. Because she had another weakness: she loved to make people happy, she loved to give. Within a short time I had collected such an extensive wardrobe that even a spoilt princess would have been jealous.

You can get used to the high life incredibly quickly – at least it was true for me. We had never been poor at home. I had always been given whatever I needed, but this mindless and totally useless expenditure of money created a peculiar feeling: the dangerously seductive state of almightiness.

One night when Estrella happened to have a night off – she sometimes did allow herself the luxury – we had dinner in a small, intimate and extremely exclusive restaurant, somewhere in one of the tucked-away nooks of the old city where she hoped not to bump into any of her clients. The French wine she ordered in my honour stirred deep in her soul, and she let more come to the surface than usual. It was the first time I had heard her complain. She complained about the men who "are harsh, insensitive and selfish, always thinking of their own pleasures", saying "if they've paid that extortionate amount, then why don't they do it in a way that would give the woman some pleasure, because then it would also be a thousand times better for them too."

The residue of many unpleasant experiences must have collected in her to have such a generalized and disparaging opinion of the male gender. Unfortunately I didn't have any great wealth of praiseworthy sexual experience either that would have allowed me to disagree or at least to provide her with some hope-inspiring comfort. My first intruder, Louis Moreno, was a borderline case – it needed a drop of good intention to place him outside the category Estrella described. But, even with the greatest of good intention, I wouldn't have been able to list among real men the next two or three of my grammar school classmates who had attempted.

Here in Seville I had had some experience. I had given myself to a son of this Torreador-blooded people out of daring curiosity about his valour. He was from Doña Alicia's studio and had waved his red flag of male virtue with the definite intent of provocation from the very first moment. And then, when battle was about to begin, he had flashed his sword with the ruthlessness befitting a real toreador, but unfortunately bled to death before time and was forced to leave the arena in shame. The second attempt didn't prove much more successful either and, when I politely mentioned it, on the grounds of my rights as a woman regarding orgasm, he accused me of the typical nymphomaniac tendencies of the females of my nation. And so I also had something to complain about. On top of that, I too had been glugging back the familiar-scented Bordeaux, to dampen my homesickness. In a state of heightened emotion we experienced the joy of finding one another in this feminist experience. We held each other's hands and shared that 'yes, thanks very much but we're just fine without men' feeling.

This was the first scene of that new and strange play that I was acting out in the costume of La Gitanilla on the stage of Seville.

We took ourselves home by taxi. My relaxed limbs and pleasant tiredness drove me to bed. After Estrella had had a shower she knocked on my bedroom door and asked if she could sleep with me. She said she needed my nearness. I made space for her under the duvet, and she lay down next to me, hugged me and quickly fell asleep. But I simply couldn't cross over into dreamland. The closeness of her naked body kept me whirring. Then she started to stroke me. The soft warmth of her breasts pressed into my back and the touch of her fingers gently stroking my belly, breasts, neck and lips initiated pleasant waves of excitement. I was totally confused. I would never have imagined that a woman's body could bring such stimulation. I thought only men could do that. Maybe she's awakening a latent lesbian tendency in me? I don't want to be a lesbian! I quickly chased away the thought. I didn't want anything to ruin this increasingly wonderful sensation that Estrella's experienced hands were bringing to life in my body. She stroked me in a different way than a man. Her touch was much softer, warmer, more subtle and refined. I had to recognize this was not the innocent touch of a friend who wanted company but obvious stimulation to stir the senses and awaken desire. Suddenly I felt like caressing her. I went with it but some subconscious inhibition excluded all eroticism. I moved my hand pretty much mechanically up and down her hot thighs, waist and back. Estrella had no inhibitions. With her searing breath, burning wet lips she travelled over the whole of my body, stroking me in places that gave birth to the greatest pleasure. She knew my sensitive spots better than I. With strokes of an unknown taste she guided my body that was shuddering with an almost painful, building excitement towards wondrous release. We fell asleep, our closely fitting bodies snuggling tightly to one another.

The next day as the sober morning light stole into my room we looked a little uncomfortably at our telltale nakedness. We tried to find escape into the cover of polite courtesy of everyday activities just so we didn't have to talk about what had happened in the intoxication of the night.

"Shall I make a coffee?"

"Yes, please."

"I'll make breakfast, ok?"

"You can have a shower in the meanwhile."

I managed to suppress my pricking conscience for a while with the explanation that the whole event could be attributed to the relaxing effect of the Bordeaux, and I tried to push the story into the fog of oblivion. But the experience had been far too intense and pleasant to be able to stop thinking about a repetition, and I kept catching myself waiting to hear that ecstasy-promising knock again. It happened three days later, this time on a bright afternoon. I arrived home from the studio and had just showered off me all the dampness that had poured out during dance. I was already feeding my skin with body lotion when Estrella, who had slept off her night's adventures, came into my room. Feint traces of sleep remained on her eyelashes but her body had a freshly washed fragrance. She stood next to me.

"Please, let me…" taking the box of cream from my hand. I shivered even before she touched me…

I was amazed to experience that I had become much braver and freer. I gave myself over to exploring Estrella's body with curious excitement. The slight tweak of remorse that arose was just enough to make the game more exciting. I think that giving pleasure provided more joy than receiving. Her body quivered under my strokes like the strings of a harp touched by a skilled hand. A true Venusian body, each and every cell crafted by the Creator for passion and lust. Stroking and touching was an indescribable delight as, with contact, that enormous and secret something awoke which made her body and soul open and radiate that sublime and blessed feeling of happiness that nothing else in this world can bring forth.

I began to understand those men who paid insane amounts for even a fraction of this feeling. I was certain that she never opened for them this much. I was in a privileged position because she loved me, and I loved her too.

After we had discovered one another we seized every opportunity to offer pleasure to each other. Yes, the joy of giving, I think that is what made it so exquisite, to give pleasure, with gentle and sensitive attention. For Estrella these secret games of female tenderness served to balance her hard life, while for me it was a new and strange feeling, one that increased the number of incomprehensible factors in my life.

This was the second act.

❖

In April, that which Estrella had so protected herself against happened. She fell in love. Miguel was a lively man, five years younger than her. The intoxicating freedom of the "Feria de abril" pushed them into each other's arms. The "spring feria" is a popular festival in Seville, the little sister of the Rio de Janeiro carnival. The whole city moves out onto the streets for days and sings, dances and has riotous fun, dressed in medieval costume. For some reason the fine-boned young man with a masculine gaze dressed as Christopher Columbus caught Estrella's eye. He was standing on a raised platform observing from a long telescope the waves of the crowd as it heaved here and there. In a silly and playful mood, Estrella moved into view of the telescope and, after successfully attracting the young man's attention, she showed him something – with a naturalness befitting her profession – that would have made even the original Columbus fall off the bridge. Then she boldly went over to him and offered herself as "a token of her devotion to the glorious captain". Miguel accepted this fateful gift and fell fatally in love with her after their first time together. Estrella also started to hold this forbidden feeling though she tried in vain to hide it from me... indeed from herself too. They fooled around together all day, took rides on every merry-go-round, aimed at coconuts, and released balloons. They displayed the unmistakable symptoms of falling in love. In their happy abandon they left me totally alone and, when we bumped into each other, she stood next to me for just long enough to whisper in my ear, "Don't be angry with me, I so needed a little madness". With that, the crowd and the feelings would sweep them away once again.

Miguel was happier than if he had discovered America together with all the treasures of the Aztecs. And Estrella, well, I'd never seen her like this.

The celebrations came to an end but Estrella had no desire to return to work. She just kept saying, "I'll just have a little time off. I deserve it, don't I?"

They made love day and night, stopping to eat and drink for no longer than was absolutely necessary… And the holiday did not want to end. Her clients inquired after her but she always found an excuse. Sometimes she was ill, sometimes she'd gone away.

"I'm just incapable of meeting with them," she confessed. "I feel that if one of them touched me, I'd be sick."

Her enraged clients threatened her with all sorts. One even said that if she wouldn't sleep with him, he would have her killed. But Estrella did not waver. She kept saying, "I'm thinking of selling the house. We can move somewhere else. I've got enough money for us to live for the rest of our lives – the three of us together. We can go to some village… we'll buy a gorgeous house with a garden…"

Some inexplicable sadness took root in me as she wove these plans. I knew she had enough money to do it at any time, but somehow it still all seemed so unlikely, so dreamlike.

One time she didn't come home for two days. On the second day Miguel desperately started to look for her. I was surprised as I was sure that they had been together somewhere. But when he said he had had to travel alone to Madrid for two days, I had a bad feeling.

We hoped she had decided to start working again while Miguel was away and that she was having fun with one of her wealthy clients. But she didn't come home on the third day… or the fourth either… My premonition solidified into serious worry and torturous tension. On the fifth day Miguel notified the police of her disappearance. And two days later they found her body in the river. Her jealous client had kept his promise…

This is how act three ended. With this brutal, violent and absurd conclusion. One in which the main character is not transfigured into a tragic heroine as she steps through death's door, where death does not become the tool of cleansing and redeeming catharsis. It is nothing more than senseless and irreversible destruction.

The police dragged me off to identify the corpse. I went like a sleepwalker. I was totally unable to comprehend what was happening. My consciousness became some strange, out-of-body state. My mind simply denied the thought of death.

I still couldn't believe it when I saw the swollen and purple body. I just stood and stared with expressionless eyes at her terribly twisted face, the blackened blotches and the scratches on her neck. They asked me if I recognized her – but my words were frozen inside me. All I wanted was to scream so that I could wake up from this nightmare and take refuge in Estrella's warmly embracing arms and listen to her calm and regular breathing. Then fall into a different dream.

Stomach cramps made me double up, and I started to vomit. They covered up my mess and supported me out of the mortuary. It was as though my fountain of tears had dried up. I just couldn't cry... or think. My body continued to do its duties mechanically but it was as though my consciousness was removed from it all. Everything – the police interrogations, the investigation, the funeral, the meetings with Estrella's devastated family and the undead Miguel, the court proceedings that followed – all was stored in my memory as foggy threads of dreams...

Then suddenly everything just came to an end. I had nothing left to do that would have allowed me to escape from my thoughts. I was left alone in the empty tomb of a flat that had become so gloomy – alone with the horrific sight of Estrella's decomposing remains in front of me and the memory of her pleasure-giving body, her look radiating the joy of love, her lips opening in laughter. I could find no connection between the two.

Where had Estrella gone? What they found was just a dead body, a lifeless object... They hadn't found Estrella! That Estrella, who had loved and hugged me only a week earlier, who had driven men crazy and given so much pleasure. That Estrella had disappeared.

The great questions of existence engulfed me all at once with suffocating power. What is that intangible something we call life? What happens after death? Where were we before we were born? Is there any meaning to this whole shit? Is there a God... or is it only abandoned, merciless people that exist? Why did God let her die now when finally she loved? Now when she could have started a new life, now that she was truly happy? Why? Why?

In the shadow of those incomprehensible mysteries that towered above me I felt small, insignificant and abandoned... and then I was swamped by my tears. I was able to cry at last... but I couldn't stop. And even if I managed for a while, my sobbing broke out again and again with unbearable strength. For days on end. I didn't know who I was crying for – Estrella? Or actually me, left alone without her? The unfortunate Miguel? The broken love? I didn't know... All I knew was that the weeping didn't make me feel any better. The tears weren't the beneficial and cleansing kind. They were the type that serves to increase the bitterness, to swell the anger and hate. A dark desire for revenge was starting to ripen in me, and the plan of how to achieve my revenge was also born.

I prepared for this new act with the cold-bloodedness of an assassin. I wanted to be not only the main character but also the single omnipotent director of the play. I chose my costume from Estrella's working clothes. It was an outfit I found the most appropriate, and I dressed myself in it with a meticulous sense of ritual. I made myself up in the most provocative colours, poured two glasses of gin and went out onto the street.

I went with the first man who spoke to me. I don't remember what he looked like, I only remember that we were together the whole night. I gave my body for him to possess as often as he wanted, and when he had tired I initiated once again, only stopping when he begged for mercy. I didn't accept any money from him. The money didn't interest me. My revenge was about something else. I wanted to squeeze as much lust as possible from this body condemned to death from the moment of its birth. This is how I wanted to get even with death and to confront the One who had created the world to be so unjust. I wanted to take my vengeance out on God. On the God I knew from Grandmother's sickening and vacantly praising descriptions. On He who only asks from us while denying us everything that is beautiful and good. He who constantly demands obedience and devotion from us.

That which Grandmother had so unceasingly warned me against gave me great satisfaction.

I began to taste all that she had called sin with cold determination. My depressive apathy gradually transformed into lascivious pleasure – a type of dark delight. It was similar to what I had experienced after Grandmother's religion lessons, as I was tasting the forbidden fruit in the room above hers. And yet, back then it was different somehow. Beautiful and exciting, it had put no extra burden on my conscience than any other childish prank, just like grinding pepper under an adult's nose. But now my desire for revenge had reached almost cosmic proportions. I wanted to punish the unjust despot of the universe by going against his will.

Some guilty feelings rumbled inside me after my first experience. I asked myself what my parents would say if they saw me in this situation. But I had no inclination to answer the question. I tried to annihilate all such killjoy thoughts, even the very first shoots. And the next evening I dressed up in my character once again, downed my two glasses of gin and went out onto the street… And it went on like that for weeks. I never dared count how many men pleasured themselves on me in that crazy period. And now I probably wouldn't be able to – I don't actually remember most of them. They included rich businessmen, rugged sailors, poor working men, penniless students... Since financial considerations did not restrict me, I offered myself to whomever my whim chose, and this filled me with a peculiar feeling of superiority. The fact that these sex parties rarely gave me any bodily fulfilment, and absolutely none for the spirit, did not disturb me. They provided a different kind of satisfaction; I felt I was defying death. However, after a few weeks the engine of my desire for revenge started to run out of fuel. I began to make my peace with the world, and the thought that it might be time to stop occurred increasingly often. But I still carried on. Only my motivation changed. I had discovered that men were crazy about me and that, if I so wanted, I could be totally irresistible. The yearning for adventure also drove me on. The thrill of getting to know someone – and perhaps the subconscious desire too, that I may actually find the mythical Mr Right. But the love of my life just did not want to surface. I started out on my path to conquer, time and again. The suspicion that the right one was not actually hiding among the men of Hispania rose increasingly often. Should I be searching for him in my own country?

Slowly the year that I had requested from my family drew to an end. On the rare occasions I rang my parents they asked ever more anxiously when I wanted to go home. Every time I reassured them with 'soon' or 'just a little more to learn' (though I hadn't been dancing for months) and 'I'm having an amazing time here'. As soon as I put down the phone I felt terrible. I hated lying. But the thought of going home seemed not a jot more attractive. I had grown into my costume of Gitanilla and wouldn't take it off. I decided several times to give it all up and go back to Marseille, but somehow I still found myself on the streets in the evening. The passion for hunting burned bright in me. It chased me into more and more adventures until one particular incident speeded up the course of events.

One night I was walking along the banks of the Guadalquivir curious about who fate would bring me that night. A black Mercedes braked sharply next to me, and a bearded man motioned that I should go closer. His face didn't inspire much trust so I carried on walking. The car started moving – and I thought that it would drive off, but instead it stopped next to me again. The doors were flung open, and three blokes leapt out. They grabbed me, covered my mouth and stuffed me into the back of the car. There was nothing I could do. I tried to tear myself out of their hands but they were far too strong. I continued struggling in the car, but the bearded man held a knife to my throat so I thought it prudent to remain silent.

When I had recovered my senses I decided to change tactics. I started to play the obedient little girl and asked where we were going.

"We're taking you to have fun," said one and chortled. "You'll have an experience that many women would envy." All three laughed raucously. "Of course, only if you do what you're told, because if not..." and pressed the knife tighter to my throat...

I reassured them that I loved having fun and that they really did not need to coerce me with a knife. I wanted to use the tactic of total cooperation to worm my way into their trust, and then to attempt escape at a suitable moment. The car came to a halt in a dark courtyard. I stole a glance around, but escape was out of the question. We circled up a dimly lit spiral staircase to the first floor and arrived at a long corridor with doors on both sides. They shoved me into one telling me to wait patiently, and then locked me in. I had a quick look around. It was an airless room with not one window. It might have been a sort of bedroom because there was a large double bed, a bedside cabinet with two glasses on it and a glass wall cupboard that served as a bar.

A little while later the key turned in the lock. A one-legged man with a monkey face limped in, supporting himself on a crutch. He measured me up, and then his mouth stretched into a wide grin. Unfortunately he liked what he saw. He glanced at me lecherously and started to compliment various parts of my body. He didn't express himself particularly poetically, but he was certainly making an effort to chat me up. The problem really started when he approached me – I instinctively recoiled, but was stopped by the wall. He comforted and encouraged me, just like you would a child before an injection... he said that if I was a good girl, then he'd pay me lots of money for the night. I told him that unusually, I didn't feel on form and that if he wanted maybe we could put off this promising encounter until another time... but he thought now was the right time. He unbuttoned his trousers and even showed me what he wanted to pleasure me with. He really did have a big one. I hadn't even seen one that large on a photo. Actually to be honest I didn't believe it was possible that it could be that size. When he realized he couldn't convince me even with this hard argument, he made to paw me. My leg went to kick as a reflex, and I caught him right in the shin. He shouted out like a wounded animal, his crutch slipped out of his hand, and he fell to the ground with a dull thud.

His bodyguards must have been waiting outside the door because they rushed in immediately. One grabbed me and the other caught my face with his fist. Only after they had repaid me did they pick up the one-legged man and his crutch from the floor. They carried him out of the room and locked me in again. I knew I had signed my death warrant. My whole face was throbbing from the blow. My mind weighed up the situation with cool calm. What could they do with me? Either rape me or kill me. Both in the worst-case scenario. Well, I had needed adventure, and I had got it! I poured over how I could escape, but there didn't seem any hope. On edge I awaited the next instalment. Nothing happened.

I collapsed onto the bed and waited. This nervous waiting became more and more unbearable, grinding down my remaining strength. I felt exhausted and only wished for one thing: not to think about anything. I don't know when sleep engulfed me or how much I slept. I only remember my dream. I was walking in the forest with Dad. We came to a clearing where colourful butterflies were fluttering about. I started to chase them. They were strange butterflies – they resembled birds. They had the wings of butterflies but the heads and beaks of birds. I couldn't even catch one and I stumbled further and further into the thicket. All of a sudden I realized that I had ended up in a terrifyingly dark forest. I tried to get back to the clearing but I couldn't find the way. Then a one-legged man stepped out from a twisted tree trunk. He stretched his crutch towards me, but the crutch was also his hand, a large and hairy monkey's hand that grabbed at my breasts. I turned around in horror and started to run, but he popped up in front of me again and again. Wherever I ran, he appeared before me. I shouted for Dad desperately and collapsed onto the ground. Then a gentle hand touched me on my shoulder. I looked up slowly. Dad was standing there, smiling. He lifted me up and hugged me tightly, and I burst into tears...

Rough hands ripped me out of my father's arms and from my dream. The sight of my kidnappers' grinning faces woke me back into my awful reality. One of them told me to pull myself together and go with them. I followed them in a kind of stupefied surrender, like the condemned to the place of execution. Like one who has had enough time in prison to make friends with the thought of death. A dull fog hung over my mind, and my face was swollen from the beatings. Through the single window on the corridor I caught a glimpse of the blue sky rising above the red roofs. It seemed so stunning, so distant, so inaccessible.

The spiral staircase dragged us down into the underground where they shoved me into a fitness room. The iron structures with their weights, pulleys, chains and benches reminded me of a medieval torture chamber. Indifferently I allowed them to strap me to the wall bars, my arms and legs forced apart. The one-legged man sat undressed to the waist on a bench opposite me. He was torturing his grotesquely swollen arm muscles with two large weights. Streams of sweat were making their way through the thick, dark fur on his chest. A flash of memory from my dream made him even more repulsive. At his command one of my torturers took out a knife, using it to slice off my clothes, grinning lewdly. As I stood there, tied up and naked, Estrella's words about "this merciless world outside the law that had driven out conscience, humanity and forgiveness" popped into my mind. Then I saw her dead body – and the reality of her words sunk in. The fear of death shot through me like an electric shock. My body began to writhe and twist but the ropes were strong. Desperate and helpless, I burst into tears. The picture of Jesus tied to the cross appeared before me, like the one I'd seen in the Zeffirelli film. His face filled with suffering, he still managed to look on at his torturers with a pure and forgiving look. In the reflection of his eyes I felt so inferior and so damn selfish. And… guilty!

At that point the proud Laurianne, the arrogant Laurianne, the broken, abandoned and miserable Laurianne, began to plead and beg for forgiveness from the One upon whom she had wanted to take revenge not long before. And that embittered Laurianne promised everything just to be free of her torturers. My tears gushed forth relentlessly. These were the tears of regret, the tears of true repentance, and it was as if I heard the voice of Zefirelli's Jesus saying: "You are forgiven, but sin no more".

My torturers started to touch me. They snatched at my breasts, poked between my legs… But I felt nothing. The connection between my nerve endings and my brain seemed to have been broken. As if I was watching my body from an out-of-body consciousness. The one-legged man, who had been masturbating for a good while, reached for his crutch, struggled up from the bench and made towards me. Oh God, no, not that! Disgust and terror thrust into me like a sharp dagger. My body started to shake madly… And that is when I saw the door open and a stout, bald figure enter the room, rush over to the one-legged man and whisper something in his ear to which he angrily stuffed his pride and joy back into his trousers cursing blindly. He limped out.

For a second I was relieved. The other three did not stop their fumbling but that was nothing compared to the danger that the approach of the hairy-chested monster would have meant.

The one-legged man returned accompanied by a tall, dark man in a suit. They stopped at the door. I couldn't hear what they were talking about, I could only see they were pointing at me. Then my captor motioned for them to release me and ordered me to get dressed and go with the suited man. There was no question of me dressing but I grabbed my shreds of clothes and wordlessly followed the recently-arrived man, trying to work out what would happen next. It couldn't be worse than here – I thought – and anyway, my new owner was much more trustworthy, actually he was positively attractive…

He didn't speak to me until we were sitting in the car.

"How did you end up in this monster's cave?" his face was serious, his voice somber but pleasant.

"They kidnapped me… off the street…"

I certainly didn't want to explain what I had been doing on the street, so I passed the ball back to him.

"And what were you doing there?" I asked because curiosity was biting me as to the run-up to the turn of events that could easily have been in a cheap Hollywood movie.

"Strange," he said thoughtfully. "I had just started to wonder about it too. I could say that it was pure coincidence, but I haven't believed that things happen "accidentally" for a long time now. So let's say that Fate led me."

"Just in time, too…"

"Yes, that's why it seems so strange for me too. A bit like a miracle. Tell me, do you believe in miracles?"

"I think that I do now, yes…" But he still hadn't revealed how he had come to be there.

"I was driving to work. I had an important meeting to go to, but I was already a little late. The traffic had been redirected because of road works and I ended up in this small side street. And then all of a sudden I found myself in front of a familiar house and I remembered that a client of mine lived here who owed me a fair amount of money. I had been there once but couldn't remember the address. But I did recognize the house. After a brief internal struggle I conquered the me that wanted to hurry onwards and decided that if fate had brought me here anyway, then I should ask for my money back. My one-legged debtor was rather surprised to see me, as he'd hoped I wouldn't find him. He lamented his current lack of money at the moment saying I should be a little patient because he would definitely pay it back. I threatened him. I told him I knew about his dirty dealings – and that I could expose him at any time. He got frightened and started to plead to give him a week at least and in return he offered a small present, a delight, a "real sex bomb" with whom I could have my way even right then and there. I told him no way and that I was in a rush. But somehow I did become interested in this "real sex bomb" so I decided that, as how I was already there, I'd at least have a look. When I saw you there, naked and tied up, your face bruised, I was overcome by a peculiar feeling. So I suggested to the monster that I let him off his debts if he gave you to me. Obviously he agreed without thinking."

"So that means I'm now yours."

"Well, we could say that." I saw him smile for the first time and his perfect teeth made him even more attractive. "But you can rest assured that I won't be exercising my right of ownership. I didn't buy you for myself… I just wanted to free you from his clutches. He's a dangerous, heartless man. You might not have lived to see next week."

I thanked him for his noble gesture and ensured him that I would repay my ransom as soon as I could, but he asked me to leave him the joy of the total act. Then he added, "As your saviour I would like to ask something of you. I would like to get to know you. Don't feel you have to but, if you'd like, come to mine. They will look after you for a while, just until you recover a little."

I must have been a piteous sight, I'm sure. It's true that I'd promised to give up this way of life and go home, but I couldn't have set off with a face like this anyway. But that wasn't the main reason I accepted his invitation. I felt something unusual in this man. He was different from anyone else I'd met during my year away, and this mysterious difference had piqued my interest.

❖

Enrique's house was actually a small palace. The bare brick walls of the Mudéjar-style house that faced the street betrayed nothing of the interior but as I entered a picture from an Arabian fairy tale opened up before me: carved columns, colourful tiles, geometric designs, voluptuous curves, walls decorated with Arabesque motifs, a horseshoe-shaped interior courtyard with niches, a crystal-clear swimming pool bordered by dwarf apple trees in the centre of the patio...

I pondered that if such a charming fairytale world was hidden behind other of the plain buildings, then I really had seen nothing of Seville. I had admired many splendid buildings during my time here but this kind of riches in a private house totally amazed me. I expected bare-bellied, wide-hipped harem women to come dancing out at any second. And I didn't have to wait for long! Enrique introduced me to them. There were three of them. True, their belly buttons were not on show – they were wearing normal European clothes. But I was still astounded. Particularly when I saw each of them greet him with a long, passionate kiss that would be perfectly natural as foreplay. I did not yet understand the relationship of these four, and Enrique made no attempt to illuminate me. He entrusted me to the women and left claiming urgent business.

Concha, Carmela and Cía behaved with surprising kindness. They prepared fragrant bath water, dressed me and gave me lunch. Concha was the most communicative, and I quickly made friends with her. She enlightened me about their way of life. I found out that all three were Enrique's lovers and that Enrique didn't live with them, only coming when he wanted to be with them. I just couldn't get my head around it.

"And you're not jealous of each other?" I asked with more than a touch of surprise in my voice.

"We were at the start. At that time we weren't living together, and our jealous outbursts caused Enrique and each other – and of course ourselves too – quite a lot of headaches. But with his extraordinary ability he was able to make peace. To be honest we could never really be angry with him. Slowly we made peace with each other too and, although it may seem strange, we grew to love each other. Then Enrique had this mad idea that we should move in together into this gorgeous little nest that he had just inherited from his grandfather."

"And you don't feel the need for one man who is just yours?" I continued the questioning.

"I could at any time. I'm free, and Enrique is not jealous. But I haven't yet found anyone who would be worth exchanging him for. He has raised the standard too high. He has a divine talent for love. He treats women with incredible sensitivity and... he can love with such total devotion. Unfortunately there are not so many of these men running around not the streets of Seville. I feel privileged to know him, that I can love him and that he loves me... and that through him I know these other two wonderful beings. Because this living together does have its own delights," she completed her startling statement with a cheeky wink.

All the time she was talking about Enrique her eyes were sparkling with a devotion that seemed more than love. During another of our conversations she also disclosed that there were nights when Enrique made love to all three of them individually, for two or three hours. Well, well. That's what I call performance!

"And you know what I've realized?" she continued in a confidential tone. "Love is not like a fruit which, if you give some away, then less remains for the other. Intensity is what matters in love. I never felt that he loves me less because he loves someone else. He has a little less time for me, but then two hours with him is worth more than a long and boring married life with someone else."

Enrique came again two days later. He invited me into his room to talk. I had awaited this meeting excitedly. This neo-romantic knight had so intrigued me. A man about whose legendary male prowess his women tell. A man who was able to just appear unexpectedly when there was the greatest need for him, save the abducted princess from the sword of the monster, and then disappear again. The inner world of this remarkable man, who could be seen as an extreme rarity in this weakened civilized modern male society, caught my interest.

"Enrique, tell me what you feel for the three C's."

"I love them very much," he said in the most natural voice in the world.

"All three?"

"Yes... why? What's so strange about that?"

"I don't know. It's just slightly unusual. And you can really love all three of them in the same way?"

"I don't love them in the same way because they're not the same. They awaken various shades of love in me. Concha, for example, is cheerful, playful, flirtatious, openhearted and warm. Her joyful intimacy inspires me to tender abandonment, makes me forget my worries and conjures life into a merry celebration. Carmelita is hot blooded, free spirited and unbridled, like a fiery colt. Wild forces course through my veins in her passionate embrace. While Cía is a delicate soul, sensitive, deep and secretive like the moonlight shining on a lake at night. The poet in me comes to life in her arms, and the gates to life's great mysteries open in front of me to which lead only two paths, two paths that are intertwined: art and love.

"And you don't think it's a sin to love more than one woman at the same time?" I threw him another of my prepared questions.

But as soon as I'd said it I realized just how stupid and false it sounded in the wake of his enlightening and deeply honest answer.

"I don't always love more than one at the same time," he laughed, purposefully misinterpreting my question. "I often love them separately too."

"I wasn't thinking of that…"

"I know what you were thinking. Loving, at the same time, separately, one after the other, or in any form is never a sin. But having sex with some-one who you are not in love with… Yes, that is a sin. To sleep with someone for money, for other advantages, selfish reasons, marital obligation or simply to satisfy your sexual urges, that is sin. Because then you are betraying your own soul. If the inspiring and uplifting power of love is not present, then your act is debasing and humiliating, not only for you but also for your sex partner – even if bodily pleasure explodes for a few moments. Because that is betrayal, against your true self, and thus against your divine being – and this can rightly be called sin."

Enrique's words affected me deeply. It was as though by using 'you' he was purposefully directing them at me. Secretly I had hoped that this freethinking person would have some snappy philosophical theory that would render my sexual excesses acceptable, but these few words were more devastating than Grandmother's complete theory of sin because I sensed the truth in them. And it made me shudder.

Later I realized that Enrique's theory was not merely a personal life philosophy that pretty much everyone develops for themselves based on their knowledge, experiences and desires. His perspective was rooted in the Far Eastern spiritual tradition that he knew so well and used with such obvious success. I found a whole row of books in his library about Tantra and the Tao of love. Totally new for me, they were sometimes shocking but definitely attractive in their approach to love life and sexuality. I threw myself into the study of these books with excitement, and soon realized two things: just how pathetically little I knew about the subject, and how much it interested me. It's true that a certain intellectual thirst for knowledge spurred me on. That I would actually use any of it to develop my own love life never crossed my mind. But I was at least able to discern that the eastern view was far more mature and profound, and much closer to understanding the secrets of love, than any of the western sexologists fumbling around in the dimness of psycho-physiological science. This harmony, this happy agreement and this bubbling joy for life that ruled in this special three-plus-one family was mainly thanks to Tantra.

"If at least a third of the world's population knew and used Tantra, then the whole world would be our little paradise," said Enrique one time we spoke.

"Your books say that special abilities are needed to practice Tantra."

"Only at higher levels. But you can develop them. That's what's amazing. At the beginning you only need a minimal amount of giftedness that almost everyone has. The rest is study, practice and experience. If you had known me ten years ago when I started, ..." he smiled rather shamefacedly as though the admission had taken him directly back to those days. "Imagine a shy, twenty-five year old young man who struggled with early ejaculation and sexual inhibitions, whose chain of sexual disappointments made him increasingly withdrawn and incapable of living... That was me at one time. You know, Laurie, I'm always filled with compassion when I see just how many people suffer pointlessly because of love or the lack of it when practically everyone could be happy. All they need is a little knowledge. But unfortunately the secrets of love are not taught in any school though it should be the first and most important subject for people to learn. There are few, very few, who have this knowledge and it is difficult to find them."

"Did you manage to find one of these sages?"

"I met a number of people who had some idea about these things. Some of what was once completely secret knowledge can today be found in books – you might have seen a couple in my library. But this is only a fraction of the insight. The complete knowledge is only in the possession of the true greats, the real masters... and I don't know where they are hiding. But, you see, even a fragment was enough for me to change my life and my fate, and it also taught me how to distinguish good from bad, the true from the false, value from worthlessness. But I know there is so much more. I am no longer interested in what the tantric books say, but rather in what they omit. I have already discovered part of it through my own experience but there are still things that you can only receive from a Master... and I haven't been able to find that Master yet."

The true depth of the meaning of Enrique's words was not clear to me at the time – I lacked knowledge and experience. But the atmosphere in the house suggested something of these secrets about which Enrique spoke.

One night I awoke from my dream to happy laughter and playful shrieking. Curious, I peeped out of the window. All four of them were out in the patio, totally naked, playing like little children who were free after a long and boring maths lesson. They were romping about, chasing one another and splashing around the swimming pool. The sight was touchingly beautiful, and I kind of envied them. They could be so childlike. I watched their games with reverence. And then I saw the kids became curious teens. The noisy chasing quietened into excited meetings, and they touched each other with a shy curiosity as they tried to discover each others' bodies. I thought I saw the sparks flying off them when two bodies came into contact. As desire burst aflame from the sparks the teens grew into affectionate youths. Their cheerful laughter subsided into sighs of pleasure. The desire to dissolve into the other was already burning in their eyes, but they knew they still had to wait until their senses fed by the body's fire were filled to overflowing and in flooded their soul. They knew that the delay increases the delight and brings greater ecstasy.

I felt the overwhelming urge to rush to join them. I felt I belonged with them... and I also felt that I didn't... But it would have been so great to partake of their delights, and share the joy with them that the mere sight of their game had conjured up in me... My One Thousand and One Nights nostalgia had been woken. Here it was. My charming fairytale world had come to life – and all I needed do was to enter. I carried on a superhuman battle in myself... and in the end I resisted. Something in me said that it might disturb the "normal life" that I had sworn myself to on the occasion of my crucifixion. And so I experienced that which every desperate person does, as they grab at the last straw of prayer, thinking that she definitely has to give or promise something to God in exchange for mercy and, having promised every last thing, regrets it... but is too proud to break the promise.

So I just stood there and admired the soft waves of the entwined bodies made light from the watery embrace, the harmonized dance of mature and experienced lovers. Then I stumbled back to bed and tried to escape the living temptation by returning to my dream world. But the sounds of delight were not invented as a sedative...

❖

The next day I decided to say goodbye to my hosts and go home to Marseille... before it was too late! I wasn't sure that I'd be able to resist such temptation again. And anyway more than a year had passed since I had left home, and I owed my parents a return.

It was with an aching heart that I left that little paradise and its wonderful inhabitants who I already loved too much. And the books containing knowledge yet to be discovered, the scents of which I had only recently discerned. The prospect of the boring everyday life awaiting me at home did not make my farewells any easier. Yet, I felt I had to go.

I now know that my "accidental" encounter with Enrique was an opportunity that I was unable to live because I was not yet ready for it. I had to return to everyday life... to learn...

9. Love Art

If I had to divide my life into periods, I would undoubtedly do it based on my relationship with women. Every girl, every woman I fell in love with opened up gates of new dimensions in front of me. Each of them taught my eyes to see a different face of beauty; each made me face different kinds of hardships and pains. And each relationship was somehow the denial of the previous one, the way aesthetic movements followed one another in the tide of the history of arts. Maybe it was the discontent and rebellion against imperfections that impelled me to seek out a new direction.

The time defined by my unrequited love towards my childhood ideal, Ylva Ekberg, can be considered as the first stage of the alchemical transformation of the soul. This was the time when the phantoms of false ideals and chimerical fancies burned to ashes in the purgatory fire of suffering. As a matter of fact that was what prepared me for my first initiation, the blessed Carina Dahl period of my life when I grew into a man. The time when I realized that the joy and happiness I had always longed for does exist. After this short and delightful period, the restless life current pushed me into the arms of Sibylla Hultgrens, who cast me into the horrendous underworld of Hades. There, similarly to novices of the ancient Egyptian Mysteries, I was submitted by the Great Initiator to tests, facing dark forces and death on my way. Only when I was beyond all hope did He kindle Christa Forshman's lantern of love, and that light helped me find the way to the Kingdom of Dawn. It was there Linnéa Svenson was waiting for me.

The period linked to her name enticed me with the illusion of a newly found Paradise. Paradoxically, the main motif of this time was searching. What was I searching for? What are we all searching for? In most cases we don't even know. To tell the truth I didn't know either. I just felt the urge to seek, an ancient instinct that smoulders in every person and drives us towards new journeys. We are travelling – every one on his own path – towards new continents, or mountain tops that seem unreachable, towards the dazzling constructions of success and power, or into the centre of the spiral of our inner galaxy. And what do we hope to find at the end the journey? Happiness? Maybe. The promise of happiness is an everlasting driving force. We give many names to happiness during our short life. At the dawn of my time with Linnéa, I simply called it "love".

These periods can easily take you prisoner. We like to linger over these times. Joys fascinate us, and for a while we forget we are eternal travellers and that we have to move on... For a long time Linnéa's world was my world. I found in it the two things that most interested me: love and art.

❖

After one and a half month break we met again in Paris. She was going to perform in the Théâtre de la Ville. I decided to go and see the performance but I kept it a secret. I wanted to surprise her.

The small auditorium was already packed when I arrived. I chose a seat in the last row. I felt as excited as if I was the one to perform. I had never seen Linnéa dance! Three musicians were sitting on a podium covered with oriental carpets. Their music saturated the theatre, conjuring up the atmosphere of an Indian temple, exhaling an aroma of sandalwood. Like a vision, she appeared in the light. A dazzling goddess adorned with lavish jewels and vividly coloured clothes – I hardly recognized my sweet Linnéa. Her beauty touched me. The perfection of her movements, the flawless harmony, gentle expressions of her face and eyes were beyond earthly, radiating rather a transcendent femininity. It was in that very moment that I had the chance, for the first time, to sense the perfection of Beauty and the beauty of Perfection.

Though I could not unravel the message her symbolical movements and delicate gestures wanted to convey, I understood their essence. They evoked in me memories of a world hidden in another dimension. A touching moment, similar to the one when a wanderer returns home after a long journey. I waited in the dressing room for my goddess, her cheeks flushed from the heat of the dance and the applause of the audience. I had spread a path of flowers that led to my hiding place. I was waiting for her behind the wardrobe, sheltering behind a huge bouquet of love-scented flowers. She picked up the flowers one by one, as if she was still dancing her ritual. Then she saw me. Her eyes opened wide. Tears poured out. She fell into my arms without a word. I could hardly imagine a more sincere love confession.

There was another reason for her surprise that she only told me later, when we were in the intimacy of her room and in each other's arms.

"Do you remember my first dance? I evoked goddess Parvati's ardour and love towards her spouse, the great Shiva. Before stepping on the stage I had felt the dance could only be true and genuine if I offer it to you. I imagined you sitting in the audience and revelling in my dance just as Shiva delights in his beloved's dance. And you really were there! I don't know... it is like a miracle... the sort of miracle Indians put so much faith in."

The miracle of love, I wanted to say. I wanted to say but didn't because I knew Linnéa did not like clichés. I hugged her close and hid my face in her ambergris-scented hair as I struggled desperately against my tears – a demonstration of emotion not befitting the great god Shiva. I managed to suppress my tears, but not my desires. My hands caressed her passionately. All I wanted then was to experience with her the wonderful pleasure, something for which even gods have to leave the heavens and visit the earth to taste. But Linnéa was in no hurry.

"Not now, Bald," she whispered into my ears. "I am tired, and I want to be completely present when I am yours for the first time."

She nestled her maddening nakedness into my embrace. She soon fell asleep with her lovely breasts resting in my thirsty palms. She must have been completely exhausted. I was unable to tear myself away from her tempting velvety warmth and to drift into sleep. Her body's scent ignited fiery fantasies in my mind. It was such a delight!

In the morning, our bodies searched the other, waking moments delirious with dreams. As her eyes met the rising sun Linnéa slipped out of my arms and said, "Come, let's have a walk in nature. I cannot stand this concrete jungle. I know a lovely place. You want to come?"

Of course I wanted to. What else could have I done?

I just had to order patience to my desire. It had to wait while a lazy bus rolled us through the morning turmoil out of the town, until we thoroughly admired all the waterfalls, fountains, and grass carpets patterned with flowers of Sceaux Park. Until we found a quiet corner, far from the alleys, where we could finally bask naked in the warm embrace of the June sun. And still I had to wait. Linnéa wanted to enjoy the homecoming to her heart's content. This was her real home, the freshly scented nature. This was the only place where she really felt complete.

We made a bed of moss for our love in the shade of ancient trees, and wove a blanket of fresh petals to cover it. We were preparing to offer the most ancient sacrifice on this luxuriant altar of the pagan oak temple. Rays of light peeping thought the leaves cast undulating islands of gold upon Linnéa's body. First I navigated that angelic landscape with the caressing softness of a bellflower. Only then did my fingers dare to touch that body-shaped miracle. Now it was me who did not hurry. As if time had changed its pace. I eagerly looked at the intoxicating sight, but my body waited patiently till her blushed cheeks, glittering eyes, and wet, opening lips silently permitted fulfilment.

After all the tension of this slow approach we merged with each other in such pleasures that even gods must have looked down from the heavens with envy.

❖

Linnéa was in perfect control of her body and senses. Desire could never drag her into ecstatic unconsciousness. She was willing to open her body to love only when she found the environment suitable – and she was extremely sensitive in this matter. She undoubtedly favoured the outdoors. We travelled a lot and inaugurated different spots as our love nest. We loved each other in flowery fields, on rocky mountain peaks, riverbanks and sandy seashores, amongst poppies scattered around wheat fields, or in intoxicating acacia forests. On the rare occasions we made love between four walls, she needed something special to be turned on – an exotic atmosphere, or some inventive games. She often asked me to play on her body with a silk scarf or a peacock feather… and she loved the touch of my freshly washed hair on her body.

The intercourse itself was an insignificant intermezzo, between a lengthy prelude and a prolonged postlude. She was sensitive to even the tiniest changes in our mood. A hint of disharmony could easily ruin her erotic feelings.

"You are only interested in the penetration," she voiced her displeasure at times. "I feel you only caress me to saddle me and mount me, but foreplay has its own life that for me is as important as the riding." (Actually it proved to be far more important).

She employed these poetic exaggerations sometimes, but the charges were not completely unfounded. My wild sexual battles with Sibylla had made me forget what I had learned from Carina. It took me time to once again direct my passionate temperament into extended foreplay and the joy of gentle touches. As part of my training, she sometimes stated in advance that there would be no penetration, and then played the most exciting erotic games with me for hours.

Linnéa was a chronic perfectionist, and this showed itself in her understanding of art too. She did not allow compromises. She only accepted the perfect. She rejected and despised anything that was blemished. She never improvised or danced freely, only ever performing dances of perfectly chiselled and practiced elements. She hated amateurs, but she could be completely captivated by what she considered to be a masterpiece – and she was an excellent judge of that. She was no snob though and valued mediocre artists' achievements just as highly as she criticized great masters' weaker works.

As for the arts, a kind of master-apprentice relationship formed between us. Obviously she was the master. She took me under her wing, regarding my aesthetic instruction as a serious matter. I trusted her artistic senses and accepted her guidance. She took me to concerts, theatres, and operas. We walked together through the most famous art galleries in Europe, and wondered at hundreds of architectural masterpieces. We talked about every artwork, deconstructing and analysing each one, trying to reach their essence through the act of transfiguration. This is how I became familiar with the fine mechanisms of achieving aesthetic pleasure.

There was one thing though that she never would have accepted: the natural aesthetic potential of a woman's body. At least she never allowed me to be absorbed by other women's beauty, to access an aesthetic experience through admiring their figures. When she caught me in such contemplations she closed off. And then lengthy and tiresome acts of conciliation were necessary to redeem myself. I could admire other creatures of nature like trees, animals, mountains, clouds to my heart's content. But women... that was forbidden. The only exception to this rule was her.

She did not even allow me enough time in front of the Venus de Milo when we visited the Louvre. Interestingly she let me watch the Mona Lisa and the Virgin of the Rocks for as long I pleased — Da Vinci had dressed them! Women with large breasts irritated her as well as any display of sensuality. Obviously she was repulsed by "vulgarity". The problem was that she found every display of sensuality to be vulgar — and only recognized the most carefully disguised forms of artistic eroticism. Toulouse-Lautrec and Rubens were certainly not among her favourite painters but in a way she forgave Gauguin his particular attraction to the naked women of Tahiti. Maybe it was Degas's dancers who represented an acceptable degree of nakedness.

I was unable to find any truth in her perspective. I rendered homage to the charms of women's bodies with exceptional wonder and devotion — and most of the 'vulgar' displays that so disgusted Linnéa, filled me with worship. I admired women who dressed sexily and boldly put on make-up. For some reason I felt in them a live and open femininity that was not present in those women who only believed in "natural beauty" and who hid even that at times. I never believed the notion that covering certain parts of the female body would create the legendary feminine mystique. In fact I was certain our body is nothing more than an enigmatic herald of a mystery beyond the body that can neither be shown nor covered. It simply exists. As with all mysteries, its main appeal is that it wants you to discover it. It wants you to see what is really beyond the physical existence of our body. Something that springs from far greater depths.

❖

Though I got close to many branches of art under the tutelage of Linnéa, in the depths of my heart I remained a musician. This was the period when I discovered Indian music. I collected so avidly that soon I had a whole record library. Obviously I did not only enjoy listening to it — I wanted to learn to play it too. I had fallen in love with the sitar.

Hervé – a member of the trio who accompanied Linnéa – was kind enough to teach me. He had been a student of the world-famous musician Ravi Shankar and always talked about his master with such admiration and love. A kind of humbleness radiated from his words that revealed more than a simple master-pupil relation. Though this way may be natural in India, it seemed strange to me at the time. Later I realized that in their culture the teaching of music differs greatly to the education in Europe. The master is not simply a teacher, but a kind of initiator; he opens up the secrets of music to the student and, along with these methods, he also offers a part of his soul to the disciple.

We travelled a lot in those months. We wandered through Europe, and I indulged in the joy of incessantly changing landscapes and meeting new people. Linnéa's beauty and refined femininity did not conquer half as many men's hearts as I had imagined. Her personality radiated a kind of cold reserve that easily disheartened every man who might have contemplated approaching her. She wanted to be loyal to me and said she needed no other man.

My monogamy did not stand on such firm ground. My love for Linnéa did not prevent me from being interested in other appealing women. Being on the road continuously gave me the chance to become acquainted with the concept of what beauty is in different nations – but I only allowed myself to admire it from a respectful distance. I did not want to hurt Linnéa. I did not even dare to dream she might understand my needs, so I conformed to hers. I made great efforts and strove to play the role of the loyal partner perfectly. As long as I could...

❖

I met Éva in Hungary. She was the sister of Hervé's Budapest musician friend, and we stayed with them in their beautiful house in the outskirts of Buda for five days on one of the tours. Éva had just turned sixteen. Only her girlish features and short tomboyish hairstyle gave away her age – her figure and gestures suggested a grown woman conscious of her sensuality. She looked at me as though she had been waiting to know me for a long time. I sensed a strong calling in her eyes. As we did not speak any common language, we just looked, secretly eyeing each other up. But these glances said more than any spoken language could have.

After lunch on the first day, Linnéa went to sleep to recover from the journey. I did not feel tired so I decided to have a walk in the orchard. I sat under an old apple tree, rested my shoulders against the hollow trunk, and enjoyed the combined relaxing effect of the full stomach and the afternoon warmth. I must have fallen asleep because I opened my eyes to meet Éva's scrutinizing gaze. She was standing behind a fair-sized sketching board. She was drawing me. When I saw her, I started to sit up but she motioned that I should stay still. It did not take long. After she had finished she sat beside me and showed it to me. It was a pencil drawing composed of brave strokes. I recognized myself in it: my features, composure... except she had forgotten to draw any clothes on me! She was generous in her drawing of my muscles. Neither had she been stingy with the graphite for my reproductive organs!

She smiled at me questioningly. As though she was asking me whether I liked the man she saw in me. Yes, yes, I nodded appreciatively. But I liked the girl who sees me this way even better. I only imagined saying this; I could not convey this message with a simple nod. I tried with other forms of body language. We pressed close together, tighter than the interpretation of her art required. My heart was beating wildly – not only because of Éva but also with fear. I knew that Linnéa could come out any moment. I could not stand the tension. I pulled back from her, stood up and indicated that, unfortunately, I had to go. She held me a bit longer with her eyes, then stood up. Slowly but suggestively she reached up, picked a golden apple and handed it to me, presumably aware of its deep symbolic meaning. At least the gesture seemed so obvious to me that I could practically hear the hiss of the snake behind the tree. After a little hesitation, I took the apple and rolled it in my palm in confusion. I did not know what to do with it. I almost forgot that, beyond its mythical meaning, it does have a primary purpose – to be eaten with relish and it is supposed to supply our body with essential vitamins.

Éva picked one for herself too. She caressed it with her finger pads, her movements so sensual they gave me goose bumps all over my body. She raised it to her lips and kissed it. She took the first taste with eyes closed, biting into it greedily, and then she opened her eyes. I began to munch mine too. An interesting game unfolded. We stroked each other's body with our eyes while eating our apples. Snake-eyed remorse pierced my skin, although nothing had actually happened. I had just eaten an apple... and apples exist to be eaten.

The next day Linnéa went for her usual after-lunch sleep. Deceiving myself that I only wanted to delight in the afternoon sun, I went to the orchard again. But this time Éva did not come out. What a pity! I arranged my body in a perfect drawing position. After half an hour of boring sunbathing, I started back, a bit disappointed, to see my sweet sleeping partner. From the hall I saw Éva's door was ajar. I felt a strong temptation to peep inside but resisted heroically. Only a few moments later Éva appeared in the doorway and beckoned me cheekily. I approached cautiously, carefully watching our door all the while. She took my hand and, with a gentle but definite motion, pulled me into the world on the other side. She led me to a large easel that held an imposing tempera painting. She must have finished it recently as in places the paint was still glistening. At first glance it seemed like a surrealist vision. It depicted a couple intertwined like the trunk of a tree, their legs like spreading roots penetrated the dark ground, their curly locks floated like the crown of a cedar above clouds of implausible shades. The two intertwined bodies were painted with almost realistic precision and radiated inspiring sensuality. I identified myself as the male figure – there was no ambiguity. The woman, needless to say, was Éva herself. This recognition awakened perplexing and inexplicable feelings in me.

She showed me other paintings too, mostly of couples and male or female nudes. The same counterpoint between visionary representation and realistic eroticism marked them. Her works spoke of her exceptional talent and an artistic maturity rare at her age. I attempted to praise her with nods and sounds of admiration but quickly realized she was not in the slightest bit interested in her works being praised. That is not why she had shown them. She actually wanted to reveal herself through them. The kind of praise she needed was very different from what I had just expressed. But, to be honest, I did not dare to give it.

❖

The next morning Linnéa went to rehearse with the musicians. I stayed at home. I was thinking about lazing around in bed but so much for plans... A gentle knocking startled me. 'That must be her,' crossed my mind. And it really was her. She stepped in wearing a T-shirt that hardly covered her groin. Her nipples pointed through boldly. She just stood there with indecently naked thighs, her questioning eyes wide open. Somehow I had to answer that unvoiced question but I did not know how. Civil war had broken out in my mind, and I had no idea how the battle would end. I should have suspected though. Well, known actually, if I had been honest with myself. The outcome was obvious the moment I accepted the apple she offered me. And when Éva depicted our union, like our ancestors painted the killing of an animal, mystically evoking it, I should have known that my Fate was already sealed. Forces supporting my attraction to Éva held far more power than those backing my loyalty to Linnéa. And yet, how many times we fight battles to the bitter end even though we know we are going to lose. To save at least a smidgeon of our honor! That is why I did not give up and that is why I decided not to give Éva the slightest hint of the surrender she was hoping for.

Now, playing on new turf, Éva's confidence shook, and I knew she needed an encouraging gesture, some reassurance. I knew I had to do something, I just did not know what. I was like someone who gets to the pantry and completely forgets why he went there in the first place. Éva saw my confusion, smiled and came towards me. I realized I was naked. Suddenly I sat up and prudishly covered myself. Éva broke into laughter and sat on the edge of the bed.

'It is still not too late.' Thoughts whirled in my mind. 'I still have time to stop the whole thing. Linnéa may come back any moment. And even if she doesn't, she will know… She will notice it, sense it… She senses everything… I have not touched her yet… I can still stop it… it's not too late…' But it was already way too late. My hands slipped onto her thighs, and the explosion broke out. Waves crashed above my head. Passionately I pulled her close to me. My lips approached hers, but did not kiss her. Not yet. I just drank in the intoxicating scent of her accelerating breath. She put her arms around my neck, pressed her breasts close to my body, her hips started to move, inviting and supplicating. She offered herself impatiently, circling me with more and more yearning. At times she pressed her thighs together tight, then she opened them, eagerly awaiting me. But I did not touch her until she took my hand and pressed it to her hot and luscious loins demanding me…

Éva was sexually mature. And sensual in a way that could make any man go mad – just like our mythical foremother must have been. She experienced pleasure with such great intensity! More than I had ever seen before. At the culmination of her delights she moved and jerked with loud screams, scratched and bit like a hungry tiger. Passionately but not painfully. Her hunger was insatiable. I gave up first. She would have continued. I tried to explain to her with hands and feet that Linnéa might come home any second. I cruelly robbed us of the afterplay. I knew it would certainly have exploded into the next foreplay.

As soon as she left and I was alone, my inner battles resumed. What was that? And how on earth will I keep it a secret from Linnéa? I have never lied to her before… I can't do it now… Maybe I'll spoil everything. But what if I tell her about everything. No, no, that is not possible, I know exactly what would happen then… No, that can't happen. I was in a terrible mess. Finally, of the two bad options I decided on the easier: I stayed silent.

That night Linnéa did not have a performance, and we decided to have a walk in the city. After a romantic dinner in an exclusive restaurant – candles on the table and gypsies playing Hungarian folk music – we strolled along the Danube. We admired the millions of lights dancing on the water and in the sky as though we had never seen anything similar before. I felt really in love. I pulled her close to me and kissed her passionately. After the initial surprise, she answered me, and we continued ever more heatedly. Then we looked at each other dazed, as though we did not understand what was going on. We giggled and looked for a dark corner but the Hungarians had illuminated the banks respectably. We had no other choice; we hopped into a cab to get under cover as soon as possible, boldly touching each the whole way back home to reassure ourselves that something of that unexpected initial flame would remain alight.

We tore off each other's clothes impatiently. The memory of Éva's body was still burning my skin, her scream of delight echoed in my ears. I let lose my passions – the way I had always wanted to. Linnéa was caught up in my passions within moments, something that normally only happened after hours of artistic foreplay. And amazingly she indulged in the pleasures with a sensuality I had never seen before. This new side of her captivated me. I was overjoyed to recognize in her the woman capable to burn in passion. She only needed a real man to awaken this in her. At the end, her face radiating happiness and a grateful expression, she breathed, "Oh, this is wonderful. You entranced me with your strong masculinity. I felt so liberated. I felt so… feminine, like never before."

Her surprising confession touched me. At other times she had often degraded my passionate outbursts as wild, barbaric, violent, and brutal. But now…

I had no idea what was happening. What had made that time so extraordinary, right after I had cheated on her? And what did we have to do so it would always be like that?

❖

I did not have chance to be alone with Éva again. Linnéa was always with me. But whenever our eyes met, there was a spark in the air.

When we said our goodbyes she embraced me more passionately than was appropriate and, before we left, she pressed something into my palm. As soon as I felt the peanut-sized smooth stone in my hand I knew – it was the moonstone from her necklace that we had accidentally torn off during our wild lovemaking. Éva looked at me with sad eyes, and my heart was heavy as we parted. I understood what she had articulated: maybe we will never meet again.

❖

Linnéa was sulky and depressed the whole journey. She attributed her bad spirits to being tired. But in Prague as the hotel door closed behind us, she sprang the question on me.

"What happened between you two?" Her inquiring eyes – always active when another woman was around – had picked up our innermost feelings as we bade our farewells.

Although I could have kept quiet about what had happened, there was no way I could deny it. I confessed everything. It was a cruel and depressing moment. Linnéa was devastated. Her bursts of emotions tugged her between two extremities. At times she flew into a rage and her eyes flashed terrifyingly with anger, at times she sank into quiet apathy and kept repeating like a lunatic:

"It was so wonderful, but you had to ruin it. It could have been most precious, but you killed it. It will never be the same."

I explained in vain. I tried to make her understand with desperate reasoning that nothing had changed between us, that we still loved each other, that we were deeper in love and had connected more passionately than ever. But my words fell on deaf ears. She sat there, sunk into herself, and kept repeating, "What could that little slut have given you that you could not find in me? Why would you sacrifice something that was so very beautiful?" She kept suffocating in heartbreaking sobs.

Our time in Prague was hell. We drove each other mad. She danced at her performance as though she was trying to stifle all her anger, desperation and sorrow, pouring them into her movements. There was not one moment when that happy and pleasant smile appeared upon her lips, the smile without which Indian dance is no more than a soulless play of a puppet twisted by strings. It was terrible. I felt responsible but, except for blaming myself, I could do nothing.

I decided not to follow her anymore on the tour. I flew home from Vienna telling her I needed some time alone to make things right in my inner world that had been turned upside down. Then, maybe… we'd see. With frozen hearts we said goodbye. I could not have felt more worthless.

My family's place did not turn out to be the best location for my inner contemplations. My two sisters' children were spending their vacation at ours. The five youngsters, under the direction of their enthusiastic grandfather, had changed the house to a permanent battlefield. On the other hand, I was happy that the grandchildren had managed to teach my father how to play at last.

So I retired to the enormous, old plane trees in Hoglands Park to ponder the big questions of life. I was certain that all the sorrow had been caused because I did not understand or know something, and that was why I had done something I should not have. I was sure there must be a secret as it was neither natural nor reasonable that love, which should make every man happy and free, would cause so much pain – at least that was the conclusion I had come to.

But the plane trees remained stubbornly silent. They did not reveal any secrets. They just stood there, wearing hundreds of years of wrinkles on their trunks. Reborn every year, conforming to the capricious seasons with a wise acceptance, mute witnesses of the change. They could have told me so much though. How easy it would have been to find answers to my troubles if I had been able to read their encrypted messages – like the alchemists, who always realized secret knowledge by observing nature.

In those times nature was no more than a stage for the drama of my emotional life. I was looking for the answers elsewhere. So my contemplations – actually nothing more than brooding on past events – were fruitless. They did not make me any cleverer or calmer.

I would have liked to talk to Carina but she had moved away from Karlskrona. All her neighbors knew was that she had gone somewhere abroad.

I visited Grandpa. He was always able to support me during my emotional turmoil. Well over eighty, he had long, white hair. Time had chiselled its hieroglyphs on his sunburnt face, on his proud forehead. Although his gait had become stiff, he retained his elegant posture and fresh mind. The sea had taught him many secrets of life. As I complained, he listened wordlessly. Just like the ancient trees of Hoglands Park. Then he spoke in an encouraging tone.

"Do not blame yourself for something you are not responsible for. Do not burden your conscience with imaginary sins. It is not you who spoiled what was between you, nor was it what you did but how she understood it. It is never the deed that causes problems but the way it is interpreted. Or misinterpreted. Jealousy is the most dangerous enemy of love. Your grandmother learned this quickly, and we had a life I would never exchange for anything else. Not one moment of it. And I'm sure she felt the same. And remember, you can only ruin something that was corrupted from the beginning. What is perfect stays perfect. An apple that has been touched by seed of decay will inevitably rot. But a healthy apple stays healthy, even if time consumes its juice and wrinkles its skin."

❖

Three weeks later Linnéa came to Karlskrona. We decided to try and restore the construction of our relationship that had been rocked to its very foundations. We made our peace. The scenery of our spring of love was like a balm on a fresh wound but it could not provide complete healing. Something had gone irreversibly wrong. She was unable to forgive me from the bottom of her heart. And the thought that if I had done it once, I would do it again infected her mind with agony. She became clingier and even more jealous. Though I really tried not to give her any reason, her imagination did it for her.

Naturally I followed her everywhere again. I went on tour with the group and at times I even joined them in the performance. I loved Indian music. I loved playing it. Yet I felt a growing emptiness in me.

We did everything we could to fix our relationship. We spent most of our time together, and tried to please the other with every little thing we could. We held hands the whole day, only that we made love less and less. There was always a reason: "there is not time for it now", "I am tired", "this is not the place for it", "I have to get up early".

But the lack of erotic fulfilment was not the main reason I felt something was missing. The source of my depression was in something else, something lying hidden in me for a long time to which, as long as our relationship was cloudless, I had paid scant attention. But now the feeling started to grow inside me that I was actually living Linnéa's life, not my own. The continuous tours and performances – attractive though they were – gave me less and less joy. Linnéa was perfectly satisfied by her work. She found happiness in it. She was certain she had found her true life mission. Meanwhile I became increasingly convinced that there was something else for me out there in the world. First this feeling took the shape of a barely noticeable pining for a change. But later this feeling transformed to a more pressing urge for seeking. A void opened in me that nothing could fill. When I looked around there was nothing that made me think, "this is my life". What made me despair the most was that I simply could not imagine what was missing, what would satisfy me. I just felt that something needed to happen.

I tried to explain my feelings to her, but she just could not understand. How could she have, if even I did not understand? In the end all she concluded was that I did not love her anymore, that I wanted a new relationship. She said that, since our unfortunate visit to Budapest, she had felt I did not love her anymore. That was simply not true. Éva just helped me bring to the surface what had been lurking inside me for a while. But how could I have explained that to Linnéa? To prove her mistaken I stayed at her side for as long as I could. But when the civil war plundering my soul became unbearable I informed her about my desertion.

I planned to start a new life after arriving home. I would accept the cantor position I had been offered for ages in the nearby community of Jämjő. That way I would be paid and still have enough spare time for study and research. I wanted to read philosophical works, religious and scientific theory. To find answers to my questions concerning the meaning of Existence in the hope that, at the end, it would shine light upon the meaning of my own insignificant life too.

Linnéa was desperate. She claimed I had made up all this nonsense just to get rid of her and end our relationship. She cried, begging me not to leave her. Though I felt my heart would shatter into pieces, I knew I still had to go. I promised her that we would meet as soon as possible, and she could visit me in Karlskrona whenever she wanted. At the bottom of our hearts we knew that it was over. That made the separation so terrible.

❖

It felt good to be at home again. I am not the homesick type but, after the tiring nomadic life, I started to appreciate the regenerating effect of the familiar. I found the cool peace of the church gratifying. I spent much time in there, especially in the beginning, practicing the organ for hours. I was responsible for the children's choir and I taught them simple hymns. Working with them refreshed me.

Reverend Danielsson's sermons did not awaken any religious awe in me. Though I found some creativity in Jesus' teachings – there was definitely some substance there – I found the theological explanations to worldly matters childish and out-dated. During the service I had the impression I was watching a film set in the Middle Ages; it may have had a magical atmosphere but it had absolutely nothing to do with our busy lives and modern sufferings marked by so many products of scientific discoveries. I was searching for theories that provided an answer for the mysteries of *my* life, of the world *I* was living in. In my frequent conversations with Reverend Danielsson he never managed to give any satisfactory answers to my questions.

I was not in the least surprised that the younger generation had abandoned the church leaving the older alone in the shabby pews. Those whose mission was to build the bridge between the scriptures and the ever-changing world did not possess enough competence, knowledge, or sense of vocation. I no longer doubted the existence of God. I felt that there must be something or someone overseeing the universe, controlling and guiding it, although no one gave me any useful suggestions as to how or where I might find Him.

I had many enjoyable discussions with my former pal, Arne Larsson, who in the meantime had graduated from theology and become a vicar in a neighbouring village. However, he was also unable to answer my profound questions about life. As for his own life, he said he had found its meaning and I could see he had because there was a peculiar light shining in his eyes all the time. He was satisfied with his job, his life and especially with his pretty, young wife.

A few years earlier I would never have imagined the bohemian, adventurous Arne would drop anchor in one harbour. But he said his wife provided everything one can get from a woman, so why would he turn to someone else. "In times of hardship, we pray, and with the help of God we can solve every problem as our love is strong," he said, a deep conviction in his voice.

I did believe him – but that was his life, his conviction. I needed something else. If only I had known what!

"God shows everyone his own path when the time comes," he encouraged me. "I found mine. You will find yours. All you need is time and faith."

Arne advised me to visit the youth Bible study lessons, as "they interpret the Word in a more modern way" there.

So I even went to a few youth meetings. They really were attempting to make the outdated theological dogmas more current and relevant to present day conditions. They even tried to modernize religious practices – that basically meant they sang silly little songs accompanied by guitar and drums, their eyes gleaming with devout love. They feverishly described the "wonderful changes" in their lives since they had "accepted Jesus into their heart". But actually I only saw polite attempts to accept each other. The "real love" they talked about was still missing. They were just unbalanced youngsters skimming the surface of the real issues, driven by a search for companions under the umbrella of religion and a desperate need to belong somewhere. Nothing there indicated a true search for the meaning of life, for genuine values. They kept repeating unexamined quotations from the Bible and, in their childish fanaticism, they were even ready for violent fights to defend their convictions.

I did not feel at home in their company. At one meeting I met my former classmate, Freja Olofson. We were both surprised to see each other. It turned out she was also searching, and that we had a fairly similar opinion about these youth Bible parties. She had been on the quest for answers longer than me – so she already had more in her bag! She said she was primarily interested in oriental spirituality and longed to travel to India where she hoped great masters who had attained a state of ultimate wisdom were still living. She was convinced they would be able to provide satisfactory answers to questions concerning the meaning of life.

She had also been practicing yoga for a while. She started it during her university years in Göteborg, did an express course and now practiced at home alone. I was interested in that yoga thing. I had read some oddities about it so I asked her to teach me a few things as I wanted to try it too. She lent me a few books about yoga and showed me some postures, breathing exercises, and concentration techniques. Some were quite similar to what I had done with Sibylla.

I practiced rigorously every day – that was what the books suggested. I forced my body into strange, twisted positions, I breathed assiduously, and tried to stare at the candlelight as long as I could without blinking or being drawn away into my thoughts. I managed to overcome the urge to blink, but the thoughts... Well, they kept dashing and running around like wild animals in a forest fire. If nothing else, at least these practices helped me discover the extent of the chaos ruling my head. After a while though I really began to feel their effect – they made me more calm and balanced. But, in the absence of more impressive results, somehow these sitting practices began to occur more and more rarely, until a time came when they stopped altogether, replaced by 'more important matters'.

Meanwhile I continued my search with Freja. We bought books, explored every corner of the libraries for rare editions, and attended lectures and conferences. We went almost everywhere they discussed matters of spirituality, God, or parapsychology. Freja was my proud guide in this paranormal labyrinth. She had already tried everything from Silva Mind Control to Dianetics, Reiki to regressive hypnosis, astrology to tarot, so she had some idea about almost everything, as well as an astounding thirst for knowledge and a passion for research anybody would be jealous of. I remembered she had read all the philosophers during our years in secondary school, and was able to have serious ontological arguments with Spinoza, our mouse-faced philosophy teacher.

But, when I asked her about philosophy, she just brushed it off.

"I grew out of it. You know, I always had the feeling that western philosophers are still in the dark. They approach reality like the six blind men in the tale who, after touching different parts of the elephant, try to guess what it might look like. Well, our philosophers are just the same. They are experts in certain aspects of reality. They build whole citadels of wisdom, but I always feel they lack something – something basic and essential, and that absence weakens their whole structure. At first I believed I would be able to discover what is true and congruent with reality. If I'd been able to put the pieces together then I'd have a complete picture in the end. But I was forced to realize it's pointless to identify the ears, tail, trunk, tusk, legs, and side of an elephant separately – I would still be far from knowing what an elephant actually looks like. And I have not even touched on the essence of the elephant… what makes an elephant an elephant. Do you see what I mean?"

"I think so." Her logic seemed stable enough. "And the Greeks?"

"Plato was close to the truth but I didn't get the whole picture even after reading him. The others, well, they got stuck at the elephant. I wouldn't include Pythagoras because he was no ordinary philosopher. He was initiated to the secret knowledge. Unfortunately we do not know enough about him to understand him perfectly. You know, more and more I have the feeling that they never write down the really key ideas. Maybe because, at the end of the day, we cannot understand the deeper truths intellectually anyway. So there's no point searching for them in libraries. We need something else. Initiation. A spiritual path that does not only describe reality, but leads us to it."

I remembered Carina had also told me about spiritual paths and initiations. But at the time I had been occupied with more worldly pleasures. Now as my thirst to understand had uncovered a void in me, Carina's mysterious and challenging words filled with a deeper meaning. A desire awakened in me to find such a spiritual path – one leading me to the understanding of life's great secrets. I wanted to meet someone who possessed this hidden knowledge, a real master who until then I had only met in books. Someone who would show me what is invisible to the naked eye, who could make me understand the things that dwell beyond the borders of rationality, who would be able to tell me about the mysterious force that pushes a man and a woman into each other's arms, who could talk to me about what magical touch makes the flower of love bud. And what makes it wither so quickly…

Unfortunately, I was being tossed about in the fashionable New Age mishmash with Freja – and I could find neither the path nor the person. Only well-polished theories everywhere. Promises of easily attainable paranormal abilities, spiced with a spoonful of secretive mystery, and a wide repertoire of extraordinary and first-class meditation delights drowned in a love sauce.

After a year of assiduous and hopeful research, I started to grow tired of it all. I felt I was arriving at a dead end. A whole year had passed since Linnéa and I separated. Since I had renounced a more or less functioning relationship – for the sole reason to unearth the meaning of life, to find my own place on this planet. After that year I was more confused and perplexed than ever. I had no idea who to turn to or what to do. I did not expect much from my journey to India either, the one Freja and I planned for autumn. I felt the spiritual ideals I was chasing fled farther and farther, slowly fading into the mirage-like fog of non-existence. It felt certain that the growing distance would prevail over their force of attraction and finally I would give up.

I began to search for Carina, the only person whose judgment I trusted. She seemed to have vanished into thin air though. I could not find a trace of her anywhere. The thought that I would have to live my life without knowing who I was, where I came from, and what I was doing on Earth saddened me. That was when I decided to try the last of the possibilities. I turned to the one we usually turn to when we are let down by everybody else, when we reach our human limits. That was the third time in my life I sank into prayer.

"Lord, all I ask is that You show me the way that can lead me to You. Nothing else matters. If I find You, then I have found everything because You are the question, and You are the answer to all questions. You are the secret and through You all secrets will be revealed, Amen."

❖

Two days later – to my great surprise – Linnéa called me. I was glad to hear from her. She told me that she missed me and wanted to meet up. In fact she had found an occasion for it too. She had been invited to perform in Copenhagen but Hervé, the sitar player, was in India and so she was wondering if I could take his place. I agreed immediately. It was a common habit of mine that, whenever something was not going well in my life or I was in a desperate situation, I was happy to leap out of my everyday and distance myself a bit. That is why I was so delighted about this opportunity – even if the direction did seem to be going backwards, to a part of my life already considered closed.

❖

Linnéa had been invited to an event called Knop, Sind, Ob Messe (Body, Soul and Spirit), a kind of spiritual bazaar. Various stands lined the enormous hall on Falkoner Allé. It was interesting to see the whole range of New Age products in one place. All those areas I had encountered during my spiritual investigations were represented: palm reading, tarot cards, astrology, Hare Krishna Kirtan, vegetarian foods, spiritual books and music, Reiki demonstrations, crystal ball readers, priests conferring blessings and reading from the Bible, clairvoyants, masters of acupuncture, Taoist healers and other similar curiosities.

I was surprised by the Copenhagen residents' keen interest in this event. The traffic was similar to that of a large shopping centre, and almost everyone found something to try in this esoteric cocktail.

My attention was drawn by a booth imitating the inside of an Indian temple. There was a low altar-like podium framed by candles with a sculpture dressed in jewels and splendid Indian clothes standing in the centre. At least it seemed like a sculpture from afar. As I got closer I realized it was actually an attractive girl, her face painted the colour of marble, who was standing there without even the tiniest movement, frozen in the position of a dance mudra. I was curious how long she could stay so still. She changed position about twenty minutes later, assumed a new hand position and became a rigid statue once again. Her beautiful blue eyes radiated an unworldly tranquillity and playful childish purity. She captivated me. I was still staring at her when – half an hour later – she changed position again. Beside her a man and a woman wrapped in each other's arms were moving into various yoga asanas on a colourful carpet.

The unique atmosphere of the stand enthralled me. It was a true oasis of quiet amidst the surrounding hullabaloo. Everybody who walked past had a surprised look. A plump, baby-faced girl introduced herself as Kristine. She noted my interest in the performance and explained they were a Tantra group from Copenhagen, and that the living sculpture symbolized one of the ten cosmic forces, Tripura Sundari, goddess of beauty, harmony and love.

On hearing the word Tantra, my heart leapt. Suddenly everything Carina had told me about Tantra flashed before me, and I listened with heightened interest. She answered all of my questions with an astounding ease, even those I thought rather tricky. After just ten minutes of talking many things became clear to me that I had long been searching for answers to.

She charmed me not only with what she said, but also with her warm nature and cheerful seriousness – and the attractive femininity that radiated from her whole being. I was sorry I could not stay any longer but I had to meet Linnéa. Kristine told me about their dance performance the next day and I decided I would definitely go.

My meeting with Linnéa stirred up many memories and emotions. Long-forgotten feelings seemed to awaken, as grudges had been worn smooth by time. We even played with the idea of maybe starting over again. Linnéa had not had anyone since we'd finished and felt awfully lonely. I did not have anything to be proud of either. Although I had tried to get close to Freja – we did have a slight attraction and common circles of interest – our time together lagged so far behind my experiences with Linnéa that in the end I had given up on such attempts.

And now, the intimate atmosphere of the hotel room, the proximity of her body, and recalled events of the past chased us into each other's arms again. We almost made love... But we changed our minds. We thought it was rather just a momentary flame – she driven by her loneliness, I by my desires that so readily fly into passion. We decided to wait. If our emotions turned out to be lasting, then we would have all the time we needed to start over. We were free.

The next night we went to the dance performance of the Tantra group. I was fascinated by the show. Not by its artistic values but rather by its message of love, of harmony channelled by all those nice, youthful bodies. By their experience of complete fulfilment and mutual devotion. The last scene in which a naked couple painted golden bronze presented a choreography of slowly changing erotic positions was both touching and uplifting.

Linnéa was not at all impressed. She said, "This is not dance. It's not art, only cheap and meaningless self-exhibition."

This time she could not convince me. I realized her Gemini mind, programmed for intellectuality, prevented her from feeling with her heart that which lies beyond the borders of rationality. I sensed it, and nobody in the world could have taken away this from me. Not even Linnéa. Suddenly the recognition shook me that it was precisely our most fundamental ideas about life – about love, sexuality, human relationships – that divided us like a gorge. And the bridge that love built above it was not stable enough to resist a stronger whirlwind of emotions.

I wanted to congratulate the group on their performance – and greet the mermaid I had met the day before. The dressing room was packed. I thought they must be the other members of the Tantra group who had also come to celebrate the success. As I looked around my heart suddenly leapt with surprise and joy. Carina Dahl was there! I had been looking for her for so long. As we jumped to each other's arms, I realized just how much I had missed her.

"I was looking for you everywhere. You just disappeared. I thought the earth had swallowed you up."

"Heaven swallowed me up," she smiled at me with a mischievous wink. "Come, let me introduce you to my sweetheart." She emphasized the word sweetheart with joyful satisfaction. Erik was a remarkably tall, bald, handsome man with a blond beard. Carina said she had been living in the Danish capital for five months. She had met her splendid knight after her summer holiday by accident. Erik had been a member of this Tantra group for two years.

"I found what I was searching for," she whispered into my ears with a glowing face.

I did not understand exactly what it was that she had found, but I hoped she would tell me when we were alone. She introduced me to the group, moving among them very comfortably. We invited everyone to the Indian dance performance that was to take place the next day.

I met Carina the next morning. She told me with a touching, childlike enthusiasm how she had met Erik, and she praised his masculine-tantric abilities at length and in an explicitly sensual manner. Carina was deeply in love, and I was glad for her. She had always been cheerful, happy and radiant, but now... Now it seemed as though she had been reborn. Yes, that was definitely my feeling: she had been reborn.

I told her about my inner struggles, and the lack of success in my research. Carina was listening with such joy, as though she was hearing a presentation about the greatest successes of my life. At the end she said she felt I was ready for the spiritual journey.

"This is exactly it," I burst out. "That is what I cannot find. I cannot find the man, the master that you talked about who will give me a map for this journey, who can help me remove the veil that hides my Self from myself."

"You have only been searching for a year," she responded seriously. "I had been looking for twelve years until at last I found him. Because I have found him now. I am certain. The people you met last night are the disciples of a genuine tantric master. I haven't met him yet – he lives somewhere far away, in an Eastern European country. But, as much as you can judge a tree by its fruits, he is the Master I was always looking for. The one whose existence I believed in, and who I know I will meet soon."

"So you are the lucky disciple who is ready to meet the Master. But how much time needs to pass for me to meet mine and when will I be ready?"

"Bald, in the last twelve years I tried many things, met many people, Indian gurus, Tibetan Lamas, and their western disciples. Several of them possessed a fundamental and authentic spiritual knowledge. But this spiritual school is honestly the best I can recommend to you – and I reckon you will like it. I have no doubt that your path is Tantra, but whether He is your master or not, I cannot be sure. You need to decide that alone. Karlskrona is not far. Come over sometimes, meet up with these people, participate in our activities, practices and meditations – and time will tell."

I trusted Carina so simply rejecting the idea was unimaginable. Still, I was in no hurry to decide. My many unsuccessful attempts had made me distrustful and cautious.

The whole Tantra group came to our evening performance. Linnéa enchanted them – they congratulated her enthusiastically and invited us to a party afterwards. Linnéa was a bit reluctant but I was delighted to accept. I hoped I would get the chance to observe them more closely.

I started to have the feeling that Carina was right. The people I met were so great! Cheerful but not big-headed, openhearted and warm but not sentimental – and extremely direct and liberated. According to Linnéa they were licentious but that was her opinion. The girls' attitudes reflected their naturally sensual, feminine nature. That may have seemed vulgar in Linnéa's eyes but for me it was the most beautiful and true manifestation of the feminine. The same as it was with Mette Hansen who had attracted my attention with her glamorous grace during their performance. Now she performed such a marvelous belly dance that my eyes and mouth were gaping from start to finish.

My indispensable friend Carina, who always pays such exquisite attention to everything, introduced her to me – and then kept Linnéa occupied so I could exchange a few exciting and promising words with Mette.

I think that was the moment I came to a decision.

It had always been my attraction towards women that lured me to necessary and unavoidable life experiences. I remembered Carina's words "Karlskrona is not far". Maybe I would not have to wait twelve years… Was it possible that Carina's master was my master too? I had no idea. All I knew was that in Mette Hansen's passionate eyes I found the fountain from which I desired to drink the first secret teachings of Tantra.

10. "Escucha tu corazón!"

I would never have thought that going home could be such an uplifting experience. There are times when you have to remove yourself from the things that have become habitual in order to be able to rediscover the wonder in them.

My home received me with an unhoped-for warmth, with a sheltering familiarity that stirred a whirl of forgotten memories. The large salon with its white curtains billowing in dense waves that always filtered the bursting sunshine into such a pleasant brightness; the piano sunk into his black loneliness, whose familiar but still freshly tinkling voice rang out as my hands raced across its teeth shining with youthful whiteness; the heavy copper mortar inherited from great grandmother that sat regally, with such proud dignity, on the shelf next to the ultra-modern coffee maker as though it simply wanted to draw attention to the time-defying quality of real values, among the many trendy kitchen utensils; the pale pink of my beloved room with the small rhombus-shaped mirrors above my bed that over time had shown so many of my different faces – and from which a woman maturing from her shocking experiences was now looking back at me. Tensely I observed this face, relieved to see that Seville hadn't engraved on it any disturbing marks.

Mum welcomed me silently with a hug and happy tears of relief after her fearful worry – as mum's usually do – always sensing more than they actually know about what is happening with their child who is so far away. Dad, his eyes wide open and wonder written on his face, looked at me and then shouted, "Mamma mia... Laurie, you have... You've become a woman."

My mother's father, the ageing big shark of the Marseille business world – as Estrella would have called him – expressed his happiness with the satisfied rubbing of his palms. Hopeful that I had finally outgrown the period of my youthful follies, Grandfather had decided that the time was right to start my initiation. He wanted to carve a highly influential figure out of me using the pattern that had proved so successful for him. In the interests of this sacred duty he sacrificed his peace and quiet retirement in the country villa for a while to reconnect with the high-voltage currents of the financial world. He took me everywhere with him: business meetings, economic-political conferences, and strategic development discussions. Within a short time I was given the opportunity to become acquainted with all those important persons who held the invisible strings in their hands, the people who directed the economic and political life of the city – actually of the whole of Provence. And there weren't many of them. In actual fact there were surprisingly few – and they certainly weren't those to whom the unsuspecting citizen casting their 'democratic' vote had entrusted the leadership of the city. Behind the sparkling superficial events, these people were casting totally different nets of interest – nets by no means woven on a democratic basis! Grandfather taught me how to tap into the main veins of this invisible and complicated powerhouse. In the meantime he also counted on being able to make me love the glittering lifestyle of the elite, and that I would choose a suitable husband too from this circle. He proudly introduced me to all those – he considered – were possible suitors.

I can't say I disliked this. In Seville I had become accustomed to a glamorous lifestyle, dressing to please in fancy evening dress and enjoying the pleasant swarm of men looking for my favours, and now there I was floating around at home on the surface of the cream of society. What was more, I was far safer here than among the filthy rich sharks of the Seville underworld. My grandfather had unequalled ability as well as a wealth of experience in business. It was an understatement to say that he adored this life. Actually business was his religion – though I can't say "money was his god". Money was merely a tool for him, a handle that controlled the complex mechanism. Something else drove him: the seductive experience of success. He immersed himself in large and risky businesses with the ardent passion of African hunters going after big game. At an early age he had completely eradicated the word failure from his vocabulary, and it seems he made a lifelong pact with success.

How he and my grandmother – for whom life on earth was nothing but the opportunity to prepare for eternal life – managed to live together with such deep understanding was always a great mystery to me. He believed in nothing but the single earthly life and was totally devoted to it. To his mind carving out a career represented the basis of existence, and almost its only meaning.

It is a strange religion that has its own promised lands which its believers desperately desire, its own laws that easily bring the uninitiated innocent into material disaster, and its own little priests who know this and that – and who sell this knowledge for sizeable sums writing 'how to be a success' books, holding courses and meetings. And then there are the true greats, the masters, who just listen and act. They rarely pass on the really big secrets as an initiation – and only to the chosen ones. And Grandfather was one just such master.

Money and business interested me far less than the sociological phenomenon of the business world itself along with its own unique laws. Grandfather basically misunderstood my fascination. He thought he'd found in me the perfect disciple – and the only reason he didn't present me with all the tricks right at the beginning was because he worked methodically. He wanted to serve theoretical knowledge together with the opportunity to put it into practice and, as he sensed that financial matters interested me little, he wanted to dangle the other key of success in front of me: opportunities offered by position in society and influential connections. So he insisted that I study law and took me to every major gathering and party.

It was at just such an occasion that I met Vincent Guillou. Shareholder and member of the board of an oil importing company, this 28 year-old man was regarded as a business natural. His strong personality, charm, intelligence and attractive appearance made him a successful negotiating partner. He spoke excellent English, Spanish and Arabic, and I felt he was warmer hearted than the others spinning in similar circles. The rushing stream of life swept him before me at exactly the moment I was crying out longingly for a true, deep and loving relationship. I was searching for the kind of man who was attractive enough for me to ceaselessly desire togetherness with, intelligent and strong enough for me to look up to, and understanding enough to accept me as I am... In every respect Vincent seemed suitable for this role.

Even on our first meeting I was pleased to discover in his eyes the spark that the fiery arrows of Amor can ignite. A light that was so obviously different from the burning fire in the thirsty look of those males primarily desiring satisfaction – in spite of the fact that both burn similarly both blaze, and men cannot really distinguish between the two... and un-fortunately neither can women. And what did I feel? It was good to be with him. I could be proud of him and I felt loved, admired, even adored. He proved to be an experienced and attentive lover. And I experienced with him those sensual delicacies enjoyed only by those bodies attuned to each other over the course of a long relationship, having discovered each other's ways and moods.

I had got what I wanted... So I was happy and content. I could live the privileged and envied life as the partner of a young, good-looking, rich and loving man. When the other students were complaining about their lovers and husbands I could only smile sympathetically. Vincent could not be accused of any of those faults that made my female friends grumble. I was still getting flowers from him after two years while most men stop all such efforts immediately after completing the manoeuvres of a successful conquest.

Vincent worked a lot and was often away but he spent all his free time with me. In winter we went to the Swiss Alps skiing. He loved that especially and was able to experience the joy of dazzling snow in the sunshine with such liberated enjoyment that he reminded me of a playful puppy. He taught me to ski. He made me love the steep slopes, tempting with their promise of the crazy swishing speed under impatient skis, and he helped me discover the pleasure of listening to the wind rustling through the pines and the unforgettable taste of grog sipped by a merrily crackling fire...

One summer we went on an outrageously expensive cruise that was nowhere near as refreshing as our Swiss holidays. Neither the group of filthy-rich people tortured by their wealth nor the typically kitsch entertainment could win me over. I survived it once but I certainly did not want to hear of wasting Vincent's short time off on something similar the following year.

When he could he took me with him on business trips. And so I had the chance to visit Greece, Turkey and the Arab states. I came back a little disappointed as, with some childish naivety, I had secretly been hoping to discover the magical world of One Thousand and One Nights. I found nothing at all however. I was saddened to see that the combined forces of advancing western civilization and the local religious fanaticism was gradually destroying the truly great values of Arabic culture.

Only one country left a deep impression: Egypt. Maybe the breath of the ancient culture still breathing there touched me in the silence of those enormous stones. A strange and disturbing feeling engulfed me at the foot of those mysterious constructions. It wasn't the tour guide's impressive numerical data and archaeological discoveries presented expensively to western tourists peeping from behind cameras and videos that amazed me. It was something else. I sensed the enormity and majesty of the human spirit in those enormous, majestic edifices set between wonderful giant statues. It was as though the light of intuition illuminated – just for a fleeting glimpse – the Biblical assertion that "God created man in his image and likeness", elucidating its hidden meaning for a moment. Unfortunately it was too short for my mind to be able to store it. I tried in vain to re-evoke the knowledge but nothing remained, only an intangible feeling that I was completely unable to crystallize into any sort of certainty. I was unable to forget it though. And that was so unsettling because in the light of that brief recognition my everyday life – along with all its petty problems, selfish pleasures and vain dreams – seemed so insignificant and utterly meaningless. I sensed that another way of life may exist other than this 'normal life' I had managed to create for myself since taking my vow in Seville – and I hankered after a life that provided the soul the opportunity to spread its wings and reveal itself in all its majesty and mightiness. Because at that moment I realized the soul becomes stunted by a life restricted to satisfying needs and chasing after transitory pleasures, becoming like the caged bird searching for security instead of flying free. I felt the desire to bring something totally different into existence, build a pyramid, discover a new America, create a masterpiece that would defy passing millennia, something, anything… just to be able to step away from the mass of people living to experience merely fleeting pleasures so that my life might attain a genuine value… So that it would truly be worth living.

I tried to explain to Vincent what an incredible influence these mysterious stones had had on me. He replied that yes, he felt the same way – and proceeded to speak with awe about ancient cultures with technologies far more advanced than our own… Then I realized that he had no idea. Unfortunately I didn't have the means to make him understand either, and he didn't have enough empathy to sense what I felt. A completely new feeling that I myself couldn't catch in the net of words.

❖

After our trip to Egypt, Vincent asked for my hand. He would have liked to get married as soon as possible. I didn't refuse him but for some reason I was in no rush to stick my finger into a ring. I asked to wait a little, until I had finished university. I didn't feel the need to tie us together officially. We were already like a married couple – I practically lived with him… He, however, wanted something secure. He felt that while I was flying free his happiness was somehow endangered. I can't say that he doubted my feelings nor was he worried about competition – he was aware that few men were able to offer what he could. But he did sense my un-predictability. And that is exactly why he wanted to tie me to him some-how.

"I don't understand why we have to wait until you finish," he rebelled. "Almost all the people in your year have already got married. You know, I'm not asking you to have children yet, but I would like to feel that we are bound together, that we are each other's…"

"But we're already each other's, my love. Why do we need a paper for that?"

I couldn't honestly provide him with any explanation as to why I was putting off marriage. He was a "really good catch". My whole family adored Vincent and they were perfectly satisfied with my choice. And he knew that too, so when he saw that I was procrastinating, he turned to them for assistance. He hoped that the united force would somehow succeed in persuading me. This move irritated me. *Because if I didn't want something, then God himself could not persuade me!* I fumed to myself. *Well, okay, that's an exaggeration; he had succeeded once or twice, but a son of man? No way!*

Following our trip to Egypt I increasingly noticed my reluctance to attend business meetings – with Grandfather or with Vincent. And the glamorous parties no longer attracted me either. I started to be bored of the company. It bothered me that I had nothing else to talk to these people about but business and gossip. Business itself was becoming less and less interesting – and I had always hated gossip. The hypocrisy and continuous role-playing began to exasperate me, though I had somehow accepted it at the start. I had taken it as practically normal, so much so that I sometimes found myself appearing in various roles: the "successful businesswoman", the "femme fatale", the "acclaimed artist" – all of which were enviable roles. I, however, no longer wanted to wear any mask. I wondered increasingly often about who I really was and what would remain of me if I stepped out of character and removed all costumes. The glamour and the luxury that had succeeded in blinding me for a while now represented nothing more than glinting of shards of broken crystal. Empty and worthless. I had quickly discovered the laws and rules of this world – and they no longer attracted me. I was forced to recognize that I did not belong to them in spirit.

My reluctance to accompany him to business meetings and gatherings caused Vincent genuine pain. He liked to have me at his side and was proud of me, like one might be of a rare jewel. Yes, I think he loved me as a person loves a valuable item… It dawned upon me that something was missing from this love though I could never express exactly what it was. He worried about me, protected me, admired me, idolized me and regarded me as his, but I don't think he ever really loved me! I couldn't even explain these fine subtleties to myself, but somewhere deep inside I felt something was lacking.

The hairline division that lay between us totally unnoticed at the start started to deepen, and the arguments and rows springing up from trivial matters brought it to the surface. After the first flames of infatuation had receded, Vincent became increasingly demanding and impatient. His headstrong Aries personality did not get along easily with my Leo wilfulness. This slim gap was slowly widening to a dark abyss we were forced to notice… and that we attempted to fill – with compromises, of course. I conceded, and so did he. And so we managed to attain some sort of balance again that was not natural equilibrium stemming from completely loving selflessness, but rather a sweat-soaked effort that was calculated, tinged with the desire to improve and the attempt to change.

Soon events transpired that rocked that delicate stability once more. Antonin invited me to an Indian dance performance at the Moulin. At the time I was meeting with him fairly often to go to concerts, to the theatre and talk at length about the arts. He was the only person around, able to satisfy these needs of mine. Vincent tolerated him but wasn't happy about our friendship. He wasn't jealous, simply unable to comprehend what I could possibly need from Antonin, and why on earth I'd spend my time with such profitless things.

Vincent wasn't the least bit interested in the arts and ranked artists among the lower forms of society. Sometimes I took him with me to the theatre or to concerts. He came along, sat them out – out of love and devotion to me – but I could see he gained little joy from them so I stopped torturing him. I was deeply sorry though that I was unable to share my aesthetic experiences with him.

Anyway, this particular performance had a very peculiar effect on me. I had seen Indian dance on television but this was completely different. A live performance. The performers weren't Indian – the three musicians were French, the dancer Swedish – but the mood they created swept me away on a genuine space and time journey to ancient India, to a time when people were so much more genuine and perfect, and far closer to the gods. The time when Ramayana and Mahabharata were written. I was amazed to discover that the dancer knew those secrets I had discovered in my ballet dance period. She understood the power of movements and was able to create with them in that invisible dimension that I then called the world of the soul. I practically saw mysterious snow-covered peaks where supremely powerful gods reside be born in the wake of her movements – each and every one bursting with creative power. I could see the rushing holy river that thousands travel to in hope of cleansing, and the thick forest where dangerous predators lie peacefully in front of the crossed legs of the meditating hermit... I was surprised because I didn't yet know that what I had believed to be my own secret was actually the very foundation of sacred dance.

This world evoked by the performance seemed familiar, so very familiar. For a moment I felt it was so much more my world than the one in which I was actually living my everyday life. And once again that incomprehensible and disturbing feeling I had experienced at the pyramids swept over me – but perhaps it had become just a little more tangible. It projected pictures before me of a world that called me, tempting like a beautiful memory. An irresistible urge awoke in me to learn this dance with its magical powers so at least I would be able recreate in myself the world that no longer exists... because it had disappeared. Just like that of the One Thousand and One Nights... or the dinosaurs...

Antonin also loved the performance. But he said that though the symbolic content of the movements and hand gestures had little significance for westerners – since they were linked exclusively to Indian mythology – the dance was, of course, in itself of high aesthetic value and also exceedingly noteworthy culturally. Somehow I saw more in it than its pure aesthetic and cultural value. I could not explain what was drawing me in.

I met the dancer after the performance, and we spoke a lot. Our conversation made my desire for the Indian dance experience even stronger.

So I decided to travel to India for at least a month. The girl gave me her own dance teacher's address and wrote me a letter of introduction too.

While my parents were not exactly overjoyed at my most recent delusions, Vincent was totally dejected. In vain I tried to explain to him that I was only talking about one month, saying, "surely we can bear one month apart, and if not, then you can always come and visit me". He protested virulently but I had absolutely no intention of abandoning my plan. So he started to plead. I felt sorry for him and promised I'd think about it... Thinking about it just made the urge to go more definite. My final decision completely crushed him – and I had no idea why my absence for one month would be such a great tragedy. One single month, thirty days... But he sensed that it was not about 'one month' at all. This was no mere excursion from which one simply returns and then continues in the same rut. He realized one dangerous step can lead to unpredictable changes in the course of fate... And indeed he was not mistaken.

❖

My plane left from Paris, and Vincent drove me to the airport. He was sad and silent the whole journey. Although I tried to be nice to him and somehow cheer him up a bit all my attempts failed. He could remain so terrifyingly silent – that was his way of voicing his deepest displeasure. But when we parted he hugged me to him tightly and let me on my way with a passionate, 'I love you' kiss. I felt better, became somewhat emotional, cried a few tears and... then felt totally fine.

Even while checking in I was already observing my fellow passengers. Were they looking ahead to their journey with as much excitement as I was? Because it is extra special to travel to India. It really cannot be compared to travelling to say New York, Rome or even Casablanca. The ticket to Kolkata had a distinctly different feel – mysterious and exciting... At least that's what I thought.

The winds of India were already blowing my way on the plane. I was sitting next to a slim girl with a pleasant face and a Mireille Mathieu hairstyle. She didn't appear particularly talkative. As we took off she closed her eyes and sat like that for a long while. She wasn't sleeping as her head didn't drop once, nor did it flop to one side. She only opened her eyes when they served lunch. I noted that she was given different food from me. She must have noticed I was staring uncomprehendingly at her tray because she started to explain that she didn't eat meat, had been vegetarian for five years and felt "so much better for it". We introduced ourselves. Benedicte told me she was a Parisian but that she often went to India to visit her master, a certain Sathya Sai Baba to "refill with his effusive divine love" and "to drink from the infinite spring of love". I was curious who this person might be, someone she was speaking of with such devotion... When I asked her she suddenly became very talkative and, her eyes sparkling feverishly, she told me incredible stories. That Sai Baba was the real incarnation of God, like Jesus. That he had come to cleanse and prepare humanity for the coming of the new age. That he already had several million disciples around the world. That he was capable of performing miracles and could conjure up various objects, jewellery and holy ash with healing properties out of thin air. That he was able to help his disciples out of trouble if they ask for help – even if they were on the other side of the world. And that apparently he had also resurrected from the dead, just like Jesus...

I listened sceptically all the while accustoming myself to the idea that I was travelling to India and that in India laws of physics do not work as they do elsewhere – at least that was the impression after reading Paul Brunton's Secret India shortly before my departure.

Well, I thought, I'd definitely take a look at this miracle guru for myself, if I had time.

❖

I devoted the whole of that short month I spent in India to learning dance. I didn't visit Sai Baba and I hardly saw anything of the plethora of sights that India has bedecked itself with over thousands of years. I thought that maybe next time when I had more time – and then I heard my friends saying: "What? You didn't see the Taj Mahal? You didn't visit Khajuraho? You didn't go to Benares? How come? What, you mean you didn't even dip your toes in the Ganges?" Well, no, I didn't. I didn't actually move out of Madurai, the small south Indian city where my dance teacher, Leya Singh, lived. During the time I had there I wanted to master as many of the basic elements of the Kathakali dance as possible. It was way more difficult than I had imagined. The playful lightness, that smiling, twinkling happiness that radiates from the dance is very misleading. It requires enormous effort, incredible self control and, of course, many years of dedicated practice.

The month was just enough for me to be amazed at how many body parts I have and that in order to pay enough attention to all of their movements to be able to put them together into one dance – and to smile – was still far beyond me. I practiced as much as I could but after four or five hours a day my body totally gave up its service.

I decided to spend the remainder of the day studying and fearlessly plunged myself into the jungle of Indian mythology. I hardly need say I got totally lost among that wilderness inhabited by the various gods, goddesses, demigods and demons. I realized pretty soon that it was hopeless trying to unravel the meaning of the many colourful and otherwise magical tales and stories without an experienced guide. I had recognized that, although the actors were gods and demons, the stories themselves were actually about human life, actually about humanity – and this was how they provided valuable beacons to help people decipher the profound life wisdom stemming from the ancient knowledge hidden within us. Despite having too little understanding to comprehend this type of wisdom it still attracted and stunned me.

I also studied Leya Singh's family life too. They go to bed at night, get up in the morning, work, eat, go to the temple, love each other and argue just like Europeans – but they are still worlds apart... I mused over where this difference lay. Perhaps in the fact that their everyday lives were much more closely interwoven with their religion than ours. They paid homage to their gods not only with the candles lit in the temples, the offerings of flowers and foods, and with prayer, but also in the most insignificant movements of daily life. From dressing to eating, from washing to having tea, an extraordinary sacred awareness pervaded everything. And that was true for dance too. You simply cannot dance Indian dance with automated body movements while your mind wanders somewhere else. This dance demands total awareness in every moment. This seemed the hardest for me until I realized that I didn't have to practice this absolute concentration only during the dance, but in every moment. I started to play a sort of game with myself. I tried to pay as much attention as I could to whatever I was doing. If I was eating, then I tried to contemplate the taste of the food. If I was getting dressed, I focused on the feel of the clothes, the style of the motion and its rhythm – and I was astonished to discover that the totally 'banal' things we usually simply skim over could actually provide exceptional joy if we but paid attention to them.

The whole Indian way of life turned out to suit me down to the ground. I somehow felt it was more mine than my life at home. I couldn't explain why logically. I just... felt great there.

The month came to its end and, with nostalgia and the promise to return for a longer period, I bade my farewells to the Singh family of whom I had grown so fond.

❖

I found it difficult to reconnect with my other life, the one awaiting me in Marseille. I sat with a faraway look in my eyes in the university lecture hall between the other students who were paying attention so seriously. The odd snippet would slip in through my ear. A fragment of a sentence from a tedious and endless PhD dissertation about the legal basis for the seventeenth and eighteenth paragraphs of the Criminal Code expounded by a Sorbonne professor Dr XY with a pathos worthy of a Hamlet monologue. And increasingly those stubborn resurfacing questions circled in my head as to what on earth I was doing there. What kind of evil spell had brought me to a place where I really shouldn't be? What kind of punishment was it that I should be there mugging up on feeble laws that could easily be changed with a new government when there was actually a completely different kind of law that I was interested in, the eternal and perfect law of Life! I should be attending a university where they taught the mysterious laws of the workings of the world... so I would be able to understand why, with what concealed purpose does Fate apportion cloudless happiness to some and excruciating suffering to others? Why does it gift some with the ease of a prosperous carelessness and smite others with distress and an empty stomach? What criteria does Death use to steal its victims? And why did I feel that something was missing from my life when I had received all that anyone could wish for and more?

India had had a greater influence on me than I had realized. Questions that had never before arisen started to engage me. My view of the world had changed dramatically since Seville. Then, when the first wave of important questions arose after Estrella's death, I had felt that life was terribly unfair and I had rebelled against it. Now I was certain that it was fair, but totally unfathomable, at least to me. Something suggested that the understanding of these enigmatic laws was somehow connected to India, so I started searching in that direction.

I studied the traditional writings of Indian wisdom: the Vedas and the Upanishads. I was disappointed to find that they were just as much double-Dutch to me in the French translation as if I had been reading them in Sanskrit. I realized their creators had by no means tailored the spiritual level to that of the present day circle of readers with their reduced intellect. So I turned to more accessible writings. I began hunting for the writings of sages and yoga masters who had lived more recently. And I found a few. One, Paramahansa Yogananda's Autobiography of a Yogi, grabbed me especially. In the book the author tells stories about his master Sri Yukteswar that are totally unbelievable for a person with a western mind educated in scientific materialism. Yet his words emanated a kind of truth beyond logical principles, and a certainty streaming from experiences that delicately and practically imperceptibly disarmed all doubt.

So I closed the book with the determination that, if even just one genuine sage lived in India, then I would find that person!

❖

Vincent had comforted himself with the hope of our approaching marriage so my most recent plan caught him like a blow below the belt. I tried to reveal my thoughts and feelings to him honestly. I had supposed that this way he would, at least to some extent, understand the challenges arising from the depths of my soul. I even hoped secretly that maybe he would be assaulted by an interest in the most profound meaning of life... and that he might accompany me to India... so we could search for answers together. But things worked too smoothly in Vincent's life for him to start scratching his head as to how it all worked. The only problem was the one called Laurie. But the solution to this was also clear for him; I just had to grow up a little. Then the fog of this mystical imagination would simply disperse – and I would land with both feet firmly on the ground... It was that straightforward!

I resigned myself to the fact that the search to make sense of life is a very personal journey. One we generally only attempt when the thought of life's pointlessness has fundamentally rocked our belief in our daily lives. And Vincent still had that to come.

Making plans come true is no easy task when, alongside the difficulties of the problem itself, you also have to struggle with the opposition of loved ones. This really does test the strength of your decision.

I left France with a heavy heart as I set off to the East again, but India greeted me with warm friendliness. The colourful and noisy clatter on the streets, the loud and cheerful honking of the many battered tricycles and motorized rickshaws, along with the joyful cordiality of Leya Singh's family quickly swept away the tension I had brought from home. I only spent three weeks in Madurai. Leya was clearly astonished at how much I had developed in the previous six months saying she was convinced I had been an Indian dancer in my past life. I smiled at her conclusion but was delighted by her words.

After I had once again gathered a large amount of practice material, I bade farewell to Leya and set off for the north. And, since it was on the way, I went to Puttaparthi to Sathya Sai Baba's ashram. After everything that Benedicte had said I was very curious about the guru and would have liked to talk to him. But, since he didn't receive me personally, I only saw him at the public darshan. From his short speech I found out that only one religion exists – the religion of love; only one caste exists – the caste of humanity; only one language exists – the language of the heart; and only one God who is ever present and to whom there is but one way – the way of love. Although I could not deny that these were beautiful thoughts, I had heard them too often for them to awaken new feelings in me.

He patiently strolled among the several thousand disciples and visitors gathered there who were sitting in long, straight lines awaiting the grace of the guru with excited devotion. He touched some of them with his hand

and spoke a few words to others. Some people prostrated themselves in front of him and kissed his feet.

He passed in front of me too and stopped for a second before continuing. The excitement of the long wait made this brief encounter special and, although I did feel the "universal love" she had spoken of radiating from his eyes, I was also certain that he was not the figure I was searching for. I was sure he was not my master...

But I didn't regret stopping in Puttaparthi, partly because I was satisfied I'd seen this man who had become so famous and adored by so many, and partly because there I met Uri, a lovely Israeli man. Uri was to play an important role in the next developments of my life. We had pretty much the same opinions about Sai Baba so we carried on our search together. Uri planned to travel to Rishikesh and, since I didn't have a fixed itinerary, I went with him.

It is quite amazing how Fate, using brilliantly designed manoeuvres, brings together people who have something to share. Many times I played with the thought that if I hadn't met Benedicte, I wouldn't have visited Puttaparthi, so I wouldn't have met Uri – and then I wouldn't have reached the place I did... Sometimes a meeting is only a matter of minutes, even seconds. If I'd got there ten minutes later, we wouldn't have met and then things would have taken a completely different course...

❖

The modern part of Rishikesh, city of the wise, is no different from any other bustling Indian city. But, as we walked along the long bridge over the peacefully flowing holy river, full of rubbish, and into the old town, it was as though we'd arrived in another world. There are no cars in this district. The law severely punishes the sale of alcohol and meat products. And the place fills the visitor with the ability to turn inwards and immerse oneself in meditation, providing a mood that is even able to subdue arrogant western tourists to a certain respectful restraint. Until then I would never have believed that the atmosphere and spirit of a place could have such a strong effect on a person. I had regarded pilgrimage as ridiculous since "God is present everywhere". But maybe there really are places where God is a little more present!

When we inquired about accommodation we were directed to an ashram where we were given a strange room – it resembled a three-storey cupboard. The bedroom was on the upper shelf, the living room on the middle, and there was a totally darkened concrete crypt below that was for meditation.

After the long and tiring journey the top shelf tempted me – and I didn't wake up until the next morning. And only then to Uri's impatient knocking which was furiously trying to communicate to my consciousness something like "we didn't come to Rishikesh to sleep". He had got up at dawn to meditate and since then had been humbly waiting for me to return to the world of the open eyed.

We spent the rest of the morning sightseeing. Then we got hungry and ended up in restaurant on the top floor of an enormous three-storey, for a long and seemingly hopeless wait. I realized that not only physical laws work differently here, but time is also measured in a peculiar way. It appeared there was much more of it here than in Europe.

So, some three quarters of an hour after ordering, the warm-hearted waiter, a smile from ear to ear, returned with something totally different than what we had asked for. Since only our hunger was greater than our irritation, we didn't dare send back the food. We weren't sure we would actually receive what we asked for anyway after another forty-five minutes. So we decided to eat what we had and, after eating, we waited again... We even started to feel hungry again. But we still hadn't managed to pay. From time to time the good-natured waiter smiled encouragingly over at us that "I'll be with you in a minute" as he carried on calmly and happily. Well... The lesson entitled "patience grows roses" was the first of our teachings here in the holy city. We were just about to go over to the waiter to pay when I noticed a tall, well-built man with glasses enter the restaurant. He was wearing the orange robes of a swami and was accompanied by three pretty girls who were chatting cheerfully. They sat down at a table by the window but somehow their presence filled the entire room. They certainly weren't bored as they waited. They might have been telling jokes to each other because intermittently they fell about in cahoots of laughter. I completely forgot myself, I was watching them so intently. It was as though the orange-robed man sitting with his back to me felt my stare. He turned around, looked at me for a long time and then smiled slightly. When the waiter – obviously a millionaire in terms of time – finally brought the bill, I asked him about the man with glasses. He bent down to my ear and explained in a conspiratorial voice that he was a European who taught Indian yoga in a way that was not at all traditional, that apparently he wasn't afraid to sleep with his female disciples... and that I should keep away from him. And he also remarked that he was very successful and had many followers.

When I asked how to find the ashram he shook his head while explaining, regretfully mumbling to himself: "No good, miss, no good...".

Somehow the waiter's words didn't put me off. The man didn't seem the least bit dangerous. Actually he was rather appealing. His face radiated warmth, good cheer and a joy of life. I felt love in his look. Not that universal or rather impersonal love I'd seen in Sai Baba's eyes but something totally other... something human.

I discerned from Uri's face that the merry group had won his approval too. So we decided we'd look at the other ashrams too and, if we didn't find anything of interest, then we'd definitely visit the European swami. After three days of searching we ended up at the infamous swami's ashram after all. We were greeted by an amazing sight – the famous swami was riding on an A-frame ladder, his hands lifted to the sky! On TV I had seen Indian fakirs meditating on the top of trees or on one leg, standing on a riverbank their hands up high, motionless, for years... But I never would have predicted these traits from the smiling-eyed man I'd seen in the restaurant three days earlier... Then, as my eyes adjusted to the dimness, I saw that he had a screwdriver in one hand and was changing the light bulb!

He greeted us with a smile and told he'd been waiting for us. He'd noticed us in the restaurant and knew we'd find our way to him sooner or later. He asked to be excused for a couple of minutes while he completed his spiritual task.

"I have to make light," he added with a cheeky grin.

I looked around. There were five others in the room cleaning and putting up pictures.

All of a sudden there was light and the swami came down the ladder.

"We're just moving into this hall. We have to tidy it," he explained, and then added, "We're also starting a new life. You've arrived at a good time."

For a second his "we're also" rang in my ears. Why, who else was starting a new life here? He told us a beginners' group was starting in two days time, and he would be happy if we came too.

"And what's the course about?" Uri and I inquired curiously, practically at the same time.

"Something you'll both like very much."

"What makes you think that?" We looked at each other with surprise.

With a serious look on his face the Swami looked deep into my eyes, stroked my hair gently and said, "You'll see."

That piqued my interest. He was so certain of himself. I'd have liked to speak to him alone as I thought a few well-directed questions would help me discover whether or not it was worth being involved with him but, with his refined senses, he deflected me.

"I know what questions are bothering you. Come to the first gathering. It'll be a theoretical presentation. There I'll try to answer everything. And then, if you'd like, then we can talk."

❖

Swami presented a new face at the opening lecture. He spoke in a serious tone, as people usually speak of great and sacred things, one that doesn't tolerate banter. His pervasive, almost hypnotic voice attracted attention like a magnet and captured me for the entire time he spoke. His words evoked thoughts with a magical force, and these thoughts, like sunrays, illuminated the dim recesses of my consciousness. In their exploding light for a second I saw myself! And I understood myself. In the mirror of recognition the human being stripped to his naked essence stood in front of me. The eternal creature chased along the night of unconscious sufferings and joys by burning desires and painful longings towards the dawn light of the spirit – the first moment of wakening to consciousness, when all the small desires unite into one powerful aspiration: to know the Creator! This is the first step on a genuine spiritual path. The spiritual path that Swami was talking about. And he spoke of God too, but in a way I'd heard no one else speak of Him. Swami's words made His presence come alive in everything around. In the light of the gently flickering candle flame, in the charming petals of the orchid, in the fluffy cloud sailing across the piece of sky framed by the window, in the exalted, attentive eyes of people... and in me too, somewhere deep in my soul. He not only spoke about things... he evoked them with the creative power of his words, bringing them alive. And that is how he evoked love too. As he was speaking the energy of his words brought the mood of romantic twilight rides back to me. I felt completely in love. I loved the man dressed in the orange robe whose deep blue gaze hinted at the infinite. I loved the open-hearted Uri who was watching so intently, the gazelle-eyed Indian girl next to me and the purring Siamese tomcat in her lap. That well-meaning waiter who had unintentionally brought me here... and the Ganges rolling along with its wise calmness... and the shining white peaks of the Himalayas rising in the distance... and Him who called all of this into existence...

"This is Tantra." Swami's closing words reverberated in the ether, echoing in me long after he finished. "The alchemy of love, the shortest and steepest road leading to spiritual perfection. The hero's way. The way for those who are brave enough to sacrifice their imagined self on the burning altar of love and to face their own true divinity gleaming under the ashes."

❖

The Swami had been right. After the talk I really didn't have any questions left. Everything seemed so clear and comprehensible, life so simple, beautiful and promising... For a while... Until the next day. Because then I had to make a decision... and so the inner struggles began. Swami planned the course for six months but I couldn't stay that long. I would have had enough money, it is incredibly cheap to live in India, but university was waiting for me, my finals, and Vincent, who phoned every day to tell me how much he was missing me... and of course, my parents... It was easier for Uri. He said nothing else interested him. This course was now the most important... and he was staying.

The call of duty is a great tyrant. All I wanted was to stay but I still decided to go home. I'd go home, finish uni, sort out my affairs and then come back six months later for the start of the next course. When I said goodbye to Swami, he told me:

"Take something from here that reminds you of your promise. You will need it..."

I wondered what to take... a moment later I knew. I hugged Swami and laid my head on his broad chest. He hugged me tightly to him, holding me for a long time. I looked deep into his eyes when he released me. That is what I wanted to take with me as a reminder: that warm hug and that deep, sea-blue gaze.

"That'll be enough," I said in a voice reduced to a whisper by the emotion. "Yes, that'll be quite enough..."

❖

It wasn't enough. It's incredible how easily the tumbling events of daily life push those uplifting feelings of our rare celebratory moments into the background. With its demanding aggressive reality our being locks the whole lot up as a lustreless museum piece on loan, hiding it under a dusty glass that separates past and present. And often we don't even know if it ever actually shone with true light or if our exploding desires dressed the banal in shining clothes.

My last classes at university, my nervousness about the exams, combined with preparations for my finals that transformed my nights into day; Vincent's loving adoration and marriage proposals that were reborn like the phoenix rising from the ashes after my every attempt to refuse them – all this, topped by our stormy fights, terrible arguments and passionate makings-up, slowly but surely frayed away the memory of the city of sages.

And then there was Antonin, who had discovered both a talented new dancer and a fantastic idea for a performance: a dance duet he planned portraying the entire scale of the relationship between man and woman – from indifference through the hell of anger, jealousy and hate, to the tender, passionate and playful encounter, and finally the ecstasy of sacred union. Of course I accepted! I craved the stage lights like the parched ground the summer rain.

The show required a huge amount of work. Not so much the creative process as the forgetting. I had to renounce all those dance languages I had gathered since my childhood. Antonin did not want to see ballet, flamenco or Indian dance, just Laurianne. I had to learn to free the power of dance working in me… It was a tough and blessed task as not only did I have to shed my body's habitual forms but also the costumes that had grown to fit my personality. Only then would the pure dance pulsing deep in my soul be free to break to the surface. And thus everything became smoother. Yvan, my partner, was talented and ambitious. He found it extremely easy to evoke the negative states but, like most artists, he feared approaching the positive feelings – the phantom of sentimentality alarmed him. Somehow we were unable to find the final scene which really had to bring some sort of resolution. Finally it was the spirit of Indian dance that provided the saving grace. We portrayed the mutual adoration of a god and a goddess in the finale, thus lifting it to a cosmic – Yvan thought mythical – level, and so we managed to avoid the "trap of human sentimentality". And the closing scene also pleased Yvan. And Antonin too. It was a divine success!

Then came the premiere and the success, along with invitations, a tour, the bohemian life. In the meantime Grandfather was paving the way for my business career, and Vincent for our union. He had sold his bachelor pad and bought a splendid family house so large that a brood of children would have fitted in along with us… and we set the date for the wedding…

That morning the postman brought a letter. It bore an Indian stamp. Uri had sent it – six months after we had parted… It was 25th August 1997, the hardest day of my life. I opened the envelope with shaking hands. There was a folded piece of paper inside with Uri's writing drawn in rounded letters as though they were decorative embroidery on a white canvas. It was a while before I realized that these were words and sentences that actually had a meaning.

Rishikesh, 12th August 1997

Dear Laurie!
I know I don't deserve to be forgiven for not writing to you once since you left. But maybe you understand… When such wonderful things happen to us unfortunately we are liable to forget about everything else, our friends too – and so many amazing things have happened to me since I've been here! I can't even begin to describe the feeling when, after a long, long, seemingly hopeless search at last you find what you wanted so desperately, when things that seemed like a such a difficult mathematical equation before, gain their meaning all of a sudden. When finally you manage to take the reins of the horses pulling the carriage of your life all

over the place and bring them into patient submission, and you see clearly where you are headed and why – it is a fantastic experience! Laurie, you can't describe it, you can only feel it...

I hope you are well, and that things are going great for you.

I spoke to Swami yesterday and he asked me if I knew anything of the "charming French girl" I entered the Ashram with six months earlier... My face burned with shame when I was forced to admit "Nothing". It was such a divine clip around the ears – like I often get from Swami – and I'm so grateful to him for it. If he hadn't asked about you, then maybe I wouldn't be writing to you now...

Well, the next beginners' group starts on 14th September – the one you promised you'll come back for. I won't be here any longer. I have to return to Israel for a while to get some money. Write to me at my home address if you forgive me.

Loving hugs,
your (un)faithful friend
Uri

The letter pierced my heart. I read it again with a lump in my throat, my eyes bursting with tears. And a third time too. Desires forced to be forgotten broke up with renewed strength, and that deep blue look in which I thought I had once seen the infinite flashed in front of me...

Then Grandfather popped into my mind. I'd spoken to him the previous evening. He'd organized me an 'outstanding' position as legal advisor at one of the most successful companies in town, with an enviable salary and various other advantages. The next day I was supposed to go for a meeting with the chief legal advisor... Me? A legal advisor?... The opportunity that I had nodded "Yes" to the day before suddenly seemed so utterly ridiculous. There was no way I could see myself in that role – sitting behind a desk piled high with papers day after day... no. The telephone shook me out of my reverie. I heard Antonin's voice breaking with excitement say:

"We need to speak...now...in person...I've got extraordinary news..."

I didn't even try to refuse. And ten minutes later he was rushing through the door, breathlessly informing me that an agent from a top Parisian acting agency had been in touch with him who had seen our performance and wanted to organize a six-month tour in Europe and the US...

"This is a once in a lifetime opportunity, Laurie darling. Aren't you over the moon?"

Somehow I couldn't be delighted. Maybe if the offer had come two months earlier… but now… Everything at the same time!

"Yvan is ecstatic with joy… I have to give the guy an answer by tomorrow. But really there isn't anything to think about!"

I still asked for little thinking time though, at least until the evening. He left a little deflated, but full of confidence. I hadn't even got back to my room when the phone rang again. It was Vincent. He wanted to come round to pick me up right away as he'd seen an absolutely beautiful wedding ring in one of the jeweller's that he wanted us to look at together. I asked him if we could put it off until the next day saying I had had a very busy day. He agreed reluctantly, but I thought I sensed vengeful tones in his usual, "I love you, my darling".

Overwhelmed, I collapsed onto the bed. And the phone rang again. This time it was my banker grandfather. He was just phoning to check I wouldn't forget to be at the meeting at eight o'clock the next morning…

"Yes, of course. I'm not an idiot!" I slammed down the receiver in irritation.

An enormous avalanche engulfed my head. I felt I would break under the weight. I had to choose between all these opportunities that were piling up. One – and quickly. But my mind was denying any sort of cooperation. I tossed and turned, my mind dull and exhausted hoping with great naivety that maybe someone would actually remove this huge burden from me. After a while the germ of an idea stirred in me that actually I had to do something. Perhaps if I went out into the fresh air… maybe to the sea… that might help.

I called a taxi and asked to be taken to the cliffs of the Calanques. The midday sun poured its searing blessing on me so I escaped into the cool dimness of the Grotte de Méjean. I loved this place. It was as calming as a church. A pagan church. I had often come here with my father when I was a child, and I always imagined a mysterious world started at the end of the long tunnel, at the point where the glint of light shone bright. It was a wonderful and dazzling place like the one my father's father, my world-travelling grandfather, told stories of. He was a great story teller. Often four or five people would stand around hungrily devouring his words like children before leaving his shop happy and content, some overpriced and worthless trinket under their arm. Suddenly I felt I had to speak to him.

I found him in his shop but it was by no means quiet there as he had many customers who were inside escaping the midday heat. He was wiping the barrel of an old musket with an oily rag "so it would shine". He noticed something was wrong so he washed his hands and sat me down on his knee as he had done in my childhood, so I could tell him what was lying heavy on my heart.

I told him what an impossible choice the day had presented me with. I explained all the pros and cons of each opportunity inside out. I hoped that he would understand the situation and then would decide what was best for me. He listened patiently for a while before placing his index finger on my lips and whispering,

"Listen to your heart, my little one. Choose with your heart not with your mind."

It was as though I'd already heard that somewhere before... Where was it?... Suddenly I knew! And then I jumped out of Grandpa's lap, gave him a kiss on his surprised cheek and rushed away...

On my return home I flicked through my diary until I found the entry on 17th December 1992: Doña Esperanza's prediction!

With increasing astonishment I compared the events of the past five years with the gypsy woman's prophecies. There was the "beautiful friendship" and the "death that changes your life", "a young and wealthy man who will love you very much and will be jealous", "a great journey" and "the decision". When I got to this point, I was in no doubt that it was referring to the "now". Unfortunately the prediction finished here... But how accurately she had foretold the rest! She could have let the next bit slip too! Only the wise and useless good advice, "La mente miente. Escucha tu corazón." But how?! Will somebody please give me an answer for that?! How on earth am I supposed to identify the "voice of the heart" among all those conflicting cries? "Escucha tu corazón!"... If only it were that easy!

Disappointed, I closed the diary. I felt exhausted. I lay back on the bed and closed my eyes, my thoughts whirling around. The picture of the quietly flowing Ganges appeared before me, and I looked down from the long, narrow bridge. Then I saw Swami on the bank dressed in his orange robes, the lenses of his glasses twinkling playfully in the sunlight. I walked towards him, going faster and faster until I was running, only stopping in his open arms. Waves of indescribable happiness flowed through me...

I no longer know if it was a dream or a vision, or simply the play of my awake mind. But I do know that the next minute I felt clearly what I had to do. I just couldn't understand how the decision had caused so much difficulty. There was no question of choice here, only my mind had tried to make me believe that there were various "opportunities" from which I had to "choose". One single moment, one honest moment, was enough for me to recognize the only real course.

With a calm confidence I sat by the telephone and picked up the receiver. I called Antonin, Grandfather and then Vincent. I said pretty much the same to all three. I informed them with cold-blooded objectivity that I would be travelling to India in the next ten days... for an unspecified length of time... My decision was final, and all their attempts to persuade me otherwise would be pointless... Then I pulled out the phone. That was enough for one day.

I only told my parents the following day. I needed fresh energy for that. Mum cried so hard for two days that her eyes became purple. Then she ran out of tears... and words too. She locked herself in her room and suspended communication with me. My father, out of respect, stood on his partner's side but I sensed from a couple of his glances that, from the depths of his crazy heart, he thought me right. It was hardest of all with Vincent. He was totally incapable of accepting the thought of my leaving. He did everything to try and talk me round. From pleading and crying to the coarsest curses and accusations, he used the whole arsenal of emotional blackmail. The fights stretching on into that long night destroyed any feelings I had left for him until only one remained: pity. But that could not put me off my purpose. In the depth of my upturned soul there was the certainty I was doing the right thing.

My adventurous and spirited grandpa was the only one who was honestly happy at my decision. He told me not to worry about money. He would gladly support my trip.

Ten days later I was sitting on the Air France plane bound for Delhi. As the midnight Paris shrank to a pinhead and its lights were left behind far below, I understood why the human soul links flying with the concept of freedom.

SECOND PART

"Your task is not to seek for love,
but to find the barriers within yourself
that you have built against it...
The way you make love
is the way God will be with you."

Rumi

11. The seed matters

I crossed over to Copenhagen every weekend. The tantric yoga classes for beginners were held on Fridays. Friday soon turned to be the most important day of the week. A red letter day that I awaited with childlike excitement. The classes surpassed all my expectations. A new dimension opened up before me, a dimension I had only suspected might exist behind the doors. I plunged myself into the discovery of this new world with eager curiosity. My physical perceptions were of no use in this expedition. I needed to revive those refined senses, hibernating somewhere deep in the dark dens of my unconscious, waiting for the warm sun of spiritual awakening. Yoga practices, under the expert tutelage of Erik, provided the way.

The inconceivable something I identified as *me* started to pry apart the barriers forced around it by my superficial viewpoint, and this refined observation, attuned to the highest frequencies, revealed ever more of my *real self*. I managed to discover the invisible cloak – woven of the finest threads – that enfolds and permeates the body like lines of magnetism do metal. I discovered the buttons on this invisible cloak, the vibrant petals of flower-shaped power centres – the chakras – that pump energy through the channels of the ethereal body like the heart pumps blood through the arteries. The yoga exercises I had once practiced without much success now became effective in the possession of these secret keys. Through them I was able to stimulate my chakras, direct my energy round intangible circuits, and to connect to the inexhaustible resources of the Universe.

Everything looked so wonderful in the torchlight of this newly acquired knowledge! The big whys and hows of life seemed to have found their answers. I realized I am more than a mass of flesh glued to a skeleton and stuffed into a skin-case. More than a transient body haunted by the phantoms of death. I am a perfect copy of the Universe, a true microcosm. The man created in the image of God whose existence is the embodied miracle. Irreconcilable opposites unite in me. I am mortal and immortal, limited and omnipotent, fallible and perfect. All in one.

At the beginning though, it was a mere theoretical understanding – one that would require years of practice and experience to grow into certitude, to become a living reality in my inner world. However, I did not know that then and, as soon as I found answers to some important questions of my life, my mind was already swaying self-contented on the tepid waters of half-success.

As the Greek fires of the first euphoric moments faded, I was forced to realize that believing in human perfection and manifesting this perfection are entirely different things. In fact, these are two opposite poles: the starting point and the final destination of the spiritual path. From the point where I was standing, only one side of the coin was visible. In the fate-mirror of actual facts I could only discern the mortal, fallible human struggling with his annoying limits. The other side – the one facing the infinite – was yet hypothetical.

I thought that the moment a man sets on the spiritual journey all his problems would be solved in a flash. My naive imagination depicted the spiritual path as a pleasant route winding up through gently sloping, flowery meadows – and in its tantric version there would even be women with splendid breasts and luscious lips waiting for the traveller under the cool shade of trees laden with sweet fruits.

Well, that is not exactly how it happened. Fate made me face faults and limitations that I completely and successfully ignored before. Recognizing them now was painful, but there was no turning back. I had tasted the apple of knowledge, and I had to leave the Eden of mindless joys. I found myself trembling alone on the seashore of my fearful depths and heights.

Well, not exactly alone. Mette Hansen accompanied me. Although she seemed to conspire with Fate: she played the mirror.

❖

I ought to say a few words about Mette Hansen. She was the first woman with whom I tasted the exquisite pleasures of conscious, tantric love. I want to talk about her, but words fail me when I try to explain the essence and nature of our lovemaking. There is no point describing it like "my fingers slid eagerly along the velvety skin of her thighs, her lips opened, in a silent calling". The meeting of our bodies was a mere projection of the real lovemaking experienced in that invisible dimension where all "matter" is pure energy and no human language has the words to depict it.

If I only mentioned her keen glance and her hips swaying with maddening eroticism, I would still be far from reality. Not only her curves radiated sensuality but her whole being, especially the magnetic field that surrounded her body. With this invisible radiation that infiltrated everything, she was able to stir powerful waves of delight in me even before our bodies touched.

This subtle erotica beyond bodily sensations that was stronger than any physical lust surprised me and overwhelmed me. I felt like the time my grandfather had taken me out to the roaring sea to teach me how to ride the furious waves with the boat: I had to pay absolute attention to the froth tossing us up and down to be able to direct the prow in the right direction. One moment of hesitation, and waves collided above our heads. Staying above the heaving billows of pleasure unleashed by Mette was just as hard a task.

I suffered a grave defeat on our very first tryst. When the long-awaited moment came, and I immersed in Mette's moistly sparkling rose petal, I simply exploded. Despite all my efforts, my vital juice flooded out of me in seconds. I could hardly understand how it could have happened. I just knelt between her thighs shattered. I looked at her panting lips and eyes opening wide in surprise, the puddle on her stomach, and I could not believe it. This had never happened before! Just like a callow teenager who touches a woman for the first time! To make matters worse, it happened on the very day of the course when Erik spoke about sexual continence, explaining for a whole hour just what a grave and irrecoverable loss ejaculation is for a man. He kept emphasizing that controlling our sexual energy was essential to the practice of Tantra. It needs to be kept at bay and transformed into a more elevated form of energy, and no ejaculation is allowed during tantric lovemaking. And there I was. It had just happened. I felt even more ashamed as we listened to Erik's lecture together.

Ironically that was the first time Mette had visited the beginner class. I had been attending those classes for one and a half months hoping to see her but she was in an advanced class. They met on Sundays when I had to be in Jämjö at the morning mass to do my magic with the organ, and provide some devout atmosphere to Reverend Danielsson's mothball-scented sermons. Meanwhile, however, I could think of nothing else but Mette. The tempestuous belly dance she performed during our meeting set my imagination alight for weeks on end.

And at last she arrived. While Erik was talking, I tried to let her know with unambiguous glances that I would like to put this wonderful and exciting theory into practice. Her expression contained not a trace of refusal. After the class finished she came over to me and embraced me like a friend.

"How long are you going to stay in Copenhagen?" she asked, and my wayward imagination already fancied recognizing sighs of pleasure in her voice.

"I have to leave for home tomorrow, unfortunately."

"And where do you intend to spend the night?"

"Usually I sleep at Carina's, but I don't have to."

"You can come to my place, if you would like. I live alone."

I couldn't wish for more, I almost cried out. But I calmed myself and said simply, "If this is an invitation, I most certainly accept it."

"No, not an invitation. That sounds too formal. A calling, let's say."

Everything started out so perfectly! I was so pleased! And now, there I was, sitting dismayed and drained, among the scattered pieces of my masculine pride.

"If you want, we just have to wait a bit and then I can start over," I suggested faint-heartedly.

"Not today, Bald. If you lose it, then it's over. I don't doubt your body could start over after some time, but it's not the same thing. You need much more energy for tantric love – without that it is nothing more than simple intercourse, and I do not want that. You need to regenerate, at least for a week. Next time, be more careful. I will be too."

I felt terrible, but I could do nothing. In tantric circles it is not the "how many times" that matters but the duration of the "one time". "Keep your chin up," she added to encourage me. "It's not easy in the beginning, but you will learn. I can teach you. If that is what you want," she told me, looking deep into my eyes.

Then she held my face with her hands and kissed me at great length making me ready again. But we did not start over. Mette would not have compromised.

My failure took a toll on me. Not only did my pride suffer, my self-confidence also took a heavy blow. Every time I thought of our next meeting, I was filled with anguish. I was worried I would blunder again. What troubled me most was the idea that somehow I was not suited to tantric yoga, that I did not have the appropriate qualities. Until then I had considered myself a strong and experienced man – twelve years had passed since Carina initiated me into the world of delights, and I had not been idle since that time. It is true that never before had I met a woman with such incredible sensual powers, not even Éva Zoltay possessed that power, though she had much to be proud of. Was it possible one needed more for Tantra than I had?

After three days of agony I decided to visit my grandfather. He was delighted to see me. He guessed straight away that I was going to talk about something exciting again. He listened to my account of events with juvenile curiosity, like he always did when I talked about my love adventures. Once, long ago, I had listened to him with the same eagerness. How marvellous it was to relive this experience with changed roles.

"The Almighty must love you very much," concluded my grandfather after a few moments of reflection, "because He always finds you these wonderful women."

"You can't complain either."

"No, of course I can't. God would certainly punish me if I did. But still, He spoils you a little too much, don't you think?" he asked with a mischievous smile. "You may even find the Island of Delights one day."

"Come now, what would I be doing there with your lewd goddesses if I can't even cope with this one single daughter of man?" the bitter self-mocking burst out of me.

"Oh, come on. What's with the long face? God would never put a burden on us that we can't carry. How gladly I would carry your burden," he added wistfully.

"But what should I do then?" I interrupted him. "I hardly touch her and I feel like exploding."

"Listen to me then. First you need to learn not to keep your thoughts where your loins are. Listen to your heart, try to feel the warmth inside it, and you will see there will be less pressure down there. You need to love the woman, Bald. That is the only way. Love her in a way that you feel your heart would melt, your spirit would expand and transform into a cloud that surrounds the one you love. It will be easier this way. If at any point you feel the volcano is going to erupt, then you just stop. Hold your breath, remain still, and pump the energy upwards" he demonstrated it clutching his fist rhythmically, "exactly like the heart pumps the blood. Feel the pleasure with your whole body so that each and every cell will receive it, not only your groin because it simply can't stand such intensity of pleasure: it spews it out and then you are cut off. If you learn to distribute it in your whole body, from head to toe, like ripples circling towards the shore when you throw a stone in a lake, then you will be able to enjoy the intoxication of love unrestrictedly."

"I wish it was as easy as it sounds."

"It's easier than you imagine. You need a little practice, and a bit more attention. Be very careful, especially at the beginning. Don't let your horse run away with you however strongly he desires the speed, rein him in till you get used to this new feeling; then, when you sit secure in the saddle, you can loosen the reins, and let him break into a trot, then gallop if he feels like. Then let him pause if he needs rest. It's good to catch your breath from time to time on a long ride"

"But, please, do tell me, haven't you ever let it go during making love?"

"Ever?" he laughed out loud. "If I had never let it go, as you say, now who would be asking me this? It did happen a few times because I let it. When we were planning your mother and your uncle, but no other times. How do you think I have ammunition at this age, when other 80 year olds need to be fed and wear nappies? A man's sexual energy is like the monthly wage, Bald. You need to make good use of it so it lasts till the end. Every man receives a certain amount of it when he enters this world, some less, some more – each according to his merits as the Almighty judges it. When it's spent, then it's over, and the once proud weapon will only be useful to urinate with, you see? You can neither multiply it nor borrow it. After the cartridge box has been emptied, your soul dries out too. And that is the time you really start getting old. And die slowly. If you want to live long and stay young even in your old age, then be very careful of your reserves."

"Grandpa, have you ever heard about Tantra?"

"About what?"

"Never mind. But tell me, where have you learned these things?"

"I learned a lot from the Indian girl I met in Bombay. You remember? I talked about her."

"Yes, I remember something."

"What a beauty, good heavens! Fiery like a Malaysian tiger. Sweet, like a juicy mango, and mysterious, like the exuberant jungle where she first lured me to make love. She taught me how to love, how to make love, and would have taught me many other things had I stayed with her. But I did not stay, however much we loved each other. She offered me her life. That means a lot in her culture: loyalty until the grave. I couldn't accept it. I could not offer her my own life. Something kept me back, however strongly one part of my soul desired it. But the other part turned out to be stronger. There were periods when I regretted my decision to refuse her and blamed myself for it. Now I know this is how it had to be. My life had to take another path. And maybe love till the grave is more valuable than loyalty till the grave. I learned much from her – and what I did not learn from her I mastered with experience. Thank God, I had my fair share of experiences. Practice makes the master, even in love. Never forget!"

❖

The next time we met Mette also explained the theory before letting me touch her. She basically said the same things as my grandfather, she just used a more scientific terminology. She outlined the basic principles of tantric alchemy, namely how one can transform sexual energy to another kind of energy, for example will power, love or mental power. She told me that with creative visualization one can direct energy from one centre to the other; and explained what happens in the body during lovemaking. She lectured me about that biochemical transmutation through which the physical material – in our case the semen – turns into energy, and about the process of sublimation, which is the transformation of the transmuted sexual energy into other energies vibrating at higher frequencies.

I did my best to pay attention and overcome the deep-seated hatred of chemistry I had held since school. Luckily, as a result of my grandfather's allegorical explanations, I already understood the concept, so Mette's theory was easier to grasp.

Physical education followed after the chemistry class. I definitely enjoyed that lesson more. With an erotic massage that seemed to make my blood boil, Mette demonstrated how each cell of the human body is capable of producing pleasure. After she had turned my whole body into one erogenous zone came the real ordeal: lovemaking. I gave my best. I felt a bit as though I was in the conservatory, sitting in for the end of term exam where I had to demonstrate the knowledge I had acquired during the year – in front of a highly esteemed committee. I was anxious but strove hard to put into practice everything I had learned. I concentrated, pumped, slowed down, sped up, breathed deep, transmuted, sublimated, but I still had to stop after three quarters of an hour – I was very close to the point from where there is no turning back.

Mette was satisfied with my development. It is true that there was an obvious improvement compared to my previous performance of three minutes, but by tantric standards I was far from even a satisfactory quali-fication.

Afterwards, I did not improve by such leaps and bounds. I had to fight for every inch of advance.

In the meantime I consulted Erik and Carina too. They gave me useful pieces of advice. I really did try to use them but, in spite of all my efforts, our encounters were more like continence trainings even after four or five months. The ecstasy of tantric love I read about and heard about from the more experienced seemed to elude me. There was one time though when we managed to get close to this ideal state. It happened after making love for two and a half hours. We both had been navigating around the highest peaks of pleasure for a long time when I felt the waves of orgasm taking over Mette's trembling body. I was completely carried away by this feeling, but this time there was neither explosion nor did the waves of pleasure subside in seconds like other times. They were overwhelming us with renewed forces again and again, even when we remained in a motionless embrace. That was the first time I felt where tantric love starts, why the duration of lovemaking matters so much, and how remarkable an experience orgasm without ejaculation is. After that I felt like I could fly for days. Mette too, but unfortunately we were unable to relive this experience again. We recreated the same circumstances, but to no avail. It was a unique moment. A gift. A proof that ecstasy does exist.

By then I was living in Copenhagen. I felt I needed to move there, not only because of the tiring weekly travels, but also because I wanted to spend more time with Mette; as practice makes the master. I had also hoped my decision would please Mette.

She had been happy when I told her about my intentions, but in her delight she also presented me with a surprise. She told me that even if I did move there we would not be together much more because she had a lover, Valther, and she would share her time between us.

"You're not angry, are you?" she smiled at me with an innocent look. "I've wanted to talk about it for a long time now, but I didn't feel you were prepared for it."

"No, I'm not angry," I groaned. I felt I'd been punched in the stomach. "So now you feel I am prepared?"

"I don't know. You have to answer that question yourself. You would have found out anyway when you moved here. That is why I'm telling you now."

"But why do you need two lovers?" The words broke out of me in an injured tone of voice, but I regretted saying it out loud that very moment. I was sure she would throw insults in my face about my not so admirable erotic performances. But she did not lose her cool.

"You know, I have been with Valther for two years, and now I have fallen for you too. What should I do? Which of you should I give up? And why?"

"How can you love two persons at the same time?"

"If your heart is open, you can love even more persons. You will see."

She disarmed me with her honesty and natural joviality. I couldn't be angry with her the way I should have been in a situation like that.

She had another surprise for me the next week.

"I talked to Valther. He lives alone in a two-room apartment and he said you're welcome to move in there for a while. In fact, he can even get a temporary job for you at the company where he works."

She spoke with such innocence that a woman's two lovers living together sounded like a most natural matter. "So Valther knows about the two of us?"

"Of course."

"Isn't he jealous?"

"Not anymore. He was when you first showed up in my life, but when he saw that my affection towards him did not change he calmed down. Since then he's fallen for another girl too, Conny. So now he understands me better, and Conny too – she also has another boyfriend."

So that was how I moved in with Valther and became familiar with this strange group, where love spread like a chain reaction, and where the basic unit was not the couple, as it is in all other communities, but the triangle. Valther and I quickly became friends. We never argued about Mette, although there were many delicate situations. Once when I was just about to visit Mette I found Valther in the bathroom, dressed up and prepared to leave.

"Where are you going?" he asked me politely.

"I just thought I would go and visit her, but it's okay, you should go."

"No, no. I saw her yesterday afternoon, so you should go. She will be pleased to see you."

"You know what?" I laughed out. "Let's toss for it."

We did, and I won.

"You see," he said satisfied. "I knew I was right. I am going to visit Conny now that I'm all dressed up."

Another time Mette popped by unexpectedly as we were just having dinner. Valther and I exchanged confused glances. She apparently enjoyed the situation. She sat down to eat with us in the highest of spirits. After dinner I politely left their company to give them some time. A little later Valther sneaked after me. I was just getting dressed.

"Where are you going?" he asked in surprise.

"For a walk. I think she came to see you."

"You're crazy, I arranged a meeting for tomorrow morning, I'm sure she came to see you."

"We'd better ask her" I suggested.

By the time we got back Mette was already preparing to leave. "Sorry, but I really have to go, I just came over 'cos I missed you guys and wanted to see you." Then she kissed and hugged us both and dashed off.

❖

In spite of all my chivalrous courtesy at the bottom of my heart I was still anxious to outdo Valther. Not because we had to share Mette, but for the simple reason that his masculine prowess was stronger than mine, and Mette was able to experience with him the authentic tantric ecstasy we had shared only once. Maybe I was even afraid Mette would lose her patience with me. She never managed to console me with her reasoning that she and Valther were an experienced couple and that, in time, we would be too. I started to lose hope. We had been together for almost a year, and that amount of time should have been enough to get accustomed to the other. I had to face the facts: the problem was with me. I could not properly handle sexual energies, and I could not entirely let go during lovemaking. We had to stop too often and this blocked the free and natural flow of emotions that would have led to the cosmic experience of uniting our souls. This matter also troubled me because I remembered that once, long ago, when Carina first initiated me into the secrets of love, I had been able to control my energies more effectively. Now I felt something had gone wrong. I suspected it had to do with Sibylla who had done everything she could to exhaust me. There were days when she had squeezed out my vital juice three or four times. The urge for ejaculation became so strong under her domination that now my body could not kick this habit in spite of all my struggles. I was most careful while making love but all in vain. The thirsty Succubi, outwitting my will, appeared in my dreams to steal my energy. The most annoying part was that they did not even take the effort to camouflage themselves as desirable women and compensate me for the loss with the ephemeral and illusory joys of an erotic dream. Grim, choking, slimy, reptilian-like bodies clang to me and sucked out my energy like leeches. I was only able to tear myself out of the claws of these nightmares after the sheets under me were soaked. I woke sweaty, exhausted and desperate, as I already knew what losing my vigour meant. Friends of mine with more experience gave me useful advice. I tried to follow them, but that still did not solve my problem. Even practicing yoga more intensively was of little help. The binding that chained me to astral demons feeding on my force was too strong. I thought this binding happened during my time with Sibylla. But I was wrong, it was from before that. No endeavours of mine or those of my environment could dissolve it. Not even the patient love of Mette.

Carina suggested I ask the Master for advice. The Master of the Tantra yoga school lives in Bucharest. Meeting him had long been on my mind, but I could not bring myself to travel to Romania for it. Now the thought started to occupy me more seriously.

Erik had met him on several occasions and encouraged me.

"He will certainly help if you ask him to. That is the calling of spiritual guides, to show you the way, to help disciples overcome obstacles. They take this charge voluntarily, out of compassion, sacrifice and love. We only have to be honest and open in asking their help, because asking for help is equal to accepting him as your Master, and you becoming his disciple."

"But I do not even know him!"

"Exactly! You have been attending his courses and trying to reorganize your life based on his teachings for a year now. It's high time you met him."

❖

It was in May 1996 when I travelled to Romania to participate in the spring camp of the Tantra yoga school. And, of course, to meet the Master.

Four of us went by car: Erik, Carina, Valther, and me. Mette did not come. She was keeping her days off for the summer camp. We arrived at dawn to the mountain resort that was situated in a picturesque gorge. A feeling of profound wonder overcame me the moment I got out of the car.

The scenery bathed in the dim light of the drowsy dawn left a mystical impression on me. The lively murmuring stream running between large boulders, the pyramid-shaped limestone peaks emerging between the darkly greening forests, the sweet and mild breeze tickling the wet foliage, the merry concerto of the awakening forest, the perfume of the dewy grass and the blooming trees, the sulphurous breath of the thermal springs all united in a perfect harmony, and played the symphony of nature delighting each of the senses. One had the impression, that nature itself was following some heavenly command when creating this scenery.

The organizers of the camp had chosen a perfect place for yoga practice, meditation and love. There must have been about three thousand of us. Maybe even more, but it seemed as though everybody knew each other and I had just landed into a large and happy family. I soon realized it was not that everybody knew each other, but all related to each other with an astonishing familiarity. What surprised me most was how easily I became accustomed to that atmosphere. I had always found it tough to make friends, but now I was able to approach anybody with an open heart, like an old friend or a dear acquaintance. For a while I believed it was the spirit of the place that made people this amiable. Later I realized what an important role the tantric spirit had; it filled all participants' heart like the intoxicating scent of the acacia woods filled the valley.

I tried to make the most of every moment, to live deeply every experience, and inhale as much as I could from the love-scented air. Though I had little time to sleep, somehow I did not need much. We recharged ourselves from other sources.

In the nights the four of us visited the thermal pools dotted here and there between the trees. It was during one of these nights when I came to know Gina, well, when I made love to Gina – we got to know each other later. It was one of those mad and unforgettable nights one rarely has in a lifetime.

The pool we had chosen that night was a naturally formed rock-bed enclosed by concrete walls with a generous spring that donated steaming, sulphurous water. About ten people were in it when we arrived. The water came up to our necks but there was no room to swim. A few candles flickered in the niches of the rocky wall. Though dancing flames cast a faint light on the people's faces, darkness reigned under the surface of the water. The moon pried through the foliage at times, and let its rays chase the rippling froth of the brook meandering nearby.

We took off our clothes and sank into the pool. The warm water entwined our body with a blissful caress. We talked for a while and shared our experiences of the first days. Carina and Erik complained about their insatiable sexual craving.

"I don't know what is going on," said Carina in a voice feigning indignation meanwhile hiding her riotous spirits. "It's like somebody fumigated the air with aphrodisiacs. We can hardly separate ourselves from the other to take part in the activities of the camp."

"We should import some of this air to Copenhagen, so don't even think about having a calm and peaceful life at home," smiled Erik at her, and I saw in the glances they exchanged that their desire was rising again.

Valther and I withdrew a bit to "let the youngsters have some time". We engaged in a conversation praising the feminine virtues of the hosting nation's Latin-hearted daughters, though, so far, we only had the chance to admire these virtues from a distance. We were just pondering how we could enjoy a few hot experiences before returning to the cold north when I noticed that although Valther was politely nodding his head to me, he was actually looking elsewhere. A long lock of blonde hair spread out on the surface of the water was approaching him. A charming face captured my friend's disbelieving eyes and lured an excited smile onto his lips. That very same moment I felt fine hands touching my shoulder and starting to caress me giving rise to a soft, thrilling sensation. I resisted the temptation and did not turn back. I closed my eyes and let my imagination draw a body for the sensually caressing hands. Those were skilled hands and revealed much about their owner. They knew exactly how to touch for how long, when to grasp and when to be smooth to produce pleasure. Her hands slipped under my arms and onto my chest, her bosom touched my back for a moment, not more than a split second, then escaped, as though my skin would have burned her tender nipples. I leaned back searching for them unconsciously, but as soon as I found them they fled again. Touched and withdrew. This is how our bodies met, playfully chasing, addressing the other in the most ancient of the languages. My hands could not stay idle anymore. I reached back slowly and felt the silkily soft skin of her hips that swelled below her slim waist. My hands lingered there with delight. The gentle, playful touches gradually matured to sweet caressing. Her hands enclosed me in a tenuous embrace. She clung close to me, and slid up and down on me, engaged in a maddening Thai massage, her panting lips danced on my neck, seeking my ears. I did not see her yet I felt I knew much about her. Not only about her body, but her character, thoughts, and desires too. I already knew the ancient language of the body, and she revealed a lot about herself, with her playful approach. I realized, she was a gentle, emotional, brave and openhearted woman who knows exactly what she wants. She could easily control herself, was experienced in love and had a profound understanding of the masculine nature. I knew all this even though our bodies were still asking questions.

Then questions became more daring, the responses more promising. Her legs clasped my hips, she pressed her thighs to my bottom and started to move her hip gently. Waves swept high in me. I looked around. Valther and his companion were looking at each other with transfigured expressions meanwhile exchanging hushed, mesmerizing words. His blond fairy did not seem to be as pushy as my assailant. In secret I was happy they had chosen this way.

Erik stood a little way away, his back leaning against the rocky wall. Carina was embracing him with her head leaning backwards and eyes closed. I saw the vibrations of hidden pleasures playing upon her slightly opened lips. I knew these telling signs well, and I knew exactly what was happening under the tacit surface of the water

I too decided to knock on the door of pleasures. I slowly turned to face my playmate. Perplexing sight! I almost broke into laughter when I realized how far imagination can venture from reality. She was beautiful and... bald! I had not expected anything like that. But somehow it suited her: the charming features of her face, her plump lips drawn with sensual lines and her dark eyes under the shade of long lashes became more accentuated this way. I looked at her smiling face in wonder, as until that moment I had believed luxuriant hair was an indispensable ingredient of the feminine beauty. I would never have believed a bald girl could be so enticing. And her breasts! Huge, splendid hills, tempting like two redolent melons. Almost unconsciously I lifted her out of the water to contemplate them to my heart's content.

She looked back at me with smiling eyes, but still we did not speak. We understood each other perfectly without saying a word. I started to caress her again. My hands lingered over her mountains at length. I gave my hands free reign, as they had never touched anything like that. Then I felt other parts of her body desired their share too. My hands began to move downwards. The door was open... calling me... waiting for me to enter. But before I conceded to the calling, I let my fingers admire her swollen lips. Then I stepped over the mysterious threshold... We stayed that way for a long time, wrapped in each other's arms, almost motionless. Her face lit by the dancing flames of the candles and the silvery moonlight seemed dreamlike. Her smile became more beautiful with every second – an angelic smile springing from the depths of an exulting spirit.

I do not know how much time might have passed in that ecstatic timeless state. I noticed people coming and leaving. Boys, girls, lovers moved around us, talking, playing, caressing, and who knows what else they were doing under the water, their silent accomplice.

❖

Would anyone accuse Gina of looseness? That she just gave herself to an unknown man. I have to object – Gina did know me. To be more precise: she recognized me. Her intuitive abilities sensed from the very first moments our paths crossing was no accident. Love at first sight? It was more than that. She recognized the possibility of a relationship that will bear exceptional spiritual fruits, and she was not wrong. True, it did not start with polite introductions, romantic walks, or sentimental shenanigans; she chose the most elemental form of making acquaintance. Well, who cares! People are different. Fortunately. Gina was not burdened by paralyzing prejudices. She had the courage to follow the desire of her heart. As for me, I can hardly imagine a more marvellous experience to start such a relationship.

❖

We had been in the camp for four days when the Master arrived. He held a lecture about the art of blessing. That was the first time I saw him. Though from afar I could not discern his features, his voice captivated me. A strong, masculine voice with metallic overtones. One that penetrates to the bottom of the heart, one in which inconceivable and stirring warmth vibrates. While he was talking, I had the feeling he not only sent off simple sound waves, but also finer waves of energy that carry their own secret message directly to the soul. Though he spoke in Romanian and I did not understand a word, the experience was so captivating I was barely able to pay any attention to the English translation.

It seemed impossible to get near as many people surrounded him. The truth is I did not really try because I had heard that during the camp he only accepted to meet people who had urgent matters to discuss with him. Somehow I did not feel my matters would be that urgent. I did not even know what to ask him. I felt happy and satisfied in this extraordinarily spiritual atmosphere. My problems that at home I had considered grave now became ridiculously insignificant; I did not deem them worthy of the Master's attention.

Moreover, the troubles with my sexual energies seemed to be resolved instantly. I could perfectly control myself and sit confidently in the saddle even after three or four hours of intense lovemaking. Though Gina was not as eruptive as Mette, she burnt smoothly and steadily like the fire in the furnace of an alchemist. She could lead me to the source of the eternal life's elixir almost every time; a state to which I can find no better expression than *the ecstasy of love*. Her Taurus personality that bore the refined marks of Venus enabled her to do this. That is why I felt I had everything I could wish for, and I no longer felt it necessary to speak with the Master. I did not admit it then, but I was also a bit afraid of such an encounter. Fortunately, there is always someone who knows what we need better than we do.

One day we went to the market to buy some food. I was busy tasting the goat cheeses. There was one that seemed conspicuously like cow cheese. Everybody was selling goat cheese as that was what most of the campers were looking for as it was known to be healthier. In those days even cows were giving goat milk! I was just trying to figure out how goat the goat was, when I heard Gina shouting out: "It's him!" I saw her running over to a grey-haired man wearing a brown leather jacket. He was at another counter picking out dried basil from a large pile. Then I recognized the Master. I am certain I would have walked past by him had I been alone. Probably all I would have noticed were the two attractive fairies walking next to him.

Gina waved for me to go over. The Master looked at me with a searching gaze, and I felt very ill at ease. I stuttered a greeting in French. He did not return it but spoke to me in French. He asked which country I came from, and how my practices were going. I had the feeling he was not paying any attention to the answers, just looking through me. Still, I thanked him and told him I was making progress with occasional troubles at controlling my sexual energies, but they seem to be solved. I also told him I had nightmares at times that had been tormenting me since my childhood and that during those times these difficulties emerged again.

"With such a wonderful woman, you will only have divine dreams from now on," he answered and smiled at Gina. "but be careful not to only dream, but to realize them also." he continued. Still looking through me he added, "It would be better if you moved to Bucharest for a time. It would be good for you." Then he took out a bunch of basil from the pile that he had bought and handed it to me. "Do you know what is it?"

I knew because I had seen it at Gina's.

"Folk wisdom holds that it protects from demons." I thanked him for his gift and held the strong-scented bunch of basil in my hands confused. We accompanied him to his car. I only managed to collect my thoughts after he left.

Gina danced with joy, but I felt very strained. This meeting caught me unprepared. I was angry with myself for being so thunderstruck. There were so many things I should have asked him. To let such an occasion go to waste, how dumb I was!

Gina tried to console me, "Calm down, it is not the number of questions that's important, but how you interpret what he says."

"But everything we talked about was trivial," I replied. "He didn't even pay any attention to what I said."

"That's exactly it. He was paying attention to you, not your words. And he said precisely what you needed to hear."

"What did I need to hear? That I will have nice dreams? He just said it.

He was making a joke just to please you."

"I know the Master never says anything just for the sake of saying something, and when he is joking you can hear the most essential ideas. That is when you need to keep your ears open. So remember everything he said and you will see what he meant by it."

"Are you saying he was serious about Bucharest?" I asked scratching my head.

"Oh no," she laughed, "he just wanted to please me with that."

❖

They say nothing lasts forever. Maybe it is not completely true, but the camp was over, for good, and I had to return to Copenhagen. It was like arriving to a foreign planet, and I struggled to get back into my everyday life. The people's distant civility and their indifference hiding behind their politeness upset me. The spirit of the camp was still burning in me, and I wanted to love and embrace everybody, to talk about my wonderful experiences, but I kept hitting walls of a cordial and discreet refusal. For a time I still thought I could simply stop an unknown girl in the street to tell her what beautiful eyes and splendid breasts she had. Unfortunately most of them turned away and quickened their step even after a simple smile. When I tried to tell my colleagues at work about my experiences, they politely informed me they were not really interested in my private life.

Mette on the other hand was too interested in my private life. I had to tell her everything. I even told her about Gina. I saw signs of jealousy flashing across her face, but she collected herself and made no condemning remarks. We made love and everything was perfect again. She announced with satisfaction, "I have no idea what they did to you in that camp but it's like you are reformed. I hope it stays this way."

"I hope I will improve even more," I retorted, feigning discontent. But at the same time I was over the moon. The truth is that nobody was as surprised as me. I had no problem with continence anymore. I was completely in control of myself no matter how passionate our lovemaking was. Even after three hours we only stopped because we were as hungry as wolves. I was afraid it was only the effect of the camp and that it would pass with time, and thus I would return to my old self. But after a few months I realized the results were permanent. My nightmares also ceased. From then on, only beautiful women visited me in my dreams – a few times Gina too – and the sheets stayed dry every time. I was able to control my sexual energies even while sleeping!

For a long time I wondered what could have been the grounds of this transformation. Gina's tantric virtues? Or the Master's magical words that in secret had had an effect on me? The bunch of basil I had hung above my bed? Probably all of them together, and something else too. After I replayed my conversation with the Master a few times in my head, a sense started to grow in me that he did not just look through me but had permeated me, repaired something in me, like replacing a faulty component, and that was why I was functioning much better. I heard only real Masters can do that. It seemed incredible to me, something befitting an Indian myth. I did not discard the idea however. The results spoke for themselves.

As the date of the summer camp was getting closer I was more certain of an idea – one to which I had been averse at the beginning. I would move to Bucharest for some time. I wanted to know more closely the man who now I also called my Master.

12. To be a woman…

Everything was so great in the beginning! The spiritual atmosphere of Rishikesh quickly dissolved all those tensions I'd brought from home and at last I found harmony with the World and with myself. The seeds of wisdom born out of Swami's teaching quickly sprouted in the soil of my soul and the flowers of the spirit were already blooming. I tended them with the solicitous love people reserve for rare and valuable plants they have procured at great effort and sacrifice.

Everything was so great in the beginning! My body delighted in the asanas, and every breath of the pranayama was like inhaling the life-giving golden rays of an invisible sun. My mind, that flighty wild horse, was ready for duty and trotted in regular steps towards the wondrous light of the breaking dawn. Day after day I spent long hours in meditation. I was searching for the mysteries of my infinity, trying to find the secret path of the soul's labyrinth to the hidden centre. The true centre of my being which is simultaneously the cause and the aim of all existence.

Everything was so great! Swami's reassuring presence, watchful eye and wise instructions directed me through the unpredictable terrain of my inner journey like a guiding light. The most deeply concealed secrets of Creation were revealed one by one before my feverishly seeking consciousness… I already knew that the visible is merely the herald of an enormous reality invisible to the eye. I had realized that the splendid teak tree under which I mediated so often and with so much joy was simply the material mirror of the true teak tree, of that invisible energy sphere endowed with unique characteristics and qualities, just like the human soul. I had learnt much from that tree: persistence, calm, unbreakable power and the desire to protect. It was not only my beloved tree that I saw this way, but all other creatures of nature. I was starting to feel the meaning of the word *transfiguration* discussed in tantric writings. I glimpsed what it meant to see beyond the material form, to see the soul of things with my own soul. I saw the World in a new light and this fresh vision was stunning…

Everything was so great! For a while… Maybe six months. And then modest waves with silent murmurs began to break towards the surface from my depths. A suspicion. It slowly became outlined as a feeling before crystallizing as a thought. Something was still missing from this, "Everything was so great!" I didn't know exactly what it was, but I sensed something was lacking, and the sensation became more and more acute. It was the kind of feeling of lack that acts as the alarm bell of change ringing in us whenever it is time to move on. A feeling that persists until we have built a new castle of peace from the scattered stone blocks of the old balance. One that again deludes you for a while with the happy thought of attainment – until that too is swept away by the next wave of development.

When this disturbing feeling of something missing had become so strong it prevented my deepening in meditation, I turned to Swami for help... and again my world turned upside down.

Swami's advice was simple but shocking.

"You need to awaken the sexual energy in you."

"But the sexual energy in me is quite awake!" I protested in surprise.

"Yes? When did you last make love?"

"Since I've been here... in India... well, I haven't made love."

"Six months..."

"Yes, six months."

"And you say you're sexually awake! A sensually active woman makes love every day!"

"But what can I do if I haven't fallen in love with anyone since I've been here? And the men don't really approach me either..."

"Why do you think they don't?"

"I don't know... perhaps because... they don't like me."

"Because you keep your distance from them. Because you're not open enough. Because the Woman in you has fallen asleep, like Sleeping Beauty in the cursed palace. You direct your energy elsewhere. You've become a real 'yogi', a student of exemplary discipline... You do your asanas beautifully, your will power is admirable, and you're progressing nicely with the meditation too. I certainly can't complain about it. But you've forgotten something – the most important of all. You've forgotten that you were born a woman. Your real strength, which is indispensable in your spiritual growth, lies precisely in your femininity. That power is related to the universal female principle, Shakti as Tantra calls it. You must become the perfect embodiment of the divine Shakti here on earth. There is no other way for you to attain Perfection! The Creator blessed you with enviable erotic abilities, and Nature carved a stunning body to go with them but, for some reason, you refuse to be aware of this. Don't forget that whatever nature – in its generosity – gifted you will be taken away if you don't use it. Beauty too, if it doesn't radiate love, if it doesn't offer delight it will be quickly withered by the restless Time. Let your body serve Life now while the time is ripe because it is way too late once Death has cast its eye upon it."

In stunned silence I accepted his words, words that fell on me like a rain of stones. His reference to death was painful – it ripped open old wounds in me as I remembered the personal sexual revolution against Death I had once initiated in Seville, a battle, Death nearly won. And now Swami was asking the same from me! Right now when I thought the quiet aloneness of meditation was enough to deserve God's grace? This confused me completely. But I had so much confidence in Swami that there was no way I could contradict him. So I just asked why he hadn't warned me of it before.

"Other things had to mature and become clear for you first," he replied calmly. "You did well, but now you have to move on… You've started out beautifully on the spiritual path, but the road will get steeper, and you'll need a more powerful engine and more fuel to go further."

"What do I need to do?"

"Love! And make love! Let that be your spiritual practice for a while. And remember the tantric saying: *The day that passes without making love is a wasted day.* Let that be your guiding principle. You'll see it will be of great help."

"And if I still don't find a prince able to awaken Sleeping Beauty?"

"Just open the castle gates. Then you'll see. Daring princes will flood in. And then you'll be able to make your choice between them."

"What if I still don't find the right one?" I objected, more for the fun of it as I was already starting to make friends with the thought of my new spiritual task.

"Are you looking for the right one?" he asked smiling. "The only *right one* is the universal male principle personified in Tantra as the great god Shiva. It is He you need to look for because He manifests in every man to a greater or lesser extent… You have told me so many of your wonderful experiences of transfiguration. You've successfully seen beyond the form of things, plants and animals, recognizing their true being – apply this to men too. You'll experience surprising things. And remember, Shiva will manifest for you in men to the extent Shakti becomes alive in you. That is the great secret of Tantra."

❖

I immediately set about putting Swami's instructions into practice, starting to observe men with different eyes. I was pretty surprised to find almost all of them had something attractive – a facial feature, a gesture, a look, a smile. All possessed something remarkable, even lovable. Then, after digging a little deeper, I started to discover what they all have in common and what makes them a *man*. I tried to discover the secret of this universal something, laying beyond their body-mind individuality that one can like or dislike.

226

I searched for the hidden masculinity in each: in the men of the ashram, the big-mouthed tea seller, the beggar shrivelled to his bones sitting by the bridge railings, the orange-robed gurus – and even in the one-legged waiter in the restaurant. After a while I came to the conclusion that this concealed maleness is exactly what makes a man attractive to a woman. And even if it manifests in certain characteristics, it is not actually the characteristics themselves. Traits are always personal while masculinity is universal.

It is true that *universal masculinity* does not express itself in everyone to the same extent. There are those in whom it is stronger – and they are the ones who always make women's hearts beat faster. And there are those in whom it hides behind less masculine characteristics. Here the woman needs a greater skill to transfigure in order to discover it. Of course, transfiguration abilities can be fine honed. I was so successful that before long I imagined I could love almost any man. That's what I imagined...

Swami was right about Sleeping Beauty. It's amazing how men sense when a woman is open. I had only just altered my perspective and begun to look at men with more interest when a group of admirers suddenly appeared on the scene. Powered by the joy of this discovery I started to flirt. In the end I chose only five. Those five who had dressed transcendental masculinity in more attractive costumes. I prepared feverishly to accomplish the spiritual task Swami had set me. My room, that had been perfectly suited to an ascetic, underwent a total transformation. I replaced my mat – used exclusively for meditation and sleeping – with a splendid double bed appropriate for fighting great battles of love. I concealed the windows behind deep red brocade curtains so the filtered light would have an aphrodisiac effect. I liberally sprinkled my new honeymoon bed with all sorts of fragrant wild flowers and draped colourful silks around as though they were each hiding hundreds of secrets. The greatest secret was, of course, me... Then I opened the castle gates to those princes thirsty for my treasures. I didn't want to waste one more day.

But spiritual practice is never an easy task, particularly not in its tantric form however tempting it may seem at the beginning. Difficulties arose immediately. My body was used to lovemaking lasting between ten minutes and half an hour and just couldn't stand the pace. At first I was unable to adapt to the new requirements. After the first orgasm – which happened fairly quickly – I carried on lovemaking only out of good will. I really didn't want to dampen the men's enthusiasm but after the second or third round I was forced to ask for mercy.

The other problem was that I did not feel right anymore with some of the boys after two or three occasions though I'd definitely found them attractive initially. I just couldn't figure out what was happening. I turned to Swami in my confusion and confessed I was unable to follow his instructions. If possible, I said, I'd rather return to my ascetic way of life because this Tantra thing was not invented for me". Swami asked me to recount my experiences. After listening patiently he said, "The first thing you need to learn is sexual continence. You mustn't lose your sexual energy in explosive orgasms any longer. There is another type of orgasm you should learn, the implosive tantric orgasm. This will direct your energy inwards and upwards, and will reverberate in your whole being. You can experience as many of these as you wish, you will not lose your desire. Your emotions will actually become even more powerful. This will indicate that you're on the right path. When you've mastered this it'll be easier for you to attain the wonderful state of continual orgasm. That is the entrance to the sanctuary of tantric ecstasy. Ask the more experienced girls for advice. They'll teach you exactly what you need to do... And one more thing, I didn't tell you to sleep with everyone. It's not enough to be sexually open. You need to open the gates to your soul too. You may love more than one man – if you are able to – but only make love to those you love. There are no exceptions to this rule!"

So I had misunderstood again... although Enrique had warned me about this already. The Seville case had repeated itself with a few minor changes to the script. Unlearned lessons, always avenge themselves sooner or later.

Swami's new guideline hit my group of admirers. After a strict examination only one person remained on the list: Niels Henriksen, a Danish man I was strongly attached to emotionally. The announcement was painful as two of the guys had fallen totally in love with me – at least that is what they claimed. For a long time they did not want to let me go, but there was nothing I could do. I adhered to my most recent guidelines.

Niels had an enormous sexual appetite, and I urgently had to learn the secret of the tantric orgasm so I could keep up with him. My more adept female friends assisted me greatly in this. And not long after I realized with satisfaction that "this Tantra thing had been invented for me" though. Everything was great again! My relationship with Niels flourished. My erotic appetite had reached real tantric heights and, though I wasn't making love every day that was still the most erotic period of my life till then.

So everything was great again... for a while... until another conversation with Swami awoke in me again the need to step forward. I had asked him something I had been curious about for a while.

"Swami, who was your master, the one who initiated you into Tantra?"

"I received my initiation to be a Swami from an Indian guru who lives here in Rishikesh, but my real spiritual teacher, the one whose teachings I follow, lives in an Eastern European country, Romania, where I was also born by the way."

As I asked him to tell me about his master my heart was beating with excitement like one usually feels just before a great secret is revealed.

Swami closed his eyes and went into himself. A new light illuminated his face – the light of a smile coming from a deep and invisible dimension. A few moments later the curtain lifted again at the infinite blue windows to his soul, and Swami started to speak.

"I had been searching for spiritual knowledge for ages when I finally found him. At that time few knew about him, but my soul was thirsty for spiritual knowledge and instantly recognized him. I saw in him the true guide, the initiated adept whose lamp of wisdom can illuminate the secret path leading to the world of spiritual light. I placed my life in his hands and started out on the way with him. My instincts did not mislead me as his teachings became reality in me after a while, and my life finally gained meaning. He helped me to bring treasures from the depths of my soul into the sunlit world of my consciousness: secret desires, the most beautiful feelings, everything I really am. And he taught me to boldly affirm my true self, my emotions, my desires and my convictions before the whole world if necessary. He cast me into the lion's cage of superhuman trials and left me there alone so I could learn to fight alone, so I would be able to find for myself the spring of divine strength, the only source that gives true strength for every fight. Moaning in my torture I fought superhuman battles, trembling in despair, until I finally realized there is nothing superhuman for one who has found connection with the Omnipotent inside. He taught me to direct my life, in every moment, according to the highest principles and ideals without compromise. He showed me how to differentiate between valuable and worthless, important and unimportant... He helped me discover the value of time and taught me not to waste my energy satisfying the thousand armed desires of my lower self. He urged me to always keep the real aim clear and shining in front of my spiritual eyes, and to allow it to lead my every thought, feeling and action. That is why I stayed with him, and that is why I accepted community with him even in the darkest days of persecution under the communist regime, when the triumph of the spirit – that he was so convinced about – seemed like a crazy hallucination. At a time when many of his followers denied knowing him, and even the handful of people who had stayed with him were no longer able to gather for the secret meetings. They were harsh, testing times when doubt and faith were fighting out their ancient battle inside me. But somehow faith proved to be the stronger – and I committed myself to the persecution and prison with him and stayed the course.

"Then I watched the collapse of the communist regime right at the moment foreseen by the Master. I watched as hundreds, thousands and tens of thousands opened towards his spiritual teachings. And I saw as he changed a derided and poor country into a flower-garden of spirituality within only a matter of years… and I looked on as people from all over the world gathered, attracted by his spiritual power. He never performed grandiose or spectacular miracles. But the little miracles of the numerous souls transformed, lives improved to be more worthy of humans and more divine, far outstrip any kind of showy miracle. I saw all this happen, exactly as he had predicted, even when it had seemed the most incredible madness. Predicted? … No, it was much more. He planned and implemented it all with immense effort, out of his boundless divine love and compassion for people suffering because of their ignorance. Seeing all this, my soul began to cry. Because of the shame of having been blinded by the difficulties and doubting the Master's words and with joy that his words had finally become true. Now I know there are no obstacles on the path of those carrying out God's will. The extraordinary life path of a man with unbreakable faith stands before me as an undeniable evidence."

"Swami, I… I would like to get to know this man."

"Yes, you should meet him. After all, he is your true spiritual guide. I am merely the messenger of his teachings.."

"Does he come to India?"

"No. At least he hasn't been here yet. You have to travel to Romania to meet him. In two months time there'll be a yoga camp at a seaside resort. You would benefit from participating. And there you could meet the Master too"

❖

Practically everyone from Swami's Rishikesh ashram moved to the Romanian seaside for the August camp. Swami too, naturally.

I awaited the event with childish impatience, imagining a thousand variations of what it'd be like… Not one was right. Surprises, challenging experiences, humiliating incidents for my ego… a true spiritual camp.

I faced the first surprise when a Danish and an Israeli friend took me to the beach. Hundreds of meters long, it was crowded with thousands of people sunbathing, completely naked! Women, men, young people, old, children, dogs, cats together, in the most natural harmony. Karen – who had been before – had advised us it was unnecessary to bring a swimsuit because we were going to a place where you could sunbathe in the nude. But I had certainly not expected nudism would be so widespread in Romania. I had never once undressed before in a public place and looked around with slight embarrassment before peeling off my bra. Karen strongly encouraged me to continue the process with courage, but I didn't want to consider revealing my lower part too – "Oh yes, so all the acne-ridden adolescents can stare at my fanny."

But that afternoon when we returned to the beach I did feel sorry for my fanny after all. Just how selfish of me to deny her the pleasure of being stroked by the sun rays! As soon as my bikini bottoms were off, I was filled with a novel and strange feeling of freedom. As if I'd been liberated from some weighty burden I'd previously stuck to purely out of habit but had finally realized its oppressive nature. Now, the coastal breeze which tempered the ardour of the sun was finally able to play with my whole body freely, and I was filled with irrepressible joy.

What I really wanted to do was frolic with those mischievous Dalmatian puppies determined to tire their sun-tanned, handsome owner with their ceaseless desire to play. On the first day Noa was unwilling to take her swimsuit off. It seemed Jewish religious rules sew prejudices to one's skin with stronger threads... but of course these fibres could not endure more than one day. The next morning she was freely and happily wandering on the beach, proudly receiving the gazes scanning her attractive figure, already unable to imagine she would sunbathe in swimming costume ever again.

I survived the first test of my prejudices regarding sexuality successfully and relatively easily. But the next tests were to be more problematic. A beauty competition was organized for the yoga camp participants and, bowing to Swami's persuasion, I entered. I passed through the preliminary selection, and we started preparations putting together brief choreographies for the parade. I made friends with some of the girls, and we swapped dresses, jewels and ideas. An extraordinary atmosphere developed between the participants. I didn't sense any kind of competition at all – it was more like preparing together for a special celebration – an exaltation of female beauty. I felt magnificent...

Until I discovered the competition included stages in which we had to appear on stage totally naked... in front of over a thousand spectators!! And in front of the Master! That was too much for me. I was totally outraged. I was astonished the rest of the girls accept it all as natural and self-evident – as if they were being asked to be naked alone in their own bathrooms! I looked for the stage director and, barely concealing my agitation, I declared that I was stepping down from the whole thing. To my surprise she showed no sign of being upset. She took my hand and led me to the auditorium. We sat down on a bench, and she asked in a calm, cheerful voice:

"When you sunbathe on the beach, don't you take off all your clothes?"

"Well yes... but it's different on stage!"

"Why would it be different?"

"Because... on stage... on stage everybody will be looking at me..."

The woman burst out laughing.

"Looking at your bodily charms, I imagine they do on the beach, too." Then she continued more seriously, "It's no different on the stage either.

It's only your preconceptions and deeply rooted inhibitions that make you believe it is, regarding nakedness as a sin, and believing that certain body parts are inferior or something to be ashamed of..."

"No, no. It's not that." I tried to explain, but had to admit she had hit the nail on the head. "But the female body looks better in an elegant dress than naked."

"I would actually say it the other way around – an elegant dress looks good on a beautiful woman's body. But here it is not the dresses that are important. This is not a fashion show. It's a celebration of femininity. Believe me, nothing is more stunning, more wondrous in the whole world than the naked female body, the body of a woman who accepts and who loves herself, who wears her nakedness with radiant dignity. If you don't believe me, ask any man with a healthy appetite, and you'll see that I am right."

"Yes, but there's some... intimacy in nudity, something personal. We usually keep that nakedness for those we love."

"Yes, you see, that's exactly what it's all about. This is the key, and you have expressed it perfectly. Nudity is an expression of love and a profound and mysterious symbol at the same time. The symbol of complete openness, unconditional devotion and full honesty, when all the masks are removed and we present our true selves to the people we love. And why would you not love those people sitting in the audience who have come to bathe their souls in the waters of Beauty? Why wouldn't you love them? And why wouldn't you love the Master? What do you want to hide from he who sees everything anyway, including the most deeply concealed places of your soul? Why wouldn't you open up in front of him and the others? Why would you not experience the joy of devotion that comes from female love? So you can share your body's most valuable treasure with others – your beauty – and awaken people's wonder, bringing to life in them the divine state of awe, helping them to get closer to God? Why not? The magical power of their adoration makes you more stunning, more radiant, you know. This is a great mystery! Why do you think a woman who loves and is loved becomes so gorgeous, so incandescent? Because there is someone who looks at her with wonder. A gaze that ignites the mysterious light inside which is the real source of all beauty. This transfiguration is the enigmatic transformative power of which Tantra speaks. The effect is only multiplied when not just one person, but hundreds, even thousands of people marvel at your beauty."

Her logical argument unwittingly hit the Leo's main weakness of character on the head: the desire *to be admired*. This wasn't what convinced me though. It was the power of her own conviction – stemming from her knowledge about the secrets of the female soul and from a wealth of experience – that had an irresistible influence on me. I decided to participate in the competition after all. The first night of the three-day event began excellently. The uplifting, jubilant ceremony was followed by a personal introduction. I was in my element in front of the microphone. I provided some spirited answers to the presenter's questions and felt I had already won the audience's favour.

The test of femininity and sensuality followed. I watched the girls going up before me with interest. Then the competitive spirit in me began to wake up, and I was reassured to find most of them had some fault with their figure – they were usually fuller than the norm, their movements on stage betrayed their inexperience. I exploded onto the stage with increased confidence. My movements – performed brilliantly, with perfect body control – were awarded an enthusiastic round of applause from the audience. I was certain of my success and confidently awaited the results. But my name was not on the list of girls going on to the next round. I was sure there had been some mistake and went to examine the results. My score was too low to go further... Feeling like the victim of a terrible injustice, I shared my opinion – spiced with some pungent remarks – about the jury with the director.

"Do not forget that this is a test for the female sensuality not a dance competition," she said in a calm but firm voice.

"That's why I find the results so unfair. Girls were eliminated who have much more sensual and feminine bodies than many of those who went through."

"Sensuality is not merely a matter of the figure, but rather a mysterious force which, if awakened, makes the being radiant. Your figure is stunning, and you danced faultlessly, but your body did not radiate. Your movements lacked sensuality, eroticism. Don't forget, one of the most important elements of femininity is bold sensuality."

"But sensuality is not the same as a vulgar wiggling of the hips!"

"Real eroticism is in itself never vulgar, regardless of whether it is bold or provocative. Vulgarity is born only of the limited or perverse imagination of the viewer. When you are more open and let the inherent *power of Eros* express itself, you'll see things differently."

This was the second time I'd been accused of not being 'open'. First the Swami, now this woman. I didn't know what they meant by being open... that I masturbated on stage with no inhibitions?

"Tell me," she continued in a slightly more confidential tone. "Do you pleasure yourself?"

"You mean, do I..."

"Yes, like that. Do you stroke yourself? Do you awaken joy in your own body?"

"I prefer men to help me in this matter."

233

I wriggled out of a straight answer as my attempts as a young girl flicked into my head. Times when I had first tried to ask my body about pleasure, my fantasy ignited by an erotic part in a novel. Then I added, "And men satisfy me completely. I don't need to masturbate."

"They are two entirely different things. A healthy woman needs both. If you keep the erotic energy in you awake with regular self-excitation, you will be able to offer much more delight to men. And you can awaken certain energies in yourself that men are unable to. They can offer you other kinds of pleasures but for that you first need to awaken yourself."

"Okay, I'll think about it."

"Don't just think about it, do it. It's only the doing that brings results. And another thing, learn not to oppose things you don't yet understand. Learn to accept the advice of the more experienced. Be humble, because that is the only way you will learn... that is, of course, if you genuinely want to grow. If not, then stay self-satisfied in your turtle shell!"

Her words were hard as steel – she deliberately sharpened them to break through my "amour". Injured pride needled me to retort with heated coarseness, but... I could not. Suddenly, I felt no trace of ill will in her address. Sobs constricted my throat. She hugged me, gently pressing me to her. As maternal warmth poured out from her enormous breasts, my tears exploded with uncontrollable force. As if something had torn inside me. She began to stroke me soothingly. I thought of Mum because it was the kind of loving touch only mothers can give properly. Sometimes it's so nice, even if you are a grown up... and even if you have been born an arrogant Leo... When we parted I sighed deeply. I would never have thought it would be so difficult to be a woman... or so miraculous...

One afternoon after the meditation there was an announcement for me. I went to the organizers' desk to find an envelope had been left for me. They said it was from the Master. Excitedly I opened the envelope. An invitation, in French, to the Master's villa for six o'clock the next afternoon. Thoroughly surprised, I was, of course, happy too because the main reason for my coming to the camp was to meet the Master. But that he would actually invite me... Well, that was a surprise. I had seen him a few times at communal activities, but had always put off asking for a personal meeting with him for some reason... and now he had summoned me! I assumed he had noticed me during the beauty pageant, but I wondered why he wanted to meet me. I prepared feverishly for the big moment, carefully planned what I was going to tell him and dressed prettily. I rang the bell at the villa gates at the appointed time precisely. A burly, bearded man opened the gate. After I showed him the invitation with the Master's signature, he led me into a spacious lobby, where another twenty-five girls were sitting! When I learned they were also there to meet with the Master, I felt somewhat brought down to size. I'd imagined that if he'd invited me, then he would be paying attention to me only. Unsure what to do, I stood for a while, until a well-built blonde girl made space for me on the couch. I waited tensely. Half an hour later the door opened, and everyone looked up. A red-haired girl came out – with a smile stretching from ear to ear and an unearthly gleam shining in her eyes – followed by the Master, who was in very homely attire: dark purple dressing gown and slippers... He looked around, motioned to one of the girls, and the door closed again. The quiet waiting continued, but time dragged much longer. An hour and a half later the door opened again... the girl came out, her smile from ear to ear, an unearthly gleam in her eyes... The Master motioned to another girl, and the door closed again... I began to run out of patience. If this goes on, I'll be spending the rest of the camp here, I thought, becoming a little irritated. Then I started to meditate to calm myself. Less than five minutes could have elapsed when I heard a strong male voice calling my name. The Master was standing in the doorway, gesturing toward me. Immediately I jumped up and went towards him. In my hurry I stumbled over the foot of a meditating girl and nearly fell flat on my face. I was terribly ashamed of my clumsiness.

The room had a special atmosphere. The thick drapes completely closed out the afternoon sun, and a lamp threw a pale blue light around the room. The Master sat me down on the bed, and sat next to me. I tried to gather my thoughts and remember what I wanted to ask him. He spoke first, with quite good French: "Have you ever had a continuous orgasm?"

His question caught me totally unprepared, and for a moment I was completely confused again.

"What?... No... I don't think so..." I answered weakly with excitement.

"Would you like to experience something like that?"

"Yes... I've heard about it... the girls talked about it... That it is something very special... I hope that someday I can... I will succeed. I try to..."

Without any explanation the Master seated me in front of him in meditation pose, took my hand and closed his eyes. I observed his face for a while, and then I shut my eyes too. My thoughts swirled wildly, my heart pounding loudly. I was simply unable to impose peace on myself. A little while later he opened his eyes and said:

"You still have to open a lot, erotically..."

This was too much for me ... now the Master too! I felt I was going to explode. But he went on calmly:

"And you need to eat more, you're extremely thin," he said stroking my thighs.

"I don't want to put on weight... I feel good as I am."

"When you've gained ten pounds, then you'll feel even better. You'll see..."

I had absolutely no intention of seeing but I listened. The Master stood up and picked up a large box of chocolates from the table.

"This is for you," he offered it to me. "And this too," he continued, pressing a picture the size of a postcard into my hand. I glanced at it. It was a portrait of him.

I realized our conversation had come to an end and it was time for me to leave so I thanked him for the gift and went towards the door. Before he let me out he said, "Be happy and laugh a lot. Don't forget it's all just a game. A wonderful divine play."

❖

I fled to my room to try and put an end to the confusion in my head. I didn't recognize myself. I, who had always been spirited, calm and self-confident. I, who never lost my self-control even in the toughest situations, had now become like a ship off course, tossed this way and that between my wildly-thrashing emotions. I was unable to spit out one proper sentence, incapable of squeaking out a single question from the speech I had planned so carefully. To behave so dumbly and clumsily when the Master should have been seeing the results of my spiritual practice! And what did he see? A jittery, frightened filly falling over her own feet! No wonder he gave me the chocolates as a present. The only thing he didn't say was, "And be a good girl now and make sure you don't get chocolate on your nice little dress". I was even more bothered that I hadn't really felt anything I thought I should feel being so close to a master: a little mini enlightenment, an outpouring of divine love, or something. I didn't feel anything I'd expected to in my first meeting with the Master as Swami had described. Nothing but great confusion!

I longed for the calm, reflective atmosphere of Rishikesh, the strength and security exuded by my favourite teak tree and Swami's watchful deep blue eyes. But even Swami wasn't the same here anymore... He had taken off his orange costume and he'd become so... European! I hungered for Niels's iron hugging arms... but he wasn't here. He was due to arrive two days later. He had gone home to Denmark and planned to come down to the camp for the last week before returning to Rishikesh. I was so looking forward to seeing him. He represented my last refuge.

Niels duly arrived – with his former lover. They'd reconsidered their relationship... Now that was just too much. Anger bubbled inside me like molten tar. Right now, when I most needed him, when he should have been cheering me up! Now when I needed to share my pain with him. I didn't want any of that! Let him go and have fun with whomever he pleased! I was not interested. Let him leave me alone! Naturally I presented it totally differently to him – as befits a student advancing on the spiritual path. I told him he should spend time with his old-new girlfriend for the week because I needed some time alone and deep meditation to be able to process the spiritual experiences I'd had during the camp, and that we would meet in Rishikesh. With its naïve purity his honest spirit believed what I had said, and he really did leave me alone. Now that made me even more infuriated. Secretly I had hoped he would not be able to simply leave me to meditate alone while everyone around me was merrily making love.

The suffocating shadow of bitterness engulfed me when I saw him walking along the beach with his dreamy girlfriend, their arms wrapped tightly around each other. How unfair we can be sometimes! The fact there had been a period in Rishikesh when I'd kept five lovers, like a proud lady of the night, seemed totally natural, correct, even praiseworthy. But then, seeing him happy with someone else... the basest jealousy started to burn me, like a strong acid. Now I understand that it was the vitriol of inner alchemy that, although it causes pain, acts as a healing salve... It cleanses the soul from the pollutants of base and selfish passions to enable us to free ourselves from unnecessary weight and thus rise above to the spiritual realm. At that time however I knew only the corrosive pain that had overturned my spiritual peace. I neglected my yoga practice, somehow I wasn't in the mood for it and during the group meditations I reluctantly took part in murky thoughts and ambiguous, disturbing emotions kept me at a distance from the state of divine peace meditation assured at other times.

Only the evening breeze could act as a balm for my wounds at times. The sight of the sky as it melted into a single dark infinity with the even breath of the sea, finally allowed an uneasy ceasefire to take hold in my world of warring emotions. I liked to sit out on the calm, relaxing beach freed after dusk from its daytime busyness. My consciousness focused on the infinite, I searched the secrets of memories from a distant past and the possibilities of ideal future perspectives. My unconscious fingers sketched pictures of unknown meaning into the quiet sands. Only the sight of lovers walking by called me back into the world of sweetly tempting forms. With a misty, nostalgic look I followed them balancing along the white foamy line where earth and water unite, making towards the tempting dimness behind the end of the beach. And I saw the sea smooth with a few conspiratorial strokes, their embracing footprints.

On one occasion a warm, male voice brought me out of my reverie. I didn't understand what he was saying. Seeing I hadn't understood, he asked me in English if he could sit down beside me. His face seemed harmless, his gentle Bambi eyes mirrored goodness and timidity. He must have spent a long time gathering his inner strength before he dared come over to me.

"Of course," I replied with cool politeness.

He sat at a distance that excluded the danger of touching and started to stare seriously at nothing in particular. We were silent for a good while until he finally picked up the courage to speak.

"I've been watching you for a while. Your fingers playing with the sand and random shells tell me something is bothering you... Can I help? ... Maybe..."

"I don't think anyone can help me... Maybe the One Above."

"The One Above usually helps through other people... Maybe if you speak about it... if you can talk... Sometimes that helps."

"But I don't even know you."

"No problem. Just tell it as though you were talking to the sea, and I'll listen as though the sea is listening."

His familiar look and comforting voice seemed to give me confidence. The honest desire to help made his shy eyes glow. I had nothing to lose, so I started to speak about my camp experiences, my internal fights, my thirst for spiritual peace, actually about everything that reached my tongue. I'm not sure if he understood everything because he didn't speak English well but he didn't ask anything. He simply listened. Like the sea. When I eventually ran out of things to say he was still listening. Then he gathered the courage to speak again – and he really needed that courage as it was a rather daring suggestion. He asked me to join him on a trip to northern Moldavia after the camp to visit some beautiful monasteries, adding he thought the elevated and pure atmosphere of these living centres of spirituality would help me regain my peace. It was an attractive idea and, after a few moments consideration, I accepted his offer. He was glowing with joy. I also felt better already. Maybe because I had been able to give someone a touch of happiness.

❖

Doru was right. The trip to northern Moldavia had a positive effect on me. The refreshing sight of the modestly beautiful landscape, the peaceful calm of the monastery gardens, and the incense-filled air of the churches so painstakingly painted both inside and out, along with the company of the reflective monks re-established my inner balance. As it turned out though, this was not the real reason for our journey...

We were to witness a strange scene in one of the monasteries. It happened on a Sunday afternoon. A disturbed-looking woman of around thirty-five was brought into the church by her relatives. They claimed "an evil spirit had taken possession of her", and that the only person in the area who knew how to "exorcise the devil" lived in this monastery. I had never seen an exorcism. Neither had Doru. We nervously awaited developments. Father Teodosie – who was leading the ritual – was well over sixty. His thick white beard stroked his broad chest, a pair of lively greenish eyes shone out between the delicate wrinkles of his face. Although he had a little difficulty walking, his bearing radiated dignity.

Her eyes flashing all over the place, the woman allowed the two assisting priests to lead her to the centre of the transept but, as soon as the elderly priest started to speak, she was immediately gripped by coarse cursing and vulgar swearing pouring out in a inhuman throaty voice as though the words were bubbling up from deep in her belly. When one of the priests poured holy water over her she threw herself onto the floor with a terrible frightful groan. Her body started shaking convulsively, her face became twisted, her eyes swam in blood, incomprehensible fragments of words burped forth from her throat, she sprayed spit everywhere...

My stomach turned as I struggled with a suffocating desire to wretch. The shocked relatives stood deathly pale, their hands switched to automatic drew fast crosses on their chests. Though Father Teodosie spoke the words of the ritual in a calm, powerful and slightly raised voice, the sweat streaming down his forehead betrayed his inner efforts. The two assistants were giving their all, but the whole scene had no more effect on them than if they had been helping to slaughter a pig on the farm.

Then all of a sudden the trembling ceased, and so did the moaning. The woman's body stretched out wearily on the floor as though it had exhaled the spirit. A frozen silence settled over those present. A little later the woman slowly struggled up and looked around blankly. The two assistants helped her to her feet. Her relatives were still staring, terrified, and didn't dare go near her. Shortly after a woman with a black head scarf – she must have been her mother – rushed over and hugged her, and both started to cry. Father Teodosie sank into a high-backed chair, and his eyes closed immediately.

Doru respectfully watched the scene and said nothing. The whole episode had thoroughly disturbed me. I had absolutely no idea what had happened. I would have liked to speak with Father Teodosie but they told me it wasn't possible. Probably the next day. They said he always spent the rest of the day deep in prayer and resting. I convinced Doru to stay for another day. This man had aroused my curiosity.

❖

Father Teodosie received us the following day. With Doru's help I told him I had witnessed the scene the day before and would like him to tell us exactly what he had done. He recounted that after thirty years of strenuous spiritual practice the Saviour had appeared to him in a dream one night and blessed him with the ability to exorcise evil spirits. At first he had doubted the dream, frightened it was "a trickery of the Evil", but then one day he saw a possessed being at a market who "blasphemed the Lord with vulgar curses", spitting in the eye of those who tried to calm him down. This was to be the first time he put his powers of exorcism to the test, and he had been successful. News of his ability spread rapidly through the surrounding area, and since then he had driven evil out of many people.

As he spoke, his eyes resting on me throughout, enormous spiritual strength radiated from his look. It seemed to be tinged with a little innocent mischievousness. His voice however bore witness to honest humility. He said it was all the work of the Redeemer, that he was merely a channel for His power and deserved no personal recognition for it. After he finished he suggested we pray together. I agreed with pleasure. I asked God for humility similar to Father Teodosie's in my prayer.

When we finished I had a strange idea. I showed him the picture I'd received from the Master and asked his opinion about this man. Although Doru had made me promise – hand on heart – not to speak to anyone of either yoga or the Master because the Romanian Orthodox church by no means held the Master's work in high regard, it was such a split-second impulse I was unable to resist it.

The old priest contemplated the picture before saying, "He is not a man of the church, but he has God's grace… the goodness and strength of the Redeemer floods from his eyes. Who is this man?"

Doru's eyes scrunched up in fear, reminding me not to say his name. All I said was that I had met him recently, and that he guides many people on the way towards God.

"Yes… there are few such people. Too few," he said dreamily, more to himself, and then gave the photo back to me.

We were given a little blessed icon as a gift and, before we bade our farewells, he said to me:

"The Good Lord also loves you very much, and smoothens your way with wisdom. Be strong in your faith and love because it is your love that will lead you to the Almighty."

Then he blessed us both and told us not to forget to look for him if our path took us this way again.

"You're sure to find me here because I still have much to live in the service of our Saviour."

❖

Father Teodosie was the first man of the cloth in whom I felt the power of the Holy Spirit. My meeting with him led me to an unexpected decision. I decided to move to Bucharest for a while so I could be near the Master. My new understanding alchemized the unpleasant events at the camp into an illuminative life experience.

I no longer yearned for the peaceful life, but rather for the Master's disturbing proximity. I wanted to be next to this white lighted sun because I knew that there I would not be able to sweep my weaknesses under the carpet, or to cover my other selfish intentions. I'd have to face my real self every single day and there – I felt – I'd be able to learn the most difficult and miraculous lesson of my life: how to be a woman...

13. Lessons

As the once yellow tram lurched between the tightly clustered houses of the outskirts, with heaps of junk growing here and there, I started wondering whether it really was a good idea to move to Bucharest.

I only relaxed a bit when we arrived in front of a freshly renovated, two-storey building that ruled with noble dignity over the low-roofed houses.

"This is our ashram." Gina proudly presented as she placed her fingertip on the doorbell with a sensual gesture. She had told me there were several ashrams in Bucharest – places where those people live who want to dedicate their life to spiritual practices under the tutelage of the Master.

We stepped into a concrete backyard closed off from the inquiring gazes of the noisy neighbours by a high steel fence. I was surprised to see that, in contrast to the general atmosphere of the city, there was complete order and tidiness in the building. No rubbish lying around. No unclaimed, dangling slippers. Not even a match or a speck of dust. This was a relief. Another surprise came a bit later when Gina showed me the numerous signs and then read out all the 'do not's' in the ashram.

"Strict rules are necessary where many people live together," she explained, seeing my stupefied look.

I was given a room with two boys who spoke no English except for yes and no. Their French was even worse, and as my knowledge in the art of telepathic communication was barely that of an amateur, our main means of communication was gesticulation. My roommates worked in the printing house of the ashram. They were simple, trustworthy guys who always followed the requests of the 'thinkers' on time and with utmost care. They did not complicate their lives with sophisticated intellectual reasoning, most of their sentences began with the phrase, "The Master said..." In spite of this, I learned more useful things from them than I had imagined in the beginning, when I was still fairly convinced that we wouldn't have much to talk about even if we spoke some common language.

Differences between the Balkan and the Scandinavian mentality caused a few difficulties at the start, but with time I learned how to sustain a Balkan behaviour only as much as the situation required, meanwhile keeping the righteous side of my Scandinavian self intact.

❖

My first meeting with the Master in Bucharest was a shaking and shocking experience.

One day, after lunch, I forgot to wash my plate. The person in charge of the kitchen immediately rushed to the Master to report the delinquency, carrying the material proof – the plate bearing the traces of the spinach I personally ate. The Master summoned me to the scene of the crime and proceeded to give me a tempestuous dressing down the like of which I had never heard before. Even innocent bystanders buried their necks in their shoulders, as though a tremendous thunderstorm had caught them in the middle of an open field. I was crushed and buried under the avalanche of his heavy words. My self-esteem, or just a flicker of it, tried to come forth with some kind of explanation, but I was to bitterly regret it the next second, when the hailstorm of the mastery words crushed me down with a renewed force. Glasses clinked alarmed on the shelves, and the kitchen girl, who never imagined her well-meaning intentions would cause such a catastrophe, took fright and glanced at me apologetically.

Those around were looking at me with genuine compassion as I stood there mourning the ashes of my pride, and as I slunk out of the canteen with the fading promise of "never again" on my trembling lips.

I was lying in the room, broken, when Gina found me. My wounded pride made me mutter the back-story of my miserable state in a rather accusatory tone. I voiced my strong dislike of the kitchen girl, and declared the Master's scolding unfounded and unfair. I had no idea why anyone would deserve to be admonished in such a manner for one single dirty plate.

Gina did not share my agitation. "The Master doesn't usually rebuke someone without reason, especially not unfairly. I am certain his thundering admonition was not merely for this small transgression. He must have been aiming at something else with the laser beam of his words. He probably noticed and wanted to eradicate seedlings of some destructive tendency rooted much deeper – your mistake might have been just a hardly noticeable symptom. All he did was to make use of the first occasion for this painful but necessary surgery."

As my temper subsided, I placed myself under the microscope of self-analysis. I suddenly remembered: my roommates had told me more than once that I always left my belongings strewn around and that I was inclined to neglect my daily yoga practice. Looking at my history I was able to diagnose myself with a severe case of untidiness and disorder that my father's treatment had been unable to cure in my childhood. And since then the matter had become even graver. Finally, I had to admit the Master's diagnosis was correct, so I ordered my own treatment that very moment. I was already well aware of the importance of discipline on the path of spirituality.

I started with the small things. I organized my wardrobe, my bookshelves and my papers. Even my father would have been proud of me had he seen me. After that, I asked the Master to determine my daily, obligatory hours of spiritual practice, and I solemnly swore to follow all his instructions without discussion. Following the "ask and you shall be given" divine legacy the Master dictated my tasks: five hours and forty-five minutes of yoga practice every day. That was my spiritual task for the next twelve months!

At the time I did not realize how difficult this job I had just undertaken was. If I had, I may not have even started as even in my most active days I had never practiced for more than three hours a day. In the first weeks, with the momentum of a beginner, everything went well. I felt the refreshing effects of the hard work, and the results of the practices I was doing with such enthusiasm were inspiring. In the second month I needed greater willpower, especially when I put off the practices till night when I was already tired, and that happened more and more often.

In the third month I would have done anything except yoga, but I endured it heroically. I did the exercises faithful to my promise – though my thoughts kept wandering farther and farther.

The fourth month was a period of inner crisis. My reserves ran out, my mind rebelled, and I searched everywhere for loopholes: Exercises made painfully and without concentration are of no use, I reasoned. They were pointless and would actually have been harmful to continue with them. Spiritual practices like that are nothing more than a torturous burden. It would have been good to take this load off my shoulders, to be free again like before, to have time to live, love and make love, to follow my heart. That is what Tantra tells us – and that is why I chose this spiritual path, to become free through it, to take delight in life and its gifts. Yet here I was. Six hours were being stolen from my life every day. It was worse than being locked in a monastery. There at least you can turn your back on life, but here life went on around me; trees were blossoming, marvellous feminine curves were highlighted with light dresses, and I had to sit eyes closed between four walls, for five hours and forty-five minutes every day – and eight months and three weeks still to be accomplished). I felt it was an inhuman task to undertake.

These thoughts led me to the conclusion that I should give up and move back to Copenhagen. I felt if I broke my promise, then I would not be able to live in the ashram any longer. I was still hoping I would unexpectedly get sick, or be completely exhausted, or something similar. Anything which would give me grounds to give up without damaging my reputation. Unfortunately nothing like that happened. In the end I realized I had to choose the only possible way out, the disgraceful retreat. One night I confessed my plan to Gina. She scolded me and told me never to think about anything like that ever again. She explained how privileged I was to be on such a path, to have the guidance of the Master, to have the opportunity to develop under his direct instruction.

"You cannot even imagine how many people yearn for such an opportunity," she said with noble passion in her voice. "You too. Through how many incarnations have you desired and prepared for this moment? Would you really quit after all this for an easy life, out of weakness or cowardice? You call yourself a man? Would you just break the promise you made to the Master? Do you know what it means? It is a cowardly submission to demonic forces which continuously tempt your faith, willpower and perseverance. Now tell me, how do you think you can dominate immense powers that lead to higher levels of the cosmic experiences of Tantra if you cannot even cope with your own wandering desires? You have to train yourself! You need to keep the fire of your spiritual efforts alive as long as it burns through all the negative karmic debris! Otherwise, you will never get further than being a mediocre dilettante of Tantra, and you will trail on the path, powerless."

Her mention of demonic forces made me reflect. I knew the disciple who fails a spiritual trial would remain, for some time, in the hands of the demon that had tempted him. I had already encountered these not so benign creatures in my life, and not a cell of my soul desired meeting them again.

"All right, all right, you've convinced me. I will continue until my last breath, but to be honest I don't know how long I can take it."

"God would never lay a burden on you that you could not carry. He gives you strength to overcome the obstacles, you only need to believe."

"I wish it was like that," I sighed.

"I will help you if you'd like me to," she spoke softly, looking deep into my eyes.

I immediately concluded what kind of help she meant, and of course I did.

"Now forget about everything," she continued. "Forget about the practices, forget about the past. Do not even think about the future. Never mind yesterday or tomorrow, what has passed and what will come next. Focus only on the now."

It was not too difficult – the now suddenly became very exciting. Her hands boldly started caressing me, her voice was mesmerizing. Fire, like liquid flowed from her eyes into mine, electricity crawled all over my body. Then she took my hand and began to direct it. My fingers exulted in touching the smile of her lips, the blush of her cheeks, the gentle vibrations of her thirsty skin. Her awakening breasts and radiating nakedness made me forget about everything else around me. That was the first time I felt the timeless now state Gina talked about. As we played on, more and more emotions managed to free my mind from the trap of time.

We made love only for a short time that night. Gina knew my yoga for the day still had to be done, and mercilessly stopped me just when it was at its best. Hunting pleasures was not her intention that moment – all she wanted was to put me on the right track of spiritual practice and, as an experienced tantric initiatress, she had found the most suitable method. She managed to make me see that a simple yoga practice can also be as wonderful and ecstatic as making love, but only if I concentrate on the now every moment, on my emotions and state of mind that appear during practice. I realized the success of my asanas were hindered by my own thoughts like "I have not developed for a week now" or "there is still a lot to do", "I have to wake up early in the morning", and "if I don't go to bed soon, then I will be tired all day", or "I would rather have a walk now". In fact it was my mind wandering and roaming about in the past or the future that made my tasks insufferable. Present is always ecstasy!

I felt illuminated by this recognition. And I was utterly grateful to Gina.

From that moment on, yoga was among my greatest joys. The discovery gave me new strength, and results were immediately visible. I admit I still had some difficulties. Many times I had to reach into my depths to complete my practice, but I never again entertained even the slightest thought of giving up – and that made my job much easier. In the end this is how the mind works; if it knows something cannot be done, sooner or later it will no longer even consider it.

I can barely describe my feelings during the last days of the twelfth month; it was a real celebration. A festivity of victory and thanksgiving. I had triumphed over my weaknesses, and just like in fairy tales when the conquered fighter's strength flies to the victor, I felt immense strength in me, and I was certain I could accomplish any task however difficult it might be.

I was delighted to share this achievement with the Master, and thanked him for his help. I was honestly grateful for him giving me such a hard time, as now I had reached the finish, I felt reborn. I told him I wanted to travel home to Sweden to visit my parents, and after my return I would like to put more energy into music and the arts. The Master answered that my parents were all right, I should leave them alone, and I should not distract myself with music because I was needed at the building site of the new ashram.

"But I do want to go home," I insisted. "I haven't seen them for more than a year. I promise I'll help with the ashram after I come back."

"All right then," nodded the Master. "If you want to go that much, then you should go. But be careful."

I had no money for the trip. I hoped I could borrow from someone.

Asking for money did not go as smoothly as I had thought. Nobody around had enough money to cover my expenses – even my more affluent acquaintances told me they had just run out of money. I asked more than twenty people and could not think of anyone else who could help me. Gina was not happy about me leaving, but in the end she took pity on me and asked one of her friends for the money for my flight.

❖

The family reunion did not go quite as I had imagined. Although my parents were happy to see me, when they found out it was only a short visit and I was planning to return to Bucharest, the storm broke out. The division of household jobs was perfect. While my father roared and thundered, my mother's eyes provided floods of tears. Up until then they had overlooked the "senseless adventures" of my life and my "useless way of life" hoping I would eventually grow up and conform to society and a normal way of living. But when they realized I had no inclinations for either, they grew desperate. I explained in vain that there are other ways of living which are just as natural – and that they conform to the social norms just like the way they live, only on a higher level. They still did not understand. My spiritual values were totally outside their sphere of interest and experience. I told them about the spiritual path, the understanding of life's big questions, the Master, the practices, and everything that was an important part of my life. It was pointless. They only found validity in the values accepted by their immediate surroundings, the manifestations of which are a "successful career" and a "peaceful, balanced family life".

My father moaned mainly about my disinterest in my career. He might have made peace with my decision not to enlist as a soldier, as he had once dreamed of, but the fact that I was even neglecting my musical career made him bitter. My mother grieved over my lack of desire to settle down with a family; she would have liked her only son to increase the already populous gaggle of grandchildren.

We called a ceasefire in the interests of domestic peace, deciding we needed to avoid such topics. But then the cold war started. Behind many over-polite utterances, I was chilled by the icy breeze. My spirit – that had become used to the Balkan currents of emotions – could no longer stand this cold Scandinavian climate.

❖

One day I visited Arne Larsson. Time had made my once adventurous friend into a happy, balding family man. He had a respectable belly and two golden-haired daughters with mischievous eyes. He jovially spoke about his parish where he was respected and loved. Arne did not learn about life from books and this helped him to find the way to his flock's souls more easily. His sense of vocation, originating from divine inspiration and deep calling, turned him into a genuine spiritual pastor. He did not hide his sparkling wit under his minister's cloak – not even when preaching. He changed the centuries-old god-fearing spirit in his church to an impassioned, cheerful way of loving God, and laughter moved between the imposing walls. "God has a sense of humour too, you know," he explained, quoting his kindred spirit Anthony de Mello, "Why else would he have created man?"

I talked to him openly about my experiences. Although he did not understand everything – and did not agree with many things – he accepted my ways and lifestyle with a goodwill proving his wisdom.

It was good to see that real friendship continued to exist, no matter how different our paths were and even now that we had no shared adventures. As tangible proof of our indissoluble friendship, he even gave me money for my journey. I knew I could no longer depend on my parents, and was happy to accept the gift. He did not let me leave without an enormous dinner, and two glasses of fragrant red nectar Lord Jesus himself would not have refused.

On my way home I took a short detour to the beach. I sat on a bench, and stared at the foreboding, restless sea. No part of me wanted to go home, and the next moment the thought cut to my heart that I did not even really have a home. Arne's warm family nest came into my mind: his pretty wife bustling around the kitchen filled with the scent of cakes, his golden-haired little angels chattering, and the flames flickering behind the bars of the cosy fireplace. Depressing feeling settled on me like a heavy shadow. The feeling of loneliness and homelessness. My life in Bucharest with its spiritual ideals was suddenly banished to the background by tangible shapes, seductive tastes and scents. I stepped onto a path once, but where is the guarantee that I will arrive somewhere? Who takes responsibility for this? The Master can only show me the way, but I have to walk it alone. What if I do not have the strength to endure until the end? What if there is nothing at the end? What if, while chasing the fata morgana of the absolute truth and spiritual self-fulfilment, I waste my life? A life that at least seemed real. Leaden clouds of doubt covered the light of my spirit. The shadows of the night bore a frightening uncertainty. Yet, I knew there was no return. I knew the family nest – that seemed so seductive in my lonely state – would only have been able to make me happy for a short period. My restless spirit would drive me away, towards some unknown, intangible destination. But as this destination did not have an outline, not even a hint of its existence, I felt nothing, except emptiness. Even thoughts seemed to elude me.

I felt dazed and must have dozed off for a second because I was awakened by the light of sunrise flooding the horizon, as the golden sun emerging from the sea spread a brilliant carpet across the surface of the water. I started swimming towards the sun. Blood and strength pumped in my arms, an unfamiliar delight twinkled in my heart. A large, dark cloud crept nonchalantly in front of the sun, and the golden trail vanished into thin air. It was a heavy sea. The waves started breaking over my head, higher and higher above me. I tried to swim, struggling impotently between the mountainous waves, but I could no longer find my way. Scared, I looked around for the shore. All I saw was infinite water – all around me – and indigo clouds whirling above my head. Fear of death consumed my heart and desperation paralyzed my arms. Then I saw a silver-winged seagull emerging above the water, circling, and then flying off into the distance. I began to swim towards it with all my might. The presence of another living creature between the furious elements gave me new hope, and this hope gave me strength. Waves crashed in my face and my hair fell into my eyes, but I was heading towards the dot of silver light hardly perceptible on the dark horizon. The dot kept getting smaller until the darkness absorbed it. Clouds began to lift at the point of the sky where I last saw it, and the sun appeared out of the clouds flooding the water again with its warm, golden light.

I woke up shivering and soaked to the skin, my drenched hair flopped into my eyes. Cold, misty drops were drizzling down, and somewhere far out in the sea a little pinprick shone, maybe the lights of a ship or a lighthouse on one of the islands.

I shook off the water and decided I had better go home.

❖

The next day I reserved the flight to Bucharest with the money Arne had given me. The thought of our separation melted the icy temper of my parents, and I felt much better. My vision on the seashore had left a mystical sensation in me. I was fully aware it was a message sent from the secret shrine of my higher consciousness. Even if I could not interpret it, I knew the clouds were disappearing and I reckoned I could see a way ahead. Still, it did not alleviate the harshness of the lessons awaiting me, but at least I knew everything that happened to me had a meaning and purpose. I understood the need to learn and from then on I no longer felt attending school as an obligation; I simply followed my inner impulses.

After I had successfully completed my yearlong spiritual practice, I felt as though I was entering a higher class in the school of life. One where I definitely needed the extra energies I had gained, because the lessons became harder, and the knowledge about the anatomy of my soul became even more complex. The lessons were not without pain either as the scalpel cut into the tissue of my very mind, and the invisible soul-surgeon used neither tranquillizer nor anesthetic.

With a conscious alertness I had to experience my depths, to face my unhealthy dispositions, my abscesses of imperfection and grotesque character flaws being opened up on the operating table of precipitating events. I was forced to begin the self-healing for which I knew I would need all my stamina.

❖

As soon as I got back to Bucharest reality caught up with me. On the bus from the airport to the city my wallet, along with all the money Arne had given me, was stolen. The money that would have helped me to settle my debts. Anger burst out of me like destructive lava. I cursed and blamed the country, its people, the thief... Everything and everybody – except my own carelessness.

After the flames of temper subsided, all that remained was the paralyzing ash of hopelessness in my mind. I had no idea what to do in a foreign country, in the middle of a foreign city without a penny, and, of course, carrying a huge debt. As I did not have money for a tram either, it took me an exhausting hour to reach the ashram. I forced a few a smiling grimaces to the people I met, then escaped to my room and closed myself in. I tried to find some solution before meeting Gina. The only remedy of the situation was to get a job urgently and get together enough money to repay my debts. Though Gina was not happy about the news, she was not upset about the debt. She simply listened to the story, her mind musing over the roots of the happenings. Then she asked:

"What did the Master tell you before you left?"

I admitted he had objected to my departure, but let me go in the end and said if I wanted go to home so much then I should, and that I should be careful.

"You see," she said with eyes shining, like someone who had just found the key to something mysterious. "The Master told you to be careful. This was not a simple formality, but a serious warning."

"Are you saying he foresaw the events?"

"I wouldn't know whether he foresees something or not, but I know he senses the harmony of things perfectly and, if he had an objection, then it means your return home somehow did not fit into the natural flow of things. You forced it, and forcing is a false note in the symphony of life that sweeps towards unpleasant surprises those who lost the harmony. He, considering your right to free choice, could not forbid you to act against your will. He could only warn you."

After I talked to Gina, two more details came to my mind that had escaped my attention until then: when I went to buy the plane ticket, an old woman's purse was stolen on the bus. That time, I reached to check my wallet and held it tight until I got off the bus. The incident had completely slipped my mind. I also forgot that a few days before I had overheard a discussion about professional thieves who often choose as their hunting ground the lines to and from the airport in the hope that most people travelling have money on them. I felt there was somehow a connection between these two events and my misfortune, but was unable to figure out the nature of their interrelation – I decided I would pay more attention to the Master's words in the future.

I met him the next day.

"How was your journey?" he asked with the slightest smile on his lips.

"Illuminating," I answered. Self-mockery was blatantly present in my voice.

I realized he was not asking me as a simple formality. The Master was interested what conclusions I would draw from my experiences. I told him everything: meeting my parents, my visit to the shore, my money troubles, and I recounted the spiritual conclusions I had arrived at.

The Master did not make any comment on the events. He reached into his bag and took out a few banknotes.

"Take these and settle your debt. "

My first reaction was to protest vehemently, but then I remembered Gina's advice never to refuse what the Master gives, whatever it might be. I accepted it but felt ashamed. I told him I accepted it only as a loan and would repay him as soon as I could.

Next morning I volunteered at the building site to work as I had promised the Master.

❖

I had never done any hard physical work before – and I had never imagined it would be so hard. I was assigned to work eight hours a day, but due to the enthusiasm and working capacity of my co-workers we often worked 12-14 hours a day. The heavy bags of cement and wheelbarrows full of concrete exhausted my muscles within no time, but I felt too embarrassed to rest especially when I looked at the others who were working with such joy. I drove myself as hard as I could. I shovelled mountain-high heaps of sand and carried unwieldy iron pipes, my knees nearly collapsing under the strain. At night I collapsed into bed dead-tired with aching muscles, and in the mornings I felt I had to fight a supreme force of gravity to drag myself out to the building site.

After many of these heroically accomplished working days Gina deployed her charms and all her tantric knowledge in vain – I was numb to all seduction. Even if at times she could light some desire in me, I was unable to live up to my potential in these love games, especially when facing such a superior vitality. Although she never complained, I felt lousy after these encounters. I have to admit, they not only stood far from tantric lovemaking – they were not even worthy of an ordinary sexual intercourse.

In addition to all that, I had neither the time nor the energy to practice yoga, read or anything else I thought necessary for my tantric practices. I would have gladly escaped from the building site, had the Master not paid off my debt. But I felt it was my obligation to stay there as long as he saw fit. Although at times I complained to him that doing this work left me no time for what was important for me, he seemed not to hear me. He had a completely different opinion of what was important for me and gave me not one word of encouragement that I might leave the site in the near future. So I stayed – and felt like a martyr.

About six months later my situation had improved. My body had become accustomed to the heavy work and my muscles were much stronger, so the work felt nowhere near as strenuous. The building was ready so we started the interior work. My pleasure-giving abilities had developed too, though still far off mark in terms of Tantra or considering Gina's demands.

That is when Ramona appeared on the scene. Well, that's when we got close to each other. She had actually been there for some months and, though we had been working on the same building, I had barely noticed her. We had hardly even said hello on the occasional times our paths had crossed and we had never talked to each other. I did not even know her name.

Until one time she succeeded in making me see her.

I had just finished working in a room and was cheerfully stretched out on the freshly tiled floor, allowing my body a little laziness when Ramona came in carrying a tin of paint and a paintbrush. She was wearing a flimsy, light green dress splattered with paint. Her make-up showed great care and little expertise. When she indicated she wanted to paint the sash frame, I moved not a muscle as I told her to feel free to work on whatever she liked as I had already finished my task. She sashayed smoothly to the window, stood on a chair and began to work. She painted with practiced, graceful movements. I watched her out of the corner of my eye and saw her looking at me occasionally. After a while she started to chat about trivial matters – with a startling warmth in her voice. I responded politely. (My Romanian was pretty good by then.)

When she gained a little courage she told me she had seen me before and wanted to get to know me, but had never found the right moment. She even blushed a little, admitting she had only come to that room because I was in it. Then she suddenly went silent, turned back to the window and, absorbed in the moment, began to paint the frames again – without realizing there was no more paint on the brush. I looked at her with growing interest. As the sunlight streaming in through the windows lit her shapely form, she seemed attractive. I only had to slide a little towards the window to peek under her dress, and I was well rewarded for that effort by the exciting sight of the swelling mounds at the meeting of her fleshy thighs, partly covered by a silk bikini. Her loose clothes also allowed me an impressive view of her impressive breasts.

The sight of naked skin kindled my passion in seconds. I slowly stood up and stood behind her, very close. The brush in her hand stopped moving. Her body trembled gently, but she did not turn round. My nostrils flared as I inhaled her natural scent mixed with perfume and the smell of paint, and then suddenly I reached up under her clothes, and with a gentle but definite movement I scooped her breasts into my hands. She muffled her shriek, I greedily pressed her quivering body close to me and felt all her instinctive resistance melt away.

I watched in delight how desire overcame her under the siege of my purposeful fingers and lips, how the awakening ancient forces of nature pushed apart her thighs and compressed every thought into one desire, into one silent supplication. I yielded to her impatient urges ecstatically. She received me in sitting on the freshly painted window ledge. After that we matched our bodies, our energies and fantasies in every possible position. Ramona was tremendously generous and complying. It was staggering how she could laugh so like a child while we were rolling about in the puddle of paint! When we finally tired of the chase we spread out on the floor, exhausted from the heat of the game. The room looked like a bloody battlefield. It took us two hours to wash off the mess of that crazy afternoon. The tiles were beyond repair, so the next day I had to break them up and lay new ones.

From that day on many rooms under construction became silent witnesses of our secret rendezvous, but we did learn not to use paint during our erotic games again. Ramona fell deeper and deeper in love with me. Her body opened up at my approach as though I had put a spell on her: any moment I wanted I could make her mine. I felt splendid in her loving embrace, and in secret I wished the construction works would never end...

I did not say a word to Gina. For some reason I did not dare confess this adventure. Ramona knew about my relationship with Gina. She even mentioned to me every now and then that it would be better if I talked about us to Gina. Yet I kept stalling. Until the time when Gina caught us... in flagrante!

Chills run through me to this very day when I think of that painful shock I saw form on Gina's face. She looked at me incredulously, not believing her own eyes. It was all done in a second. She closed the door and ran away.

In the evening I visited in her room. I did not want to explain. There was nothing to explain.

"How long has it been going on?" she asked with a barely noticeable shake in her forced calm.

"Well, about one and a half months."

"One and a half... Well, that's just great," she took a deep breath before continuing, "You know, Bald, I do not care about you and Ramona. You are a free man, you have the right to do whatever you feel like, but why didn't you tell me about it? Why did you keep it a secret? For me the most important things in a relationship are being open and sincere, and the mutual respect."

"I know, I made a mistake. I should have told you about it."

"One more thing, I do not even understand why you feel the need for two relationships when you cannot even satisfy one," she was having a hard time keeping her temper. "Keep two lovers only if you can make both of them happy, and if you can love both of them. Otherwise you aren't fully present with me, and I am certain this troubles Ramona too."

"But you also see that things have started to be better between us," I tried to defend myself, but Gina was not finished.

"Just think about it and make up your mind. You need to decide, me or Ramona. But I want to see that you make at least one of us happy."

Hearing the ultimatum in that form, my masculine pride sprang to its feet. I may have expressed my views with more vigour than I should have. I told her categorically that I had no intentions of giving either of them up, saying it was high time she grew out of her hysterical fits of jealousy.

She said no more, and I was satisfied I had been able to make her see my side. I was wrong. She just did not see the point of continuing the argument with me. But I only realized that when she took my hand the next day and said, "The Master wants to speak to you."

I knew she must have told him everything, and I also had a vague idea about what would come next. I quickly tried to figure out a defence strategy. I pre-composed a few contra-arguments I considered acceptable, and evaluated the possible attenuating circumstances. But the moment I found myself face to face with the Master and his razor sharp gaze, the words froze on my lips.

"There are complaints about you, again!" I was overwhelmed by his thundering voice, a tone that burned even the thought of apology to cinders. "I thought you had become more serious by now and finally understood why you are here – and that spiritual aims guided you in your actions. But now I see you let your animal instincts drive you, and you are indulging the demons of egoism again. For how long do you want to vegetate in this miserable state? For how long do you plan to wallow in the mud of your inferior desires? Did you think that using Tantra as an excuse you would be allowed to indulge in uncontrolled lust and use the loving attention of the girls here to give full vent to your bodily desires? That is what Tantra means to you?! Is this how you interpret the spiritual path? You seem to have expelled not only your spirit but also your soul from your acts! Do you know what you have done? You have violated the very spiritual path, the path that creates the greatest miracle love. You think just because you were born to this world with a handsome face, you can get everything and every woman has the duty to worship your masculinity? How dare you assume the right to tread on another's sensitive soul! You thought that is masculinity? Well, it's not! Only the lowest of the low behave like that. Those, who are drunk with the thought of their own wit and use the kindness, self-sacrifice and love of others for their despicable and selfish purposes. These worms of the earth think they can escape the consequences of their acts. But this is not mindfulness, not even cunning, but the most pitiful, pathetic stupidity."

His words felt like sharp arrows piercing through my flesh. I would have sought refuge in a mouse hole had I been able to, but I had to stand there with naked conscience in the cruel hail of arrows that felt like would never end.

"When will you finally grow up? When will you tear away the chains of your own greedy interests? When will you become a man?! Here you stand in front of the door leading to infinite spiritual values, and instead of stepping in, you waste your time and gifts on worthless sex parties. When will you learn to *love*? When?!"

He was capable of pouring rebukes with frightening force. Lights of an all-knowing mind condensed into a divine flash of lightning because his words, bolts like well-aimed bullets, besieged the weakest points of the bastions of my ego until the Babelian tower of my conceit, arrogance and empty desires were all reduced to dust.

Based on my reading I had imagined spiritual masters as warm hearted, white-bearded old men who meditate serenely in the circle of their disciples, respond wisely to their questions and gift the most diligent with flashes of enlightenment. But my meeting with this flesh and blood Master had quickly demolished my misconceptions. This Master showed a face, rarely mentioned in books. Amongst all of his faces this terrible one was the most astonishing – and it somehow reminded me of the wrathful deities of the Tibetan tradition.

I stood in front of this phenomenon uncomprehendingly until I realized there was not the slightest trace of anger in these stormy outbursts. They contained only compassion springing from the depths of his soul, and were filled with love to have such striking power – the kind of love that does not spare (because should not spare) the worthless and harmful flaws. This love, like the sun that brings fertility, animates the seeds of the spirit laying somewhere deep inside.

I only understood this when someone else was targeted by the arrows of lightning. While I was standing in the fiery circle, I was in no mood to analyse these observations. At such times I felt like a defendant who just heard the death sentence – with no appeal – someone who in the momentary enlightenment of his awakening spirit recognizes the weight of his own actions. Only after the Master's rebuke did I realize just how appallingly selfish I had been with Ramona and that I really was interested only in my own pleasure. She had unconditionally placed before my feet everything that was beautiful in her: her body, heart and soul. But I had given her nothing except my lust.

I had never presented her with anything. Not a single flower, a kind word, or anything that would have let her know she meant more to me than mere breasts to grab or a groin to take delight in. That she was more than a body I could use any time I wanted, like an inflatable doll, something I could stuff under me on the hard floor of the paint-smelling room, on the unplastered stairs, on dusty cement bags.

That was our only meeting place: the building under construction. We met nowhere else. Not once did we walk on the flower-scented park paths under the shade of trees fading into the twilight, nor fondled in intimate, candlelit rooms because... in secret she was just an adventure for me, nothing more. Because I could not accept her, because I considered her to be below my rank, and because at the end of the day I did not even love her. She was only good as long as I could feast on her body occasionally and suck in the warmth of her soul. The recognition was devastating. I knew I could not continue this anymore and that I had to tell her truth. And I knew she would suffer miserably, and that I also knew I was solely responsible.

The next day I bought Ramona a bouquet of flowers. I found her in the exact same room where I first took possession of her body. She was sanding a bookshelf when I went in. A fine layer of dust covered her face, even her eyelashes. Her eyes filled with happy tears when I gave her the flowers. I had never seen her so happy. There is no pleasure in my memory of what followed. I tried to express myself as considerately as I could. But facts were facts. She listened to my awkward confession without saying a word. Her lips tightened and large teardrops began to slip from her eyes drawing wet stripes down her dusty face. Then there was a point when she could restrain herself no longer. She leaned on my shoulder and just sobbed loudly. She was so much in love with me that she could not even be angry. I felt like a lowlife, a despicable worm, just like the Master had said. But Ramona did not reprimand me as the Master had, although I would have felt better if at least she had let rip... She simply embraced me passionately, and cried. Then she suddenly stopped, took a single flower from the bouquet and handed it to me.

"Do not forget me," she said in a faltering voice, "And in case you change your mind, I... am... waiting for you."

She smeared her tears away with the back of her hand, picked up the sand paper and walked out of the room. As she left, her gracefully swinging hips still managed to awaken desires in me, even at this most unpleasant hour.

With a sudden determination I closed the door so as not to be disturbed and knelt down to pray. My supplication broke out from the deepest parts of my soul like a fervent outcry. I vowed I would only stop when God responded to me, when I felt finally the love the Master had talked about, when I sensed how a tantric man should love a woman.

I prayed for twenty-four hours without stopping – I did not eat nor allow my eyes to rest. I felt nothing but my will stretched to its limit and the unquenchable desire to feel the genuine tantric love. A strange thing happened in the twenty-fifth hour. My mind calmed and became like an infinite lake smooth as glass. Then somewhere from very deep, I heard an enigmatic rumble and as the muffled sound reached the surface it turned into a crystal-clear sentence ringing in the stillness of thoughts.

There were only a few words, yet they were as brilliant as if they had been written in golden letters on the infinite blue sky: The Master is the answer! For a moment this odd, inner phenomenon astonished me so much I did not even think about the meaning of the words. Then thoughts began to wave around this seed of idea that seemed as pure as crystal. What is this sound? Where does it come from? Is this my voice? Who else's? "The Master is the answer" But what is the question? Tantric love. Suddenly the Master's face became distinct in front of my mind's eye and a new, startling idea caught me: "I am the Master". The Master is inside me. My imagination almost unconsciously began to play a game; I pictured my hands as the Master's hands, and I imitated the gestures of the Master. I pictured my legs to be the Master's legs and I walked the way he does. My head, my body and my eyes were his. I sensed my voice to be his voice and like a thunderclap this voice spread throughout endless space. Together with this voice I expanded, becoming boundless, and embraced everything around me: stones, trees, animals, people, clouds and stars.

Then I knew that this all-embracing expansion is love itself. I felt my heart to be the Master's heart, my spirit to be the Master's spirit. Then I saw beautiful girls running towards me, all of them longing for my embrace. I enclosed them in my arms, each of them one by one in a joyful and loving embrace. But my love towards them was not a purely physical love, that of man for woman. It was more abundant and more expansive. I loved them like parents love their children, like siblings and friends love each other, like flowers love the bee, and oceans the river, like nuclei love the electrons, the Earth the Moon, and the Sun the planets. I loved them like Shiva loves Shakti, and like the Master loves Woman.

I spent three hours in this state of being one with the Master, in this tantric samyama. After those three hours passed, I began to feel again that my hands, my legs, and my head were mine once again. Yet I was surprised to discover that in some other way I was not myself after all.

Something had happened to me. Something wonderful. Something had died in me, and something had been born. My heart was no longer the heart it was before. This heart knew that the Master loved me, and this heart yearned to love like the Master's heart loved.

As far as I remember this was my first mystical experience, and my first real and spiritual meeting with the Master. Its effect lived on in me for a long time after and I saw the world with different eyes. Everything was most beautiful, more loveable; a world and its creatures that are in need of help. And I realized what unselfish love felt like.

14. Power of the snake

The Master assigned the largest and busiest ashram of the yoga school as my living quarters. Board and lodgings were free but, alongside the obligatory spiritual practice, everyone had to undertake some kind of job, an individual duty contributing to the life of the ashram. Some worked in the kitchen or cleaned; others worked on the building site or in the print office.

I arrived in Bucharest with my plans ready. I expected to be working with the yoga school's dance group. From what I had seen at the camp performances there was a lot of polishing of the dance group to be done and I was convinced these duties would suit me perfectly. My imagined role as dance instructor already filled me with joy and pride; I would be able to offer something truly useful with my work. Indeed the outline of a new performance had even begun to form in my head. Obviously only after some very tough work as I would first have to prepare the group for it.

I presented my plan to the Master with great enthusiasm, but he seemed nowhere near as keen. He listened to it all calmly before saying he didn't think it was needed at the moment, and first I should try to fit into the ashram life and learn Romanian. My task would be assigned me by the head of the ashram.

Despite my deep disappointment there was nothing I could do. Reluctantly I went to see the head of the ashram who assigned me to cleaning. My job was to keep the entrance and main staircase clean which meant I would have to sweep and mop the stairs. Four or five times every day! The area was used not only by the ashram inhabitants, the practice halls of the yoga school were also in this building.

I really did not want to accept the job. It seemed so... humiliating. I expressed my vengeful dissatisfaction, asking the director to give me a more worthy job. I said I wouldn't even mind if I ended up in the kitchen.

"I'm sorry, this is what the Master wanted. I can't do anything," shrugging her shoulders, indicating she considered the case closed.

When I first started mopping the stairs I nearly died of embarrassment. I wasn't only seen by people I knew, but also by all those strangers attending classes. I hung my head the whole time I was working so no one would recognize me. The view of the world was so peculiarly different from underneath! People appeared very large, proud and important while I was just small and insignificant. I felt terribly humiliated.

My situation caused me genuine trauma, and for weeks I didn't even feel like meditating. I was irritable, spoke to no one and hardly ate a thing. I went about my allotted work with a bitter taste in my mouth and often caught myself just standing, mop in hand, astounded at where I was. I increasingly felt I was in this place as the result of some incomprehensible mistake. What on earth was the point of me being here? – doing something I had no affinity for. The whole thing was like a bad dream I would have liked to wake up from sooner...

But my dream showed no sign of coming to an end. Again and again I found myself on the stairs next to the bucket of water, wearing rubber gloves, always just looking up at people who seemed to walk by me with cool indifference as if I wasn't even there... Then one day I made up my mind. I threw down the rag. I wasn't going to do this any more. Either I've gone completely mad, I thought, or I'm the victim of some hypnosis. No normal person does this. I renounced my Marseille life, leaving a potentially good marriage, a promising career and even the most important thing in my life – dance. Then I left the profoundly spiritual atmosphere of Rishikesh with the reassuring presence of Swami... and what had I achieved? I'm mopping stairs in a foreign country... for free... I'm cleaning up the muddy footprints of people who don't even notice me. At home in France ridiculously wealthy men competed for my attention while here the guys dressed in torn clothes, lime in their hair, who were working on the building site hardly ever deign to notice me...

"Hurry up with the cleaning. The people will be coming out of the yoga classes soon!" The commanding tone of the head of the ashram woke me from my bitter turmoil. I continued with the teeth-gritted obedience of a slave, dark thoughts swirling in my head all the while.

When I went into the toilets to empty the bucket I met one of my fate-mates. There she was, singing happily, caressing the inside of the toilet bowl with reverent movements. She was dressed elegantly and carefully made up, as though she was ready to go to the theatre. I must have had a haggard expression because she anxiously inquired about my health. We had never spoken before – somehow I'd not been in the mood to talk to a toilet cleaner, but at that moment it felt good to pour out my heart's misery to someone.

"You shouldn't think like that," she said when she had sympathetically listened to me. "All jobs are equally noble and, if you do them with love, then anything can be a genuine balm for the soul."

"But how can you love doing this kind of work?" I spluttered bitterly.

"I always clean," she continued in a confidential tone, "as though I'm carrying out a sacred, sacrificial ritual. Before I start I entreat God to help me clean this place and these things, in a way that my heart also be cleansed from dirt and the deposits of negative emotions. And believe me, so much in me has changed since I started thinking like this. At the beginning it was hard for me too. I felt so humiliated that I had to clean the toilets! So I started to pray and implored the Omnipotent to show me how to relate to this work, so it wouldn't be such torture for me. That night I had a strange dream; I was cleaning the toilet and in came a lad, an extremely good-looking man. We got to know each other, he started to chat me up, I let myself be tempted and... we made love. We made love divinely, here in the toilets... And from that moment on I always clean them as though I were preparing the place – and myself – for a secret and sacred lovemaking ritual. And you know what happened last week?" she asked laughing. "I was cleaning the toilet when in came an extremely good-looking bloke. We introduced ourselves, he started to chat me up..."

"And you made love... here in the toilets...?"

"No, we didn't. We haven't yet... but I hope we will," she added winking playfully. "And I hope it won't be here in the toilets."

This strange story cheered me up somewhat but I didn't pay it any special attention until the evening. I remembered it again after I'd gone to bed, and then I began to wonder if I should also learn from it, even if it came from a "toilet girl". The next morning I dressed beautifully, carefully putting on my make up before I started work. I imagined ascending the stairs with my divine partner, going towards the holy altar of our consummated love. I tried to polish the cement with the utmost dedication but I still hadn't managed to completely eliminate my feelings of discomfort... What I did achieve, however, was that the bystanders – especially the men – began to notice me. Some smiled at me, some stroked me and, there were even those who made positively flirtatious remarks. I was starting to feel better.

One month later I was totally at home moving around in the stairwell. Through some inexplicable miracle I had begun to love my job. Actually I was even quite proud of it. I no longer worked with my head bowed and ashamed – I was already able to smile with a calm naturalness at whoever looked at me. I finally managed to feel the sacred state too that my fellow 'sufferer' had spoken of...

Using my body to its full advantage, I worked with attractive, sensual movements, gradually developing a cleaning choreography for myself – sometimes I even added music. Slowly everyone noticed "the French diva who cleans dancing". People noted my cleaning times, and many came by even if they had nothing particular to do in the building. Sometimes such a large group gathered to admire my work that it was difficult to go up the stairs. Then the ashram's management introduced a new rule: people were no longer permitted to stop on the stairs. This was announced by a forbidden sign at every turn of the stairs. Of course, people took little notice of the signs and carried on standing and watching. Someone was appointed to keep discipline and ensure compliance with the new rule. And because people couldn't stop any more they walked up and down around me. Seeing this, the director banned me from being in the stairwell before and after courses. I had to organize my cleaning schedule around the times when there were few people on the stairs. Of course, those who had become accustomed to my old timetable still hung around waiting for the cleaning show to start.

❖

A wonderful and surprising process occurred in me during my stint as a cleaner. Finally I realized why the Master had chosen the stairs as the venue for my first performance of my stay in Bucharest.

So my encounter with this kind of work – that at the start I had so condemned and regarded as so "beneath my status" – had simply been a painful but necessary operation. Invisible hands were trimming the negative aspects of my Leo sign: pride, vanity and the ridiculous and pathetic need to be on the top or at least in the centre. Then, as the first germ of humility appeared in me, and I recognized the true master teaching in the "toilet girl's" admission, I was suddenly able to re-evaluate everything with one stroke. I began to discover the joy of selfless work done for others and the miracle that lies in the transfiguration of life situations. I felt just what magical and transformative forces even seemingly insignificant acts can provide if we link them to our inner spiritual processes. And I discovered something else too – and this was perhaps the most important of my stairwell lessons: the amazing power of femininity opening. To see the men swarming around me gave me a pleasant feeling tinged with excitement. It was thrilling to see their blatant desire to approach me. Of course, it was no new experience – I had felt it a few times and always secretly desired it. But previously the Greek fire of pride had always burst into flame inside. But there I sensed in myself neither proud arrogance nor coquettish vanity as I realized that the admiring and lustful looks were not addressed to the person Laurianne Lamy but to the enigmatic female power, the universal energy of femininity, Shakti manifesting through me. I was finally allowing the expression of this energy through my being. And so there was no pride in me – only gratefulness, and awe of the Great Cosmic Woman, the Eternal Mother, the infinite female energy with its irresistible effect on men. The same force that once tempted Adam out of the Eden of happy ignorance into the world of knowledge that teaches through suffering and joy. A power capable of chaining a man to the seductive triviality of everyday life until struggle matures his strength, and experience awakens his wisdom. The same power that, when you change its direction, will lead you back to the Heavenly Realms of conscious community with the Creator. There on the stairs, bucket in hand, I first felt the power of the initiatress known as the cleaning woman in the tantric tradition, the dombi that is outside of castes – and therefore free of all social fetters. It was a genuine and blissful meeting with my feminine self, and the starting point of a long process leading to the total awakening of this mysterious power.

❖

Just as I had begun to perceive the stairwell cleaning as the most noble duty, a true spiritual mission, and no longer desired anything else, the Master summoned me. He told me he'd like me to take over direction of the dance group from now on. For a second I was disappointed that I would have to bid farewell to my dear stairwell, but before long my old and unsatisfied desire relating to teaching dance was reborn, and I found myself preparing enthusiastically for my new task.

Actually I was delighted that at last I would be doing something I had an affinity for, something I truly loved. I led tough dance training sessions for the group and was satisfied to see their dancing improve. I was working on a choreography that could speak, in the language of movement, about that mysterious femininity I had recently discovered in myself.

The Master came in to the practice on one occasion. The girls were performing a half-finished choreography. When they stopped they gathered around the Master, curious about his opinion. He praised some of the girls for their "beautiful opening", "becoming braver and more confident" and "increasing their femininity". But he had not one word to say about my choreography. When he finally turned towards me all he asked was:

"Have you ever danced a striptease?"

"No, never," I replied in surprise.

"You should learn how to strip. It will help you no end," he said, and I saw on his face that he meant it seriously.

I had seen some striptease on television, but it had never particularly interested me. Taking off your clothes while dancing was no great art, I thought, and had no idea why I should have been interested in it. But, once the Master had recommended it...

After making friends with the thought over the next couple of days I went to a strip bar...for the first time in my life. The atmosphere was surprisingly pleasant. There weren't only men sitting in the colourful dimness as I had imagined, I also noticed some couples. Actually three women were merrily chatting away at the table next to mine. This made me relax. I had that feeling again of being in a place where I had no reason to be. I felt everyone was staring at me because I seemed like a fish out of water. I sat sipping my pear juice as though I was on a school bench, studiously watching how the girls moved, trying to copy their provocative movements in my head.

They didn't seem at all difficult. I quickly saw through their tricks: a couple of heated hip movements, a few slow and erotic strokes of the most intimate and exciting areas of the body, a few luscious movements on the pole imitating lovemaking, open lips, an enticing look, and the men were reaching into their pockets. I planned to try them out in front of the mirror when I got home.

As I wasn't seeing anything new after the fourth or fifth performance, I didn't see any reason to stay longer, so I paid and got ready to leave. But the captivating tones of a new piece of music held me back as a new girl took the stage. She was dressed as a queen. A gold-edged, rich-red velvet cape fell in generous folds from her shoulders; the deep lace neckline of her shimmering, long, red dress suggested her generous and shapely breasts. A small gold crown adorned her plaited blonde hair and a lustrous ruby set in gold suspended on a gold chain described the beautifully arched line of her neck. She walked slowly and regally. Two attractive men dressed as pages held her cloak. She stopped in the middle of the dance floor as she cast her eye over those present with a genuine regal dignity. She had an enthralling presence. Mesmerized, I sat back down at my table. I glanced around. Everyone was motionless, watching with bated breath. Her radiant femininity made me think of Estrella. She had known how to do that, how to captivate people with her mere appearance. But this femininity was somehow different – more sophisticated, more noble… I eagerly awaited her dance.

When the music became more rhythmic this stunning queen made a sign; at which her pages removed the cloak from her shoulders with reverence, and she started to dance with slow entrancing moves. Then, at her next command, the pages brought her a large, oval mirror set in a highly ornate silver frame. She started to look at herself in it, tracing the line of her face, lips and neck delicately with her fingers. She removed the crown and her golden-blonde locks tumbled onto her naked shoulders. Her hands slowly and sensitively slipped to her breasts and started to undo her bodice. The red dress slithered from her body onto the floor leaving her in only Baroque-style, erotically cut, white lace underwear. She started to dance again, now with far more dynamism. I was amazed to note that she didn't use any of those traditional striptease tricks I'd seen the other girls employ. Still some enchanting and stirring power radiated from her body. Men and women alike greedily drank in her movements. It was as though they wanted to catch every drop of that invisibly flowing nectar. Then she stopped unexpectedly at the front of the stage and, with an enigmatic glance, looked into the eyes of the man in front of her who was watching with devoted attention. She drew her hands behind her back and untied the hooks of the lace corset.

Her body was now almost naked, revealing its Venus-like proportions. She had nothing on but white stockings, delightfully shaped high heels and the ruby at her neck.

I imagined what the men must have been feeling, and I empathized deeply with them. The spectacle had excited me too. Everyone clapped… but the act had not yet come to its conclusion. With a cheeky smile she winked at the man in glasses whose eye she had been holding for a good while and, with a sudden movement, she turned her back to him and, with her legs sensually open, stroked the length of her inner thighs and then placed her two hands onto her naked labia. The next moment, as she turned back to face the audience, she was holding a partially open, dark red rose bud in her palm. She must have conjured it from herself as the petals glistened with wetness in the light of the electric atmospheric.

This astonishing show was awarded an enormous storm of applause and hoorays. She was still looking only at the man with spectacles. She lifted the rose bud to her lips, kissed it and offered it to him as she stepped towards him. I saw tears glistening behind the lenses… The man removed his glasses, stood up slowly, took the woman in his arms and kissed her passionately. They hugged each other for a good while in front of the stunned bar guests, before the woman released herself from the embrace and left the dance floor with light but dignified steps.

That last performer dealt a healthy blow to my preconceptions concerning striptease. I sensed this was real art – and that I would be willing to dance something similar. Well, of course, not in a bar, but… let's say… for the man I loved. Or maybe in front of a few close female friends. My imagination ignited as I saw myself as the female ideal of my childhood. I was suddenly the lion-taming Lady Cleopatra in her glittering costume, whip in hand, with her lion-charming look and proud deportment, performing in front of my friends, all agog with awe… Then with a sudden decisiveness I stood up and rushed to the dressing room.

The dancer was already dressed and ready to leave. I stopped her and in one breath I told her how much I loved her dance, her figure, her radiance, her everything, and that I would love her to initiate me into the secrets of this intriguing striptease. She replied she didn't have much time because her man was waiting for her, but that we could speak a little. I invited her over to my table and wanted to order her a drink but she just asked for fruit juice. I was observing her face, look and movements. Even in her normal clothes she was a magnetic person. She spoke in a charming, warm voice, so directly it seemed we had known each other for years. And somehow she still seemed so mysterious, even secretive. She answered my questions about dance quite readily but said nothing of herself. I only managed to find out she was called Natalia and had tried her first striptease only one year earlier. I was pretty surprised – I had imagined that to attain such artistic perfection you would need years of practice, even for striptease. I asked her what did she do to make everyone look at her in that enchanted way the moment she stepped onto the stage.

"It's not a matter of *doing* but rather of *being*," she replied. "It is an inner state that I cannot teach you. But if you look inside, you will find it there. This mysterious power is in every woman; you simply need to awaken it. And the more you wake it, the more you will be able to radiate this magical force. That is you'll be more feminine."

"And what does femininity mean?" the question burst out of me.

That was the question that most interested me at the time. My views concerning femininity were undergoing dramatic transformation, and I was searching for a secure grip, some sort of standard to support my newly awakening emotions.

"It is hard to express in words…it is a rich concept. It contains warmth, playfulness, sensitivity, happiness and wisdom… loving and giving… Femininity is what makes a man's circulation increase, fire collect in his eyes, and his whole being start to shake. Yes, and you can read the level of the awakening of your femininity from a man's eyes – from how he looks at you, from how *a human* becomes *man* in your presence. How they suddenly come alive, how they awaken interest and desire in you, how they approach you, touch you, make you theirs… This is femininity. There is one more part too: mystery. The great enigma that words are unable to express, or even to describe – that only an opened and mature soul is able to sense… and experience with silent joy."

"I think I too am included in that "a human becomes man," I said laughing.

"No, you are actually *"a human* that becomes *a woman,"* she laughed in return before carrying on more seriously. "The sight of femininity manifesting can also have a remarkable effect on a woman. If you can watch with wonder, then the femininity in you will also awake because with time you always become that which you admire. This is a great secret. If you understand and use it, you can achieve anything. But beware, the opposite is also true. If you regard the beauty, charm and femininity of another woman with envy or contempt, then slowly that which is beautiful, charming, feminine in you will also die." I saw her glance at her watch as though she was getting ready to go and remembered I had one more reporter-question to pose.

"How did you get the idea of the queen?"

"I don't know… I bet I was one in my previous life," she replied with a telling smile.

"And I'm sure you were born under Leo in this life," I smiled back, but only partly meant it as a joke. "I think we are similar in many ways."

"No, I'm a Virgo… but my ascendant is in Leo, and my Venus too…" She glanced at her watch again. "Sorry, but I have to leave. You know, it's my sweetheart's birthday today…" She gestured to the next table where the man with glasses was sitting, his transformed face stroking the little rose as though he were caressing that most secret of places from where the bud had grown…

"We'll meet again," she smiled at me and squeezed my hand.

After they left I sat deep in thought for a while longer, sipping my second glass of pear nectar absent-mindedly. I would never have imagined a striptease dancer could be so intelligent, educated and… wise. But that was just another of my preconceptions, I thought. There was no reason why they shouldn't be intelligent and educated women. But that woman was still an extraordinary character. I had to get to know her! Natalia… beautiful name too, so… oozing noble femininity.

The next day I stood in front of the mirror trying out all the moves and tricks I'd spied from the dancing girls. It was easy copying the movements. Actually, I felt that with just a little practice I'd be better than them. But Natalia's enchanting radiance, well, that just didn't seem to want to appear. I tried in vain to make my glance enchanting, my facial expressions enticing and my lips purse seductively but my movements, even the most daring strokes, all seemed empty, lifeless and false. Though I tried for ages, just in case I happened to realize the secret it was to no avail. I still wasn't able to produce any results. But something else happened. I discovered my body took to the touching really well. It filled me with a pleasant feeling when my hands encircled my hips, my thighs, and my bottom, and my fingers, caressing the edges of my lips, neck, nipples and toes created a state of great excitement. The discovery filled me with joy. It was like getting to know someone else. I was stunned to realize that up until that point my body had been an unknown person for me. Although I knew it existed, lived together with it, cared for it, washed and dressed it, I had never actually become acquainted with it. Sometimes I had allowed others to explore it, so they could rejoice in its existence, but I had never discovered the ecstasy it could give me – or I could give it… Now I was somehow able to view it differently, like a man would – with interest and wonder.

Inspecting my breasts I saw their peachy roundness as beautiful and attractive… so desirable. If I were a man, I'd like to taste them. They're like some luscious exotic fruit… And my hips and bottom… what delightful and exciting arched lines they created under my slim waist… How good it feels on the palm to explore these undulations… and the little lotus flower men dream so much about… that tempts them with such irresistible force…

mmm…it's so beautiful, so mysterious like a gate leading to a hidden world… the wonderful lotus flower gate… How velvety the petals are! What a sweetly exciting feeling to touch it! Oh God, it's been such a long time since I touched myself like this… When was the last time? Maybe when I was sixteen… What if I…? …my fingers had already started the game I hadn't let them play for ten years. Timidly at first, holding back, as though a stagnant guilty conscience restrained them. Their courage increased slowly but surely until they had freed themselves of all inhibitions, drawing out delight with unbroken joy.

Re-meeting myself was an astounding and confusing experience – like rediscovering a long-lost treasure.

I wrote this in my diary about it:

7th March 1999

I'm happy! I'm happy! I'm happy! I've come to know myself. Today I realized that I am beautiful. Not because someone else said it. I saw it with my own eyes! And I fell in love! I love myself! I love the spiral curls of my jet-black hair. I love my playful eyelashes, my sensitive neck. My lips tailored for kissing. I love my generous breasts, my steeply undulating bottom and my enticingly curved thighs. I adore my stroking hands and the feeling they awake as they circle around my belly. I love it as they slip lower and lower until they reach the velvet lips. I venerate the sweet excitement my playing fingers provoke. I love to plunge between the wetting lips to explore the secret spring from which the delight of delights gushes forth. If I were a poet, then now I'd write a poem. It might be called "confession of love to myself" or maybe simply "Psalm to God"… Oh, I was so ignorant! Why did I imagine it as shameful and pathetic fun? Only meant for adolescent girls and abandoned, lonely women! How could I have lived without myself for so long? Whatever. Now I know… I discovered the secret today… My whole body is buzzing, vibrating, and I finally feel that my body is alive, my soul delighted! I've already loved myself twice today… and now I'm going to again… and after I go to bed. Now, actually now… here in front of the mirror… in a second… my fingers are already peeling open the petals of the lotus flower… Oh, God…

❖

I loved myself for a long time that night… and whenever I could in the following days. For the next week I floated in a light and airy state caused by the joy of my discovery and the excitement of this new game. I felt that, if I really wanted to, I'd even be able to fly. That my body was finally starting to radiate was what pleased me the most. Of course, not as much as I'd have liked. Not exactly like Natalia's but I could read from men's eyes that I was on the right path. I could hardly wait to meet Natalia again and to update her as to my discovery. A breakthrough that ushered in a new era for me. When I went back to the bar on Saturday night I watched the girls in a completely different way, seeing far more, noticing subtler shades. I could tell which of them loved their body and which did not. Who did it without enthusiasm, just for the money, and who with joy. I also sensed who was faking the enjoyment, and whose stroking had created genuine desire. Their auras were quite different. There were those whose courageous and provocative femininity seduced the viewer into free and healthy sensuality while others emanated wild and aggressive sexuality. Some were without any aura at all and they awoke no feelings at all... apart from pity.

I watched with interest, patiently awaiting the real one. I was sure they would leave her till last – hers would be a hard act to follow indeed. But the show ended, and Natalia hadn't appeared. Fearing the worst I asked the waiter about her and found out that "the blonde queen" didn't work in the bar. She had simply asked the boss if she could dance one number, as a present for her boyfriend's birthday. Of course, the boss had immediately wanted to employ her after her dance – offering her a pretty sum – but she had refused the offer saying she didn't intend to work in this profession. She had left neither address nor telephone number, not even her name.

I was disappointed and angry that I hadn't even asked her for her number. I had thought I'd be able to find her here any time... So why would she have said, "We'll meet again" Where should I look for her?

An unpleasant male voice jolted me out of my thoughts.

"Excuse me, Mademoiselle, would you permit me to join you?"

A swarthy stout man of medium height with a black moustache was standing next to me. He spoke French. In my surprise – and without thinking – I nodded a polite, "Yes...of course."

"Thank you," he said, throwing a sharp and inquiring look over me before sitting down confidently at the chair opposite me.

"What would Monsieur like?" I asked with a forced smile.

He did not return the smile. His black beady eyes hunted down my eye contact.

"I would like to admire your magnetic beauty from close up."

"Oh, thank you." A good dose of sarcasm vibrated in my voice. "And how did you know I am French, if I may I ask?"

"I heard you speaking to that blonde dancer last Saturday."

"I see..."

"You already captivated me with your charm then, but the courage to speak to you escaped me. But I promised myself that if I ever saw you again... then I would. And so I have waited every night... hoping... I knew... I felt... that you would come again."

A strange, disturbing and goose-bump generating force emanated from his voice. I had no sense of the wonder of a man overcome by my charms at all.

"Do you often come here?" I tried to move the thread of conversation away from me.

"No, no, I came last week for the first time... just so I could meet with you."

His eyes bore inquisitorially into mine. I didn't turn my head away. Out of pride, I guess. I didn't want to appear weak, so I withstood his scrutiny. A silent duel began. At least that's what I thought, resolving not to give in. He appeared insolent – and I wanted to teach him a lesson.

We sat motionless for minutes that dragged, looking fixedly at each other. I had to blink sometimes, but his eyelashes didn't even flutter. A strange hypnotic force flooded from his eyes. A power that seemed to enter me and travel through every last bit of my body. Discomfort started to rule me but I wouldn't give in. Then all of a sudden I felt an unusual tingling around my tailbone, and that sensation began to spread. The next moment an icy heat filled my loins. It was an unfamiliar and frightening feeling that was like the desire to pee intermingled with a strong and torturous sexual desire. Currents of cold shivers ran the length of my back. The state gradually became unbearable, and I turned away my gaze. I tried to calm my lower body, which had started shaking, and to put an end to my growing fear. I couldn't grasp what had happened. Maybe I had excited myself so much that week that now I was turned on just from the look of a man? I needed to go out quickly.

I excused myself and, forcing calm into my quivering body, headed for the toilets. When I arrived in the cubicle I was astonished to find my loins as wet as after generous foreplay... I didn't lock the door although I knew he'd follow me... Or maybe that's why...

It would be hard for me to describe that strange contradictory feeling that overran me. One part of my being protested against what I knew would happen next. But still I consciously desired it. I hadn't become the victim of hypnosis – I was totally myself. No external will was forcing me to – I myself wanted it. I wanted it because the single crazy thought filling my mind was that only a hard sexual organ boring into me would be able to alleviate my unbearable desire. Nothing else...

A lustful thrill ran through me as the door opened. The man said nothing. He grabbed my hips and with a sudden motion turned me so my back was towards him, pushed my upper body forward, wrenching my clothes up to my waist. First he dug his fingers into me, as if he wanted to take me into his possession as legitimate owner. When he impaled me it was like a high-voltage electrical current had been turned on in me. My body trembled, twitched and shook. My fingers clutched the toilet handle. My hair was hanging in the water. He thrust with growing wildness. Despite my lips being pressed together, uneven and abandoned screams escaped from my throat. I was rapidly approaching the point where the convulsive explosion was unstoppable. But before I reached the peak, he suddenly stopped the assault and moved away from me, leaving an excruciating, burning void in me. I whimpered like a starving dog. With sadistic pleasure he watched my body writhing and only penetrated me again when I asked him, begged him, abashed and humiliated. Wild strokes lashed me again toward the peak, and before I reached it he left me once more. Whimpering, vulnerable. Then I begged for his pity... this time he sat on the toilet bowl and pulled me onto his lap. I began a frantic chase, and did not stop, until finally I felt my body tense, as if trying to break in half, and my loins start those all-releasing convulsions... The relaxed muscles opened the floodgates and urine streamed out of me. I couldn't stop it... I did not want to stop it. It trickled pleasantly, washing away with it all the tension, slowly extinguishing the last embers of lust too...

Then, all of a sudden, I came to my senses, as though from a drunken stupor. I was empty and burned out. The atomic war had destroyed my body. Repulsive vultures circled above the smoking cinders. The man adjusted his wet trousers with a cold calm.

"Meet me out there," he barked and then left me alone.

I felt like a humiliated and beaten dog. In my helplessness I started to sob. I tried to pull myself together. I looked terrible. My clothes were rumpled, my hair all over the place, my face burning. When I went back in I felt as embarrassed as if everyone had seen how I had allowed myself to be screwed. The man was sitting at my table. His small piggy eyes were shining with triumphant exaltation. I was repulsed by him and, when I remembered that only a few minutes earlier I had been begging him for lust, I was filled with disgust. I didn't hate only him, but myself too. I said not a word, picked up my coat and started to put it on.

"Wait a moment, I'm going too," he grabbed my arm.

"Yes, well, after all that you can treat me like that, I suppose," I threw at him with a bitter grin in my voice.

"Well, actually, maybe we could even introduce ourselves ... I'm Alex," proffering his hand. I turned away in irritation.

"Why are you so angry? Don't tell me you didn't enjoy it too!"

"You're a beast," I hissed.

"You are too. A fiery and hungry wildcat. I think we really suit each other. Come on, I'll take you home by car."

"No need. I'll be fine."

"As you wish Mademoiselle. Here is my name card… just in case you warm a little towards me."

I've no idea why I took the card, as I had absolutely no intention of "warming towards" him. I should have refused it, or at least chucked it into the first bin I saw. But I didn't… Alex was so disgustingly sure of himself.

❖

Torturous days followed. The experience seared itself into my soul with a fiery iron. I tried not to think about it. To sweep it under the mat of consciousness. To busy myself with other things. It was all in vain. The moment I was alone Alex's repugnant face immediately appeared in front of me, his lascivious breathing buzzing in my ears.

Three days later, just as I was about to meditate, that terribly icy heat filled my pelvic area again with a torturous and uncontrollable thirst. Some eerie force crippled my brain once again. My will was transposed into one single, burning desire – to feel in me again that something which made my body shake, that maddening current. My spirit protested vehemently but the tyrannical desire proved stronger. I searched in my bag for Alex's name card with an insane awareness of what I was doing. My fingers trembled like those of a chronic alcoholic as they pressed the numbers.

"I knew you'd call. I was just thinking about you," I heard that loathsome voice say.

"Come to Pilots' Square… Now." I didn't even wait for his answer.

We went to his flat. The script was similar. He stirred my lust with demonic force, so much so that I was terrified of myself. In my agonizing tension I started to beat his back and scratch him, drawing blood. He awoke fearsome ancient instincts that I was unable to control. He hunted me to an even higher peak and, after the final lava eruption had burnt the last of my desires to ashes, the fall was far deeper, the emptiness even bleaker, the disgust more excruciating and the abhorrence more unbearable.

On arriving home I broke down in floods of tears and vowed never to meet with Alex again – even if I was climbing the wall in torment. I already had an inkling that he was trying to chain me to him with magical powers, but I knew too little to take him on. I started to pray for divine protection which did at least help me resist that wild temptation, though the anguishing desire did not cease. Whenever that icy wave flooded over me, I had a tough battle to fight to overcome it. And this fight consumed all my life force. And when I wasn't being tortured by physical desire, then I suffered from terror. I was afraid of the moment it would overcome me again.

I know, I should have gone straight to the Master to ask for advice, but something prevented me from telling him. I was embarrassed by what had happened, and of my own weakness. I didn't want to tell anyone what was happening to me. I wanted to wrestle with it alone.

Finally my roommate – from whom I hadn't managed to hide my struggle – questioned me until I confessed everything to her.

"What's he called? Did he tell you his name?"

"Alex."

"Alex Feroman?!"

"Yes, do you know him?"

"Hmmm. I've had the 'pleasure'. I should have known he was involved..." she said thoughtfully. "Well, I can't say he's not progressing."

"Why? Who is he? How do you know him?"

"He came to our yoga class, years ago. He was pretty talented and pretended to be a very avid student so the Master initiated him into many secrets. Then all of a sudden he started to spread around strange rumours: that "the Master isn't a true master"; that "he just manipulates people"; that "he hypnotizes them so he can steal their energy"; and other such rubbish. I think jealousy was the reason. Alex wanted to be a "great Tantric master" but he had no success with the girls. He just couldn't make us like him. He hung around me for a while but I refused him. There was something revolting about him, something that repulsed me. On one occasion the Master chided him in front of all the other students saying he treated women harshly and violently, that he was still trying to seduce us despite the fact we didn't like him. He warned him that if he didn't learn to love, then he would fail on the spiritual path. Then he recommended none of us respond to Alex's flirting until we felt he was approaching us with real love. I saw him standing humiliated in front of us, wild fire burning in his dark eyes. He hadn't understood the Master's warning, and I think that was when he decided to take revenge on the Master and to wage war on women. He disappeared unexpectedly and never came back to the course. But he used everything he'd learnt to achieve his goal. He practiced with intractable perseverance until he'd developed certain skills he thought he needed to ensnare his chosen female victims, to bring them under the yoke of his own will. He's already tried out his power on some of my friends – with amazing success. Of course he only achieved anything with the less experienced girls. I realized what he was doing. He'd learnt how to awaken the mysterious Kundalini power – in another person – with energy transference. You know, Kundalini is the power of the mythical serpent dormant in the root chakra which, if it scales up to the centre of sexual energy and stops there, causes phenomenally strong physical desire. That's what he used with you too. That's why you're experiencing that icy heat and urgent desire…"

"That's not the worst of it," I interrupted. "But the disgust I feel towards myself because I sullied myself with him."

"You mustn't think like that," my roommate warned me. "If your soul is clean, then nothing can sully it. And, you know, your physical reaction is a natural one too. It's not about Alex Feroman personally, but the universal male energy he employed. So there's no point blaming yourself. The energy that's awakening in you is neutral. In itself it is neither good nor bad, so you can also use it for your own purposes. You should simply give thanks that it's happened and forget about the unpleasant side of it. But don't meet with Alex again, however much you want to. Remember that the energies he has awakened in you are your own energies and you can relive them whenever you want. You can experience again the intensive desire Alex called forth in you, the one your body craves so with a man that you love. Or even alone. Because it's yours! Because it's in you! It's already alive. You don't need Alex Feroman. Do you understand?"

"Yes, but what should I do when he tries to influence me? He doesn't only ignite my desire, he also affects my thoughts too!"

"He is only able to influence you as long as you believe he can. He conquers you not with his power but with your inexperience. Use your secret mantra, the one you received on your first initiation. That'll protect you from violent, negative effects. And when the Snake raises its head, flooding you with icy heat, direct that energy up your spinal canal, right to the crown chakra. Offer to God what you feel as being too much for you. That's the safest method."

❖

I took my roommate's advice. Taming the snake was no walk in the park but I learned pretty quickly. When I sensed that tingling I was not afraid anymore. I allowed the heat to wash over me all the while directing the energy up my spine. It no longer caused such excruciating tension. Actually an extremely pleasant buzzing warmth travelled through my whole body. I imagine Alex must have been rather surprised that after one of these strong surges his telephone remained silent.

A week later he called me. He accused me of not getting in contact as though he was lecturing his wife. When I told him straight I would not put up with such a tone, and rejected him with cold objectivity, he changed tactics. He said he'd fallen in love with me and couldn't live without me, begging me to meet up with him. I didn't believe him. He phoned me every day. I did not respond. Luckily he didn't know where I lived. Ten days later I did answer his call. I spoke with ice-cold cynicism hoping that maybe if I injured his pride he would leave me alone: "Your perseverance is remarkable, but it can't touch me anymore. It's all finished. Forever, as far as I'm concerned. You've already enjoyed yourself enough at my expense. Be content with that, and don't bother me again."

"No! Please, no. Don't hang up. Listen... I want to say something important."

I sensed a genuine waver in his voice.

"I'll give you two minutes. I'm listening."

"Please forgive me. I know I acted like a jerk... but... let me make amends. I love you Laurie..." his voice quivered. "I've fallen in love... for the first time in my life... and the last time. I've done some appalling things... I know. But, maybe I can put them right... Don't push me away, please. I'm begging you... you're my only hope... if you reject me, then that's the end of me... you understand... the end..."

He broke down in tears, and I knew he wasn't simply acting. Pity started to melt my icy resolve. I didn't know what to say. I told him to call back the next day, to give me a little thinking time.

I asked my roommate for advice.

"Well, well, so here we are " she said. "The magic power of the famous Alex Feroman has broken down, and he has become the captive of his own trap. The magic he wanted to use to enslave you has now bound him. That is the punishment of black magicians that they always forget. You shouldn't give in. It isn't love, only agonizing physical desire. What he wanted to ignite in you is now cooking his innards. And the only person he can turn to for relief is the person over whom he cast his monstrous net. But you wouldn't be able to quench his thirst either because it's unquenchable. The more wildly a person tries to satisfy it, the more virulently it flares up. There is nothing you can do for him now. The energy he directed at you – and that flicked back to him multiplied – has to consume itself. It's the fire of purgatory but it only destroys that of lower rank in him: the demonic dross of his character. Only divine mercy can relieve his suffering. You can pray for him if you wish. That is the most you can do now."

I answered Alex's call the next day. Calm and definite, I told him that I forgave him for everything and that I wasn't angry with him. But that I could not love him. I also tried to make him understand it would be better for both of us if we didn't meet again. I didn't wait for his next emotional outburst. I simply hung up. The day after I changed my number and trusted that we would never bump into each other "accidentally" on the street.

15. Gifts

Being broke is an interesting experience. Though not among the pleasant ones, it is still a useful and illuminating lesson for those who step onto the path of spirituality. At least it turned out to be so for me. It taught me to see the difference between the false sense of security provided by a bulging wallet and the safety of faith in Providence. When I started the voluntary work at the construction site of the ashram I had no income. At first I was nervous and uneasy about it. It was uncomfortable to think about what the next day would bring; how I would buy new shoes or a flower for my girlfriend, and how on earth I would manage to cover the costs of the yoga camp. I did not even dare to consider how I would afford to travel home.

There was one significant benefit of this stressful situation and this was present from the beginning: I was thinking about God ceaselessly. I felt I had to remind Him of my needs time and again. It is not that He did not know about them, but there was no harm in bringing them up occasionally in the form of a prayer. At that time I was praying quite often. Initially I repeated the Christian principles to myself as a comfort: "one only has to ask and he shall be given"; it is pointless to worry about the next day; we should regard the "birds of the sky" and the "flowers of the fields" as examples. They never worry about tomorrow, yet Providence provides everything they need. As I had no other choice anyway, I began to put the above-mentioned ideas into practice. To my great surprise and my even greater delight, I realized I actually had everything I needed. No, not everything I desired. Just what I needed – and at the right time. When I was in need of money, some kind of casual job or an unselfish donation always came along, or I was presented with the very something I needed to buy. At times it was the Master himself who gave me money without me ever asking for it.

After living like this for one and a half years I was entitled to call myself master of the art of living pennilessly. I began to understand the deeper meanings of relevant Christian principles. I improved a bit the "ask and you will be given" principle and interpreted it as "be in harmony with yourself and the Universe, and then you will be given". I also found a solution to the apparent paradox between "do not think of the tomorrow" and the necessity to "plan the future". I strove to act the way every present moment required. I planned only as far as was necessary to be able to decide correctly in the present. I did not even strive to fulfil my own plans, I left to Providence the possibility to surprise me with circumstances that my mind closed in the cage of space and time wouldn't have been able to foresee. This way of life that in the beginning left me distressed and uneasy, now provided me a liberating feeling. I was calm, cheerful, and optimistic. Just like oriental ascetics or many Christian saints, I believed poverty to be an indispensable practice on the path of spiritual fulfilment. I adjusted to it with enthusiasm, so much that I became legendary among my acquaintances. I astonished everybody with the way I could renounce things, yet everything went smoothly in my life.

I thought I had attained masterly skills in this form of living, until one trial made me realize that in matters of faith I was still far from perfect. The summer camp was approaching and I needed a considerable sum to cover the expenses. I hoped that Providence, as so many times in the past, this time also would not forget about me and my rightful claim. But as time passed and I received no promising signs my faith began to shake. A week before the camp anxiety overcame me. My friends and acquaintances had already reserved their places and bought their tickets, yet my wallet was still empty. For a while I hoped the Master would remember me and take care of my situation, but I saw no initiatives from him that suggested this might happen. When I heard he had already given money to my pals in need, I felt the hopelessness of my situation growing. I was in anguish, but too proud to ask him for money. Anyway, I thought, a Master should be fully aware of the needs of his disciples, and if he does not give willingly, then why should I even ask? When only two days remained I made up my mind to act. As I did not manage to talk to him, I thought it would be wise to turn to his boss.

So I prayed to the Almighty and, referring to our fruitful cooperation in the past, I announced my wish to benefit once more from his boundless charity, according to His will, of course, but if He could take into consideration the humble wish of my fallible person too, that would make me feel extremely glad and I would owe Him immense gratitude.

Ten minutes later the phone rang and I was told the Master wanted to see me. This fast and infallible intervention of the Divine astonished me. I had always known that if you want something from a person you should turn to his superior. I whispered a short, grateful prayer from the bottom of my heart and I was on my way.

I was completely disappointed to realize the Master had called me only to send me to work. I had to accompany another guy to a cosmetics company to pick up a cargo with gifts for the summer camp participants. While the Master listed my tasks, I dropped a few hints about my burning problem, but it was as though he had simply not understood – he passed the buck with masterly skills. I sat in the car crestfallen. I was in no mood to carry cases with gifts to participants of a camp I was likely to miss.

Heavy were the boxes, yet not as heavy as my heart. Then a charming young lady came out to check the cargo. I suddenly got my act together and began to carry the boxes in threes. They were suddenly not heavy anymore. There are people whose presence can change the physical laws; this woman was obviously one of them.

After we finished she invited us to the office for refreshments. Adela was the executive manager of the company, though her direct attitude was not characteristic of a manager. Memorable, curvy thighs accompanied her brilliant sense of humour, communication skills and exceptional intelligence. Her black silk skirt covered her thighs only as much as her managerial status required; it was obvious why our cups did not want to be emptied. We started talking with familiarity and I felt great. My pressing thoughts were dismissed by her cheerful smile and playful features. Though only until she asked where we would be staying during the camp. Then I realized again how dreadfully close the date was. My friend announced the name of the villa they had rented. I thought I should bluff something, just for the sake of leaving a good impression, but the next moment I found myself confessing the sad and humiliating reality to her. My mood and confidence passed in a second, and I felt embarrassed in front of the annoyingly pretty manager's penetrating glances. I gulped the last sips as a sign I was leaving, but before we said goodbye she asked with an enigmatic smile:

"Would you accept a gift?"

"How could one refuse you?" I smiled back at her with renewed confidence.

"Let me cover your camp expenses."

This kind of gesture seemed unusual.

"I cannot accept that," I answered instinctively, or rather out of politeness.

"A moment ago you said something utterly different if I remember correctly, and I usually do," she said, amused at my confusion.

"I don't even know what to say," I said reluctantly and tried to get used to the tempting offer. "You're not good at accepting presents, are you?" she said, shaking her head, in a playfully reproachful tone. "Does that mean you are also not good at giving presents?"

"All right, you got me. I see negotiation is your profession," I replied with a relieved smile, purposefully leaving unanswered the question I myself still had to crack.

"If you have no other plans, then we could leave together by car tomorrow morning."

Of course there was no other plan. How could there have been?

❖

The three-hour drive to the seaside was the most pleasant ride of my life. I could hardly imagine a man who would have been able to resist the captivating interplay of charm and joy that moved on Adela's face. At least I could not. By the time we reached our destination I was already encompassed by a rosy cloud. My eyes were glowing, I kept confusing my arms with wings, and no one could have scratched the smile off my face.

We stayed in a luxurious villa where I had my own room. I couldn't thank the Master enough for sending me to load the boxes. I found out Adela had been married for eight years and that her husband was not really interested in anything but business — especially not in spiritual matters. However, his prime virtue was to give complete freedom to his wife who was ten years younger than him.

When asked, I also had to admit I had a girlfriend who was not interested in anything but spirituality, and that she limited my freedom as much as she found necessary for my spiritual improvement. Adela knew Gina well and regarded her highly. Next evening the three of us had dinner. I did not want to show my awakening feelings towards Adela in front of Gina. I felt rather odd in that situation. They both chatted on in a calm and relaxed manner. My presence did not seem to bother them at all.

Gina spent the night with me. After a long session of lovemaking she whispered into my ear, "You are in love, aren't you?"

"Yes, of course. You know how much I love you," I held her tight.

"No, that's not what I meant," she caressed my face. "You fell in love with Adela."

"What makes you think that?" I looked suddenly at her in surprise. I knew I had been reserved with Adela in Gina's presence.

"I saw it in your eyes."

"I am not certain," I explained. "Maybe… it's simply just physical attraction, you know, since Ramona I have not fallen for such things."

"No, Bald, it is more than a simple physical attraction. Believe me. I know that much." After a few moments of reflection she turned my face towards her and continued, "Be honest with yourself. I won't be angry. If something beautiful is to happen between you two, then so be it. I don't want to stand between you."

I clasped her in my arms tight. Her sincere devotion touched me.

"She is not indifferent either," she added.

"You reckon?" My eyes sparkled. "She did not show any signs."

"Of course she did, you just missed them. You only react after someone has unzipped your trousers."

Gina was an angel. From that moment on she left Adela and I alone more often. Her assumptions were right: from Adela's unintentional gestures, furtive glances and her jovial smile I felt she was attracted to me. One night after dinner she invited me for a walk on the shore. The sea was silent. Like an alpine lake in the moonlight. Her voice was intimate yet stirring. We walked for miles on the pebbles when at last I made up my mind to touch her. A pleasant vibration ran through my body when our hands touched, and our fingers intertwined in joy. Holding her hand filled me with joy. I stopped and turned to her. Her smile was like that of an angel, and her perfumed hair was fluttered in the silent midnight wind. She ran her fingers through my hair and leant closer to me. First our breaths met, then our lips.

"Oh, God, how long I have been waiting for this moment," she whispered with an ardent expression and kissed me again. "You are not good at accepting gifts, you see?" She looked deep into my eyes.

"And I am not good at giving either," I continued her thought.

"Let me teach you."

"I am yours," I whispered, our lips touching the other.

"Come, let's start with the first lesson."

The first lesson lasted four hours, and I knew the Almighty must favour me beyond imagination. Adela was a splendid gift for me. It was the kind of gift we do not even dare dream about, and when it falls into our lap due to some inexplicable miracle, we cannot believe it. At these times, our gratitude towards Providence is mixed with fear. Fear of the emptiness that remains once the good that was given and sweetened our lives is taken away.

Adela offered me a job in her company. "There is still a lot I need to teach you about gifts," she smiled sweetly at me. "About the secrets, dangers and wonders of a life in abundance."

She needed no special PR tricks to convince me. All I feared was that the Master would not give his consent, but my fears were unfounded. The Master was not opposed to my leaving the building site and starting a new life. He knew exactly what kind of experiences, life lessons and hardships I needed to pass on my spiritual path and he always recognized opportunities with wisdom. After my meagre years at the ashram, now with Adela I felt like a king in Wonderland, where houses were made of gingerbread, where it was enough just to think of something and it came true. She provided me not only with her generous love, but with all the earthly goods that one can wish for. She made me used to walking with a fat wallet, wearing elegant clothes and riding in expensive cars. She taught me how to move with confidence among serious businessmen and conceited men of wealth. We stayed at exquisite places and ate at classy restaurants on business trips. Adela was never thrifty, but neither did she waste money senselessly. She knew exactly when and how much to spend to manoeuvre everything around her in harmony. She loved helping others and donated considerable amounts of her money to charities. She was not the type who gave money just to relieve her consciousness like many men of fortune do. Adela believed in the generosity of Life, and her actions spoke as loud as her words. She herself became the source of Life's generosity. Probably that was the reason why the business boomed under her supervision. It was a unique experience to watch her during business meetings. Her irresistible charms and persuasive manner of talking won over many negotiating parties, especially those wearing trousers. I had the chance to admire her turning cold and calculating businessmen into considerate admirers though she never used her natural dominance for selfish reasons. She struck bargains that were advantageous for both parties. That was another secret of her success. She had some other tricks she told me about, and I learned a few others just by watching her.

She was never overcome by greed that yoked even skilled businessmen, forcing them to sacrifice their time, life and energy on the altar of success, with a craving of a psychotic gambler. She worked a lot but always left enough time and energy for her spiritual practices, for love and everything that makes life a celebration. She knew exactly that profit is not in proportion with the time and work invested in gaining it, that success is governed by hidden laws. She understood some of these rules well and instinctively knew many others. In the beginning we argued a lot about the need of financial affluence for someone on the path of spiritual truth. I held the idea that wealth is nothing more than a temptation, an insidious trap that chains you to the physical world meanwhile you strive to attain complete freedom. My pretty director argued this way: "Lack of money – if you want more than what was given to you – is a larger setback on the spiritual way than wealth itself. The secret desire for wealth, even if you try to conceal it, is just as strong as the fear of losing it. Those who walk on the path do not need to be afraid of anything, not even wealth."

❖

Maybe if these two extremities had happened in a reversed order – if I had first tasted moments of prosperity before being forced to live in need – I would have had a tougher job. The current would have seized me, and the fall would have been painful. But this way wealth could not became a temptation, a trap for me. I enjoyed it but I did not become its prisoner. I knew I could give it up at any moment. I was deeply convinced I would get everything I needed in life. I learned not to be attached to objects, or even to people. I got used to the continuous change and to Fate rearranging the scene of my life from time to time. Life is an odd theatre. No roles are taught. You always have to improvise. You can never know who will face you the next moment. There are new performers and players on stage in every episode, and you never know in advance which of them will play a main role in your life, and which of them was cast as secondary character by the Stage Director. One needs to pay attention to each and every one, and to learn to perform together with them in joy and harmony.

❖

At that time the Director gave me a rather atypical, but nonetheless exciting role: I had to learn how to act with two main characters at the same time. To respond to the needs and desires of two beloved and loving women. Not a simple task. It was not sexuality that gave me troubles, by that time I was experienced enough to manage my energy so neither had grounds for complaint. It was the emotional side of the relationship that required effort. I had to take particular care of both, so neither would feel I loved more, or paid more attention to the other. This needed real expertise. It was a true art and, like every art in life, it required talent too. I was luckier than other men I knew in that both of my lovers were intelligent and experienced. They knew and accepted each other. They did not make any scenes of jealousy, and when they met occasionally they related in a pleasant and natural manner. Although they weren't friends – they were too different for that – each respected and admired the other.

There was one fortunate advantage of this unusual situation: neither tried to possess me. They did not come forward with selfish demands, on the contrary, they tried to give their best to make our encounters unforgettable. It was touching to see and feel on my own skin that they prepared attentively to each rendezvous and each lovemaking as though it was the first time, as if they had to win my heart over and over again. Doubtless somewhere deep in their souls they also competed with the other, but the result was clearly positive. They managed to turn every tryst to a celebration. Of course, I also strove to do my best. It was easy for me as they both attracted me enormously, though they were astonishingly different. Gina continuously fuelled my aspiration towards spiritual practices and ignited beacons leading me towards the final destination of my journey. Adela uncovered in front of me the driving power of happiness, joy and laughter, and taught me how to love everything that is good and beautiful without attachment. Gina was awakening in me a thirst to divine transcendence dwelling beyond the mortal, changing world. Adela tried to open my eyes to see the immanent Divinity incarnated as the beauty and abundance of Life and Nature.

I was grateful to both of them.

❖

I played the role of a businessman near and for Adela for a year and a half. Then I realized I had had enough. I felt the same as when I accompanied Linnéa round Europe for years. It was not me, this was not my job anymore. I had other purposes in life. I learned many useful things, that was never in question, but I had to move on. In my heart I heard the sound of bells signalling that the hour of change had arrived.

I kept a sharp eye on the changes in my environment. I looked for the hidden correlations between events, meetings and information. I strove to discover the divine signs lying concealed in the synchronistic connections between things – but I was unable to discover anything that showed me the way, telling me where to go and what to do. It seemed those invisible forces, which until then with the thread of my desires led me towards necessary life experiences, had abandoned me. I had reached a junction without road signs – from where I had to find my way alone.

My birthday was approaching. I knew it is a magical moment when the cause-effect chain of our lives breaks for a second, when with conscious interference we can start on a new path, give up our bad habits and harmful dependencies, and rid ourselves of these forever. This is a time when we can be reborn.

I planned to use this day to start over. For days and weeks my mind was bent on it. I meditated, prayed, analysed myself, and deconstructed my life hoping I would find some hidden thread that would open up a way in front of me... but I found nothing.

During one of my discussions with Gina I told her I was feeling uneasy. Her remarks did not surprise me.

"I do not understand you Bald," she started in her characteristic tone that knows no opposition – and that she only used to reprimand me. "You have a master, a guide on your path who can tell you exactly what you need to do. Why don't you turn to him? He took responsibility for you, your life and your spiritual growth when you accepted to be his disciple. He can only do as much for you as you allow him. He will not restrict your free will. But you always only do what your limited mind thinks proper. At best you ask for his consent to calm your conscience. But even if he gives his consent, that does not mean it is your best choice. Why don't you ask for his opinion? Afraid of losing your freedom of choice? It's a false freedom that you worry about so much. In reality you are the prisoner of your own conditioning and limiting ideas that determine your decisions. You can only be free in the knowledge of the whole Truth. Why don't you make your decisions according to the advice of someone who has already reached this wholeness of Truth? I know, you do not trust him enough, and you cannot trust him until you know him well enough, and you can only know him properly if you approach him, and you can only approach him with an honest soul and pure love. The Master will reveal himself only to this kind of approach, just like God does."

Gina's advice, or shall I say scolding, set me thinking. I knew that in matters of spiritual practice I had to follow the Master's advice without hesitation, but allowing him such involvement in my life as Gina suggested... Well, I had never thought about it. Maybe it was true that I had not trusted him and known him enough after all. And I am certain I had never approached him with an absolutely open heart or complete surrender.

Gina had once said: a master is always what you see in him. If you see him as an intelligent person, then he will fascinate you with his intelligence; if you see him as a wise man, he will present you with the fruits of his wisdom; if you see in him a helping friend, he will be your best friend who helps you in need; if you see him as someone who has attained perfection, he will lead you to perfection; if you see God in him, God will become alive in him for you. This is one of the greatest secrets of true masters' real nature.

I started to rigorously analyse my relationship with my Master. Radical changes were necessary – at least on my side. I decided that at our next meeting I would stand in front of him as a disciple should stand in front of his master, just like Gina advised and I had read in the books: with an open heart, complete self-surrender and boundless love. I was not sure if I would succeed or not, but my resolution was strong.

❖

I visited him at his place. I asked him to see me because I needed to talk to him. He did not refuse me, in fact he accepted me cordially. That was the first time I had been to his apartment, and I felt excited as I stepped over the threshold. A pleasant scent floated in the air – I could not figure it out its source. He led me to a small room with shelves filled with books. Papers full of writing lay on the desk.

We sat down facing each other. He did not say a word, just sat and watched me with a calm attention as though he had all the time in the world. For a moment it really seemed like time had stopped, or like it did not even exist at all... An ephemeral second, like a flash of light... then I felt the passing seconds again bringing the pressure to hurry, not to waste his precious time. I began to talk. I talked about what had been occupying my mind in the last few months, about the need to find my place in the world, my life mission or at least the next step. He did not interrupt or pressure me. He simply let me talk... and I kept talking... about my life, about anything that came to mind. Probably I hoped this way he would see things more clearly and would be able to give me some helpful advice. But it is also possible that I talked to him for the simple reason it was good to be with him and talk to him, to feel some kind of unknown happiness spreading in me, to see new thoughts and a new understanding crystallizing in me... I just talked and talked.

Then I stopped. I suddenly realized how pointless words were. I fell silent, and the Master did not speak either. We sat there for a long time without saying a word. It was a special silence, not the awkward type when one feels the pressure to speak. This silence was not empty. In fact it was filled with something I had not felt – I could not feel – while I was speaking. An invisible liquid was waving around us which mediated messages between our souls, messages that silence prevented from crystallizing into words. Later even my questions went silent, and a certainty descended upon me that I knew the answers... all the answers... to all the questions... Even to the unborn ones. And together with that silent certainty love and bliss flooded me.

I felt intense love for that man, that mysterious someone sitting in front of me who was much more than the body my eyes saw. I had experienced many shades of love, but this one had a new taste, a particular flavour. I could compare it to a child's emotions towards his father. I had never been able to have it with mine because we never gave the chance to know the other, to get close to each other's souls. Still, I knew it had to be, it should have been something like that. I probably loved my grandfather this way... yes, grandpa, my first master. I felt immensely grateful for both of them for everything they did and do – I realized my tears were pouring. I was not crying, I was just so overfilled that tears erupted.

We stood up and embraced. The Master's arms had a unique grip; they were firm and masculine, yet there was ineffable warmth in them too. I realized again how unnecessary words can be at times. But before I left the Master himself broke the silence:

"When is your birthday?"

"Tomorrow," I was moved by his question as much as by his embrace.

"At what time?"

"Two forty in the morning."

"Meditate from two to three, and pay a great deal of attention."

I said goodbye. As I reached down the street I had to smile that I had not gotten any answers to my most burning questions yet again. The Master did not want to ease my situation – at least that is what I thought. Strangely I was still very content with the meeting. I felt something had happened though.

❖

I prepared carefully for the meditation. I spent almost the whole day with spiritual practices and I had an unusually elevated feeling. I was a little nervous too – a sensation hardly noticeable – that we have before great and important events.

I lit a candle a few minutes before two in the morning and sent off the light of the spirit to all the creatures of the Universe. Then I sat down to meditate. As soon as I was absorbed in concentration I saw the Master's face in front of my mind's eyes. The vision lasted only for a few seconds, then disappeared and silence settled on my mind. All disturbing thoughts vanished, and my conscience shone above the sea of my mind with the clarity of the midday sun on the infinitely blue sky. Then from somewhere far away I heard sweetly ringing sounds floating towards me. Crystal-clear like the sounds of mantras, but different somehow. They did not keep one pitch, they moulded into sweet melodies, like a whispering flute. It surprised me so much that my eyes instinctively opened up and I pricked up my ears wondering where these sounds might have come from. Silence all around me. The sounds were resonating somewhere deep inside me as though they had been born on a remote star in the infinite space of my conscience. The more strongly I concentrated the more continuous and audible they became.

Then new sounds started towards me from different points of my inner cosmos. Some of them were very deep, deeper than the deepest sounds of the organ; others were higher, meandering like winds blowing through the mountain pine forests. There were sounds high as the tinkling of tiny bells, ringing clear as crystal, and diaphanous ones like shiny glass fibres. These sounds united and resonated in an astonishing polyphonic composition. I cannot describe with words the vast joy that permeated me while listening to that stunning concert. It was as though I was listening to thousands of orchestras playing together, a symphony composed by divine perfection, each and every part and sound was clearly audible, but at the same time it was a continuously changing piece of complete unity in harmony. I felt this celestial symphony contained every song that had ever been and would ever be composed, and pieces that no composer will ever compose. Only those can hear them who listen not with their ears but with their heart. I was not simply hearing the music but actually feeling it with an inner sense capable of interlacing all my senses. This music did not simply have sounds, but colours, shapes, a sense of touch, scent and even taste.

These together brought forth majestic, exalted feelings that earthly music would never be able to. The sounds could not be compared to any earthly musical instrument either. Maybe tones of the human voice showed some resemblance. The torrent of tones gripped me with an irresistible force, and carrying me like a rolling stream of shiny waves towards the infinite ocean. I not only heard the music, I *became* the music itself. Each cell of my infinitely spreading self was a vibrating sound in that boundless symphony.

Then the sounds faded, and I knew the Great Opus was reaching its closing chords — at least for me. I did not want it to finish. I resisted. I wished it would never stop. Please let it continue forever… I tried desperately to hold onto the receding sounds with all my might, but these sounds cannot be possessed. Like birds flying away into the deep blue the notes merged back into the ether from whence they had come.

Deep silence reigned over me. I did not feel nostalgic anymore for what had passed. I knew I had arrived where I should be.

I opened my eyes. It was three o'clock sharp. And so I had already been born. Reborn! I was reborn as the feeling I had thought lost was reborn in me: the desire to play music and to compose. Ideas, plans, thoughts flooded me suddenly and unlimited enthusiasm to discover the secrets of music, to bring them down to earth, to be able to hand them over to people as a gift, at least a fraction of that heavenly music I was given to hear, tones that would live on in my memories, never to be forgotten.

Now I had a purpose, finally I knew what I had to do. I only wondered how on earth I had not managed to figure it out sooner as I had been preparing for that since my childhood. I had been neglecting my musical studies for a long time and almost completely forgotten about them. But even this had a reason: I had to prepare for the task thoroughly. I had to awaken the spiritual values in me and for this I needed all the time and energy I had. I also had to discover the path to the realm of spirituality so that the music I create would open up that path to the mysterious dimensions for others too. I knew authentic music is capable of doing that — eventually this is the true purpose of music.

❖

Three days later I met the Master again.

All I said was, "Now I know what I have to do. Thank you. That was the greatest gift of my life."

"Until now."

"Yes, until now."

He always drew our attention to formulate our ideas correctly. He was well aware of the creative power of words.

16. Kaula

Since Alex Feroman had managed to stir this Kundalini snake in me, I became truly interested in discovering its habits. I read the few books about it I found in the yoga school library but the mystery only seemed to increase along with my questions. I discovered very differing – and in some respects contradictory – descriptions about the origin, nature and form of this mysterious energy. Some authors attributed it with a simple symbolic or mythical meaning, like the snake of the biblical Garden of Eden. Some even tried to prove that actually the two snakes in question were one and the same. Others held it to be a form of inner energy, describing its nature and manifestation in the body with scientific detail. I also found works reporting its destructive nature, identifying it as a powerful "inner fire" that, if escapes the control of the consciousness, can burn the body to ashes, or cause a "short circuit" in the psyche leading to mental problems. But there are also those who classify this unruly snake as a useful creature. Most interesting to me was the account by the great Indian yogi, Paramahansa Ramakrishna, who uses symbolic language to describe the awakening of Kundalini and its gradual rise through the chakras up to the highest level. It was his explanation that brought me closest to under-standing the true meaning of the phenomenon.

I asked the Master too, but a couple of evasive answers brought me to the conclusion he had no intention of helping me unravel the mystery or ease my task. He said the time would come when I would understand exactly what it was all about through my own experience. Naturally I didn't let him shake me off so easily. I told him about my adventure with Alex Feroman, pushing him until he revealed snippets that made the phenomenon clearer. I found out Kundalini energy is simply the divine creative power hidden in human beings. Energy which, in spite of the fact tradition declares "it sleeps in the root chakra", is active in every person providing the basic energy for all physical, mental and spiritual processes. Increased awakening however leads to psychic phenomenon and results in paranormal abilities. If it reaches the "crown chakra" – through "ecstatic" unification of the consciousness and the divine energy – then the human being will attain the state of Spiritual Liberation. I also found out that if Kundalini is awakened by force, in a person who is not yet prepared, it can cause unpleasant or even damaging effects. That's why correctly performed Tantra yoga exercises gradually bring this mysterious force to life in a natural and safe way. The Master also let slip that tantric lovemaking is one of the most effective ways of naturally waking Kundalini, and that orgasm is the most easily recognizable manifestation of this waking. That it is even possible during normal lovemaking. The difference being that then it only lasts for a matter of minutes and is accompanied by the total loss of life force, while in tantric orgasm the energy is retained and increased, having a tangible positive, recharging, dynamic and spiritualizing effect that lasts for hours, even days.

During our conversation I got an overall picture of the phenomenon, and many of those contradictory descriptions I'd found in the books seemed to be elucidated. I was glad I had been so pushy and thus managed to squeeze out important information from the Master. I paid less attention to his first comment – according to which I would only be able to understand this energy when I experienced its presence in my own being. And that it could be a promise, never even crossed my mind.

Most nights before I went to sleep I made my confession. That was how I called the sacred moment when I lit the candle and, in the silently watching light, noted my more significant experiences, spiritual revelations and new thoughts into my diary. It had become a personal ritual dear to me. One I never wanted to miss.

I had stuck the photo of the Master – the one he'd given me on our first meeting – into the first page of my diary. So it was as though I was reporting my experiences to him, admitting my wrongdoings and promising to rectify my mistakes as soon as possible. Somehow I saw myself with the Master's eye too. Well, to some extent...

I have developed an intimate relationship with my Diary. Since I have stepped onto my spiritual path both of us have changed a lot. I love its ability to listen so wisely. I don't always write my feelings, sometimes I just speak to my Diary, tell it my thoughts, my feelings, my doubts and my desires. This way things always seem clearer and tensions relax. Sometimes after one of these confessions I feel I'm on a happy and cloudless island of peace, looking at waves of thought as they bob on the filthy froth, no longer able to reach me. I love that it can focus on me with such understanding and healing silence. It does not judge, admonish, advise, or even praise. It just listens, and sometimes this silence is worth a thousand times more than any lecture. It's a shame few people can listen like this. I've certainly tried to learn this from my Diary.

That night I spent a little longer than usual confessing in front of the Master's photograph as I tried to remember everything he'd told me about Kundalini. Suddenly I felt that his eyes were filling with life. I was no longer looking at the paper photo but at the living and piercing hazelnut brown eyes my gaze had met a few hours earlier. Those eyes that stirred an inexplicable feeling in me whenever they fixed on me. I felt that feeling now, too, with inimitable strength, and surprised excitement ran through me. I touched the paper with an instinctive movement as though I was looking for the explanation to this strange phenomenon on the shining surface of the paper. No, the photo hadn't come to life... but I still felt the Master was standing in front of me. Not in his physical body, but still with an almost tangible presence. If I had stretched out my hand I would even be able to touch him. Surprise froze me to the spot. I closed my eyes. The feeling of his presence intensified, his gaze even more alive, even more piercing. With my mind's eye I kept looking mesmerized at those eyes, shining with an extraordinary light, emitting a subtly vibrating power. This vibration enclosed my whole body with a stirring sensation as though invisible hands were stroking my naked skin... male hands radiating tender power... the hands of an experienced man whose touch make the hidden harp strings of the woman's soul vibrate. The vibration gradually matured into desire... intense sexual desire that was both psychical and physical. Similar to the icy heat flooding my loins that Alex Feroman's attacks had triggered in me. The similarity frightened me and for a moment the instinctive need to escape washed through me... but only for a second, as I sensed this was utterly different. This heat did not cause that unquenchable thirst. It did not gouge an excruciating void in me desperate to be filled. Instead it flowed over my body with pleasant waves to the calm and even rhythm of ecstatic melting into one another.

My consciousness experienced it as an excited witness, a dazzled participant of an incredible natural phenomenon. I was aware that I was sitting between four walls, in front of the picture glinting in the quietly flickering light of a candle. But I also knew I was somewhere else too. That I was much larger than my body, continually growing, as my expanding consciousness embraced new forms of existence. And these new forms gave me possession of new powers. I felt I was an enormous mountain. I did not *see* the mountain though... I *was* the mountain. I felt its taciturn power, its steadfastness confronting storms and tempests, its time-defying perseverance of millions of years, its life-sustaining breath. Then, some-where deep, a hushed rumbling stirred under my cliff roots that reached into the belly of the earth, and my mountain body shook. The shaking grew into an earthquake-orgasm and my consciousness began to demolish its rigid stone boundaries and spread once again. Expanding circles of waves rippled out across the infinite ocean encircling the enormous mount until I felt I was the sea itself making love to the infinite sky. Ocean currents surged, as immense rivers flooded through my veins. I was rising ever higher as the unrestrained flooding high tide, higher and higher, burying underneath and dissolving into my new self the rocky mountain I had been before. I became one with the ocean... I felt the nature of water: how it caresses everything, flows around everything, how it adapts to every shape and form, and dissolves everything into itself. Inside I felt the primordial ocean's life-giving power. Its tide-breath waved in me with the sensual rhythm of lovemaking. I felt the joy of searching for the other, the joy of finding the other, the joy of a new life being born, the joy of creation... The sheer delight of the interplay of changing forms. And then, like a lava-flow breaking upwards from the bottom of the sea, the water-me started to warm, to boil to a rock-melting incandescence. Darting tongues of flame flickered above the watery waves. Ocean of water and ocean of fire fought their fierce ancient battle in me, their clashes giving birth to immense energy... My energy.

That was the moment I realized the true nature of energy. It is nothing but enormous tension constantly trying to resolve itself. If we allow it to explode, it destroys all around. But if we gradually open its way of expression under constant observation, we are able to construct, transform and create with it whatever we desire. I also sensed how to keep this power in check knowing that I and the power are one and the same.

Then in the wake of the orgasmic clash of water-me and fire-me enormous steam clouds were sent high that I knew were also me: the freed, light and joyful me diffusing through the air like gas. Pulsing in the rhythm of love I encircled the whole planet with a protecting and nourishing embrace. My consciousness, thirsty for the infinite could bear no boundary. It expanded further, becoming the interplanetary void, transforming into the transcendental ether – the cradle and the tomb of all physical forms. Diamond-lit stars of the galaxies crowned my ether body as brilliant decorations. Then these tiny points of light started to grow, as though the mystery of the Big Bang was being played out in each and every one. They spread out until they touched each other and fused together into one infinite ocean of light. I knew I was this ever-renewing ocean of light and I was also beyond this ocean, where the creative pulsation ceases, where the Word of the Genesis stays silent, where light and dark exist as yet unseparated. Consciousness and energy, Creator and Creation – all in One. Then this infinite motionlessness was broken by a thought: "I am! I exist!" Followed by, "It was me who lived through the cosmic drama of creation in reverse. It was me who travelled the path from personal to universal, from finite to infinite, from created to Creator." And with that thought my consciousness suddenly plummeted back to the prison-cage of time and space. The world around me was revived as if with the wave of a wand. I remembered that *I* was *me*. That I was sitting here in my room at my desk, staring at a photograph in the light of a burnt-down candle. The awareness of my infinite Self was nothing more than the pale reflection of a wonderful dream, a misty memory. I stayed motionless for a while, scrutinizing the secrets of my new-born memory, until the flickering light of the candle flared up one last time and the wax-scented dark engulfed me.

❖

I assumed that my amazing experience was to be attributed to Kundalini but just to make sure – and also so I could boast a little – I asked the Master to enlighten me.

"It was a partial awakening of Kundalini," he replied tersely.

"Oh my goodness! What can it do when it awakes completely? " I thought.

"Do I have you to thank for the miraculous experience?" I asked smiling conspiratorially.

"Evoke the experience as often as you can until it becomes so familiar that you can bring it about at any moment," he said, ignoring my question. I didn't push him any further. I already knew he preferred not to talk much about the secrets hidden behind the wings. But deep in my heart I was inexpressibly grateful to him. I was aware he didn't share such initiation with all his students.

❖

I tried to create the suitable conditions to travel again the initiation route of my inner universe whenever I could. I used the framework I had already experienced but it was certainly no easy task. The capricious snake returned to its slumbering state and I found it extremely difficult to tempt it out of its nest. It just did not want to succumb to my will. Thus, I was rarely able to arrive at an objective perception from creative visualization. I did realize though that it required far less effort if I went into a Kundalini meditation after some pleasant self stimulation, and I supposed that passionate lovemaking would have made it far easier to rouse the slumbering snake-queen. Unfortunately I was unable to employ that method as my prince was still exploring some other land on his white horse. I can't say there were no willing young men around me who would have gladly sacrificed their time for such an attempt, but I wasn't truly in love with any of them. So I experimented with other possibilities and I discovered extra-ordinary things. I noticed I could wake that sleeping ancient force with dance, with certain movements I had seen often in African tribal dances. Flamenco and even Indian dance also contained elements capable of bringing Kundalini to life.

Filled with the enthusiasm of my discovery, I continued my experiments with great momentum. I worked on my new invention for months. It was, of course, nothing new. People had only forgotten about it. I gathered and experimented with all those movements, dance elements and rhythmical patterns that proved to be effective in awakening the snake. In part I used traditional elements of dance language, in part the series of movements that I myself had discovered.

I condensed the results of my search into a Kundalini dance that was at the same time a dynamic meditation. Thus I not only awakened energy – I was also able to direct it, to lead it up the spine's hidden energy channel from one chakra to the next, towards the highest level.

Only after lengthy and persistent practice did I manage to approach the cosmic state I had experienced through the Master's favour. I was starting to sense the real core of dance. I was amazed at its magical-spiritual role, a role that had once justified its very existence, and that had been completely forgotten in our entertainment-oriented culture. Only a few folk dances have preserved elements of that ancient initiatory magical dance culture. Although I would have loved to know more, I didn't know who to turn to for advice. So for the time being I confined it to my own experimentation.

I presented my Kundalini dance, a thoroughly sensual version, at the summer camp. I was dressed in a costume resembling that of my childhood female ideal: the lion-taming Lady Cleopatra. I had a whip, and there were lions too. They were the ferocious wild animals of my primordial powers, brought to life through enchanting dance and intense concentration. They were no easier to tame, bridle and bring under control than real lions. There, on stage, they brought their savage energies to life with more intensity than ever before. For a moment I was gripped by fear. I was terrified they would not succumb to my will. That I would be incapable of making them jump through the fiery ring of my higher chakras. In the end the risky show did succeed, but I suspected the Master also had some part to play in it. At least that was what I felt when I glanced over at him and noted his attentive look radiating concentration. I felt the need to draw strength from his gaze, and from the eyes of the audience too. This was the very secret I had discovered early on, in my first performances.

My dance had a stunning effect. Some of those who came to congratulate me told me enthusiastically that, while watching me, they had felt their own Kundalini energies awake. I was delighted to hear that. The enormous spiritual opportunities hiding in dance filled me with mystical excitement.

Among those who congratulated me one person really raised my interest. A man about forty, with a thick black beard and dark brown hair falling in generous curls to his wide shoulders. He was only a little taller than me but his fine figure made him extremely attractive. Eyes conveying exceptional intelligence complemented his distinctly masculine face, and those eyes also whispered unusual and mysterious depth too.

He introduced himself as Gregor and claimed he had discovered something during my stage performance that he had been "hunting for for a very long time".

"And what might that be?" I asked with genuine curiosity.

"The extremely rare fusion of spiritual power, artistic perfection and female sensuality," he replied with calm objectivity.

His words filled me with joy as I felt they were the words of an experienced man with spiritual knowledge and artistic sensitivity. He said he did not want to hold me up any longer as he saw there were a good number of people waiting behind him to congratulate me. He invited me to dinner the next evening so we would be able to "continue our conversation". Our meeting gave me a strange feeling of déjà vu. My first meeting with Antonin Gautier after Miss Giselle's ballet performance popped into my mind. And it was not the first time I'd had that feeling. I had started to realize that certain moments and events of my life repeated themselves, obviously in other places and with different actors but still according to a virtually identical script. It was as though I was advancing on a spiral, returning to certain points from time to time. But each time I lived out these events with the benefit of richer experience behind me. I was having the feeling again of something being repeated, sensing the meeting indicated the first beat of a new and unexpected life experience. Just like when I'd met Antonin years before. Both had appeared after a pivotal performance and both… seemed so familiar, right from the first moment. Although I was pretty sure we had never met before.

I remarked on this at dinner the following night.

"I had such a strange feeling yesterday when I saw you as though we have already met somewhere before…"

"Yes, we have met," he smiled mysteriously.

"Strange," I pondered. "I don't remember when or where. I thought I had quite a good memory for faces."

"In northern India… but it was a very long time ago. I'm not surprised you don't remember…"

"Northern India? I was in Rishikesh two years ago… perhaps…" I searched my memories with all my strength.

"A little longer ago than that," he laughed. "Some five hundred years ago!"

"I have to admit you have a better memory than me," I laughed back.

"Memory can be refined. My ability to remember was not always so long distance either."

"What do you do?" I brought the matter to a serious topic. "Tell me something about your life!"

"Which one?"

"Well, this one… the present one."

"I'd rather you tell me about yours. I promise I'll tell you everything you'd like to know at our next meeting."

So there would be a next meeting, I thought jubilantly. I definitely liked this man and I concluded from certain signs that I could count on a certain amount of interest on his side too.

"Why are you so secretive?" I asked, attempting a slightly confidential tone.

"Maybe so I can raise interest in the subject of the mystery," he replied with an ambiguous smile that made it impossible to decide when he was joking and when he was being serious.

We had a very pleasant evening together. After he had accompanied me back to my accommodation, we parted with "I'll look for you".

The camp went on for another ten days… and I waited hopefully every day. But he didn't come looking for me. I looked around for him everywhere, but in vain. He was nowhere to be found. The final day drew to an end, and with it my hopes. I sat on the train, disappointed. What a pity, I thought. He was a man after my own heart. You don't meet them every day… and I hadn't had a real lover for such a long time…

On my return to Bucharest I was occupied with my work, so I didn't have much time left to dream about long haired, bearded men with ambiguous smiles. I was planning a new performance with the dance group. I would have liked to experiment with the results of my Kundalini studies on the others but for that I still had to teach them so much else first. I ran into an unexpected difficulty. What I found naturally easy, others required long and enduring practice to master. My greatest test at the time was the lesson of patience…

❖

One day I found a message on my phone. It was sent from a withheld telephone number and written in French:

"Be at Pilots' Square by the metro entrance tonight at nine. An old acquaintance would like to play with you."

My first thought and hope was that it came from Gregor. But I hadn't given him my number. Oh, why! I listed all the people I knew it could possibly be but couldn't think of anyone. Who was this playful acquaintance? Had Alex Feroman got hold of my new number somehow? The fact I'd already given him exactly the same spot as a meeting place increased my suspicion. I had absolutely no desire for such a game… and that late hour was peculiar too. Maybe it would be best if I didn't go to the rendezvous at all. If that someone really wanted to meet me, then he would definitely get in touch again. Or he could call me. He knew my number. Yes, that's the best thing to do. I'll stay at home and wait.

But curiosity consumed me… so at five to nine there I was, walking in the square…

It was a pleasant September evening. A moonlit night, perfect for a romantic meeting. There weren't many people on the streets. From time to time a speeding car broke the silence. A policeman was standing with an armed soldier in front of a bar not far away. A beggar crouching at the foot of the metro entrance railings stretched his hand towards me and muttered something when he saw me. I reached into my pocket and pressed all my change into his palm. He thanked me loudly. It seemed strange that he was doing overtime at such a late hour. Hardly anyone was around. As I moved on I felt a flat object under my foot. I bent down and picked it up. It was a small penknife. I looked around to see who it might belong to but saw no one else in the square so I decided the owner must already have been far away. I tried it. It worked and was quite sharp. I looked at it a little longer, closed it and then slipped it in my pocket. What else could I have done? I glanced at my watch. It was nine o'clock on the dot. A black Mercedes braked beside me. A man in a leather jacket got out of the back seat and motioned that I should sit in the car. The feeling of déjà vu brought back terrifying memories and I was overcome by fear and the instinct to escape. I went on walking, planning to run, but the man grabbed me by the arm and repeated his command. I couldn't wrench my hand free from his clutch. He was holding me with an iron grip. A bearded man leapt out of the front seat, the barrel of a pistol pointed towards me from under his long raincoat. He tried to make me comply in his quietly threatening voice but I ripped my arm out of the other's grip with a sudden movement and set off running. They dashed after me and caught me. When I shouted for help at the top of my voice, the man in the leather jacket covered my mouth. They dragged me towards the car. I caught sight of the men in uniform running towards us. The officer shouted, "Stop" and the soldier fired a warning shot into the air. The bearded one suddenly released me. Then I heard the hellish sound of the pistol and watched as both men in uniform crumpled to the ground clutching their stomachs with a grotesque movement. All my energy drained away, and I let them gag me, tie my hands behind my back and bundle me into the car. It was almost as though I'd been hypnotized. The driver calmly started the car as though nothing had happened. The murderous iron-barrel was pointed at me again. I thought it better to remain compliant. They had managed to convince me what they were capable of.

As the first waves of terror subsided, my brain began to weigh up the situation. Alex was definitely under suspicion now. I thought him capable of organizing just such a kidnapping. What a nice little "game"! The uniformed men lying on the street came to my mind and the beggar… yes, the beggar! If he'd had any sense, he would have noted the car registration! Hope lit up, and I started to wait for the sound of police sirens following us. But we had already been travelling for a while… and nothing had happened. Slowly the city lights faded… As we were racing along a busy highway I suspected there was a long journey ahead. Maybe it wasn't Alex. Maybe the person I was supposed to meet had not even been there yet. And these blokes had just kidnapped me. I had no idea what was happening.

After about an hour I noticed that the armed guard was nodding off. Time to escape! I had already calmed myself, my brain worked with clear purpose. First of all I had to free my hands. I remembered the penknife that was lying in my pocket – and a warm up exercise Antonin had used with us once; we had to stand up from a sitting position so slowly that the watchful referee did not notice us moving. I managed to stand up in fifty-five minutes then. Now my task seemed somewhat easier. It took me half an hour to reach into my pocket, fish out the penknife, open it and cut the fairly tight ties. My hands were free, but I didn't know what to do next. Then I suddenly had an idea. I pretended to feel sick and gestured that they should stop the car as I had to get out. The driver braked without a word. The armed man got out, and the bearded one removed the gag from my mouth. Holding my hands behind my back as if they were still tied, I struggled out of the car. I looked around. We were in a mountainous area with dark forested slopes rising steeply, a full river was winding its way along the valley floor. At the edge of the road a few steps away I noticed a large stone. I went over to it and bent double as though I had to vomit. The leather jacket turned his head away in disgust. Then with a sudden movement I grabbed the stone and hit the armed man's hand with all my force. He screamed terribly. I caught his weapon while it was still in the air and pointed it at him. The other two jumped out of the car immediately. The leather jacket man, who was clutching his fingers, hissed through his clenched teeth that there were no bullets left anyway. The bearded man took out a revolver and came towards me. He ordered me to throw away the weapon as it was empty anyway and I supposed that since he was coming towards me so cautiously – as though he wanted to hypnotize me with his look – he was just bluffing. I held the barrel up and pulled the trigger… it clicked an empty click. They overran me at the same time – all three of them. They brought me down mercilessly, tied me up and then shoved me back into the car. Left bitter by the futility of my escape attempt, I had no energy left to resist. I sank into myself and took the only option I had left. I began to pray silently. And then they covered my eyes too.

I had no idea how long we were travelling for but from the sounds I heard I concluded we had passed through several towns. Then, finally, the car stopped. I heard the creak of a door, and then we went up some steps… another door opened… more steps… a long corridor… another door. When they finally removed the blindfold I found myself in a windowless, whitewashed room with a mattress and check woollen blanket. Nothing else. They took away my telephone and penknife, and then locked me in. A small bathroom with toilet and basin opened off the room. I washed my hands and splashed cold water over my face before going back into the room and stretching out on the mattress. Before five minutes was up the door opened and a bearded Arab man dressed in a white robe came in carrying a tray piled high. He set it down on the mattress.

"Your dinner, Mademoiselle," he said, and bowed low.

"Tell me. What do you want from me?" I asked in a reproachful tone.

"You are the house guest of Ahmed al Khan," he replied politely. "My Master sends word that in the morning, when the sun rises, and you feel fully recovered, he would like to spend time with your good self. Until then, feast well, and rest after your tiring journey."

I wanted to ask more, but he indicated his mission was already complete. He left, locking the door behind him.

My stomach was rumbling madly. I started eating with a greed unbecoming my situation. Ahmed al Khan had certainly guessed my tastes well. The lentil cream soup with lemon, the Mutabal and Fateh were among my favourite foods.

The world looked different with a full stomach. Even imprisoned! I was surprisingly calm, and had even dared to start hoping my "host" was not some one-legged, hairy monster. I had ascended several spirals higher since my experience in Seville, so why would it not be just a little different this time round? I myself have changed a lot.

Sleepiness engulfed me. I pulled back the wool blanket. A black book was lying between the mattress and the wall. I picked it up curiously: a Bible in Romanian. Well, well…. was this Arabian Casanova that respectful with the religious needs of his victims? Or was he merely providing the opportunity for a last prayer? I shuddered at the thought, quickly ushering it away. But I did open the book, just flicked it open and started to read.

"Then upon Jahaziel the son of Zechariah… came the Spirit of the Lord in the midst of the congregation. And he said, Hearken ye, all Judah, and ye inhabitants of Jerusalem, and thou king Jehoshaphat, Thus saith the Lord unto you, Be not afraid nor dismayed by reason of this great multitude; for the battle is not yours, but God's…"

The words made me feel strange, but I was too tired to strain my head thinking about them. Dreams took over.

I awoke to a key turning in the lock. The door opened. I must have been asleep for a long time as I felt fully rested. Two veiled women entered. They motioned that I should stand up. One held a dark-blue satin scarf. They blindfolded me. Then they took my hands and led me out of the room. I allowed things to simply happen. For a second I had the feeling I was watching a film in which I was the main character. The thought filled me with calm and a peculiar happiness. The whole thing was like some strange game.

They carefully guided me down some stairs, and we went through a door. The cold air made my body, still preserving the memory of the warm blanket, shiver. We were outside. Then another door and many, many steps up. As we walked through another door, I was greeted by warm, damp air, and the strong scent of plants. It was as though we had entered a hothouse. I could have removed the blindfold at any moment, but, for some reason, I did not. It was an incomprehensible game, but I was starting to accept the rules.

I felt the touch of delicate women's hands. With slow, almost ritual movements they removed all my clothes. I was standing there totally naked… somewhere… I did not know who was around me… who could see me… what they planned to do with me… And strangely my situation did not bother me. Actually I was excited in a very pleasant way.

The soft hands led me onwards. My bare feet searched out steps, going down. Then my feet met with balmily warm water. I stepped further in until the water reached my belly button. The hands started to wash my whole body, gently stroking it. There were four or five people around me. Naked bodies touched mine. They led me out of the pool, lay me down on a soft surface and massaged me from head to toe with fragrant oils. I did not want to think about what might follow. But this… this was extremely enjoyable. Then they stood me up, dressed me in delicate, silky clothes, adorning my neck, wrists and ankles with jewels and escorted me out of the hothouse… Steps, doors, corridors and more doors. Suddenly the hands which had guided me thus far – and that I trusted to some extent – abandoned me. For a second I felt so alone… Then I felt a hand take my right hand. But this was a different touch: a man's touch. It felt pleasant, soft-skinned, but with a firm grip. A hand suggesting tenacity and resolution. Strong fingers wove into my left hand too. As we held hands, I tried to conjure up a picture of the man standing in front of me, whose breath I sensed on my forehead. Whose body was emitting an unknown, exciting scent. Whose hand suggested strength yet tenderness… even playfulness. Yes, that hand betrayed much about its owner. That should be the way to start getting to know everyone… play of hands… and blindfolded… It is certainly an unusual experience… The man's palms stroked the back of my hand, then started travelling up along my bare arms… my shoulders… my neck… my face… my nape… and, with a gentle movement, they removed the material covering my eyes.

"Gregor!" I shouted out in surprise, happily relieved. I jumped round his neck and hugged him tightly. It was an instinctive explosion. I only remembered afterwards that our relationship was not yet quite so intimate. We had only met twice... and then we had not even touched one another. Too late to worry about that. I had already hugged him, and he had hugged me too.

"Welcome to the Isle of Delights." He smiled at me after I had removed myself from our embrace. "We call it Kama Pura. By God's will you're here."

"God's will you say!?" I said, feigning offence. "Some wicked villains kidnapped me! You dare say welcome?!"

"God brought you here, the *wicked villains* just followed his orders" he retorted, and that familiar, ambiguous smile spread across his face.

"But I don't understand why you had to kidnap me with such violence. I would have been delighted to come, had I known it was about 'delights'... and... you."

"Violence?" he laughed. "You are the only one here who was violent. No one else. I sent a car for you, and bodyguards, so nothing would happen to you. I prepared a pleasant reception... and you..."

"Well, what about the guns?... The police...?"

Placing his index finger on my lips he said, "Come, I'll show you something."

He led me into a room with rows of velvet-upholstered chairs and a small stage. We sat down in the first row. The auditorium lights went out and stage lights illuminated the stage. First to enter were my bodyguards: the bearded one with the pistol, the leather-jacketed one, his hand in bandages and the driver. Then the beggar, the policeman and the armed soldier, the Arab who had brought my dinner, the two veiled women, and the five women of the harem...

"Usually people applaud the actors," Gregor threw in, and started to clap.

The 'actors' bowed. The stage light beam was turned on me, and those standing on stage began to clap. They were applauding me. My eyes filled with tears. I had no idea what was happening to me... should I be laughing or crying? I only knew that I already loved these people.

The group of actors paraded down to the auditorium, and then the lights went out.

"It's not finished yet," said Gregor.

Space music started up. A picture was projected onto the white background: dark sky with shining stars. The stars began to dance and to swirl as they changed into letters forming a golden title:

THE WHOLE WORLD IS A STAGE

The music became the sound of children laughing, and the letters disbanded. The next picture: black women's shoes on the pavement… she stops… coins fall into an open palm… thanks from twisted lips… long black hair bouncing… a face appears out of the dimness… my face! Wow! They filmed it all!

Excitement ran through me, and my gaze was fixed to the screen: hands playing with penknife… breaking car… scuffles… weapon firing… police helmet flying, hitting the kerb and stopping…

The pictures flashed past. I watched with baited breath. I watched the face – *my* face – and the changing emotions that were reflected so clearly: overshadowed by fright, twisted in fear, bitterness, dismay, cunning watchfulness, cold determination…

It was strange looking at myself… Myself? That person who half a day earlier I had identified as myself, who twelve hours earlier had been struggling, cursing, fighting, crying, suffering and praying. About whom I could not say in my heart of hearts that it was *me*.

As I watched myself being tricked, it all struck me as utterly ridiculous. I had believed it all to be merciless reality – when it was all just an innocent game! How frightened I had been. Fear had ruled me. How cruel the instinct to survive and the imagined danger had made me… I may even have been capable of killing. That thought made me shiver as the recognition flashed through my mind like lightning that we humans are like this almost every moment. This is how we think, feel, and act. We forget that life is just a game. That we are merely players upon a wonderful great stage. We suffer, go mad, hug, hate, hurt, kill – unconsciously. How much more beautiful we could make this play, if we have to play anyway! It all depends on us! Life assigns the roles, but we choose how we act them out…

If only I had been able to see myself like this yesterday, from the outside, as though I was watching a film. I would have acted differently. Far better. Like children play… and those in love.

The true meaning of Shakespeare's words hit me, like a startling recognition, an enlightenment for the whole of my life: All the world's a stage… and we are all merely players!

I experienced inexpressible gratitude to that great literary initiate, who had managed to put the greatest mystery of life into words. Gratitude also to Gregor's group who had been able to transform this great mystery in me into living reality.

And yes, this certainly was real theatre. Antonin should have seen it! This was the genuine "Realithéâtre" he had been searching for, but had not found. These people had succeeded. They had discovered the "living play" that theatre has been looking for centuries. In comparison even the most daring interactive, modern performance is merely a weak experiment. This was true art... It is true art, because it is initiation... because it leads to catharsis... Because it leads to enlightenment. And it was still theatre, even if several actors play for only one spectator. Spectator? Who is the audience here anyway? And who is the actor? Since all the players are both audience and actor in one body... Only the roles are different... Just as in life.

The light in the room came on again. Gregor motioned for the group to come closer.

"This is the drama group of Kama Pura," he said with a sweep of his arm.

"And who was the director?" I asked curiously.

"Emanuel," replied Gregor, pointing towards a tall, dark, blue-eyed lad.

"I was the Great Director's earthly representative," interrupted Emanuel, his hand outstretched. "Actually it was Gregor's idea. I only directed it."

"Tell me, how did you manage to work out exactly what I would do? And my reactions too?"

"What happened was just one of the possible versions of the script. God gave people free will, and so that precisely what we gave you too. We worked out numerous versions, and then there was the "Great Director's" version too, which, of course, we had no idea about."

"What would have happened if I hadn't given money to the tramp?"

"You wouldn't have found the penknife. You'd have had less chance of escaping."

"And the rock which just happened to be there when we stopped?"

"That was the Great Director's variation," offered my bandaged friend. "And my karma that was expressed through you."

I blinked guiltily towards him, and asked for forgiveness for my thoughtless act.

"No problem," he reassured me laughing. "Every job has its risks. We're used to them."

"And what was the Bible all about?"

"Well, that was part of the Omnipotent's work too," replied Emanuel, glancing towards Gregor.

"Yes, I thought so."

"It wasn't in any of the variations. But we hadn't checked the room thoroughly enough – one of us had left it there after a twenty-four hour prayer practice in that room."

"To be honest it's typical of God," offered Gregor. "He grabs every opportunity to convey His message to his creations." His observation was received with general cheer.

"He always presents us with surprises, so we don't forget for a minute who the real director is."

"And where did the Bible open?" asked one of the cameramen. "Unfortunately we couldn't film that."

"I read a part from Chronicles II in which the Lord uses one of his prophets to comfort the Israelites before battle. Telling them they should not be afraid of the overwhelming force they faced since it was not them, but God that was fighting."

"Fantastic!" enthused Emanuel. "You see… that's what's amazing in this kind of theatre. It's the unexpected things that make the work perfect. We can do whatever we want. God still has the last word."

"And what other variations were there?" I was still curious.

"One possibility was that you wouldn't show up for the meeting at all. And then you wouldn't have come to Kama Pura."

"So it was a kind of spiritual test too then?"

"A spiritual test, and, of course, a mirror for you – just like every initiatory mystery play. Another possibility was that you realized who it was about from the keywords hidden in Gregor's letter to you. And then you'd have been able to pretend to us. That was perhaps the best scenario – that you acted the whole play as though you didn't know who had initiated it. So we wouldn't know you knew… There was an empathy test too in the play. If you had paid just a little more attention to the people, not only to their exteriors, making preconceptions based on the gun and the leather jackets, you'd have sensed that they were not bandits but people similar to you. Peaceful companions on your spiritual path, and that it was all just a game."

"Well, yes. I certainly have to work on developing my empathy. It was never one of my strong points. But this morning I realized it was just a game so I allowed things to take their course."

"Yes, the last test. It was the most difficult and you passed. We purposefully left your hands free. You could have taken off the blindfold at any moment."

"And if I had taken it off?"

"You wouldn't have been allowed to stay in Kama Pura… That's what the Master stipulated… That was his input."

"So the Master knew about it all too?" I asked in surprise.

"The Master knows about everything," Gregor informed me with a playful smile. "That's why he's a master."

As I began to see the events more clearly and to understand them, I was increasingly amazed at the perfection of the interconnectedness of events. I had one final question, for Gregor. It actually was a rhetoric question. I meant it as a lead in for the surprise I had for the group.

"Tell me how you had the kidnapping idea."

"I sat down to meditate. I visualized your face in front of me, and waited. I allowed the idea to be born. A play that would be most suited to your personality. When it flashed before me I had no doubt. I knew it was the right one."

"I've got a surprise for you too," I turned ceremonially towards the group. "Seven years ago, in the beautiful Spanish city of Seville, a girl was walking on the street. It was about nine o'clock at night. A black Mercedes stopped beside her. Three figures in leather jackets jumped out. They grabbed the girl and forced her into the car. That girl was called Laurianne. Seven years ago I lived out this script, identical at almost every step. The difference was that they were real baddies, with real guns, who stroked me with real punches. My host was a proper Arab, a hairy, one-legged man, a true savage and, if the 'Great Director' hadn't stepped in at the last minute, then there would have been no performance here today…"

Stunned silence met my words. Everyone was staring in front of them, as though some miracle had happened… Actually it had… I think these are the real miracles… Finally Gregor broke the lull.

"So that was also the work of the Great Director! And I was so proud of my fantastic idea!"

❖

The series of unexpected turns had not yet finished. The director of all things gave me a new surprise at lunch.

I was already eating dessert when someone covered my eyes from behind. A fine female hand with a soft touch and unusually long fingers. I was sure I recognized these fingers but just couldn't bring to mind the face they belonged to. Then a velvety alto voice whispered in my ear.

"Welcome to the queen's birthday."

Then I knew exactly who it was.

"Natalia!" I cried out in joy and leapt up to hug her. "I didn't dare hope we'd meet again."

"I knew we would. I reckoned that sooner or later you'd find your way here."

"What made you think that?"

"There are some things a person senses," she replied smiling mysteriously. "I knew your place is here."

"And when is your birthday?"

"27th September… Today… and thank you for my present…"

"What present?" I looked uncomprehendingly.

"You. You are my present. I asked God if you could be here today. And I got it. I've thought lots about you since we met. And I've waited quite impatiently for Fate to finally bring you here."

"I've thought loads about you too... I can hardly wait to show you what I learnt from you... there..."

"You'll have the chance. We're going to be living together," she replied, and squeezed my hand. "Come on, I'll show you our room."

The first chord of our burgeoning, wonderful friendship rang in that squeeze.

❖

I moved into Kama Pura permanently. For a long time I had the feeling that, as a result of an extraordinary time travel, I had arrived at the era of spiritual renaissance. The atmosphere and inhabitants of Kama Pura reminded me of the image that esoteric traditions paint of the coming 'Golden Age'. The people living here were testament to an elevated spiritual level. In their everyday lives, work and relationships they reflected most noble values. They gave themselves completely to achieving shared goals, aimed to attain the highest spiritual ideals, and accepted one another totally. This, along with their mutual understanding and love, the lofty sacred seriousness of their spiritual practice, and the constant good mood and boundless cheerfulness that characterized their life together all made me think that if there was an earthly paradise, then Kama Pura certainly deserved that title.

The complex itself was built on foundations in the form of a mandala. The square area of roughly one hectare was staked out with metal fencing based in concrete. This perfectly imitated the outline of mandalas. Young trees lined a circular path inside the fence. The next element of the mandala structure was represented by the three large buildings in this square figure. The fourth side was closed by a tall hedge. The internal courtyard this created had been made into a stunning Japanese garden with a Shiva lingam carved of shining white marble rising in the centre and wonderful sculptures of naked couples around the garden. The men lived in the building on the right, the Vira Loka, which had several workshops on the ground floor along with sound and film studios.

We girls lived in the Shakti Loka in the left wing of the complex. The kitchen and the dining room were here too. The top floor was made entirely of glass – a hothouse full of exotic trees, bushes and colourful flowers with three small pools set among the lush vegetation. A shrine to the beauty of nature. The inhabitants of Kama Pura loved this place especially, and its name, Fragrant Garden, suited it perfectly.

A circular tower rose in the middle of the central building: the Tantra Loka. It had two impressive round halls. The lower was the Mandalas Room where we gathered together for communal spiritual practice. The walls were decorated with colourful mandalas symbolizing the ten cosmic powers, the ten Mahavidyas of the tantric tradition. Above that was the Shiva shrine which we only used for special meditations and rituals. To me this was the most beautiful place in the whole spiritual complex; colourful mosaics of the Shiva yantra created the floor; stained glass panels incorporating mythical elements from Shaivism adorned the arched windows; and reliefs evoking the erotic carvings of the Khajuraho temple were set on the walls between the windows.

The two wings of the central building housed more workshops, rehearsal rooms, library and the studio theatre. The fantasy rooms of the top floor were designed for couples to meet. The Arabian Room was here, along with the Indian, Japanese, Chinese and Egyptian Rooms. There were also several decorated in modern, western style, each with suitable props for erotic games.

I stumbled from one dream to another as Natalia led me around this incredible temple to spirituality, the arts and love. At every turn I had the feeling that every single detail was built organically into this superbly designed 'whole'. It was harmonious and balanced – a perfect artistic creation.

The complex had been designed by Gregor, based on the Master's advice and inspiration from the sages of Shambhala with whom he had apparently been in constant contact. Though born in Romania, when still a child Gregor had moved with his parents to Germany. Particularly attracted to the eastern arts, he had studied art history and sculpture at the University of Berlin. On a visit to the land of his birth he met one of the Master's female disciples and, through her, encountered Tantra yoga.

After the end of the Ceauşescu regime, he had moved back to Romania and become acquainted with the teachings of Kashmir Shaivism, the highest spiritual school of the east under the guidance of the Master. He had thrown himself into studying the writings of the Kashmiri sages with greedy enthusiasm, helped by the fact he had already learnt Sanskrit in Berlin. Using these effective spiritual methods he quickly attained excellent results on his spiritual path. Together with a few similarly minded friends he founded the spiritual group, the Kaula. With superhuman work, they had established Kama Pura in less than nine years. Gregor's most fervent desire was to revive the extremely valuable spiritual tradition so close to his own soul. He used his spiritual intuition to select the members of the Kaula. New people could only join the community if Gregor felt them ready, the Master agreed and, of course, if they passed the initiation test.

When I arrived in Kama Pura there were about forty of us in the group.

Gregor proved to be a very strict leader and put much energy into establishing and developing the communal spirit. According to the tantric tradition, spiritual growth is faster as part of a loving couple than alone. And group development is even faster. But the most effective framework for spiritual advance can be created by a group made up of tantric couples. And this is what Gregor was trying to achieve in Kama Pura. Naturally you needed a certain spiritual maturity to gain entry into such a group explaining why not everyone was allowed into the Kaula. At the start I had some doubts as to whether I truly deserved to be here, and whether I was up to it. As long as I had known my own mind I had been a convinced individualist, with no desire to belong to any kind of group. I fiercely protected my own freedom, never yearning 'to become like the others'. This kind of illness of the artists was one I had to cure myself of quickly in Kama Pura. And it was not as difficult once I understood the concept of the spiritual group, realizing just what indescribable assistance such a community was able to offer on the Way.

Most of the Kaula members were artists so artistic activities obviously received an elevated role in Kama Pura life. People worked in the various workshops: the painting and sculpture studios, music, dance and theatre studios, along with places for film and literature. Each group worked on creating an artistic language to make their spiritual treasure accessible to those who possessed aesthetic sensitivity but were not yet mature enough to step onto the spiritual path. This was the exoteric part of artistic activity. There was also an esoteric thread, the goal of which was to create works and performances that spoke to initiates, works of art capable of bringing about high states of consciousness and true cathartic enlightenment.

Naturally I joined the dance group. It was led by a girl from Budapest, Amrita, who – like me – had long lasting ballet training before going on to study the secrets of eastern dance in India and Indonesia for several years. Her real name was Amália Rita but here everyone called her Amrita.

In the period when I arrived the dance group was experimenting with Sufi dances. In the theory lessons we explored the Indian aesthetic theory of Rasa and its connection with the Sufi-inspired enneagram typologies. I found it amazing to experience how similar the cores of these spiritual theories were despite having been established at various points of the earth and in different cultures.

I had much to learn. I had to catch up everything the other Kaula members already understood. This provided me unspeakable joy as the teachings of the Kashmir sages were close to my heart. Among the titans of this once flourishing and influential spiritual tradition were two who had a particular influence on me. One was a woman known as Lalla whose incredible personality and writings radiated a mystical energy, freedom and joy of life that can only be born of those people whose hearts have become one with the divine heart – only such a heart would be capable of living the divine joy of Life and god's zest for life to the full.

Up until that point I had sensed a similar soaring mystic strength only in verses written by the great Sufi poet, Jalaluddin Mevlana Rumi. I had been astonished how similarly the most sacred spiritual experiences are played out: the great mystics' experiences of becoming one with God. I realized that the meeting of Creator and Creation was the unification of two loving hearts each desiring and searching for the other bringing boundless happiness.

The other person to whom I had a mystical attraction was Abhinava Gupta, the most eminent figure of Kashmir Shaivism. His writings were inspired by the highest spiritual vision, the existence in a state of complete divine freedom. This is how he expresses the vision in one of his verses.

"Cling to nothing, renounce nothing, live in the joy of Plenitude, and be who You are."

To express the most profound truths and elevated states of consciousness he often called upon the arts. Whenever I read his poetry I feel I am holding diamonds whose light projects the great secret truths onto my mind's canvass with sharp clarity, igniting with overwhelming strength the desire to meet with the Lord of the World, the Great Lover playing in total freedom.

However, it is not easy to understand the writings of the Kashmir sages, without Gregor's help I would not have got far at all. I am grateful to him for gradually revealing all those secrets that he himself was only able to decipher based on the Master's guidelines and an enormous amount of work.

❖

I developed a special relationship with Gregor. He had an endearing personality, masculine determination, playful humour, and thoughtful kindness that totally captivated me. I adored him and thought it natural that, after a while, we started visiting the Tantra Loka fantasy rooms together. I was well aware that Gregor had a stunning girlfriend, Evelina, and I knew they loved each other, but as it was he who made the first steps, I accepted his approach. I did not regret it. The experiences I had with him were life changing. Certainly the most experienced man I had met in my adventurous life, he initiated me into the secrets of tantric love. And it was with him that I tasted my first ritual, sacred lovemaking.

At the beginning I felt strange with Evelina. But when I saw she regarded our relationship as natural, not showing even the slightest hint of jealousy, I gradually felt reassured. What's more, I felt no discomfort or tension when I knew Evelina and Gregor were together. That surprised me, but I attributed this phenomenon – so inconceivable in the outside world – to the elevated spiritual atmosphere of Kama Pura.

It was fantastic being with Gregor. To lie in his strong arms, listen to his titillating whispers, opening my body and soul for him... it was wonderful to receive him into me... and yet, I didn't really feel him as the true love of my heart. Our relationship was rather one of master and student. I perceived him more as my initiator. Of course, I only became aware of the subtle difference after a long time when I started to feel something was still missing: some deep resonance, some delicate vibration, the accord of the secret strings hidden in the depths of our souls. That string, in my soul, was still silent. Not one man had yet managed to vibrate it... not even Gregor. But I already sensed that this string existed. And I knew there must be someone on this planet able to make it sound.

Actually it was a rather unusual event that helped me realize what was missing from my relationship with Gregor. The scene was played out by my roommate and faithful friend, Natalia, with her bespectacled lover – the man who had received a birthday present in the bar the like of which few men can boast. This time he was not wearing his glasses. One night he crept into our bedroom after we had both fallen asleep. Although he opened the door carefully, I still woke up and heard him slip in beside Natalia. Their suppressed whispers together with the unmistakable sounds from lips nourishing themselves from the other's breath stirred great excitement in me. Though I kept my eyes closed and politely pretended to be asleep, my mind caught every sigh with the awareness of an animal ready to pounce, projecting thrilling pictures of all that was happening in the neighbouring bed. The sounds became louder and even more obvious. As the heat of the game swept them along they gave themselves freely to the joy of love and each other. Feeling strange I wondered if I should go to the room next door to leave them alone. But I did not, experiencing an increasingly irresistible desire to see that which was so disturbing and magnetic so close to me. Slowly I turned towards them and opened my eyes.

I have never seen anything like it. And from so close. And for so long. I would never have believed what a wonderful experience it is to watch lovers loving each other. They were beautiful as they pleased and cherished one another; as they stroked each other and replied to the touch; as they let themselves go or allowed the other free reign to the exploding desires and emotions, played together, sometimes tenderly, sometimes passionately. As they became their own true selves, undressed of all inhibitions, all boundaries and all masks. It did not even matter that I was there, watching them. Nothing else mattered, only love...

Their whole bodies and souls vibrated. Right down to the soul's most deeply hidden delicate string, the key to a secret dimension their souls had already penetrated. A dimension whose nature I was only beginning to suspect. It was as though I had listened to a wonderful symphony whose playfully dancing rhythm, melodies awaking sweet memories and uplifting harmonies had not been spoiled by a single wrong note.

They were able to tune in to the other with particular insight and tenderness. The sight filled me with the feeling of perfection and completeness. To watch them... it was a divine experience. And divine grace too. Dawn was breaking when they moved apart. Natalia snuggled in next to me and hugged me. Her body was still hot, and love-scented.

"Please don't be angry with us that we didn't let you sleep," she said. There was no guilt in her voice, rather trust in a friend's understanding.

"Don't be angry that I watched you," I replied, no trace of guilt in me either. "It was so... so wonderful. I've never seen anything like it."

"Well, I'm glad we've enriched you with a new experience then."

"And I'm glad I had the chance to know you... like this. You know I've realized you can truly know people only if you watch when they make love. I think it is the only time we can really be ourselves."

"You've got some interesting ideas," she said looking at me surprised. "I'd never thought of that. But... I think you're right." Then she continued, laughing, "I'm going to recommend to Gregor that he introduces it into the Kaula, as a method of group development. So we can all get to know each other well."

❖

The awareness this most recent experience matured in me, ignited my desire to meet a man finally. A man whose love would reach the most profoundly hidden mysteries of my soul. Make my mysterious strings sound the first notes of the symphony of plenitude...

That was when I decided to follow a tantric method that would enable me to direct the path of Fate. To find that man somewhere in the labyrinth of time and space. The Man. For seven weeks I carried out my secret ritual, every day for forty-nine days. And then...

17. Dream and reality

I dusted off my abandoned sitar. A touch of remorse mingled with the joy of getting together again. Sounds of rebuke answered when I tried to lure some notes out of it. My fingers had grown unused to these kinds of pleasures and did not want to obey me, though there were many impressions in me longing to be played out. Weeks passed before my fingers became my allies, willing to conjure my feelings into music.

Just as every process that has started will create its own continuation, my musical endeavours also birthed important revolutions. First, Fate brought me together with Alin, a musician from Bucharest. He had a cosy studio with many fancy electronic devices, keyboards and a piano. We started to work together. A few weeks later Hanna appeared on the scene. She played the flute superbly and had a beautiful voice. So our duo became a trio and, as three is the number of creation, this formation bode well for our creative work.

Hanna was the one who drew our attention to the importance of numbers. An expert in numerology, sacred mathematics, and esoteric musical theory, she was able to stimulate my interest in these subjects. I was astonished to discover how musical scales are in complete harmony with the structure of the Universe, and that understanding the laws of musical notes provides essential information about the design of the Universe and its phenomena.

I was beginning to understand the theory of resonance that serves as a basis for the existence and structure of the whole Creation and that is also the foundation on which the Master built our yoga school's system of spiritual practice.

Hanna insisted on us keeping these occult theories in mind while composing music, and being fully aware of the cosmic energy-sphere that our music attunes its listener to. Hanna not only understood music and numbers, she also had great skills with words; she spoke Sanskrit and understood the Kabbalistic interpretation of the Hebrew alphabet. I learned from her that the letters of these sacred alphabets are not mere bricks that make up words. They possess a magical power and they invoke specific cosmic energies. She also explained to me the secrets of magical syllables, called mantras according to the teachings of Kashmir Shaivism.

She was the most intelligent woman I had ever met. Her synthesizing mind had a rather masculine way of thinking. She could easily penetrate to the depths of things and extract the essence of a phenomenon even from its tiniest details. She could easily scan people with her psychological X-rays and set up surprisingly accurate profiles even about complete strangers. She said she always thought in archetypes and that it was enough to establish which archetype one belongs to in order to perceive their main motivations and characteristic behaviour. She linked everyday situations to archetypal situations and was thus able to identify the right attitude for the given circumstances. My connection with Hanna was not limited to mere conversations about theories. Now and then, in an archetypal situation, for example when we happened to be together in a room with a bed, we applied the natural behavioural patterns befitting the situation when a man and woman meet. As these experiments did not have the results we expected, we continued with them only until we realized we could not neglect the phenomenon of resonance in the matter either. We were unable to attune to each other precisely on the level that the archetypal situation would have required. Namely the sexual level. The main reason was that Hanna, like most intellectual women, concentrated a high proportion of her energies within the region of her skull, so little was left for the abdominal parts and not much more for the pectoral zone.

However, these meetings were not entirely fruitless. Thanks to the cosmic law of balance, my intellectual needs increased markedly along with my ability to see the crux of the matter, and she started to show more interest in phenomena related to the pelvic region. The archetypal focal points of pleasure began to awake in her body. But as my needs that had matured with Gina's and Adela's archetypal femininity, were far stronger than hers, I could no longer take responsibility to work on her sexual awakening.

On a musical level we were able to attune to each other fairly well and working together proved to be exciting. She was very talented and had a fine ear for music. We meditated every time before we played. We visualized an atmosphere, a mood that we tried to preserve while playing. Usually we improvised and let the music be born out of this mood. When we discovered the right tone of the music, it reinforced our specific inner mood, and the music created this way inspired us to play more and more in accordance with the previously visualized atmosphere. We also realized that listening to the recorded music evoked the same mood in us, even weeks later.

We came to the conclusion that music is not as subjective as it might seem. It actually presents a high level of objectivity. A musical piece will always tune and elevate its listener to its own spheres, provided the listener likes the piece and is willing to let it in. If the music irritates him, it will elicit entirely different feelings. Obviously, this is not to be attributed to the objective influence of the music, but to the listener's lack of acceptance.

We tried to prove our assumptions with experiments: at our summer camp concert we played three pieces, each with its own distinct atmosphere. We tried to tune the audience to the energy-spheres of bravery, cheerfulness, and love. Then we took a poll to measure if the audience felt the same as we had planned.

The results were beyond our expectations. Sixty per cent were able to define the mood exactly, twenty per cent felt something similar. The remaining twenty per cent were those who were either not paying attention, did not feel anything, or said something completely different.

So our assumptions proved to be right, and we were convinced that consciously composed music could have a precisely controlled effect on the human soul. Then I understood the negative side of it, and I was amazed how easy it is to manipulate people through music. As we did with our death metal concerts in Stockholm. How easy it was to synchronize listeners to the wavelengths of that infernal music and merge them into one raging crowd! I recalled how we got into contact – many of us against our will – with diabolical forces, and how these forces gained power over our feelings, thoughts and lives. I was astonished to realize music is one the most powerful magical tools; with its help "musicians", making alliance with demonical forces, are able to consciously destroy. This power is also used by those initiated in occult sciences, black magicians like Magnus Evans and other such patrons. This kind of exploitation of human ignorance angered me. I would have liked to figure out something to enlighten people, to call their attention to the dangers and blessings of listening to music. To tell them that sooner or later we all become alike to the music we listen to. Sublime music elevates the soul, glorious music induces noble feelings; harmonious music keeps us balanced, light-hearted and joyful. Worthless and fashionable mass music turns us into worthless mass-people obsessed with fashion; aggressive music awakens violent impulses; depressing music makes us downhearted; diabolical music makes us prisoners of dark powers.

I toyed with the idea of writing a book about the esoteric theory of music and its occult influences but knew I would have needed much more experience for that. I could not do anything about this matter except to continue with my experiments and to compose music that tolls the most beautiful emotions in the listener's heart.

❖

I had a puzzling dream a few days after the summer camp. I saw Carina Dahl sitting on a crimson velvet-covered stool, stark naked. She held her cello tight between her thighs, and was playing, eyes closed, unworldly expressions on her face. I asked her, begged her to put down the instrument so I could see her naked body. She did not listen to me and continued playing, her body undulating to the rhythm of the music. Strangely, I did not hear the cello but a whole orchestra playing wonderful, ethereal music, similar to what I had heard during my birthday meditation. I grabbed the instrument. I wanted to take it out of her hands, tear it away violently to get closer to her naked groin, to touch her. But my arms were weak, my hands could only caress, sliding up and down the lustrous instrument, as in my first lesson when I was getting to know the cello.

As I reached the sound hole, instead of the hard wood, I felt a warm silkiness in my hands. My fingers submerged between the wet lips. The instrument had disappeared and Carina's nakedness was opening up in front of me. I leaned closer and watched her labia swelling, growing as large as a human, and I felt an irresistible desire to creep into the hole, to feel the warmly pulsating walls with my whole body. I opened my way as though I was pulling apart a thick velvet curtain, my arms spread out… and… I found myself in an unknown world. I could not discern any forms or figures. A swirling, multi-coloured fog seemed to descend. As I advanced the glistening fog began to lift, or rather it took distinguishable forms, crystallizing into female statues that formed a large circle. In the centre of the circle a lone female figure stood on a tall marble pedestal. Her body and face were covered by a white veil.

I stepped closer to the nearest statue, which was shining with ebony light. As I touched her, she opened her eyes, her body was filled with life and started to move. Her face… it was so familiar! Yes, I recognized it then. It was Sibylla's face. Her figure also reminded me of Sibylla, although she was more fulsome and her breasts larger. I saw the familiar garland of skulls hanging round her neck, the snake head dagger in her hand. She began to dance a dance so wild and terrifying it could raise the dead. Fear overcame me, and I wanted to escape, but she grabbed me, turned me towards her and forced me to look into her eyes. I was amazed to see nothing terrifying in her face. There was no trace of the mad look that haunted my memories of Sibylla, nor were any clues of the subtle cruelty that once hid in the line of her lips. This was a breathtakingly beautiful and provocative Sibylla with sensual lips and a piercing but not cold look. This Sibylla was smiling! I enclosed her in my arms and she put her arms around me. Our warm embrace dissolved all my terrible memories of her. I hugged her passionately and felt her body melting and merging into mine, her soul becoming part of me, her vitality living on within me. I looked around surprised, but she was nowhere to be seen.

I moved to the next sculpture. She was shining like alabaster, her hands folded in prayer. When I touched her with quivering hands, her eyes opened and Christa Forshman's big, innocent eyes looked down on me. Immense joy flooded through me. So she is alive, Christa has resurrected! I knew she could not really have died! Wow! How beautiful she has become!

An eight-point golden star shone on her chest that emanated its own light, like the inner sun of her soul. She opened her arms and pulled me to her breast. When she embraced me, I felt God himself was holding me in his arms. I held her tight with joy, I merged her into myself and then walked on to the other statues. I touched them one by one and each came to life taking the shape of the women I had met in my life, all those I loved and who loved me, and opened up their body and soul for me. I recognized them, their features and their characteristic movements, though they were not exactly them. To be more accurate, they were themselves in their most perfect form and nature, in full harmony, within charming bodies of goddesses – beautifully the same, yet all different.

Linnéa Svenson's skin glowed with the light of a velvety red rose petal. Her body adorned with garlands, she caressed me with fingers formed in graceful mudras.

Éva Zoltay's hands flashed lightning as she danced and in her embrace all disguise and all masquerades I had woven around me out of habit or vanity were burned to ashes.

Freja's body was covered by an azure veil. She offered me a yellow parchment scroll. When I opened it a mysterious map unfolded in front of my eyes, a three-dimensional picture, like a hologram: the map of the visible and invisible World, drawn with light. As I watched it, I started to grow and expand until I became as large as the Universe itself.

My breath stopped at the marvellous sight of Mette Hansen belly dancing. My thoughts simply vanished into thin air. Spellbound, I embraced her as if enchanted and became united with her.

Tongues of flames shot up beside the meditating figure of Gina when I touched her and she opened her eyes. I stepped back alarmed, but she indicated I should stand closer. When I stepped inside the ring of fire I realized these flames did not burn and when, together with the Gina's body, they transformed into a liquid fire in my veins, such enormous energy awoke in me that I could have moved mountains.

Ramona's face was covered by a grey veil. She seemed like a sad, grieving widow. Seeing her like this, remorse overcame me for the suffering I had caused her, and the suffocating loneliness of a sinful spirit conquered me. But as she pulled aside the veil I noticed a cheerful smile opening. All the tension in me lifted, and I felt the forgiving, blissful might of her embrace.

Adela held a bowl laden with fruits and handed me a golden apple. I took it and bit into it. Tastes I had never before experienced flooded through me. I felt the unforgettable flavour of divine nectar not only on my tongue but throughout my body.

The last statue of the magical circle was the figure of Hanna. She gave me a black metallic disk that contained a geometric blueprint resembling a mandala. I did not understand its meaning. I kept staring at it. Then the lines became longer, dashing on towards the infinite until they wove into a brilliant net that connected everything in the world.

Then that picture disappeared too, and I found myself in front of a luminous marble altar that had one last statue on it covered with a white veil. Steps led up to the pedestal. As I reached the statue the veil slipped off. A stunning beauty smiled at me. She seemed familiar, as if I had seen her somewhere before, but I could not recollect who she was. Something indescribable and ethereal emanated from her. This radiation awakened a peculiar, yet unknown emotion in me, inexplicable and stirring at the same time. It closely resembled love, but it was much stronger... and greater.

She was alive – just like all the other statues. But she did not move. Only a barely noticeable, silent calling was visible in her eyes. I felt an irresistible desire to embrace her. I stepped closer and took her in my arms. I hugged and pressed her passionately until my body slowly dissolved in the light of her body. I was no longer somebody anymore, I simply *was*, I simply *existed*, for one single but infinite moment... and then I woke up.

No more dreams were projected on the screen of my consciousness that night. I was wide awake. My mind was clear as a mirror, and renewed strength flowed in my veins. I sat with eyes wide open for a long time trying to decipher the meaning of my dream. I sank into a meditative state and replayed the pictures in my mind over and over to relive these wonderful feelings. The joy in my heart intensified to exultation.

Something exceptional happened that night. Something changed in me, the light of a new way of understanding sparkled, and in this light my past and present acquired a new meaning. As though in a flash, I had been relieved of the burden of past memories to become light and free. Something had come to an end. The circle became complete and I felt something new was about to start, something more beautiful and better than ever before. I know the world had not changed, yet I still saw it differently. I beheld people differently; a new Gina, Adela, even Hanna. I saw them as in my dream: wonderful, beautiful, perfect. Actually, that is what happened: I had discovered their hidden perfection. From that moment on I could only see them in that way, and I saw that in the mirror of my eyes they also perceived themselves as miraculous divine beings – and that ultimately brought them closer to divine perfection.

❖

One day, I found a small envelope on my bed. Unsealed, nothing written on it. I fished out a folded paper which said:

Deepest desires of your heart shall lead you on your way. Follow the path until you discover what you are looking for. Be in El Paraíso tomorrow at four.

It was written by a female hand, I was certain. I puzzled over the identity of the writer for ages. I had a few secret admirers and suspected she must be one of them. Frankly speaking I did not expect much of the meeting. Still, the invitation excited me, and it kept me awake until the small hours that night. I projected thousands of ways of how the meeting would go. But it also crossed my mind that one of my friends was playing a trick on me. Nevertheless, the next day at the given time I was sitting in El Paraíso, impatiently awaiting the developments. At three minutes past four (I looked at the time every second) an extremely pretty tanned woman stepped in and, after glancing around, sat down at a table in front of me. I stole glances at her and hoped she might be my romantic playmate. She was served a large slice of cream cake, which she started to eat with relish. I had the feeling that occasionally she glanced over at me with interest. I tried to catch her eye in the hope of reading her purpose. When at last our eyes met, she smiled at me, and then continued. I was none the wiser. It was ten past four and, as nobody else had showed up, I thought I would carry on getting to know her. I looked at her provocatively. She answered with the same mysterious smile and did not look away this time. We measured each other up for long moments, but she did not stop eating – or smiling. In fact, she started to lick the cream off the spoon with such expertise that I felt shivers running through me and felt flustered. I suddenly turned my head away. I regretted it the next moment and wanted to start that game again, but she no longer looked over at me. She finished her dessert, paid, and was on her way. I felt sorry for ruining it all and could not decide what to do. *I should have been braver. I should have sat down at her table to meet her, but now it was late....* Before she went out, she looked back and smiled at me one last time. I had the feeling she was inviting me... Then she closed the door and hastened her steps. *If it really had been an invitation, then probably she would have waited at the entrance a bit longer. Or was she waiting outside?* I indicated to the waitress that I would like to pay. She brought a heart-shaped folder. When I opened it I saw it contained not a bill but a slip of paper with the same handwriting:

Northern Station, counter three.

I looked at the waitress perplexed. She said the bill had already been settled and left me alone. I started for the station. Well, what else could have I done?

Several people were waiting in line at the counter: a grey-haired man, a plump lady of about forty, and a soldier. Hoping my playmate was not amongst them, I looked around questioningly. A little later I saw a vision with long blonde hair coming towards me, the kind a man's eye espies from a mile away. She was dragging two gigantic travel bags behind her, apparently in a hurry. She stopped to catch her breath not far away from me... she seemed as though she was looking at me asking for help. She was attractive, the type you do not normally see in the streets, not even on screen... I went towards her, then came to a sudden halt. *What if it's not her and I miss my chance of meeting the right person. Or it is her after all and now she's testing my readiness to help?* I was clueless. I only knew I was being tested, but I could not figure out what I was supposed to do. In fairy-tales wanderers receive a reward when they help old women to carry the twigs: the old woman turns to an enchanting princess, and the hut into a splendid palace. So in this case would the already beautiful princess turn into an ugly witch if I helped her with her bags? I had to laugh. In the end, I did not help her, turned away and glanced at my watch so she would think I was waiting for someone.

As I turned towards the counters I noticed the ticket agent frantically waving at me. I stepped closer wondering what she wanted. She pressed a ticket into my hand and told me to hurry as my train was about to leave. Hastily I reached into my pockets, but she said the ticket had already been paid for. It bore an unfamiliar location. Looking at the departure boards, I saw my train would leave in three minutes and rushed to find it.

I had hardly boarded the train when it whistled and surged ahead. I inspected the ticket thoroughly. I was startled to see that I was scheduled to arrive in three and a half hours. I had not counted on such a long journey. Besides that, I was by no means convinced the result would compensate me for the efforts. I was also annoyed that I had to wait that long before I would discover what was going on. I stared out of the window: the plain stretching as far as the eye could see – an incredibly tedious landscape. My travelling partners were two old dames who could not stop yapping not for one second – in fact they often talked at the same time – and a college student who was trying to study in spite of the constant chattering – it must have been important for him.

At the first station a very attractive young lady entered our compartment. She had long black hair and sizeable breasts that she seemed to wear with pride. The sight put new life into my journey. I searched for some topic to start a conversation with her. Unfortunately nothing came into my mind apart from the flat formulas like 'where are you going?' and 'what a beautiful day we've got'. I was reluctant to use these. I wanted something more romantic, more original. I measured her up from head to toe. At times our glances met but she did not show any particular interest in me. She fished a book out of her bag and lost herself in the words. I admired the monotonous landscape for a while, then realized that if I really had to look at something, I would rather rest my eye upon the mounts swelling in front of me. 'Rest' may not be the most appropriate word here. I became more excited every second, especially when I read the title of the book: Julius Evola: *The Metaphysics of Sex*. My heart gave a sudden leap. Now I had the topic!

I waited for her to look up and catch her glance, then I asked her the bold question.

"Do you practice Tantra or you are only interested in its theoretical aspects?"

She smiled and said after a short pause:

"A gram of practice weighs more than a ton of theory." She quoted one of the Master's favourite phrases.

I knew at once we were walking the same path. Now things became easier, and an exciting conversation was on the horizon. Antonia proved to be a pleasant travelling companion. Besides the considerable amount of practical experience she had – its effects were visible on her – she possessed tons of theoretical knowledge too. And she had excellent communication skills. She could string words in a way that almost everything had a double entendre, allusions with an explicit erotic charge. Her style reminded me of Carina. Her figure was similar too. And familiar somehow, so after one and a half hour of journey we had become very close, diving deep into intimate waters until we realized the two chatty dames were suspiciously silent, their ears pricked to attention, so we thought it prudent to continue our conversation in the corridor.

We reached the mountains. The landscape was stunning. The autumn patchwork gown in an array of colours as worn by the deciduous trees broke the silence of the deep green pine forests' cool majesty. Here and there pointed peaks of cliffs strove towards the lilac sky of the sunset with bold momentum.

We contemplated the land in silence. The sight of nature's harmony with all its beauties kept us spellbound. In that magical moment when day and night meet, emanating a somewhat otherworldly, fabulous atmosphere, everything seemed to be filled with mysterious meanings. Unusual things can happen in such moments. We said not a word, and the silence gradually deconstructed the invisible walls we had built around ourselves with words. Her shoulder pressed close to mine. Gently, as though accidentally... and I was reminded how beautiful life is.

The train entered a tunnel, and a few moments later complete darkness fell upon us. I felt a fine hand gently stroking my face, caressing my ears and neck. It reached the back of my neck and stayed there. My hands slipped onto her waist, and I pulled her towards me. My heart was beating quickly. She did not resist. Suddenly everything became bright again. The tunnel was short, too short. My hands stayed on her waist. Her face was close to mine. We tried to read from each other's eyes the depth of our awakening feelings.

"One more tunnel," she murmured in a sensually soft tone, "a longer one."

Our accomplice, darkness, fell upon us once again, and we wasted no time. We clang to the other and our lips searched out the other's. They met, familiarized themselves, made friends, became intimate... and were unwilling to say goodbye when the darkness began to lift.

Although that tunnel was longer, it still seemed too short. We carried on hugging. Our faces touched as we feasted on the landscape.

The increasing number of lights indicated we were approaching a city.

"I have to get off here. This is where I live," she sighed and hugged me gently.

"I'm going to the next station," I sighed even deeper, pressing her to me more tightly.

"Get off here with me. Let's spend the night together, and in the morning you can carry on. I live alone, and I will feel very lonely tonight, now I have come to feel you"

She whispered her last words. Ardent desires and a promise of unforgettable pleasures burned in her eyes. I had never before felt such a strong temptation in my life to be spontaneous and follow the calling of my desires without thinking. My inner struggle did not take long though. This time my rationality won. I knew that if this was a game where I had to reach a goal, then Antonia was only a test I had to pass.

"I am sorry but I can't. Not now. But believe me I want you with all my body and heart. I am sure we will meet again, we have to."

"And if we meet again, do you promise that..."

"Yes, I promise. Be sure of it."

"All right, but don't forget your promise!"

She waved with a playful smile and disappeared down the steps of the underpass.

I slumped back down on the seat of the empty compartment with a deep sigh. How strange life is! One can never know when to accept an opportunity and when to renounce to it in the hope of a greater gift. This time I had chosen the uncertain, but I was not at peace with my decision.

I got off the train with mixed feelings. I was a little tired of the game but still curious who would be the gift. The first surprise came when I saw the blond diva I'd met at the Bucharest station getting off the train. Two young men were helping her with the bags. She looked at me for a second – a conceited smile on her face – then turned her head away. So it was her after all. One good deed deserves another, just like in a tale. Had I missed my chance, or could I still correct it? Maybe it's not too late? I started towards her, but it was too late. A tall, well-built man went up to her, picked up her bags and they left quickly.

Nervously I strolled up and down the station, craning my neck to look for somebody who might have been waiting for me. In the end I gave up hope. I was dressed for an afternoon stroll and started to shiver on the cold and deserted platform. I walked into the station building to have a look at the timetable. Still two hours until the next train back to Bucharest. I was lucky to have money on me.

A little later a balding, moustached, chubby man entered the waiting room and, after a quick scan around, he came towards me.

"Are you Mr. Balder Falkenberg?" he asked, panting heavily.

"Yes, that would be me," I answered with gleaming eyes.

"In that case, please follow me. Your cab is waiting for you."

I was more curious who was waiting for me in the car, but I was to be disappointed once again.

It was empty. We got in and he started the car.

"Please excuse me for being late, but I was stopped by the police – you know how bone-headed they can be. I told them in vain that I was hurrying to the station, but no use. They couldn't care less. They didn't let me leave until they'd checked all my lights. I thought I would never find you."

Where on earth would I have gone, I thought irately.

"Could you tell me where we're going?" I asked politely.

"I was given an address. Just trust me."

"And who charged you with this if I may ask?"

"A man. I don't know him. Bearded, long hair, you know. But he seemed like a nice guy. And he wasn't tight-fisted either if you get my meaning. I hope God gives me more clients like him."

We were on the road for what seemed like a long time. We left the city but we still hadn't reached the place.

It even crossed my mind that he was taking me back to Bucharest as I might have failed the test. So I was absolutely delighted when at last we stopped in front of a high iron gate.

"This is where our journey ends." He was informing me politely that I had to get out there.

I pulled the handle. The gate opened and I found myself in a spacious courtyard. Not a soul to be seen. The moonlight highlighted the impressive building in front of me. No lights anywhere. I walked down the gravel path and entered the building. I found myself in a large, circular hall. Light filtered through the opposite window. I faltered towards it and then through a glass door into a large inner courtyard. A white stone statue towered in the middle, sharply lit from below. Three grand buildings surrounded the court. Two were in complete darkness, but a weak light was coming from the upper storey of the third. I guessed that the top must have been made of glass. I went towards it, feeling my way up the stairs, and entered the glasshouse. The spectacle surpassed my wildest dreams: subdued lighting, a pool surrounded by an exotic paradise of plants, and in it ravishing girls playing, squirting water and chasing each other around – all completely naked. Their cheerful laughter echoed on the glass walls.

I just stood there mesmerized by the unbelievable sight. It reminded me of the idyllic picture my grandfather's fantasy painted about the Island of Delights. The atmosphere was the same, it just wasn't an island in the middle of the ocean. Everything else was identical: rich, exuberant vegetation, naked women playing in the water… and all that followed.

As soon as they noticed me, they stopped romping around. Six pairs of curious eyes turned towards me, six pairs of majestic bosoms emerged out of the water, six pairs of bold nipples winked at me flirtatiously. For a few moments we measured each other up, then two girls rushed to welcome me.

"Welcome to Kama Pura," said one of them.

"Kama Pura?" I asked in surprise.

"Yes, Kama Pura, The Isle of Delights," said the other, while she took me by the hand, "make yourself at home."

Isle of Delights! Even the name was similar. Incredible! Had I found what my grandfather had been dreaming about all his life? The piece of earthly paradise in which he believed with such moving naivety? The ideal he seeded in me during the spring of my life, that I had unconsciously been searching for since then?

My thoughts were interrupted by a tender voice. "Come closer. Let us wash off the dust of your journey."

"May I?" another voice asked and, without waiting for an answer, she started to take off my clothes. "In the sanctuary of Venus you may only enter with naked body and naked soul. You must take off all your disguises and remove all your masks."

I let myself be treated by the attentive hands, and I really had the feeling they were peeling off some kind of ridiculous costume. As soon as I was liberated, my two benefactresses led me to the scented pool. Now I was taken into the care of twelve hands. Not only hands, but other body parts were rubbing off the dust of the journey. My masculinity soon rose to the height of the situation making me feel somewhat embarrassed, but the priestesses of Venus did not seem to be disturbed. They found it a natural reaction – in fact they showed wonder and veneration which made my confusion slowly become satisfaction tinged with pride.

"Will you tell me at last which one of you lured me here? Who set up this game?" I was eager to know after we all were introduced.

"We, all of us, together," they answered looking at each other cunningly. "Today we are all yours..."

"But you can also choose one of us..."

"Today you can do whatever you want. This is the day of Tripura Sundari, the goddess of love. This is her present for you."

"You deserve it. You passed many tough tests today."

"Hmmm, beautiful tests," I answered, dipping into the lake of fresh memories for a moment.

"Are you talking about them?" motioned one of them towards my back.

I turned around and was surprised to see my three dear female acquaintances approaching from the bushes. One of them had tempted me with her cream cake in El Paraíso; the second, with her allure of a Hollywood star tried to lure me to help her with the heavy bags; and the third used one of the strongest weapons while passing through the dark tunnels on a train: the irresistible power of the awakening desire. Now, all three of them were standing there, smiling lusciously, calmly and... naked.

"You planned it supremely," I said as laughter bubbled up in me.

They chuckled, and jumped in the water. I embraced the three of them. I needed to compensate myself for what I had missed on my journey.

"You were the toughest temptation I resisted in my life," I whispered in Antonia's ears.

"I was not acting, you know," she whispered back. "The feelings you awoke in me were real, and have stayed that way."

All were curious to hear my adventures on the road. I recalled the most exciting moments in a colourful and humorous fashion. We shrieked in laughter, and I felt fantastic. I was deeply grateful for our forefather, Adam, for sacrificing one of his ribs, and his resolution to bargain Eve from God. And now comes God... who pays attention to even the tiniest details in His boundless wisdom and almighty sense of humour when drawing the jumbled lined of Fate: a hand snaked from behind my back and held a large, golden apple before me.

Déjà vu struck me like lightning. But I could not recall the first instance of this symbolic gesture. I turned back and my eyes filled with tears in the very moment. I remembered. A beautiful city on the banks of the Danube... a sunny orchard... a wild embrace... Yes, Éva Zoltay was sitting on the edge of the pool, looking at me with inquisitive, eager eyes, just as she had nine years earlier. She still preserved a teenager's charms. Her hair was longer, her figure more curved and sensual, and a mature women's confident smile played on her lips.

I sat her in my lap with a passion evoking our heated past. She clasped her feet behind my back and pressed me so tight I hardly could breathe.

"We can even talk now," she breathed into my ears. "I learned English... and Romanian too."

"You have become a gorgeous woman," I told her when I managed to get away far enough to admire her from head to toe. She stood my wondered gaze, for a while before coiling round me again.

"I have desired you since then. It was never again as good as it was with you.."

"I also thought about you a lot," I whispered back. "Do you remember that piece of moonstone you slipped into my hand when we said goodbye?"

She nodded.

"I have kept it on me since then."

"Maybe it's childish, but I have always seen it as a magical stone, and I believed that one day it would lead you back to me."

She wiped away teardrops from the corner of her eyes and embraced me tightly.

"It's not nice to treat him like only you possess him," the others yelled out at Éva with a feigned rebuke. "Tonight he belongs to all of us."

"Didn't you say he can choose someone if he so desires?" she retorted playfully. "Well, he has just chosen me."

Before letting me go she whispered in my ear: "We will have plenty of time to talk, and to do anything we want. Now go and enjoy yourself."

I did enjoy myself. I was sitting on the stairs of the pool, submerged to the waist in the fragrant water. The girls caressed me, massaged me, and fed me with fruits. They delighted me with a passionate exaltation of all the senses.

Antonia's arms twined round my neck, her lips touched my ear.

"You promised me something. You haven't forgotten, have you?"

"I could never forget a promise like that."

"Well, then go on."

"Here?"

"Here if you want, why not?" she smiled coquettishly.

"We have all the time we want... we have time for everything," I responded.

I put one of my hands on her waist, caressed Éva's apples with the other, and let my head fall back. Stars shone through the crown of the palm trees; the moon was like a huge orange sitting between the leaves. A strange, intoxicating feeling overwhelmed me. Everything around seemed so implausible and dreamlike. Still, so palpable and real.

"You could not have even dreamt of anything like this, could you?" Éva asked with a faraway look, her head resting on the steps of the pool, next to mine.

Her question hit me like lightning. Then a thought flashed across my mind: Of course I had dreamt about it! Then another thought shook me with the power of certainty: the game is not over yet!

I counted the girls. There were ten of them just like the female statues in my dream. But the dream showed me another one, standing in the middle of the circle, on the high pedestal. My common sense had a hard time believing there would be a connection between my dream three weeks ago and the present reality, but I did feel a strong urge to get out of the water and search for something.

"I'll just have a look around in this marvellous garden," I responded to my surprised playmates when I started on my way in the green labyrinth.

I found a door at one end of the glasshouse. There was a sign on it: a six-point star with the Hebrew letter Yodh in the middle. As I opened it a chill ran across my wet skin. I recoiled and wanted to turn back, but I felt like a magnetic force was attracting me and I could not move back. I stepped in after a short hesitation. I found myself in a poorly lit, cold corridor. There were doors on my right. I tried to open a few, but they were locked. On the door at the end of the corridor I found the same sign as on the exit of the glasshouse. I pushed down the handle in hope. It opened. Complete darkness received me. Only the dim light of the corridor illuminated it, as I left the door open. A thick velvet curtain hung in front of me. I looked for an opening on it, feeling my way around, but realized that it ran in a circle, following the line of the circular hall. I walked three-quarters of the circle before I found a hole. I stepped through and complete darkness fell upon me. My extended hands found another curtain. I started to feel my way around again until I found another opening. Of course, as soon as I stepped over, I was stopped by another curtain. This was made of a flimsier material and some light penetrated through it probably from the centre of the circle. The light always gives hope, so I continued my way round the circular labyrinth with renewed zeal. I passed through four curtains. The fifth was white and enclosed an octagonal structure, with a dim light emanating from its top. I padded around the wall until I found what seemed like a handle. I pulled it and a door opened. The sight petrified me. An infinitely large chamber unfolded itself in front of my very own eyes with thousands and thousands of beautiful female figures illuminated by the light of thousands and thousands of candles. My brain short-circuited. Only moments ago I had walked around this structure, and its diameter could have been no more than three meters. I felt as though I was standing at the door to another dimension. I stepped in and, when I saw thousands of naked men staring at me with a stupefied expression, I realized I was simply the victim of mirrors. The octagonal construction was in fact eight mirrors facing each other. One woman stood in the middle on an eight-petal lotus-shaped sofa, a candle burning at the tip of each petal. This recognition disappointed me but only for a moment. Then recognition came like an illumination: this is how the illusion of the world is brought forth! This is the mystery of the multiplication of the one into the many. The very mystery of the creation of the Universe. A little time had to pass before my eyes could focus on the one, the real one, the living and breathing woman in the centre. She stood with her back to me. A fine veil covered the enigmatic shapes of her body. Her long black hair fell onto her shoulders in abundant locks. Slowly she turned towards me. Her beauty... moved me. A thin gold chain ran around her forehead holding a finely elaborated ruby set in a beautifully crafted golden frame. Her regal stance emanated such dignity! What noble features, and those glowing black eyes! She was so enthralling, and so familiar... I knew I had seen her some-where before... Then I remembered: I had seen her dance at the summer camp the previous year. And I remembered I had felt something move in me even back then, a new and disquieting feeling, a gentle vibration somewhere deep inside my soul, that I had tried to silence before it grew to a stronger craving. I had thought a mere mortal such as myself would never have a chance; a woman like her was only worthy of kings and gods.

I pretty much managed to erase her image from my memory. I had not seen her again since then, but her memory lived on deep within me, and a wonderful dream had brought news of her existence. Now I knew: the goddess standing on the marble altar had assumed her face.

And now there she was, standing in front of me. More beautiful than on the stage, more stunning than her replica in my dream. I could hardly believe this time it was not a dream. I saw one of her hands reaching slowly to her shoulder and untying the golden clip of the veil. Thousands of goddesses were uncovered then, and thousands of men looked at that thousand-fold manifestation of beauty. Thousands of little candle flames were dancing like as many little angels at the celebration of a divine wedding. I can find no other words to picture the miracle that came next. Our souls and bodies merged in that most miraculous love as though we had been united since the beginning of Worlds. That was the first time I felt Time came to a halt, and barriers of space ceased to exist. Nothing remained. Nothing, except the kind of happiness and love that no words can describe...

I cannot tell how much time passed while we were in the magical sanctuary of divine love, I only know that after she led me to a room prepared for my rest and left me alone, I felt my own soul had been torn in two, and she had kept one half of it. I desperately tried to imagine again the touch of her hands, to evoke and relive the wonderful moments of plenitude when I was as blissful as only God can be.

❖

It was around midday when I woke up. Pieces of images and emotions kept whirling in me, and I tried with all my might to determine how much of the previous day's events were real. Everything seemed so unimaginable in the light of the midday sun.

I heard a knock, and Éva popped her head round the door:

"Are you awake?"

"I no longer know when I am awake and when I am dreaming."

"I will help you with that. Can I come in?"

She stepped in, accompanied by a long-haired, bearded man.

"This is Gregor, the father, maecenas, and spiritual leader of Kama Pura.

"Welcome to your new home," he said holding out his hand.

"What do you mean?" I asked in surprise.

"The Master allowed you to live here, provided you pass the initiation, and, of course, if that is what you want."

Mentioning she had something to do, Éva left us alone.

"What is Kama Pura?"

"A spiritual centre, a secret spiritual group operates here called Kaula. And from this day you can also be part of it."

"And what does this Kaula do?"

"Everything you had been doing up until now, spiritual practices, although on a more intensive level, and with far more effective methods."

"If these methods are so effective, then why does everybody who walks on the spiritual path not employ them?"

"Practicing these requires a higher level of spiritual maturity. This is the path of power, the path of the energy, and this energy can be dangerous for those who are not prepared. These methods utilize a most ancient energy of the human being, the power of desire. They transform the desire for valueless, illusory objects into a powerful aspiration to attain higher, spiritual values, to realize unity with God. One important station of this transformation is Kama, the ecstatic Delight. The Kashmir tradition knows two very effective methods to attain this. One is love, the other is art. For this reason, in the spiritual practices of the Kaula, both sacred love rituals and art practices meant to awaken higher consciousness are essential."

"That sounds very alluring, but how did I end up here?"

"Laurianne discovered you. She heard you play in the camp and thought your place is among us. She was the one who organized your initiation game."

"So her name is Laurianne," I said pensively, "and she brought me here because of my musical skills," I thought to myself

"Yes, Laurianne. But you have already met her as far as I know."

"Yes, we met, though we have not talked yet."

"I can understand," he said smiling cheekily.

"...and I still do not know anything about her," I continued.

"She is a wonderful creature. She's endowed with a remarkable spiritual power and aspiration. She is French, started her yoga practices in Rishikesh, where from she headed to Bucharest. She has been here in Kama Pura for a year now. She dances like a goddess."

"I saw her dance, last year at the camp."

"That was the first time I saw her too."

"And who... brought her here?" I asked with hesitation.

"I did."

"I see..." somewhere deep inside I felt a dull pain. "So she went through *the same* initiation ritual as me."

"Yes, all members of the Kaula went through *a certain* initiation ritual."

"Hmm, thanks," that was all I needed to know.

"Berthold directs the musical department. You will work with him, in the event you decide to stay."

After Gregor left I decided to look around this spiritual centre. In secret I also hoped I would see Laurianne. My legs led me towards the dance room. The girls were just having their break when I arrived. A few of my initiatresses were there. They quickly surrounded me, welcoming me like an old acquaintance, and introduced me to the others. They recalled details of the game cheerfully, and she... she was there too. She did not join the chatter, but laughed with the others at times. This was the first time I heard her voice. It awakened painfully beautiful emotions in me, emotions much more human. She too was different from the Goddess, the stunning creature I had met the night before, whom I hardly dared to touch for fear she would disappear, like a dazzling dream. This time I saw another Laurianne. She was a breathtakingly sensual daughter of man even in her exercise gear and without make-up.

I wanted to step closer to her, run my fingers through her shaggy hair, say something to her, anything, even if it was only a word, no matter what just talk to her, but I did not. Even the thought I had to go to her and say something to her made me nervous. I felt as though I was before a tough and very important exam, my heart was beating wildly and some odd, paralyzing force turned me to stone. I could not move. I just watched her from the corner of my eyes, hoping she would walk to me and talk to me as a proof that it was not a dream, that everything that happened in the mirror–magic of the sanctuary was real. But she neither came to me, nor talked to me, just flashed her adorable black eyes at me occasionally, making my yearning more burning.

After the break the girls returned to their dancing. Before I left, Antonia darted up to me, kissed me and whispered in my ear:

"I wasn't just acting, do not forget," and away she dashed.

I stopped at the window of the corridor and pressed my forehead to the cold glass. So most of it was nothing but acting. We would have a good laugh at it, think about it for a while then forget it like a play no longer on stage. And I, the naïve spectator thought for the whole time that it was real, while I should have known it was just a stage-play, or a dream, a beautiful and unforgettable dream. Like it was with Ylva Ekberg, my childhood love. I first met her in a similar dream. She was also playing with me, in a charming and enchanting way, but she was just acting. "The Princess of the Wolves!" She did not even recognize me afterwards, and turned months of my life into a living hell. This parallel rang the alarm bells in me. No, I will not suffer this time. I have gone through many experiences since then. I know that dreams are but dreams, and the lovely ones only remain lovely if we store them in the secret drawer of our mind where we keep our sweet memories, and don't wake them up anymore. The present moment is the only thing that matters. And there she came, the living reality.

"Where have you been wandering? I've been looking for you everywhere," Éva clang close to me. The proximity of her body dissolved my tensions.

"Why were you looking for me?" I asked, looking deep into her eyes.

"I was searching for you because..." she started, approaching my private parts with her hand "... I wanted to take you to dine," she finished her sentence laughing.

She took my hand and led me to the girls' building, where the dining hall was.

The delicious lunch and Éva's merry chatter pulled me back to reality. I was feeling much better. Then I saw Laurianne again.

She came to eat too. She was holding hands with Gregor!

The suspicion turned into painful certainty. My flickering hope faded, leaving behind bitter smoke like a burnt-down candle stump. I knew that a woman like her is a match only for kings. I saw her release Gregor's hand, and smile at me. I acknowledged her attention with a polite nod, then turned my head away with a phony coolness and armoured heart. But the armour proved ineffective because the surreptitious attacks coming from within became more torturous under the pressure.

Éva invited me to her room after lunch. I eschewed seduction by telling her I wanted to meet the musicians. I really felt that only music could help me at that moment.

I spent a pleasant afternoon in the studio. I was surprised to see that my fellow musicians were walking a similar path to the one I set out on in Bucharest, although they had already gained more experience.

I met Gregor at dinner.

"Have you met the musicians?" he asked cordially.

"Yes, this afternoon. I have a feeling we will work well together."

"And how do you feel in Kama Pura?"

"It's a great place... though there are still things I need to get used to."

He saw I was not in the mood to go into details so he interrogated me no further. To be honest I did not feel like speaking to him. I was unable to forgive him for Laurianne.

After supper I went out to the garden and sat down on a mossy rock in front of a sculpture depicting a nude couple. I closed my eyes and tried to chase away my thoughts. I wanted to meditate but I heard steps behind me. I turned and saw Antonia approaching. She sat beside me.

"Are you meditating?" she asked quietly.

"I am just having a bit of rest. I am tired of thinking."

She snuggled close to me, embraced me and leaned her head on my shoulders. I put my arm around her waist. This is how we stayed, in silent stillness. Tender warmth radiated from her body. I felt something melting in me.

"It's getting dark," she broke the silence after a long time.

"Yes, just like in the tunnel," I responded and turned her head towards me. Our lips connected.

"Come," I whispered, "I want to honour my promise."

18. Play

... and on the fiftieth day I saw him! There he was, sitting up there on the stage, on a dais decorated with flowers, playing the sitar. Tall and handsome with golden hair, attractive beard and sea blue eyes, like a demigod of Atlantis!

Sitting in the first row I could notice even the tiniest movements of his face every one of which stirred deep waves inside me. His fingers playing on the strings were stroking me, making my body tremble, scaling the length of my naked skin. The most delicate strings hidden deep in my soul replied to these heavenly sounds. The harmony between the strong masculinity of his body and the tenderness of his soul brought to life painfully sweet feelings yet unknown to me. In less than half an hour I was fatally in love. Or maybe the very first notes woven from his soul had already ignited in me that unquenchable flame. I knew I was experiencing this something for the first time in my life. A feeling, hard to define. A sweet nostalgia for memories of a distant and mysterious past interwoven with the promise of a joyous fulfillment. A moment of genuine magic. One glowing with energy and radiance, soaring high above the ordinary. Like the evening when Mum met my father. You sense true love with the very first look, she said. I felt it now! I knew it was *him*!

I would have loved... oh God... how much I wanted him to look at me. As if by chance. A fugacious glance... at least. So he would see the fire he had lit in me... He did not look at me. He was flying on the notes of his music, somewhere far away. In a hidden dimension only he could enter. And from where he was bringing us that most miraculous music.

After the performance all I wanted to do was to run to him. To hug him. To say into the microphone, for all to hear, that he was the one my heart had chosen... just like my crazy father had once done... But some strange force kept me nailed to the bench, unable to move, hypnotized. I looked longingly as the distance between us grew, and finally he disappeared behind stage... After the concert I went home terribly angry about my cowardice. How could I have wasted such a great chance?! I was already suffering as if abandoned by the love of my life. The next moment I felt ashamed. I acted like a dumb chick who falls in love with the dream figure on the cinema screen, who weaves sweet fantasies about men she can never reach. It was not fantasies I wanted but tangible reality. A flesh and bone man.

I decided to search for him the next day. I would go to the ends of the earth to find him, throw myself at his feet… or better into his arms, and pour out my soul. I would tell him how much I loved him. I would tell him that I was his and his alone, and that he could do with me whatever he decided. Embrace me with passionate love, or reject me forever… but immediately. I couldn't bear waiting any longer!

With that strong and somehow calming determination I plunged into sleep. The cool of the night tempered my inflamed passion and in the morning I awoke with a new idea: I would arrange his kidnapping into Kama Pura.

Although it required much patience and self-control, the plan filled me with excitement. I set to work with great care. First I found out all the necessary information about Balder from my friends in Bucharest. And I made sure we did not bump into each other. Then I started to plan the mystery play. I wanted to find the idea of a play that would confirm my intuition was right, to put him through tests he would only pass if we really were meant to meet, if 'God had created us for one another'. It was easy to convince Gregor. He had also been at the concert and instantly liked the 'Viking' as he called him. I was a little nervous about the Master. I knew I had a good deal of personal interest in the matter that made my judgment of the situation particularly subjective.

The Master did not show much enthusiasm for the idea of Balder moving into Kama Pura. When I told him eagerly of my feelings, also explaining my hunch that Balder and I might actually be soul mates, he cooled me immediately. He said the soul mate story was more of a myth than reality, the result of the misinterpretation of Plato's spherical being theory elucidated in his Symposium. He explained that Plato's symbolic description referred to a universal law, the separation of the male and female principles during the process of creation which gave rise to the attraction between the two that takes the form of the love between a man and a woman. This does not mean every person is merely a 'half person' whose other half is wandering around somewhere, and that people can only glimpse happiness if they join with their other half. Actually every human soul is potentially whole and complete. But this wholeness only gradually awakens as the result of meetings and relationships with other souls. So we are always attracted by those qualities in others that are waiting to be woken in us. And, since these qualities are not all found in one single person, we don't have just one soul that complements us. We have numerous other halves. That's why we can be in love several times in our life. Even with more than one person at a time.

"So eternal love doesn't even exist?" I asked a little disappointed.

"Love is eternal because it is the expression of the divine Self in our being. It is human relationships that come to an end. They can last for hours, days, years, even several lifetimes. But eventually they fade. Love, however, resurrects time and again. Love is the magnet that attracts human souls on the path of development to new experiences. Meanwhile it appears in ever more beautiful and increasingly refined forms until it finally purifies into androgynous and perfect divine love."

"I understand… Well, then, to be more accurate, I feel that man is the most suitable complementary companion for my life and spiritual development in this present period. Please let me test out my hypothesis… Please allow me to organize the initiation game!"

"Let me hear your game plan," the Master nodded.

I told him everything in detail. Basically he agreed, although he did have a couple of stipulations.

"I will choose the girls – and they may use any method to seduce him and stop him. If he manages to reach the Fragrant Garden, then the girls there must act as though it was the end of the game. If any of them do manage to seduce him, he may not stay in Kama Pura. And you may not meet with him either… Will you still take on the game under these conditions?"

I pondered for a while. The Master had tailored merciless terms. In this form, according to human calculation, it would be practically impossible for Balder to reach me. But I didn't really have a choice.

"Very well. Let it be according to your will," I answered with a sigh.

"Let it be according to God's will," the Master corrected me.

"So who will be the temptresses?" I asked. I predicted there was no way he'd leave Evelina, Natalia and Antonia out of the game.

"The first three: Evelina, Natália and Antónia. Then Diana, Éva,…

I listened to the list as though to a judgment against which there was no appeal. I knew only God could help.

❖

I set the date for the game and the Kama Pura drama group helped me organize it. The most difficult task was building the Soul Sanctuary, but it looked amazing in the end. The effect was so stunning it took my breath away when I first entered.

I prepared feverishly on the day of the game. Just like a bride in love for her happy nuptials.

When they phoned from Bucharest to say Balder had successfully passed the first two tests and was already sitting on the train I was gripped by a peculiar excitement. The joyful anticipation of our meeting was mixed with tension. I was afraid he might not succeed as the two most difficult tests were still to come: Antonia and the Fragrant Garden.

I stepped into the sanctuary and started to meditate, to try and calm my shaking limbs and galloping thoughts. When I had managed to create a little quiet within, I began the magical preparations. I offered my every action, feeling and thought to God. Then I created the space for the magic ritual, evoking the female cosmic energies one by one. And the angelic legion of Love, Harmony and Spiritual development, too.

The unique atmosphere of the sanctuary, the miraculous energy field and the presence of heavenly beings gave me a feeling I had never experienced before. It was a kind of mystical excitement, combined with increasing joy and with the knowledge that I was a part of a secret and cosmic mysterium. I was amazed to realize this was more than a mere game. It was a real "Divina Commedia", part and semblance of the Great Cosmic Play. As I saw my thousand times multiplied self in the mirrors around, I felt I was the likeness of the Great Cosmic Mother, who multiplies herself into millions and millions of beings in the grand play of illusions called Creation. Infinite joy flooded my heart.

I spent hours in this state of ecstasy. The candles burnt down so I had to light more. This physical act somehow conjured back my usual self, and I realized I was tense again. Doubt was creeping through me. *He won't succeed... one of them will have seduced him. He should have been here ages ago. It was an unfairly difficult test. To make him believe he had reached the goal, that the play had finished, when he has no idea what the aim is. That there's actually another goal that he has to search for... No... no man would be able to succeed...*

This suspicion about the chance of Balder failing grew increasingly torturous. Then I suddenly came round. Shame on me! Where was my faith! I started to pray immediately. I asked the Divine Mother to give me back my trust and inner peace. And to return the joy of being one with Her.

Thankfully my overturned serenity was gradually restored. Peace found its nest again in my soul. My thoughts become clearer and, as though giving sound to a whisper coming from deep inside me, crystallized into a comprehensible message: *Why are you so attached to the offspring of your imagination? Why do you desperately want him to find you? What if he is not the one you're really waiting for? Why don't you just let things take their course as they should? Why can't you believe that divine providence will always guide the paths of Fate with perfect wisdom? And why do you continually forget that this is all just a play? That everything is just a play. An exciting illusion. The only reality is you! You, the Great Cosmic Mother! Everything you see is merely the illusory projection of your divine imagination!*

These thoughts possessed creative power, and I slowly regained the feeling of being the Great Cosmic Woman. The creative power of God. I felt I was every woman, every opening flower, every tree and every bird. I was

Nature itself. I was all forms in which life is still dormant and all in which life already lives and pulses.

All of a sudden I saw the image in the mirror in front of me changing. A long dark line appeared, getting ever wider as, out of the dark, the outline of a human figure emerged. A naked man's body appeared in the slit. His body! His beautiful body crowned with golden hair!

As he entered the mirrored door closed again. Suddenly thousands of he's and I's filled our radiant, small but infinite Universe with thousands of tiny star lights.

He had succeeded! Thank you, God!

My throat was constricted by tears... but I controlled myself. Now I had to be strong. I had to be a goddess. And goddesses do not cry. Only mortals. Because they know... love!

I turned to him slowly. As I reached for the clip to my veil I quickly brushed away the two disobedient droplets that had managed to break through the dam of my will. As the softly falling veil stroked along my skin. I felt that my smaller me had unravelled into nothing and that the purified, divine Me was standing now before the divine Man. I didn't know what would happen next. I hadn't planned anything and wanted nothing. I allowed the secret inner voice to guide me. Now, in this state, I was able to hear it so clearly. I allowed everything to happen as it should. I experienced the meeting of our bodies and souls, the sweetness of our melting with the awareness of an enchanted observer. I saw our bodies twisting in an ecstatic dance of love. And I saw an infinite number of us replaying the eternal mystery of creation.

When I sensed our meeting had come to an end I gave thanks to God and to the heavenly beings. Then, wordlessly, I took his hand and led him to his room. I knew we had to part – my higher consciousness beckoned me. I knew we had to put an end to our togetherness so we would be able to keep this wonderful experience in its entirety and perfection. I knew all that very well. But my female side did not want to separate. With a frightening force it urged me to stay with him, to lie my body next to his, to nestle into his arms promising security, to allow the sound of his breathing to lull me to sleep. My eyes to open to the sight of him in the morning, and my body to awake to the heat of his body... God, how I would have loved that... But I listened to my highest voice. We said our goodbyes with a silent embrace, and I tore myself away from him.

❖

The moment I awoke I wanted to rush to him. But a forceful and unrelenting inner voice ordered me to stop. What on earth are you doing?

Is it not enough that you tempted him here? Is it not enough that you put him in the situation where he had to make love to you? At least now give him the chance to choose freely. You're behaving as though he's yours! He doesn't even know who you are! Not even your name! Leave him now, and leave the next step to him. Relax. If he likes you and if genuine emotions were born in him, then he will come looking for you. But if he doesn't, there's no point forcing it anyway. Give him the chance to fight for you, to conquer you. Men need that. Then he'll value you more.

All right, all right. I'll wait. Let him show me he is a man! Let him conquer me! I deserve that at least. So I muted my rebellious emotions and got on with my own life.

That was no problem until I actually saw him. The moment he came into the dance rehearsal my heart started galloping, and I was so confused I didn't know how to act. I felt so ungainly. Just like an idiot in love.

The girls immediately pounced upon him, of course. Even if I'd had the courage, I wouldn't have been able to get close to him. But I still hoped he would come over to me and say something... anything. Or at least touch me. But he didn't. At the end of the break he left, as though I hadn't been there at all... As though I was only one of many. As though? Well, I was. One of the crowd. No different from the others. The night... the special atmosphere, the make-up, the jewels had charmed him. I had seen that on his face. I had felt it in his embrace. But now in these worn clothes, no make-up, scruffy and sweaty, I was no longer the 'goddess' he had imagined. Of course he ignored me. But even so... I had given myself to him. We had spent an amazing night together. And now he didn't even deem me worthy of a kind word. Men can be so cruel!

That meeting, or rather non-meeting, threw me off balance. To Gregor's remark that something wasn't right, I just replied I was somewhat tired. He gave me a good hug, which made me feel better. We went to lunch together. Balder was there too, sitting at a table with Éva... and they were eating each other with their eyes. He barely even noticed me. He just nodded towards me and then hung off every word coming from Éva's chattering mouth. My heart squeezed tight. My first thought was that I should go over and tell him off, quickly followed by the realization that I was being an idiot. I had absolutely no right. He didn't belong to me. He was free to do what he liked...

He left with Éva. I watched them through the window as they stepped along the garden alley hugging each other round the waist. Towards the girls' building. Éva's erotic gifts were legendary among the men of Kama Pura. I knew there was no way I could compete. And my stomach clenched, bitten by terrible jealousy. Though I had been sure I was well over that nonsense. I gave others advice proudly, warning my 'less experienced' friends in a reproachful tone of the destructive effect of that damaging addiction called jealousy. And now here we are! The steadfast Laurianne, 'embodiment of selfless love', was being tortured by the ugliest jealousy.

At night I saw him again. He was sitting in the garden... alone! My heart beat loud. This is the moment to go to him! I'd go over... and hug him. No, I wouldn't hug him. We'd just speak, or at least introduce ourselves... I was about to leave when I saw a female silhouette approaching him, nestle down beside him and whisper into his ear. I could make out the figure of Antonia in the falling darkness. I watched them for a while, my heart constricted. Then I saw them hug and start to kiss. I couldn't bear it any longer. I threw myself onto my bed, buried my head under the pillow and started to sob, my body shaking silently. Why was life so unfair? So cruel? Now, when I was finally in love, perhaps for the first time in my life. Why? Why did it have to be like this? The girls hadn't stopped the play. I couldn't blame them. No one knew of my secret feelings, not even Gregor. The girls weren't to know what had happened in the sanctuary. That was my secret alone. They thought I was only acting like everyone else... like Balder... Well, nice little game! He had resisted all temptations and received top prize. And now he could safely taste everything he'd had to refuse during the game. Men are like that! All are alike! And I, the fool, had thought he was 'different'. That 'he would be with me only...'. Oh, you're such a naïve child, Laurie! I felt deep pity for myself.

❖

Hard days followed. My relationship with Balder had been reduced to a Hi-how-are-you- Fine-thanks-and-you level, in the meantime I saw him with Éva, or with Antonia, playing in the garden, chatting away, or making for the fantasy rooms of Tantra Loka. I was suffering terribly.

But I did have a secret pleasure. Something he could not deny me. I used to sneak into the music room, hide in the dim light behind a column and listen to him playing. At such times he was again the Balder who had managed to awaken in me that new and mysterious feeling. The only way to describe it was 'true love'. As he sat there without his admirers, his face transfigured by playing, I imagined we were flying together on the waves of the music. Towards a hidden dimension where we had already been together once, on our dream night. When I glanced at him I saw a mysterious, unearthly love flooding over his face. A kind of love that spoke not to *someone* but to *everyone*... Maybe to me too.

These were the most exquisite moments of my life. I always stole in carefully, like a thief. So he wouldn't see me. So he wouldn't know I was there. This secret game ignited a joyful spark of naughtiness in my heart.

Luckily sadness, bitterness and suffering are not natural states for the soul. They are merely pathological symptoms of internal disorders and, like headaches and stomach cramps, are relieved the moment the soul starts to heal.

Gradually I recovered. My unforgettable spiritual experience in the sanctuary acted as a vaccination that speeded up my recuperation. I regained my faith, I started to feel and live as though it was all a play in which the joy and beauty of playing are paramount. Not whether we win or lose. I was no longer attached to winning. I accepted my undeniable disadvantage as well as the possibility of losing. Surprisingly that made me relax. Actually I became completely free. I didn't abandon the play, but I was no longer interested in the outcome. I was glad I could play and that I could love him, even if that love was unrequited. I was amazed to find that real happiness does not depend on the emotions of the loved one, but on the pureness and selflessness of our own feelings. Mutuality may increase our joy, but the feeling stems fundamentally from our own love, not from the fact someone loves us.

I became more and more generous with my fellow players and was no longer angry with Éva or Antonia. I was surprised to discover that the fact all three of us loved the same man brought us closer together in spirit. A kind of secret unity developed between us. I had grown to love them...

I thought of my Seville adventure, of the incredibly beautiful atmosphere that reigned in Enrique's family. Then I had watched the relationship of the three women uncomprehendingly but now that I had been forced to experience it, I understood such relationships can and do exist – despite generally accepted opinion.

I developed a new secret game. One that would let me live out safely the desire of my loving heart. I kept hiding small gifts under Balder's pillow or in his coat pocket. A piece of fruit, a sweet, a flower bud. Things that did not betray it was me. He never guessed they were from me. But I still felt he received a little of me through these tiny messengers of love. I was happy for the joy he must have felt when he found them, but I didn't mind if he thought someone else had given them to him.

Since I no longer needed to grab him for myself, somehow I could act more naturally and honestly with him. I was no longer flustered when we met on the garden path, nor did I feel a fool, finally able to exchange some real words, straight from the heart. This made him more direct too. He came and sat down next to me a couple of times when I was sitting on the garden bench... and we talked. We talked about all sorts. But never about that night. It was as though that experience had been a dream and had survived in my memory only. But it was still good. His tiniest gesture filled me with infinite delight. Like removing a dry leaf from my hair or putting his coat around me to protect me from the cool autumn air. All inconse-quential really, but they made me so happy. It came from him, and it was meant only for me. We bumped into each other more and more frequently, in the garden, on the corridors or in the restaurant. I did not hurry to part. I kept talking. I told him about all sort of trivial things, just to have a few more moments of our sweet togetherness.

My jealousy subsided with time. If I saw Antonia snuggle up to him, I tried to feel the pleasure a man feels when he inhales the warmth of a sensitive female body. If I noticed him enter Éva's room, I looked for the joy Éva's passion-fuelled body would extend to his male soul.

These were difficult lessons. But in the end I did manage to learn to selflessly celebrate all his pleasures, even those given him by other women. And I was more than a little surprised to feel that in some ways I was also the 'other women'. I felt my love radiated from Éva's fiery groin, and I also nourished him from Antónia's generous breasts. It was a new, unusual and uplifting feeling.

I now know this was due to the awareness of being one with the Divine Mother that the mirror game in the Soul Sanctuary had hinted to me.

19. LIFE with capital letters

Gregor was delighted I decided to stay in the Kama Pura. I travelled back to Bucharest to fetch my clothes and instruments. I told my friends I was retreating for a special spiritual practice for a while, and I did not know when I would come back. I had an emotional farewell with Gina and Adela. Both escorted me to the train station and I promised to visit them as often as I could.

I became an official resident of Kama Pura and a member of the Kaula. In the beginning I spend my days in the music studio and shared my nights between Éva's and Antonia's beds. Yet my dreams swarmed around the unreachable figure of Laurianne.

I had to continue with Éva what we had started nine years before. This rare passion, which still flared between us, pushed into each other's arms with an irresistible power. It was an unfathomable primal force: it would have been madness to stifle it, and I suspect impossible too.

Éva's life took an interesting route after we had separated. The awakening tiger in her had immediately set out for new prey. The problem was that her expectations were too high, and for a long time she did not find anyone able to satisfy her both passionate and refined soul thirsty for erotic adventures. Until one day during her college years when Fate brought her together with one of the Master's disciples, who was teaching Tantra in Budapest. With him she was able to taste the kind of love her whole being had unconsciously been searching for. She threw all her heart and soul into the study of Tantra.

Gregor first saw Éva and her paintings at an exhibition in Budapest. He recruited her on the spot, and here, in the Kaula, she was able to plunge herself fully into the two most important things she had passion for all her life: the art of love and love reflected in art.

She had been filling her exercise and textbooks with erotic drawings since a very young age, to no little annoyance of her parents and teachers. Now her frescos and canvases adorned the walls of Kama Pura to the great delight of the residents and occasional visitors.

I asked her once why she always painted nudes.

"I believe," she answered in a contemplative yet determined tone, "that amongst all the things of Creation, the human body is the most perfect. Trees, flowers, animals, rivers, mountains may be wonderful and may inspire many to paint, but for me the greatest of wonders is Man. In a human being you can find the flower, the tree, the animal, the river, the mountain, you can find the whole of nature, but there is something more too. There is something that makes Man really Hu-man and something that keeps him divine. All these live together in our souls, and are reflected in our bodies. But, after all, what is a human? It is only a concept, an abstraction, as human is in fact man and woman. The connection, relation and tension between the two can express the infinite scale of feelings, the complete richness of emotional tonalities. That's why the human body has been and will remain the toughest challenge for me ever to represent."

Her natural and sincere admiration for the human body presented itself not only in her paintings, but in her sexual life too. This is probably why she was so easily able to transfigure her body into a temple of pleasures. These elevated erotic experiences had a highly inspiring influence upon her creative imagination. This singular harmony between her emotional life and creative work not only made her depictions more alive, more powerful, but also enriched the range of her erotic experiences. Fate must have favoured me for granting me both.

I loved to spend time in front of her paintings. Some kept me captive. I tried to discover the secret of their effect. It might have been that those paintings not only represented something, not only caused aesthetic delight, but they practically infused the observer with a strong desire to experience the type of love that the figures of her paintings radiated with such a magical force.

After Linnéa Svenson, Éva had the most influence on my artistic sensitivity, but while Linnéa taught me theories and educated me to understand and appreciate works of art, Éva initiated me for good, opening up to me her deep and abundant scope of emotions through the art of love.

Antonia opened up different dimensions in me. She made me feel the divine mysteries of boundless love. I kept my promise – the one I had made to her on the train – many times. The unconditional devotion and immense love that radiated from her whole being attracted me like a fire near a mountain hut attracts the hungry and tired wayfarer.

She and Éva completed each other perfectly, but I still felt something was missing. And I knew that something was only treasured by Laurianne.

❖

I loved working in the recording studio. First I played the sitar and organ, and later Gregor found me a cello so I had one more instrument at my disposal to express my expanding range of emotions. I continued composing music and I realized something surprising: the works I composed after making love to Éva had a completely different atmosphere than those I wrote after being with Antonia. This observation led me to further experiments. I came to the conclusion that the women we love have much more influence on us than we, men, would ever imagine, and that our longer relationships have a considerable impact on our life, field of interests, actions, our way of thinking, even our destiny.

During these experiments I also discovered I do not necessarily have to make love to someone to attain these results. It is enough to concentrate on the person and try to connect with her unique inner world. In that period I thought about Laurianne a lot and, as a result of my daydreaming, I composed exceptional pieces.

This phenomenon was so obvious that even months later, when I listened to my compositions, I always knew whether it was Éva, Antonia or Laurianne…

During improvisations I caught myself imagining Laurianne in front of me. Warmth flooded my heart, and I played as though she had been standing in front of me. I dreamt she would come into the studio one day and listen to me playing. Sometimes I went to the dance studio to see her dance, but she did not seem to be interested in my activities. Still, in secret, I kept playing, imagining she was sitting near me. My pieces were my love confessions I had tried to pour into words thousands of times, but had never found the courage. I thought she would not be interested anyway. She was too occupied with Gregor. My heart clenched every time I saw them together. It was not easy. Had I not found refuge in the embrace of Éva and Antonia, I think I would have been unable to stay in Kama Pura.

There were other girls too, searching out my company. One of them often surprised me with anonymous presents. I found a banana in my pocket, a rose bud on my pillow. I had no idea of her identity, but I was delighted by these little gifts because I felt somebody cared for me. At times, I imagined it was Laurianne, and though my rational mind told me it was obviously not possible, I still liked to think of her sneaking into my room in unguarded moments and rolling an orange under my pillow. It felt good to imagine that one day I might catch her and then...

But I was content with sitting at her table in the dining room occasionally. I had that much courage – in the dining room you can sit next to anybody you want. It was nice to talk to her. I liked hearing her voice. The way she talked to me, and the ringing laughter at my jokes or foolish remarks in French, touched my deepest chords.

Every now and then I realized I was spying on her walking alone in the courtyard so I could accidentally meet her. I always invented some burning topic to talk about just so I could stop her and simply look into her brilliant eyes.

She was never in a hurry to break off these meetings and that felt good. It gave me confidence and I became more daring. She even sat down next to me on the bench one time and together we wondered at the golden colours of the warm autumn. It gave me the chance to enjoy tiny forbidden joys – brushing my knee against hers, taking a dry leaf out of her hair. Once, at dusk, seeing her shiver in the cold breeze, I laid my jacket around her shoulders, and then for a moment, for one brief moment, I embraced her.

That night I could not fall asleep for a long time. That insignificant touch had deeply stirred me. It revived the first night I had tried to forget, a memory stored by all the cells of my body together with all the touches, flavours and scents.

You are an idiot, my rebelling senses kept echoing in me. *Can't you see, can't you understand that this woman loves you? This woman who prepared for you the most marvellous initiation the world has even seen, who offered herself as a most sacred sacrifice in that wonderful shrine, and who gave you everything a woman can... this woman desires you, wants you to embrace her... you have to act now... you have to give her what she wants, now that she is lying in her bed alone...*

Shut up! That's enough! These are mere hallucinations of maddened senses, my rational mind interrupted in a tone that suffocated any response. *We are not going anywhere, not now, not ever!*

The last word is the right word, I thought, and for the time being I managed to stifle my rebellious senses, but I was unsure I would be able to do it the next time.

❖

One evening we went to theatre. They played Midsummer Night's Dream. Laurianne also came and she sat right in front of me. The performance itself was nothing out of the ordinary, though I found Puck's actor very convincing. He inspired me anyway, and all kinds of quirky jokes came to my mind, and I kept whispering them into Laurianne's ear. She was not much captivated by the performance either, but at least we had a good time. It felt good looking at her trying to muffle her giggles. The best part was that I could lean close to her, feel her hair tickling my face and absorb the scent of her body.

After the performance Laurianne felt like walking, so we strolled to Kama Pura. Four kilometres, just the two of us!

She told me many interesting things about her life, but I was barely able to pay attention to the meaning of the words. The magical music of her voice, the exciting closeness of her body, the sight of her hair rippling in the evening breeze... all enchanted me.

We stopped in front of the entrance of Shakti Loka, and she continued her stories. I would have loved to see her to her room, to her bed, but she did not encourage me. Not with one word –although it seemed her eyes had that stirring gleam, that nowhere else can be found, but in the eyes of a woman in love. I was not sure though or just could not believe it. I was waiting for a more obvious sign, something to reassure me. When she ran out of words, I started to talk to keep her longer, maybe something would happen. When I saw her body shivering in the chilly evening air I had to let her go. We wished each other sweet dreams. I looked after her with a deep sigh, until the last of her dress disappeared behind the door. I started towards the Vira Loka with heavy steps as if struggling with gale force winds.

As I threw myself into bed heroically, my inner struggle resumed. My emotions attacked again with a renewed force. *We don't understand you, Balder Falkenberg. Do something. Do you still want her to make the first step? You have been doing this all your life. You expect girls to approach you, to conquer you as though you were a delicate virgin.* I defended myself: *This is not true at all, I definitely did take the initiative with Ylva Ekberg, and you know best what the consequences were then!*

That was a long time ago. You were still a child, now you should be a man. A real man who dares to accept himself, his feeling and his desires, who is not afraid of failure, of being rejected... Yes, Balder Falkenberg, it is high time you behaved like a man, and not like a... like a ... worm.

I was attacked at the most painful point. The word worm reminded me of how the Master rebuked me.

All right, let it be, I answered with the sulkiness of the defeated. *I will show you.* I put my jacket on and made my way to the girls' building.

I halted for a moment in front of Laurianne's door, I started to look for some loophole but my hands desiring to caress waited no longer. They suddenly pulled the handle.

The Moon peeked into the room with a silvery gaze. Laurianne raised her head from her pillow. First I saw surprise, then happiness on her face. I closed the door carefully. Natalia was sleeping in the other bed. I stood there, hesitating for a moment, until I saw Laurianne lift up the sheets, a sure sign for me to snuggle in next to her. She hugged me and passionately pulled me close to her.

"God, how long I have been waiting for you," she whispered fervently, before our lips melted together.

I felt as though I was finally arriving home after a long, long journey. The prodigal son must have been this overjoyed when his father's love embraced his soul again. I would have been satisfied with this only, such was the fulfilment offered in that hug. But when she began to untie the belt of my dressing gown desire flooded me with renewed strength. And when our naked bodies touched there was no power in the Universe that would have been able to stop me. Nothing else existed, just the two of us, and I saw nothing else except her face shining with happiness, and her tears glistening with mine.

Our time together was perfect. Infused both with the uplifting mysticism of our first encounter, and the immeasurable happiness of two people in love finally finding each other.

I completely forgot about Natalia. Only when the waves of desire subsided, and we allowed our bodies a short rest did I notice her. She was sitting on her bed watching us. She smiled, then approached and embraced the two of us.

"You are beautiful together," she said in a quiet voice filled with emotion. "I do not understand how you could have wasted so much time."

I did not understand, and I don't think Laurianne did either. One month had passed since our first meeting. The longest month of my life.

❖

In the period that came, my soul moved somewhere between the almost complete and complete happiness on the scale of emotions. My love for Laurianne now requited, gave me great momentum for my spiritual practices. The highly effective spiritual practices we did in the Kama Pura increasingly stimulated the transforming power of love in me. I felt this was the first time I had been really and truly in love. I had been searching for her in every woman until then, and deep in my heart I had always known she existed. I discovered in her all the qualities I had admired in other women. I was convinced I found my ideal spiritual companion with whom I would be able to go all the way on the tantric path.

As our bodies grew accustomed to each other and discovered each other over and over again, our mutual love became deeper and deeper. The way she loved me kept my passion burning as strongly as I had never before imagined it could burn. At appropriate astrological moments we prepared tantric rituals. The universal analogies that we invoked elevated our love sessions to cosmic heights. Laurianne initiated me into the secrets of the Tantric Maithuana. I became conscious of the invaluable advantages of a tantric couple on the spiritual journey. The Maithuna rituals brought us close to a divine fulfilment and a state of complete freedom. I felt I needed nothing more to reach the final goal than a much stronger spiritual inspiration, a thirst as strong as that of a drowning man who struggles to breathe. My communion with Laurianne strengthened this thirst for the divine each day.

❖

My love for Éva burned on even after discovering Laurianne. I still felt close to the heavens in her passionate embrace. Although I loved Laurianne more than anyone, I could not resist Éva's mythical attraction – and neither did I want to. Moreover, I observed that after making love to her I could love Laurianne with even greater intensity. Éva had the extraordinary ability to awaken mysterious powers in me giving me an incredible sexual vigour and erotic potential. I had noticed this at our first meeting when I had been with Linnéa Svenson, but unfortunately Linnéa could neither understand nor accept it. And I did not have the knowledge to explain it to her properly.

I was able to explain it to Laurianne though. She understood and accepted it. She never blamed me for meeting Éva not with one word. Interestingly, the complete freedom we each gave the other was precisely what kept us together and contributed much to our cloudless relationship.

As for Éva, well, I did not need to be concerned. She compensated herself amply for getting second place in my life.

❖

The men's meetings had an important role in the Kaula's life. They gave me the chance to discover the real masculine virtues that are based on spiritual values, which unfortunately are very much pushed into the background in today's civilized, effeminate society. The Master's endeavours to awaken these virtues of a real man in each of us seemed to be one of his most blessed activities. Gregor, just as in everything else, followed him in this too. During these meetings he often cautioned us that the spiritual, tantric road is in fact the road of the Vira, the spiritual hero.

Of course, we did not deal with these questions solely from a theoretical perspective. We practiced and exercised a lot to become a true Vira. The results were clearly visible on the older members of the Kaula. As for me, well, I struggled heroically to leave behind my weaknesses once and for all.

Sometimes we went on strenuous hikes in the mountains, combining them with intensive spiritual practices. I enjoyed these as I felt they deepened and strengthened the special bond between the men of the Kaula. In those days I discovered the beauty of an honest friendship between men who walk on the road of spirituality, and that I had always longed for deep inside.

Sometimes we invited girls to our meetings. They danced for us, then we transfigured them into the manifestation of one of the ten female cosmic powers through secret tantric rituals. We indulged them with exceptional gifts, adorned their body with flowers, and worshipped them as the embodiment of goddesses. Marvellous things happened at such times; they really did transform, their faces became heavenly beautiful, and their bodies radiated as though they had been the source of some kind of an otherworldly light. Real moments of grace – the gifts of the Great Divine Mother.

Gregor insisted that male members of Kama Pura learn to look at women in this transfiguring way even in the not so celebratory moments of everyday life.

"Woman is the manifestation of God's love for us, and as such, she is also the door to another dimension that opens to a divine presence," he explained at one of our Vira meetings. "For all our activities we need energy, strength, momentum, and the most easily accessible source of this energy springs from the women we love. Do not forget that beside all men who achieved remarkable accomplishments, there always stood powerful women full of love and adoration. But a woman can only open up for a man, can only shine in her true and complete femininity, if she feels loved and adored. Then, and only then she will blossom in the sunshine of a man's love, and become an exotic flower of brilliant colours and intoxicating scent. But in the lack of this fertilizing power of the sun, her flower chalice bearing the secret energy of life stays closed and withers like a bud left in the shade without ever revealing the beauty and wonder nature hid in it."

One time Gregor invited Laurianne to a Vira meeting. That event stays memorable to this day. Laurianne evoked Kali, the cosmic energy of time and transformation with her dance. Kali showed herself with such terrible power, that all twenty-one of us present experienced the awakening of our Kundalini, just by looking at her, admiring her and becoming one with her.

I was even more privileged than the others, as I was given the grace of joining her in love after the ritual. This was the most intensive erotic experience of my life. I felt I was holding Kali herself in my arms. Her overwhelming power flooded me as if I was standing on the shore of a sea roused by tempests, and only by concentrating all the power of my will into an upward and God-ward stream I could rise above the waves towering ever higher.

❖

One afternoon Laurianne asked me to be in the Fragrant Garden at nine o'clock in the evening because she had a little surprise for me. I love surprises, and Laurianne was full of them. She often devised something special that made our time together excitingly fresh and unique, and kept our relationship effervescent and lively.

I walked up the steps of the Shakti Loka hoping for the best, my body trembling with anticipation as I approached the top storey. The lush garden, witness to innumerable secrets, held a gift that surpassed everything I had ever imagined. The central pool was surrounded by a magic circle of candles. Rose petals floated on the water, and candlelights twinkled on its surface. Ethereal light shone above the magic circle, but the vegetation around withdrew into enigmatic obscurity.

The first beat of the surprise was that it was not Laurianne who welcomed me but Éva. A true Zen moment. My mind stood still, and I did not know what to think. I stared at Éva in astonishment, but she did not feel any need for explanations. She made me sit in the deckchair opposite the pool, outside the circle of candles. She knelt beside me, took an orange from the tray and calmly began to peel it. I used this interlude to accustom myself to the unforeseen situation and ponder about the "What's next" As for the why's, I put them aside for the moment. Answering both would have been too much for the mind. The seductive outlines of Éva's breasts were faintly visible under her crimson robe; as she directed the cool and moist oranges between my lips I was already thinking about how to untie the knot on her belt. It was then I saw Laurianne's figure emerging from the sultry twilight, wearing an orange silk robe, mysterious smile on her lips.

My mind was out of order – and stayed like that for a good while. Unexpected turns kept coming. Laurianne did not come to me but to Éva. They nestled close for a short time, then with breathtakingly slow movements undressed each other as if peeling a fruit. They picked up the fruit bowl and, hand in hand, stepped into the magical circle.

A wonderful play started. They not only fed each other with the fruits – they devised such varied and ingenious ways to use them, that for a moment I had the feeling the Creator did not create them primarily to be eaten.

I watched the two mesmerized as they touched and kissed each other in a way we men never touch and kiss a woman. And I saw a new kind of pleasure radiating in their expressions, different from the one my touches used to bring forth. It was not easy to stay put. My body was urging me, but my spirit stayed motionless in wonder watching the embodiment of some unworldly joy. The magic circle seemed to enclose them in a world beyond my reach, but the fact that I was allowed to peek into this secretive, intimate female universe was a great gift in itself. To see two women love each other, the two women I love, awakening each other's body and soul, to see how they coil round the other with that special embrace that radiates a burning lust and tender affection at the same time... I do not know if anything more beautiful ever existed on Earth. Maybe if...

Then I saw Éva step out the circle and approach me. She began to undress me. I suspected what might come and I admit I became fairly nervous. This was a totally new situation – and I had no idea how I would be able to cope with a lioness and a tigress at the same time.

My knees shaking, I stepped inside the candlelit circle. However, my worries turned out to be unfounded. Éva directed the game brilliantly. Obviously, it was not her first trio but for me this was a new experience. A fresh, exciting and soul-stirring experience. I can't deny the thought had already flashed across my mind: What if Laurianne, Éva and me...? But the thought remained just that, a thought. It had not even ripened into a fantasy. Now, that my secret hope became reality, I simply couldn't believe it. I was like a child who had just received his most desired toy. I could hardly get enough of it. It was daybreak when I let my beloved goddesses go to rest. This was the most beautiful present I had ever received from a woman... well, from two women.

20. Triangle in the circle

One night we went to the theatre. The actors of the local theatre company served up Midsummer Night's Dream, in a quite tasteless version indeed. But I didn't regret going to the performance as Balder came too and, with a gracious game of Fate distributing the theatre tickets, he sat right behind me.

Balder wasn't particularly impressed by the production either, making witty comments throughout, so it took me some effort to stop myself breaking out into fits of laughter. I had a great time, eagerly awaiting his next remark. Not only so to be amused at his ideas, but also because he always leant forwards to speak, so close to me his golden hair fell onto my bare shoulders, tickling my skin and sending goose bumps all over my body. But that was not enough for me. When he whispered something I tried to ensure his lips touched my ear for a second. I loved that pleasant sensation as it rippled along my skin. I would never have believed such a delicate, innocent touch could stir such a tempest in me.

Like a taut bow, my body thirsted after the next touch. The subtlest contact started strong waves of excitement running along my nerves. I only realized then just how much my cells had treasured the memories of our first encounter, and how much they desired the next union. If such delight begins to fly after one single touch, I fantasized, then what would it be like if our whole bodies, naked, could merge together as they had in the temple of the soul. What would it be like if, yes, we were each other's once again...

I desired that more than anything in the whole world. I wouldn't even have minded making love in one of the dark corridors of the theatre. Or if we had made one of the toilets a temple to our love... Whatever... But he showed no signs of approaching. At least he was talking to me... leaning close to me... touching me secretly. And I could fantasize about him. About us...

Despite the poor performance I felt that Shakespeare's text had managed to bring to life the mystery of Midsummer's Night and create that enchanted space and time in which the supernatural is played out. Where secret loves can be fulfilled, and where anything may happen because the veiled gates between the world of humans and fairies open for a brief moment... I even imagined some mischievous fairy sprinkling a pinch of nectar from Amor's magic flower in Balder's eyes. An elixir that would make him see me as more beautiful, as more worthy of love. So he would actually see me, notice the flame that was burning for him and because of him...It was a special night. For the first time since our first meeting I felt attractive again, stunning even. I started to trust in the magic power of love... Although it was a chilly October night the mysterious fires of Midsummer Night were blazing in me. Though the others were going home by car, I felt like walking, and Balder offered to accompany me! Yesss, magical nights do exist! Ones on which our desires can become true...

We were in no hurry on the four kilometres back. We didn't touch each other, just strolled along, our steps in harmony. And we talked... about the theatre and the arts. At least that is what our words said. But our voices, our tones spoke of something else. Love. Our love. Those unmistakable overtones were not only vibrating in my voice, but in his too. I heard and felt them!

He accompanied me to the entrance of the Shakti Loka where we stopped and talked... and talked... I didn't want to let him go. I couldn't let him go, though my teeth were chattering from the cold. He was in no hurry to leave me either... that felt wonderful. I would have loved to invite him... to accompany me further... to come to my room. But I couldn't break my promise to myself; he had to make the first move. Were he to make the slightest approach I knew I would rush to him, melt joyfully in his arms. But he didn't make any moves that would have freed me from my resolution.

In the end we had to say good night to each other. Sighing, I headed for my room, alone. Despite my urgent desire, I was alone!

I wasn't disappointed though. Actually I was surprisingly happy. At last I had seen that secret light in his eyes. The one that made me feel beautiful and... yes, desirable. I felt something in him had finally awoken... something for me.

But I still didn't understand why he hadn't made a move. In the other way, not just as a friend, but as a man approaches a woman. I just didn't understand. I knew he wasn't shy. I'd had plenty of opportunities to see the elegant self-confidence with which he twirled girls around his little finger. But now if I attracted him... and I was sure I did... Then what could be the reason? Maybe he was waiting for me to make the first move? Suddenly I realized I had to put an end to this game of cat and mouse. Tomorrow I would go to him, and...

The door opened quietly. Balder was standing in the half-light. Hesitating, with a questioning face. He'd made the first move! The rest is up to me, screamed my body and soul. Now I am free. Now I can do what I feel. Now I can repay my roommate the experience she had once surprised me with...

I lifted the cover so he could see my naked body calling him.

I knew Natalia wasn't sleeping. I felt her watching the whole time. Listening to us. And I was delighted she could also be present at the celebration of our joy. At the celebration of our finding each other. I felt it was only now we were actually meeting. On our first encounter in the uplifting magical atmosphere of the sanctuary our *divine selves* had met easily and quickly. But the *humans* in us needed some time before getting to know each other, getting close. We needed to be purified in the fire of suffering, and had to expend tremendous efforts to be victorious over all the obstacles set by the *gnome* dwelling in us. The *gnome*, that suspecting its own destruction in love resists it with all its might…

Well, the *gnome* went silent that night. So finally the *human* and the *divine* in us were able to meet.

❖

Balder was a strong man, and his love passionate and overwhelming. With his fiery embrace he was able to heat the sparks of desire into explosive lava flow within me in a couple of seconds. And he could keep me near the highest peaks with incredible finesse for hours. We discovered new hidden spots on each other's bodies which made us taste delight in its whole spectrum of shades.

My body and soul were ready for love, and our lovemaking surpassed every previous experience. If I considered the mere physical, then the sex battles I had fought with Alex Feroman were close in their intensity. But they had been torturous clashes that left searing wounds in me because the fire had been burning in my body only. Now that same fire aflame in the expanse of the soul tamed me with its sweet healing warmth and boundless love. With Alex I had had to experience the anguishing urge to receive. But with Balder I was able to live the tender and passionate joy of giving every moment.

I desired no other man. I felt I received everything from him that a man can give; I was able to give myself to him completely. I also knew he loved me… truly and honestly. But it was still different for him. Although I saw him less and less frequently with Antonia, he still searched out Éva's room often. For a long time I lived under the false impression that when two people found each other they would be enough and need no one else. This seemed not to be true for men… later I realized it doesn't apply to women either. Love born on the tantric path obeys different rules than those between other couples… and the transition between the two can be incredibly painful.

During the time I secretly loved Balder my jealousy had gradually subsided. And I had thought it gone for good. I was already able to be happy at his joy when another woman embraced him, when he embraced another woman. But now that I felt he was mine to some extent, the torturous tension surfaced again. Particularly when I knew he was with Éva.

Once I was passing Éva's room and stopped a while in front of the door. The voices I heard disturbed me deeply and painfully. To imagine my love charging another woman's groin, whispering sweet words into her ear – words that should have been for my ears only. To imagine all that, and to accept it, was no easy task. I went to my room and had a good cry. But when Balder came and smiled at me all my sadness lifted and once again I was the happiest woman on the planet. He was always honest with me. He told me of every feeling and experience as though he was speaking to his best friend. And I did try to be not only his lover but also his most understanding friend. Gradually I started to see with his eyes, feel with his heart... and, of course, with the heart of the wise tantric woman who knows we can never own anything or anybody. Only that which we give to others can be truly ours. We can only enjoy the things we let go. Everything we want to keep at any cost we are bound to lose sooner or later...

I wasn't ever actually angry with Balder. Not for his romantic adventures or indeed anything else. I think I loved him too much to get angry with him. After a while even my renewed jealousy evaporated – particularly after I was finally convinced that his being with Éva in no way altered his feelings towards me. I also noticed that, strangely, it made him more manly, more attractive and more exciting, than if he'd belonged to me only and I had unlimited power over him. I had the feeling I had to conquer and reconquer him. And that protected me from sinking into the calm passivity of ordinary relationships.

❖

There were other things too that helped us maintain the incandescence of our passion at such high temperatures. For example, we didn't live together. Gregor insisted men and women live separately in Kama Pura. He knew it was the only way for relationships to retain their freshness and sparkling energies. He couldn't emphasize enough that cohabitation and particularly sleeping together would, sooner or later, lead to a decline in erotic attraction. Even the most passionate couples were not exceptions to this law of nature – they merely lasted a little longer before their sexual attraction faded.

In the beginning there were moments when a part of me rebelled against Kama Pura's "inhuman" rule. I would have loved to spend at least twenty-four hours per day with Balder so I could reach him at any moment, always breathe in his comforting male energy, continually mollycoddle and

353

spoil him. So he would only focus on me and be with me only, thus constantly proving his love for me… Luckily I had the opportunity in the Kaula to develop in myself the traits of an elevated, spiritual femininity. I learnt to value freedom and independence, and to decline smaller pleasures in favor of greater joys.

The Shakti meetings were very helpful in this. These gatherings, attended only by women, were led by Evelina, who had been personally initiated into the mysteries of Tantra by the Master.

Here I learnt a wealth about life and love, femininity and masculinity. I was particularly amazed to realize just how much pointless suffering this knowledge could save humans.

Evelina initiated secret tantric rituals and special erotic games to develop our femininity – a most pleasant and exciting way to do it.

One time we practiced sensual massage. We pulled straws for our partners. Oh, the irony of Fate… or maybe its special mercy. I had to massage Éva… erotically.

I hadn't approached a woman in that way since Estrella, and some sort of strange guilt had been lurking in me. But it lifted at the first touches. Éva's body had an exciting and magnetic effect on me. I saw the perfect incarnation of the Goddess of Love in her. Maybe I had been unable to see it before because, subconsciously, I still felt she was my rival. But now, approaching her with a free and open spirit, she deeply moved me. She was stunning, even to a woman's eyes… I imagined what waves she must stir up in men. And for the first time I understood Balder.

There were no erogenous zones on her body: every cell of her body was ready to transform touch into ecstatic delight. But she not only experienced it, she also radiated this joy. As her body began to awake under my strokes, I was also drawn into excited trembling. It was a kind of sexual desire too, but so very different from that the presence of a man awoke in me. It inspired me to another kind of touch, another way of embracing, and promised a different fulfilment…

The meeting awoke unusual and slightly disturbing feelings in me. Were I not so wary of big words, I would say I had fallen in love with Éva. But I'd rather say I started to feel attraction to her, and I really liked her. I secretly hoped for a continuation. I hoped she had also felt how well suited we were together.

I was not mistaken. She initiated the next step.

We met in the Fragrant Garden one night… Just the two of us. She asked if she could massage me this time.

That was when I realized experience is not enough for giving love and conferring delight. You also need talent. Éva was the most talented woman I had ever met. She never ran out of playful ideas. Refined, almost spiritual passion vibrated in her touch. We experienced the most beautiful shades of all those feelings a woman can feel for another woman.

We talked a lot that night. She told me of her life, experiences and feelings towards Balder. I also shared my emotions honestly. It was interesting that precisely our love for Balder – which had somewhat kept us apart – now opened the gates for our closeness.

That was the moment I dared to say my tendency to be jealous had finally ceased, once and for all. Not long after a new idea started to besiege my mind: what if Éva... and I... and Balder... together.

Éva was delighted by my suggestion. She became really emotional and reassured me we would have a divine time. She also told me she'd been in triangle games, and that it was an "unforgettable and enriching experience".

We prepared for the ritual for a whole week – in secret, of course. We didn't breathe a word about it to Balder. Neither of us touched him for the week, but in exchange we spent plenty of time with each other. We met regularly, practiced tantric exercises to awaken the focal points of certain cosmic energy spheres in each other's body and aura.

This secret preparation filled me with joy and excitement. The emotional ties that linked us became stronger day by day.

We prepared our meeting place with the greatest care and attention; we drew the magical space with a circle of forty-nine candles, marking each with a letter of the Sanskrit alphabet; we inscribed the fiftieth letter, the symbol of transcendence, into the centre of the circle with astral light using the power of our mind; we scented the pool water with natural plant oils chosen according to the astrological moment in time, and filled it with the energy fluids of Ananda Shakti – the infinite divine beatitude. We charged the fruits for the ceremony with this energy too.

I planned the ritual, basing it on magic laws learnt from Gregor. But I entrusted Éva with the actual erotic play. She was far more experienced. She gave me a few hints early on. One was that in threesome games two should focus on the third, and that the roles change from time to time. She also warned me that if any of us felt jealousy or another negative emotion we should stop the play immediately. Otherwise we could resonate with astral forces so damaging they were capable of destroying our relationships with each other forever.

It was Éva's idea that we two should step into the magic circle first, to awaken each other's bodies before the play of three. Men love to watch two women stroking each other, she said. It shouldn't be merely a show: we should really provide pleasure for the other. That's the only way to extend true delight to the viewer. We would have to act as though he wasn't there. Only pay attention to each other. And that way it would be real.

I accepted her suggestions but, when we started to play, I couldn't resist the temptation to glance at Balder. Éva had been right. The joy shining through Balder's face was real. And so were the desire and wonder, sparkling in his wide-open eyes.

Designed only as a preparation, this couple game was to present me with a surprising revelation. While only the two of us were within the circle, playing with the water, the fruits, and each other's bodies, I had the feeling we were the two poles of creative energy and nature's forces were brought to life in our play. Forces that carry divine perfection within but are unable to break out of the circling of the created world. The light circle marking the magical space enclosed us too within the permanent cycle of nature, but the moment Balder entered the circle something shifted immediately... I couldn't put my finger on what had happened exactly, but I sensed the change clearly. Only later I recognized it was the appearance of the male principle that had had such a magical effect. Nature's duality had unified in a sort of holy trinity in which the male principle symbolizing unity was already there: the upwards-pointing triangle, the symbol of the way leading from the manifestation to divine transcendence. With the appearance of the triangle the magic circle itself was transformed. It was no longer the ceaseless turning of the wheel of nature; I felt it as a symbol of divine wholeness and infinity. I felt the triangle too contained somehow completeness and perfection. And that we three created perfect unity.

There in the stupor of the play these thoughts had not yet crystallized. What I did feel was a kind of uplifting and mystical emotion vibrating in me, one I usually feel when I can peep behind the veil of the visible to see the transcendental essence of the invisible.

To this day I can't decide what was the most wonderful that night... the physical delight raised to ecstasy, the emotional waves washing away all barriers between us, the intoxicated delight on Balder's shining face, or the fact that I had finally defeated the demons of selfishness, jealousy and possessiveness. Or the happiness of sharing the man I loved more than everything on earth with another... or maybe the magical analogy of the situation that gave our togetherness a cosmic dimension. I don't know. But I already knew that here was a game I would be delighted to play again. Any time!

21. Message from the past

Laurianne had to leave for France in the middle of December. I also decided to go home and spend Christmas with my parents. I wanted to meet Carina too as I had asked Gregor's permission to invite her to Kama Pura. I had to talk to her before I started to plan the initiation game.

Arriving in Karlskrona; I went straight to my grandfather. I found him in my aunt's house. He was not in his best shape so his doctor ordered him to spend some time in bed. As soon as I stepped into the room his face lit up with joy and his eyes started to shine as though he was awaiting a surprise. He sat up with an ease uncommon for people of his age. His long white hair, beard, and mischievous eyes reminded me of a kind-hearted Santa Claus.

I gave him my present without saying a word: three photographs taken in the Fragrant Garden during my initiation, showing ten beautiful, naked girls caressing me. Candles around the pool, and in the background, between the leaves of a dwarf palm, the moon shone like an enormous orange.

"You found the Island of Delights!" he cried out in excitement. As he eagerly drank in every detail of the picture fat tears slid down from the deep furrows under his eyes, one after the other.

"Yes, I found it. It is exactly like you described."

My grandfather was crying. Crying and smiling. I could only guess what he was feeling. I had never ever seen his eyes wet – maybe he had never cried before. Except for now, when he saw the dream he had staunchly believed in his whole life was true after all.

"I can leave now," he said quietly, rather to himself, and for a moment his wrinkles seemed to become smooth. "I can leave now."

I told him about Kama Pura, our life there, about the girls, about Laurianne and our love. I had not seen him so happy for a long time. Maybe once, long ago, out on the sea, standing at the prow of his boat his shirt unbuttoned, singing in the roaring wind. But this was another kind of joy: that of a man who had made peace with life. A tranquil happiness.

He listened to me with satisfaction, and kept nodding as though he had known all along this was how it was supposed to happen. He then slowly sailed into dreamland like a child who, exhausted by a long day of playing, falls asleep during the bedtime story.

That was the last time I saw him alive.

Three days later he was gone. When my aunt found him, his face looked peaceful, like he was just sleeping. He was holding the photos tight in his hands. In a reproving tone my aunt told the family that he was looking at porn pictures even in his last minutes. When I asked her about the pictures she told me she had thrown them out. Luckily, I managed to fish them out of the bin and in an unguarded moment I slipped the proof of his life's great dream into his pocket.

Arne Larsson preached at the sermon. I heard familiar expressions that reminded me of Christa Forshman's funeral. I knew he was thinking the same as me. But now, these words awakened different echoes in me. I was not sad for my grandfather's passing. In fact, I can say I felt great joy – an Island of Delights must exist on the other side too, and I was sure my grandfather would be sent there.

❖

I found Carina Dahl in Stockholm. She also spent Christmas with her parents. She was delighted to see me and, as we had not met for a long time, we had plenty of stories to tell. I could not talk to her about Kama Pura but, as I was inquiring about her plans, I found out she was planning to move to Romania for a while "to be near the Master". I was extremely happy to hear that, as it seemed to prove my assumption that Carina also belonged to the Kaula.

She told me one of her dreams – and it set me thinking. In the dream she was dancing in a large hall like the interior of a temple, men and women dressed in Indian clothes were sitting around her, and I was there too. She supposed this dream must have belonged to one of her past lives because my body and my face were utterly different. But still, she was certain it was me. That night, probably as a result of our conversation, I had a similar dream: we were in a circular shrine resembling the Shiva sanctuary in Kama Pura. Men and women were sitting together in a large circle. Although I did not see Carina, I did recognize a few members of the Kaula. Laurianne was sitting next to me, though with another body and face, but I knew it was her. She was looking at me in anger – and that caused me pain beyond words. In front of me a long, black haired man stood on a pedestal and I recognized him as Gregor. I saw him talking, but did not hear his voice. As far as I remember, I was not even paying attention to him. I was spellbound by the fury burning in Laurianne's eyes.

I awoke with a strange feeling. I was relieved to discover it was only a dream, but it still left me perturbed and nervous.

As morning came, I called Laurianne, but before I could say a word, she told me her dream. I was astounded to hear her telling similar things to what I myself had seen.

This extraordinary coincidence surprised us both. It happened before that we had been at the same place and met in our dreams – in fact around that time we even started to explore the possibilities of astral lovemaking – but this was completely different. This time the dreams seemed to evoke the stirring feelings of past experiences and long-forgotten memories. We decided that as soon as we had the chance we would investigate the hidden matters of our past lives.

❖

Strolling through the streets of Stockholm, my legs unconsciously led me towards Magnus Evans's luxury villa where the Nightriders club had had its hidden nest. I felt a strong temptation to enter, curious whether it was still running. I could not resist the temptation, I did not really try to. Sixteen years had passed... and I thought there was nothing to be afraid of. Or was I actually trying to prove that to myself?

I was amazed the joint was still up and running, only some of its decor had changed and obviously its members too. The atmosphere was terribly depressing. I felt a large flock of astral demons fluttering around. Although I did not plan to stay long, I met an old friend of mine and had to talk to him. I found out my former band, Atrocity, had broken up a long time ago. After I retired, they continued to glitter in the sky of the rock-world for another three years – augmenting Magnus's wealth – but then quarrelled and disbanded. Not long after, my successor as bass player died the same way as my predecessor, of AIDS, and Ramborg had been stabbed to death in a pub fight. Sibylla had been in a mental hospital since that time. Her condition was improving, but not enough for her to return to a normal life.

I was astonished to see what thorough work the destructive forces had carried out among my former companions, forces they had called upon themselves in their madness. Only Magnus's star was still shining. He was the owner of one of the largest record studios in the country – and known to be among the wealthiest men in Stockholm. In addition, he was flirting with the idea of starting a political career. He continued to finance the Nightriders with substantial sums of money. I supposed this was still the plant where he produced the supply of human raw material for his plans.

I was just about to say goodbye to my friends when I saw the door opening. Magnus whirled in accompanied by two hefty bodyguards. I turned away my head so he would not notice me, but my dear friend cried out.

"Magnus, look who's here!"

Magnus turned towards us, his face petrified for a moment in astonishment, but only for a moment. Then, with a surprising skill, he smiled a diplomatic smile and started towards me confidently.

"Well, well. The prince of the hell returns," he offered his hand while prying into my eyes, as if trying to figure out my motivation. "Great... I knew that one day you would return. You had no other choice."

"I am not here for the reason you think I am," I answered in coolly and calmly.

"You mean you can read my thoughts?" he asked cynically.

"No, but I can read certain signs."

"Hmmm, I see." With a cutting look he motioned my friend to clear off. "But I hope you will drink a whisky with a former fellow member of our secret brotherhood, won't you?" he continued when there were just the two of us.

"Thanks, but I have not drunk for a long time."

"You haven't joined some weird sect, have you?! I don't think so, you are too intelligent for that, but even if you have, it must be some momentary lapse of judgment. I, of course, can take care of your redemption, in the event you're willing to work with us again."

The offer surprised me, and momentarily I could not decide whether he was seriously considering that option or just pulling my leg.

"Well, what do you mean by work?" I asked with feigned interest.

"It is no accident that you are here right now."

"No, it is no accident," I agreed, convinced that we meant two completely different things.

"I need a music expert in the record studio."

"What's your offer?"

"Fifteen thousand bucks a month and, of course, certain other allowances."

That is really something, I thought. I could build a new Kama Pura within a year. Still, I was not sure whether he was bluffing, like I was, or he was serious. But I had an intuition so I decided to continue with this game.

"Why do you think I am in need of your money? Just like the way you got yours, I could get mine. Tantric alchemy opens up the same material resources for me, and I do not have to listen to the hubbub of dilettantes twelve hours a day."

On hearing the words tantric alchemy, his smile faded. As I had expected.

"So you reinvented the wheel, and now you're too big for your boots, huh?"

"Yeah, I discovered things. Things you seem to have forgotten. Or you are simply ignoring them on purpose"

"Namely?" He tried to show self-confidence, but I saw the shadow of anguish on his face. He sensed I knew more about the subject than he had initially believed.

"Now you are able to control immense powers by sexual magic, but if you use these powers for selfish reasons, the negative karma you accumulate will make you suffer for many forthcoming lives. You seem to ignore that side of the coin."

"I use nothing for selfish reasons. I simply give people the chance to have fun, to feel good in their skin, and I provide them the music they like." I felt anger vibrating in his voice and knew I had the upper hand.

"They like the music you and your lot make them like, and they live a life you dictate them to live. You chain them to the astral demons through addiction to the alcohol and drugs you serve them.."

"Hey, hey, hey, hold on, you take things too much to heart, don't you think?" he interrupted me, restraining his growing irritation.

"Things are even worse than that, and you know it. Consider the thousands of suicides you have contributed to. You are responsible for their souls too. I'm amazed how you could have forgotten so much about the laws of karma. You studied them yourself once quite thoroughly."

"And how would you know about that? Sibylla must have opened her big mouth."

"No, it was another mutual friend of ours. You must remember her... once you started out on the same path. She stills walks on it, under the tutelage of a real master."

"Carina Dahl!" The words broke out of him involuntarily, and he turned pale. Before long though he forced his disguise back on, and continued in a steely voice, "She was a stupid ass. She got frightened of the real Tantra and dashed away. Her opinion means nothing to me. And I give a shit on yours too, Balder Falkenberg. I practiced for years, experimented a lot, and reached everything that Tantra promises. Now I take delight in the fruits of my efforts."

"Yes, you achieved all the by-products and big temptations of Tantra: success, glory, money, power, and unlimited pleasures. Yet you forgot the most important part, the real and only purpose: your divine Self. Did you really believe that your wittiness and some occult knowledge would be enough to lead you on the path? Without the warmth of the heart, the brain is just a cold and bleak steel blade that may help you cut your way through the crowd, to the pedestal of personal glory you are craving, but all you leave behind is death and destruction. The suffering you cause will sooner or later turn the pedestal of your vanity into a scaffold of tortures. "

My words vibrated with such a penetrating power, I had the feeling that actually it was not me talking, I was no more than a surprised witness to those judgments I delivered. I sensed my Master's voice resonating in my words. For a moment I had the sensation I really was the Master lecturing an errant disciple. This unusual tone caught Magnus by surprise too. He fell silent, and his mind's ability to search for counter arguments failed. I knew my words penetrated deep into his soul. But the magic did not last long. As soon as I turned silent, his mind, well-trained in delusion and self-delusion, jumped back into the saddle and counter attacked.

"You have been completely fooled my poor boy. Let me show you the real face of things. "he pointed a powerful stream of words at me like a heavy gun." Every man is a star that has its own orbit. Every man has the right to be what he wants to be, to follow his own path and to manifest his willpower in every circumstance. This is the path of will – the only valid path. Every man has to learn to dominate the powers directing his fate, and for this, he does not need to lick any guru's feet. The guru is inside each one of us."

I was surprised by his skill in tying irrefutable spiritual truths onto false logical threads to validate his standpoint – and I imagined how easily he was able to enthral shallow-minded people with these tactics. Magnus really was the master of manipulation. What struck me most was that he not only manipulated others with his manoeuvres but himself too. I think this is how his outlook on life, built on false foundations, had solidified into such a strong conviction.

I tried to explain the basic difference between the will of our ego and the will of our deeper self-mirroring divine ideals, and that only our deeper self can show us the way we have to follow; that this is the only will that brings us harmony with the world and with all the other 'stars'. His beliefs were strong, so my effort to convince him with logical explanations seemed pointless, but I still gave it a try.

"Your theory contradicts itself. You also follow others' teachings. Your words are Aleister Crowley's words. You're simply echoing his convictions."

"You are dead wrong. His teachings merely opened my eyes, and now I can see the truth myself."

I could not undermine his conviction. At least not that time, but I knew our discussion would not be unproductive. My words had planted something in him and that something would sooner or later start to work in him, until his awakening conscience would shake the Babelian tower of his false beliefs.

I thought a lot about what Magnus might have wanted from me. Why had he insisted I be with him, work with him? Why had he wanted me to accept his ideology? Certainly not because of my musical talent. He could easily have found himself a better and more obedient professional. There must have been some other reason. He had paid unusual attention to me since the first time we met. I dare say he was afraid of me. He was deeply engaged in trying to figure out my opinion about him and his activities, even if he would not have admitted it to himself. That is why he so wanted me to join his secret order, and that is why he threatened me and lured me back. He was even willing to turn a blind eye to my violations of the oath, just to know I was on his side. Maybe this was how he wanted to prove to himself his actions were correct. He did threaten me many times, but he would have never hurt me, though he could have done it easily. At that time, the reason why I was more important to him than anyone else in his entourage was unknown to me, but not long after our conversation, light was thrown on that matter too...

22. An old acquaintance…

I had to travel to Marseille for a while to renew my identity card. After the elevated spiritual atmosphere of Kama Pura it was like entering a disturbed beehive in that pre-Christmas buzz. I walked for miles in the city, sometimes throwing myself into the bustling crowds, sometimes observing the colourful and noisy throngs of people and cars speeding past, as I leant against a tree. The throng was unable to disturb my inner peace. I even realized that if I was conscious enough, I could draw a kind of psychic strength from the sea of energy heaving around me. I was a little surprised however. Over the last few years I'd become used to using spiritual practices carried out within the calm of the soul to prepare for important celebrations. I had almost forgotten that for most people preparation is nothing more than an exhausting scramble and that Christmas itself the chance to relax.

Christmas was beautiful in my family nest. My relationship with my parents, which had been seriously damaged when I chose a somewhat alternative lifestyle against their will, had recovered completely. Now, that I spent some time with them, I had the chance to tell them more about my life, feelings and thoughts, and had enough knowledge and experience to explain my views. And they had enough patience to listen, enough intelligence to understand, and enough good will to recognize my right to determine my own life. They had even started to show an interest in yoga. I found them willing to ask for my help in matters of spirituality and health. I was surprised to find that since I'd stepped onto the spiritual path they had also started to transform. Another miracle of love…

After Christmas I visited my former producer and old friend, Antonin Gautier. He had also made a great journey since our last collaboration. His awakening occult tendencies and unconventional theatre experiments made him sensitive to the existence of an invisible reality behind the facts. This had directed him unavoidably towards esoteric studies. But, similar to many other inexperienced western seekers who have tried to gain knowledge from books, he had also been unable to discover the rare flowers of the spirit among the New Age sea of weeds. He had collected a veritable library of books dealing with the esoteric. On his shelves there was a peaceful harmony between the works of the great masters and writings by those enthusiastic authors of the New Age trying to bring the buds of spiritual traditions to bear fruit – particularly on a financial level.

"Ah yes. I was infected by the occult epidemic too some time ago," he remarked, his head slightly bowed with shame when he noticed me taking in his bookshelves with such interest. "I went out and bought all of them where I saw words like karma, magic, reincarnation, guru, and nirvana. But you know what I realized?"

"What?" I asked, feigning curiosity... I already knew exactly what he was going to say.

"Useless mishmash. False spiritual propaganda that makes people stupid. A motley crew of charlatans wanting to get rich quick. I felt sick after reading ten of them. All the authors are just advertising their own spiritual enterprise – and they're worse than the Christian sects because at least you can easily recognize those by their aggressive do-gooder intention. But these New Agers are always hiding behind the mask of universal wisdom, and somehow they manage to trap bona fide seekers that try to beware of sectarianism. It was only my natural respect for books that stopped me from throwing the whole lot on a fire. But I didn't want to give them away either. I wouldn't like to be guilty of fooling others."

I smiled to myself at his genuine indignation. He must have started his studies with the poorest of the books.

I lifted Yogananda's book "Autobiography of a Yogi" from the shelf.

"Did you read this one?"

"No, I haven't got that far."

"And this one?" I turned the cover of Paul Brunton's The Quest of the Overself.

"No, I haven't read that either. I told you, I was sick and tired of them all after the tenth."

"And you haven't read Kahil Gibran's The Prophet either?"

"Oh, I did. I loved it. An amazing work. But most of that wasn't about the occult – it was artistic, poetic."

"Yes, real spiritual art," I agreed.

"All art is spiritual in its essence" Antonin insisted.

"It should be...but we'll talk about that later." I said taking down books by Vivekananda and Shivananda, the life and teachings of Ramakrishna, two Gurdjieff books, the life of Milarepa, one about astrology and another about the Enneagram.

"If you do decide to send the lot to the pyre, it'd be worth sparing these."

"Have you read them?" he asked in genuine amazement.

"Some of them yes. But actually after just a couple of lines I can tell if the spirit lives in them, or if they are merely lifeless letters."

"So the esoteric fever has infected you too?"

I let this pointed observation slip.

"I see there's another area that has totally escaped your notice," I said.

"Which?"

"Tantra."

"I've read a couple of things about it but I was already through the first phase of my illness and tried to refrain from more infections."

"Good for you. It means you've not become immune, so I still have a chance to infect you."

"What? Do you mean... that you...?"

"Yes."

"That's a surprise... I always thought you were a woman of healthy intellect."

"That's what you thought?" I asked happily. "Maybe I'll even be able to prove it to you one day. So, tell me what you know about Tantra."

"It's a branch of Indian yoga that's somehow connected to sexuality. I've read very contradictory theories about it. It's impossible to find your way between them. To be honest it did interest me, despite being totally sick of the occult. That's why I shied away from it. So I wouldn't relapse again."

Antonin's opposition did not put me off. I sensed the natural and healthy skepticism of a genuine seeker. And something else too. An unusual talent for the practice of Tantra yoga. So this infection experiment provided me with great pleasure.

"Let's put aside all bookish theories and allow me to speak of my own experiences."

"I'd love you to. I've always been fascinated by people's experiences – on the assumption they are totally genuine."

"Let's make a deal. I'll be completely honest. I won't keep anything secret or leave anything out that might interest you. You'll have to try and restrain your constant need to contradict, particularly in areas you don't have enough experience."

"Deal. But can I ask questions?"

"Of course."

It was just my kind of game. I told him all my most intimate experiences, and he kept his word. He tried not to protest but he did reserve the right to doubt. This was the first time I'd shared my experiences with an outsider since I'd discovered Tantra. In spite of all his superficial doubts he was spiritually ready to accept the knowledge. His questions were testament to his genuine interest.

"Do you believe in reincarnation?" he asked, a good dose of scepticism in his voice.

"I don't *believe*, I'm *sure* it exists," I replied directly.

"Have you had any experiences linked to your past lives?"

"Yes. When I was a child I knew I had already lived here and I had memories that could only have stemmed from past lives."

"Have you ever met anyone who you knew you'd already met in another life?"

"Yes. More than one."

"And they felt the same?"

"Some of them."

"And the others?"

"They weren't aware enough."

"What proof do you have that it's not just all your imagination?"

"Nothing tangible."

"So how can you say that it exists with such conviction?"

"I feel it…"

"Feel is a nebulous something. You need to examine everything through a sober mind. The fact that you feel it is not evidence for me."

"I don't want to prove anything to you. I'm just telling you about my experiences. Anyway 'feeling' and 'intuition' are much higher functions than your 'sober mind'. These reality-sensing antennas reach far further in space and time, than the mind. Unfortunately nowadays this ability has declined massively, so people try and replace it with the sober mind. A bit like hearing aids do for people with damaged hearing, or glasses for those who are short sighted. But, with practice and appropriate techniques, this intuitive ability can be reawakened. I've already had some results."

"Tell me a person I know who you 'sense' you've already met in a previous life."

"Antonin Gautier, for example. Well, I don't know how well you know him," I replied smiling, as though I was just joking. But I was actually deadly serious. Like the Master, who often says truths that are hard to believe as though he was joking.

"Yeah, right. Don't tell me we were Anthony and Cleopatra, because then… Up till now everyone who's told me of a previous life was some extremely important person. I've already met three Alexander the Greats, a few Egyptian pharaohs, five Marie Antoinettes, a dozen Mary Magdalenes, two Paul the Apostles and, believe it or not, a Jesus Christ too. And I haven't even mentioned those sitting in the mad house. I think they would provide even more shocking data."

"To be honest I haven't really been interested enough in the subject yet to research my memories in the Akasha chronicles."

"The what chronicles?"

"The Akasha chronicles… Akasha comes from the Sanskrit for the sphere of Cosmic Memory. Everything about all past events, appearances, feelings and thoughts can be found there in a coded format, just like recordings on videotape. This information is 'readable' with the help of certain yoga techniques."

"And you know people who have managed to get stuff from it?"

"Yes. I've had the chance to speak to a few such people."

"It's only that their imagination was richer than the average."

"I've met some of them too. But with a little attention and some practice you can easily tell one from the other."

"I imagine you just 'feel' that too. And again you disarm all my rational arguments. You can't discuss anything this way."

"We didn't want to argue, if I remember rightly. I'm just sharing my experiences with you. And I promise that if I find out any information about our shared past, then I'll tell you immediately. Until then you can believe whatever you wish to. And after that too, of course."

"I am really curious. And I'd like to know why of all the spiritual paths you chose Tantra."

"I don't think I chose Tantra. I think it chose me. I knew too little about it when I started to practice it to be able to talk about 'choice'. But however it happened, I'm sure it was the right choice… for me…"

"I hope you don't want to proclaim it's the only true way."

"Not at all. But I would dare to say it'd be the best path for most spiritual searchers today."

"Some say that several paths lead to the aim, just like to the top of a mountain…"

"You can put it that way too. But maybe a more accurate analogy is to say that there is one aim, and one path leads there. Only the vehicles we travel in are different. All spiritual seekers have to proceed through the same stations, learn the same life lessons and develop the same spiritual abilities, regardless of the tradition or school's practical methods they use as their vehicle. Many spiritual schools are only able to take their passengers to a certain stage. Those who wish to progress further have to change their mode of transport. Unfortunately most people are too attached to their vehicle so the vehicle itself becomes more important than the goal. They get stuck somewhere, or fall into a ravine on a difficult stretch. Only those fired by strong spiritual aspiration can ascend the highest peaks."

"And the others? What will happen to them?"

"Sooner or later they'll get there too. They just roll about a while in the illusory world of suffering and transitory pleasures. Until their aspiration becomes stronger than their attachments."

"And religions?"

"Certain stretches of the way can be done on the public transport of religions. But after that the phase of individual effort begins. To go further you also need a trained guide. This is the most risky point on the journey because you have to choose. This is where the true spiritual leaders wait for seekers – and the false guides too."

"And how do you tell the two apart?"

"With difficulty. It needs a certain spiritual maturity. But if genuine aspiration guides you, not just some childish curiosity or pubescent desire for adventure, then you will find your true guide instinctively."

"Do you think there is a spiritual tradition that can lead to the highest peak?"

"I'm convinced it's Kashmir Shaivism. Its vehicles leave from peaks most spiritual traditions hold to be the most elevated goal possible."

"And you're travelling with that vehicle?"

"I'm preparing for it yes... with all my might."

"And why did you say Tantra would be the most suitable for contemporary people?"

"Tantra uses a fuel to power its vehicle that is most easily available at the present moment, one that originates from the greatest source of psychic energy: sexual energy."

"I have read that Tantra is the most dangerous of all the spiritual paths – the way of the razor blade."

"Playing with great energy can become risky. But if you follow the instruction of a genuine and experienced guide, there is practically no danger."

"Where are all these genuine and experienced guides?" sighed Antonin. "I'd love to meet one – God knows I'd love to try this vehicle... But I reckon they only exist in Indian legends."

"I know one. He is a legendary figure, without doubt, but he lives and teaches today – and not in India, but much closer. Here in Europe. You can try his vehicle."

"Now you've got me. But how do you know he's genuine? Yeah, of course, you feel it."

"It's much more than that. Jesus said, you should judge a tree by its fruit. I cannot measure the tree – I still have to grow a lot – but I've already tasted the fruit many times. I've experienced it in myself in the form of undeniable spiritual states of consciousness. And I can tell you the fruits are particularly luscious."

"That means you're also a fruit of his labours?" he asked with a smile.

"You could put it that way. Most of my spiritual achievements certainly are."

I felt his stubborn resistance weakening. His tone became light and playful.

"Do you find the fruit appealing?" I winked.

"That's manipulation!" He laughed. "You know you were always an attractive fruit. Even if I had put you in the forbidden fruit category."

"I wasn't exactly thinking of that. But that is part of it – Tantra includes everything, even that."

"You know what surprises me most in all that you've said? It's all so logical!"

"Truth is always logical. But the opposite is not valid. Not everything that seems logical is true. So never accept anything just because it's logical. Nor that which I say. But if you're interested, take the opportunity to become convinced through your own experience."

"You haven't convinced me of anything. I won't give you the satisfaction. But I will admit you've managed to awaken my interest in a subject I'd long since discarded... It wasn't *what you said*, but *who you are* that has touched me. *Who you've become* since we first met."

❖

That night I had had a strange dream. I was in a temple hall decorated with erotic statues and pictures portraying eastern deities. There were some acquaintances from the Kaula and many others I didn't know. I recognized Gregor, Evelina, Diana, Natalia, Éva, Berthold and... Antonin! Balder was there too... he was sitting next to me. We all looked different than in reality, but I still knew with a strange certainty who the figures were! An unfamiliar woman was dancing in the centre of the circle. Her dance was sensual, or rather lustful and provocative. At least that is what I felt in my dream. Balder drank in this sight in amazement, and that definitely upset me. My irritation turned into anger, and all of a sudden I wanted to leave the whole thing and rush out of the temple. Then I woke up... but deep in my soul I still felt a strange and secret pain...

I suspected it was some trace of memory from one of my past lives. Though I could hardly wait to share the experience with someone I didn't want to tell Antonin. I knew he'd say it was absolute rubbish. But when Balder called I blurted it all out. The great surprise was when we realized he had been dreaming something similar at exactly the same time. That wasn't the first time we'd met in our dreams. But I felt this dream had an important meaning. A secret message. I hadn't managed to work out the meaning even after an extended meditation. Nor had Balder. Although we both sensed it was something important... Something that referred to both of us... and maybe to Antonin too. Or even to all the other members of the Kaula.

We decided that on our return to Kama Pura we would try and leaf through the records in the Akasha chronicles about our past lives.

23. Behind the black door

The thought of uncovering my past lives kept my mind busy after that strange dream. I knew that rediscovering my past was not necessary for my spiritual development. What happened in the past cannot be changed. We need to focus on the *now* because it is the *present* where *future* is conceived, and this future depends only on us. I knew all that, but still, the secrets of the past attracted me with an irresistible force. At times I could convince myself it was nothing more than childish curiosity and I neglected the matter, but time and again I was keen to peep under the dark veil hiding bygone memories. I felt like the hero from One Thousand and One Nights who was allowed to enter any room of the palace except for the one with the black door. I could think of nothing else but the mysterious black-doored room.

Laurianne was haunted by similar temptations so one day we went hand in hand to visit the Master for advice, or should I say, to convince him to initiate us into the secret of reading the Akasha chronicles about our past lives. Following our strategy prepared the previous night, we supported our request with solid arguments. We told him our wonderful dream with enthusiasm, and exposed our firm belief that our relationship did not start in this life. Neither our zeal nor our cogent reasoning seemed to move the Master. In fact, I had the feeling he was not even paying attention to us. Although his head was turned towards us, he was just looking through us. He let us talk through our business, but all the while his gaze pierced into a vast remoteness.

"It is true, this is not the first time you are together" he spoke suddenly. "Old ties bind you, and it is time to finalize what you had started long time ago. This would enable you to unbind the knot."

"What knot?"

"Why should we unbind it?"

"What did we start?" We kept interrupting each other in our excitement.

"We want to know more."

"We want to uncover this."

"If possible."

"Through Yoga everything is possible," said the Master, then added, "but not all is permitted."

"But is this permitted?" asked Laurianne anxiously. Instead of answering, the Master took out a piece of paper and jotted down a few lines. We were on tenterhooks.

"Give this to Gregor," he handed us the slip. He wasted no more words.

❖

Gregor was glad the Master had given his permission for this experiment. He gave us all the necessary instructions but we still had to wait a month until the appropriate moment, when we could undertake the experiment. We used this period for preparation. The new purpose gave momentum to our spiritual exercises. I practiced yoga for five-six hours a day. I did asanas and special breathing exercises, and tried to stay in the state of deep meditation for longer periods. Besides that I practiced the most efficient yoga cleansing methods every day. I kept a strict diet, eating only pure, sattvic foods abundant in vital energy. Never before had I felt so clean. My astral senses refined, I heard mantric sounds with surprising sharp-ness, my mind was uncommonly calm, and I could concentrate easily.

When the day came I withdrew to a special room used only for medi-tation, well- equipped with candles, incense and other necessities. The thought, that not far from me, in another room, Laurianne was preparing for the same mysterious experience gave me strength. I resolved not to leave the room until I was completely satisfied with the result. After three days of fasting I felt physically weak but, as soon as I started the preparation with the breathing exercises, I recovered and felt a strong life-force vibrating in my body. It surprised me that, without foods, my purified body was capable of supplying my energy needs from subtle sources.

After the preliminary exercises when I sat down in front of the ritually prepared mirror, a strange, mystical feeling took possession of me. My face was lit by two candles. I placed them so their flame would not be visible in the mirror. I focused my attention on my own forehead in the mirror and sat motionless for a good while. Gregor had told me what to expect, but when I saw my reflection in the mirror fading and then disappear, I shuddered. A queer and unpleasant sensation permeated me. The sight of a corpse might cause a similar sensation, when we are suddenly confronted with our body's transitory nature – something we are generally compelled to ignore. This bizarre notion disturbed my spiritual and mental balance, and the familiar Balder-face appeared again in the mirror. I had to start over a few times until at last I was able to contemplate the eerie emptiness of the mirror with impassive calmness. Then I had to face something new: a terrifying monstrous face emerged from the dark depth. Human and bestial expressions intertwined in its frightening face. I shuddered, and the image disappeared. My face appeared again, though this time it was much more frightened. Gregor made me promise that if the meeting with the guard of the threshold terrified me, then I would stop. That would mean I was not prepared for facing certain experiences of my past lives. I perished the thought of stopping. I convinced myself it was not fear. I was a bit alarmed, or rather surprised, that's all. After a few attempts, I managed to look into the eye of the monster with cold tranquillity. I examined its expressions trying to understand its nature. The idea that it had something to do with me took possession of me, just like it was a part of me, like it was my own shadow, a manifestation of what I judge to be my bad side, the part of me I banished to the bottomless depths of my unconscious. When I grew familiar with the monster, and even started to feel a kind of compassion for it, the image faded and another face rose from the smoke-coloured void. It was a masculine face with strong, rugged features – and a look that instilled a pervading strength and vast abysses. The light-skinned face was accentuated with long hair and short beard. Strangely, I sensed that was also me. It's the same feeling as when you see yourself in the mirror, even if the face looking back was not similar to mine. I studied the face with interest, tried to get to know it better, to feel what it would be like to be behind it, I tried to feel his personality, and his soul, which was after all my soul... and yet so very different. The face disappeared like the previous ones, and a new one emerged. It had darker skin, kind features, and reflected a mysterious restlessness. Three horizontal painted lines decorated his forehead, and his dark hair was gathered up in a knot with a shining hairclip on the top of his head. The same stirring emotion took hold of me: that was me too. I saw a few other faces, amongst them a bald Tibetan, and two feminine faces with oriental features. Each was motionless. I looked upon them as though they were three-dimensional portraits. I started over the experiment several times, and the same faces appeared in the same order every time. Later, when each face and its emotions were impressed in my memory, I was able to evoke whichever I wanted, without the need to look through the pages of the whole photo album.

That is all I managed to achieve the first time. I felt tired so I had to stop. I ate some fruit, a bowl of rice, and then retired to sleep. The experiment continued in my dream. It was an extraordinary and conscious dream. I was looking in the mirror, knowing all the while that I was dreaming. The pictures appeared again, the first two more frequently than the others. This time the faces came alive, had a body, and started to move around. I woke with the certitude that these two personalities had an important message for me, so from then on I focused on them.

I gradually learned how to see these pictures in motion and to expand them into life-situations complemented by other characters. I learned how to unravel a whole story from a tiny detail or a shred of memory. Later I felt as though I was watching short video films about the more significant moments of my former lives. I realized those moments that had an intense emotional charge or were ingrained deep in my memory were the easiest to evoke. Basically this kind of reminiscence is not so different from the memories of our childhood events, it's only that now I had to be conscious that the persona in the other body was also me. In fact, this is not that difficult either; the body of the reminiscing adult is not the same as of the child he pictures, yet he can still accept the fact that the two are the same.

While I was in the dark room, one week passed in the outside world. However, inside, time changed its dimensions. There were no nights or days. Hours and minutes ceased to exist. I did not feel time was passing at all. I experienced it as a continuous presence in the moment where, in some form, past and future were also present. Time was like a long river, and I could see each and every point of it from its source to the ocean.

Not only my sense of time changed, but also the perception of my self-identity. In theory, I already knew that the part of me who says "I am" is not identical with the body that houses me, and it's different from my emotions, thoughts and even my personality. Still, identifying my former selves was a bewildering experience. Until that time I believed I was Balder Falkenberg – born in Sweden, long blond hair, loves to play the cello – and this had given me a kind of certitude in myself. I had something to hold onto when I wanted to define who I was. Now, these barriers erected by my birth suddenly collapsed, along with the feeling of security. I could not find myself. There was nothing to hold on to, and I no longer knew where to search for the mysterious somebody or something that I would be able to call myself.

It was a frightening state, at least in the beginning. That was when I realized why divine providence closes away the memory of past lives from immature souls, and I also realized what a blessing it is to see these doors open. I felt unspeakable gratitude for being allowed to pass through the door.

Memories flooded me in three ways: I saw them in the mirror, during meditation and in my dreams. Still, they were congruent and complemented each other, in a way that in the end they formed a coherent and traceable map of my destiny. I had to relive the most soul-stirring events of two previous lives in order to see the roots of my current life reaching far back into the depths of centuries. It was astonishing to discover how my decisions and deeds in the past influenced my next lives, how different processes once started, spiraled forward breaking through barricades of births and deaths. I was shocked to see that main characters of my current life had played crucial roles on the stage of my former lives. This wonderful creature whom I know and love as Laurianne today, I had already known and loved centuries before!

We had lived somewhere in Northern India as members of a tantric community, lead by a wise man with exceptional spiritual powers. I recognized Gregor's spirit in him. I managed to evoke shreds of memories about certain erotic rituals in which I participated with a pretty Brahmin girl, Laurianne's former self. She was beautiful even then. Thirst for knowledge reflected in her large, black diamond eyes, but she was inexperienced in love and spiritual matters, just like me. We were young and in love.

There was a scene that awakened an intensive nostalgia in me each time I called it to light from the obscurity of Time: I am sitting in a clearing in the forest with a sitar in my hand, she is dancing gracefully like a young gazelle moves. In the background trees with branches spread wide, far in the blue distance snow-covered peaks of remote mountains pierce the sky... I put down my instrument and we chase each other between the trees, then she collapses into my arms, eyes closed, lips opening for a kiss. It must have been the first time we met. Then we became members of the tantric community, which was to subject our emotional and spiritual maturity to rigorous trials.

One time the then-Gregor invited an unknown woman to our temple, a chandala, a woman of no caste, who according to Hindu tradition was considered untouchable. For us, followers of the tantric path, these formalities did not mean much, and we often worshipped these chandalas as the earthly manifestations of the Great Goddess.

She danced for us, and she danced naked. Her erect breasts and curved hips combined with her impudent, teasing and enchanting movements made me lose my senses. Every part of her body radiated a frightening magical force. Inflaming me, making me crazy and turning me into her prisoner... then I saw myself in her ardently embracing arms, I saw myself merged into her body, dancing that frantic dance of the unrestrained lust again and again... and I saw Laurianne, the young Brahmin girl, my love, suffering with a broken heart. She could not forgive me. Her once tender affections changed to bitter ire, and in the end she rejected me.

However, time was to heal my wounds and alleviate her anger. The Lord heard my prayers, and she restored me to her favour.

The final tragedy took place at the great celebration of Shiva, on the day of Maha Shivaratri: we wanted to accomplish the holy ritual of the Chakra Puja to invoke Shiva's ultimate grace on the whole community.

Between the walls of the temple adorned with erotic sculptures, forty-nine couples prepared to offer their holiest sacrifice: uniting in the act of sacred lovemaking. During the invocation of the five elements everything went smoothly. But when I reached out to her to awaken her body's secret points and prepare her for the acceptance of the cosmic forces, she instinctively withdrew. I saw a strange anger swell in her eyes: her bitterness, lurking deep in her soul surfaced again. Shadows of resentment appeared on her angelic face and she pushed me away. Her young, enamoured heart was unable to forgive me after all. She could not bear my touch, my hands on her body, my hands that not long before had brought forth pleasures from another woman's body, from the body of a filthy chandala.

Her refusal felt like a painful stab in the heart. The pain that emerges from the wounded pride is followed by rage and the demonic urge to strike back, like thunder follows the lightning. In the middle of the ritual of love I threw down my garland and rushed out of the temple leaving her and everybody else behind.

I knew I could no longer return to my spiritual community. I searched for refuge, comfort, healing and oblivion in the embrace of the hot-blooded chandala. I received all these at least for the time being.

The chandala was a master in physical love. I traversed heights and depths of pleasure that I would have never even dreamt about with the young and inexperienced Brahmin girl. She let me feast upon her body, but cunningly kept me away from her soul. And when she managed to make me fatally dependant on her mature and skilled body that gave me pleasures no one else could, when I ended up wanting her only for myself and myself alone, wanting her to open up her gate burning with the invisible flames of lust, for no one else but me... she took away even her body from me. The chandala served God Kama, not men, and God have mercy on those who, blinded by the thirst for lust, wanted to possess her. I was thrown into the tormenting pains of jealousy, into the hell of the insane attachment. My soul was attacked by the toxic flora of the embittered grudge and seasoned fruits of hatred and revenge. After the chandala left me I had a new demented purpose of life: to possess every woman blessed by nature with a desirable body, no matter who she was or to which caste she belonged. With the help of the tantric knowledge I had acquired in the community and my experiences with the chandala I could possess any woman I wanted, but I indulged in pleasures with them only as long as their awakening love made them my defenceless prisoners, then I abandoned them and searched for new ones. With every woman I had I wanted to take revenge upon the chandala and on my young lover who had pushed me away.

I pursued this odd pilgrimage, lurching from one woman to another for years. Though the successful revenge satisfied me for a time, I felt my soul drying out, and hatred transformed into apathy. With that surfeit of pleasures the desire turned into disgust and a flickering light of remorse smouldered in me.

The black-diamond eyes of my former love that so long ago I had pushed into oblivion started to shine again, calling me. I started for the temple of Shiva where I had last seen her. The temple was empty. I only found an old sadhu, who informed me that once an eccentric spiritual community had lived there, but that it no longer existed. A cunning demon attacked them, managing to destroy the spiritual unity of the community. The great Shiva withdrew his grace from them, the community disbanded, and some of its members headed for the mountain forests in the north.

I rushed into the woods and wandered the land for years. I desperately searched for my companions and my love with the perseverance of a madman. Without success. In the end a bloodthirsty tiger helped my soul escape from the prison of my uselessly wandering body.

The chandala whose seductive groin made me abandon the spiritual path, reappeared in my present life. Our relationship two lives ago had been a decisive turning point in the Destiny of both of us. For me it was an apparent setback that pulled me into the whirling waters of passion. It actually proved to be an opportunity to learn to ride the waves with steady feet and heart. For her it was the moment, when the seeds of Tantric spirituality were planted in her soul.

I met her in this life as a physically and spiritually mature and refined woman. As though she had to compensate me for a past debt, it was through the sacred gateway of her body that I stepped onto the path of spirituality, the path I had left because of her, lives before. This woman, who was the first to initiate me into the secrets of art and love in this life, is called Carina Dahl.

My next birth took place at the end of the eighteenth century in England. Fate, that almost compels the traveller to follow the path he had chosen in a decisive moment, inevitably pushed me towards the fulfilment of my destiny. This force now metamorphosed into a yearning for occult knowledge and inescapably led me towards the marshy grounds of magic. An infamous witch initiated me into the secrets of sexual magic.

My former lives' experiences and abilities, although only unconsciously, reached across to my new personality in the form of desires and endowments, and this made me exceptionally quick in learning. I soon surpassed my initiator, who became jealous of my growing powers and tried to destroy me. She could not – it was too late – so we became deadly enemies. We fought dreadful battles of magic. For many a year I was unable to defeat her, but in the end I resorted to a trick: I seduced her daughter who revealed me the weak points of her mother. After that it was an easy job to destroy her. But this did not mean the end of my loathsome enemy. After her death she continued to send me threatening messages through her daughter endowed with mediumistic capacities. And she hasn't ceased to do this even in my current life, in which her daughter took the shape of Sibylla Hultgrens, whose seductive body attracted me with such numbing force. There was another character in my infernal life on the Stockholm stage, who appeared between the eerie memories of my previous life: Magnus Evans. He joined me as a disciple at the zenith of my career as a magus. He was assiduous and possessed an astonishing desire for knowledge. He was flattering and servile with the strong, but extremely cruel with the weak. I had known his greed would sooner or later lead him towards practices of black magic so I decided to deny him the most important initiations. Then he changed tactics. He seduced the ex-Sibylla to be able to use her abilities of a medium to connect with the dark forces of the other world. He could even manage to persuade her to have a child whom they would sacrifice on the altar of Satan. This is how he wanted to master the most terrible occult forces. But Sibylla revealed their monstrous plan while under hypnosis, and I was able to save the child. I made all the arrangements with the authorities to have Magnus sentenced to lifelong imprisonment. I adopted and raised the child and tried to keep her far from everything connected with magic. I became very fond of her but, however tenaciously I tried, I was unable to stifle her nature, the personality she had inherited from her parents. As soon as her body was mature enough she became the favourite courtesan of the neighbourhood. It was still better than to follow the family tradition and become a witch. One day fate brought her together with a travelling monk who had a great effect on her: from one day to the next she renounced her life as a courtesan and, denying her own nature, she decided to retire to a convent. I later met this girl as Christa Forshman; the travelling monk turned out to be my best friend, Arne Larsson. Enthusiastic about his success, the monk tried to usher me onto the right path too. He spent a lot of time near me – too much time – and this led to his downfall. I turned out to be stronger. My female disciples were experts in sexual magic and, after they had been able to charm him out of his habit, he never wore it again. He became prisoner of the carnal pleasures he had tasted. The predecessor of Arne Larsson tried to triumph over forces that were unknown to him. He still had a lot to experience to become the adult and mature Arne Larsson who would many years later wear again the robe of Christ's shepherds.

I met Éva Zoltay in that life too for the first time. I set my eyes upon her during my voyage in the Middle East. I bought that Arabian dancer right away and she soon became my favourite partner in sexual magic, at least until I visited Venice where I saw the Brahmin girl again, the woman who would later become my Laurianne. Something in me instinctively recognized and sensed her.

A famous courtesan, rich men competed for her favours. She refused me in spite of the fact I promised her incredible riches only to spend one night with her. She was adamant. I asked and begged her in vain – she would not give herself to me, not once.

After my trip to Venice my life changed. An odd emptiness began to grow in me and everything that had interested me until then – magic, love, the secret knowledge – became once and for all pointless. I felt the painful absence of something, but I did not know what that something could have been, so I didn't know where to look for it. One day a beautiful dark-skinned girl with glowing eyes knocked on my door. She wanted to be my disciple. She asked me to initiate her into my secrets... the secrets of love. Dazzled by her beauty, I failed to see the germ of destruction she was carrying – had I been more attentive I would have seen it. I accepted her as my disciple without any hesitation and soon she became my lover. When the symptoms of syphilis appeared on my body a few months later I knew I was sentenced to death. She had known she was sick, but was visiting me on Sibylla's instruction. As a matter of fact she was learning witchcraft from Sibylla.

Despite my rage and desire to kill her, I decided to have mercy on her. I realized she was nothing more than an ignorant tool of my former enemy, the powerful witch that once initiated me in the secrets of sexual magic. It was her mortal revenge that reached me now through Sibylla and her infected disciple. Still, my physical destruction did not satisfy her. It was my soul she wanted and continued to fight for it in my present life, using Sibylla again. To this very day I feel an icy chill running through my spine when I think about how easily I could have lost my soul. I know only providence saved me which, for some mysterious reason, never abandoned me. Just as I had been hanging onto an invisible golden thread when thrown into dark and dangerous waters, to learn to swim, while struggling for my life. A mysterious force pulled me to the surface each time the vortices were about to swallow me, even though many of my companions have been swallowed by that unmerciful, dark funnel! It seems the Almighty had traced me a different destiny though, and all these were nothing but preparations. Preparations for a task whose importance can be best measured by the seriousness of the training...

24. Roots deepening in the past

The thought of facing my past lives awoke quite contradictory feelings in me. There was, of course, curiosity – without its beneficial propulsion no knowledge, wisdom or discovery would exist. But there was also a tension accompanying this desire to find out more. I was afraid of what may come to light. What would happen if it turned out a friend or family member had been my enemy, torturer or even killer in my past life? What would I feel towards them? Would I still be able to respect and love them?

I was most worried about Balder's past. I couldn't imagine how my feelings would change when I came face to face with that someone whose body was not Balder's. Not his personality, yet he was still him. He whom I now loved so much. But was I really loving the real him? Was it actually not that body, those eyes, that personality that attracted me, fascinated me, enchanted me and awoke in me something I called love?

I was certain that we had met before. And not only because of the unusual dream we had both had. Another strange experience had strengthened my supposition... It had happened during a paired meditation. We were sitting in a candle-lit room, looking deeply into one another's eyes. Since we were trying to sense each other's soul, I was less concerned with what I saw than what I felt. Suddenly I realized that Balder's face, or at least the Balder picture projected onto the screen of my mind, was starting to change. It carried on until it had totally transformed. It was as though his gaze had remained, but the lines of his face were different. Strangely this face also seemed familiar. Although I knew I had never seen it before I was sure it was Balder's face. Or I should say it was that someone's face I knew as Balder.

Not long after that unusual experience I read somewhere that this was a way to see someone's past-life face ...

The experience fired my curiosity, and finally Balder and I asked the Master for permission to delve into our past lives.

❖

The preparation seemed difficult. Never before had I done my yoga practice with the intensity as in that one month. But that wasn't the most challenging part; I wasn't allowed to read anything during the time, nor was I allowed to watch TV or go to the theatre, and I had to reduce my communication with people to a minimum. My only relief was that lovemaking was not on the forbidden list! I was delighted because in that period our amorous encounters always had an extra special aspect. My senses were unusually heightened as a result of the many cleansing practices, and this amplified all my sensations. As though I could see everything through a magnifying glass, hear the tiniest sounds from invisible loud-speakers. Even tastes and smells surprised me in a richness of shades I'd never before experienced. To say nothing of touch...

❖

We started our experiment on 26th February at four in the morning as that was the time Gregor calculated would be best. I spent five days in a windowless room, lighting a candle for certain practices only. The rest of the time I sat in total darkness. The long-lasting lightlessness had an unusual effect not only increasing my subtle ability to sense, but also improving my powers of imagination. So I had to be extremely aware in order to be able to differentiate genuine visions from the products of my imagination. This was the first and most important aspect for me to learn to ensure my efforts would be successful.

I carried on the excavation for buried memories on the archaeological site of my ancient past, for a full five days. During those five days the image of myself underwent startling changes. I knew I could no longer be the same person I had been before. In those five days I aged around five hundred years, and became richer with the memories of two past lives. I relived the most beautiful and the most distressing moments with the intensity of the real experience until I felt the messages and lessons pertaining to my present life spread out before me in full.

I saw friends and acquaintances appear in other costumes, disguised as other people, and was overjoyed to recognize them. I also saw myself in unfamiliar guises, playing long-forgotten roles. I saw myself struggling and suffering, hating and loving. And it was by no means easy to accept that all of it was *me*.

The destinies of the actors were intertwined in my reawakened memories like the colorful threads of an enormous tapestry, interwoven into one stunning picture by its creator's will and imagination. When the complete picture was finally revealed before me, I was filled with awe. I managed to sense something of that we call perfection.

I saw myself as a young Indian girl who was participating in devotion rituals for Shiva. I relived the unusual love that the pretty-faced Brahmin lad, the then Balder, awoke in me. Experiencing again the suffering that

381

overtook me when a cunning prostitute seduced him away from me – and the joy I felt when he returned to me. The crazed fury that flooded me during the sacred ritual of the great Chakra Puja, and the demonic power that forced me to reject him – when I should have united with him in the holiest of love. I relived the excruciating guilt I felt when my partner left the temple, when we had to stop the ritual uncompleted, as the magical order had been broken... because of us... because of me!

That Brahmin lad never returned to the temple, and I too left the community after a while.

I escaped to the mountains to atone and attain an inner triumph over the sufferance, guilt, anguishing physical desire and unfulfilled love through the power of meditation.

I meditated for many years in the quiet of the forests and caves but never managed to find the peace my soul so longed for. Though my guilt abated, the love and desire in my desiccated body still raged, and lascivious astral demons surrounded me, tempting me ceaselessly. In my despair I was desperate to end my life. I was preparing to jump off a high cliff when the goddess Kali appeared before me, scythe in her hand, garland of skulls around her neck, her naked ebony body shining. Her sensual, full lips shockingly, reminded me of the prostitute, the woman who had once seduced my love. As the goddess started to dance, communicating a secret message to me through her movements, I understood my desire to die was the greatest madness since only the body can be destroyed. Sexual desire can never be, as it is the mirror of divine creative energy that belongs not to the body but to the soul. The very living power of the soul. I understood this energy could never be suffocated, only recognized, released and... loved. I realized that for me there was only this one way to Shiva: Cosmic Love. So the dark goddess of death had commanded me to life...

I left my cave and returned to the Temple of Shiva from whence I had fled long, long before. But I found it empty. The tantric community no longer existed. I didn't know what direction to take so I started to pray to Shiva to show me the way. The moment I stepped out of the temple I found myself face to face with the former prostitute. It seemed as though her body was more radiant, her beauty more stunning than before, as though time had no power over her. I fell to my knees in front of her – I, born of the highest caste, at the feet of a chandala – and begged her to be my master to teach me the knowledge of love. As she lifted me from the ground, looking at me with sad eyes, I understood she could no longer help me. My distorted body was unsuitable for erotic love. Instead she took me to a place where the temple dancers, the devadasis, lived a life of service to the gods. And that is where I spent the rest of my days.

According to the temple's traditions the dancing women living there presented every passing man with their love as priestesses of the great

Divine Mother. My body recovered to some extent but its life energy and sparkle had been lost forever. It had grown old. No man wanted me, but at least I could watch the women and men as they joined in the sacred ritual of love and that filled me with joy. I spent most of my time praying and carrying out sacrificial rituals. I tried to appease the gods for what I had done to my body, a vessel been born for love. I had wasted a life that had been given for me to learn to love... and I hoped that at least in my next life I would have the chance to share love as those dancing priestesses of the Divine Mother's temple were doing.

The gods must have listened to my petitions because my wish was granted, even if in a slightly different way than I had imagined. I was reborn, not in India but in Europe. In Venice, the city of Venus. I was born into a poor family and ended up on the streets quite early. I started learning the trade from the bottom, with the hardest and crudest lessons life could throw at me, but within a few years I had managed to cling onto a lifeline. The richest men visited me, and I was awash with money. I bought a gorgeous house, learnt to dance and wrote poems. I was highly prized among men, probably not for my sophistication and attractive looks but because I loved men in a different way than the women around me. Perhaps because of the abilities developed during the devadasi period of my previous life I was able to be equally giving to almost all men. It was a genuine offering. Those I bedded must have felt it.

I refused only one man... without any reasonable explanation. He had come from England and offered an incredible amount for one single night. I could not give myself to him. Something in me protested vehemently although he attracted me irresistibly... Or maybe that was why. I was terrified as I realized he was the first man who could make me his slave. So I resisted. I wanted to remain my own mistress. I knew that a courtesan was not free to love. I refused him. He stayed in town for a couple of weeks, coming to plead with me every day. He even threatened me with a curse, but he was unable to win me over. He left the city totally broken.

After his departure a bitter emptiness remained in me. Though I had denied him my body, he had taken a part of my soul with him. That man was Balder. The love conceived in our Indian lives had swept us together in a more recent incarnation too. Fate had given us another chance to meet, but I had rejected the opportunity again.

Not long after the English gentleman left, a young girl knocked at my door and said she wanted to serve me. I accepted her. Maybe I liked something about her, or maybe I felt sorry for her because of her tattered clothes. Or maybe I was simply lonely. I don't know. Later it transpired that she didn't only want to serve me – she wanted to discover my secrets. She sneaked around all the time, copying the way I moved and spoke. If I had a male guest, she even spied on me in bed. When I confronted her she admitted that she admired me more than anything and wanted to learn from me, that she also wanted to be as famous a courtesan as I was. Although I knew she was not talented enough I started to teach her. She was impatient and skittish, and she was least interested in that which would have been the most important: knowledge and education.

I explained to her in vain that a real courtesan's power rests not in the loins but in the head. She, however, was only interested in quick success. The lascivious female soon awoke in her but she lacked all delicacy and feminine dignity. Extremely jealous of her rivals, she was constantly squabbling with them. Particularly if she had been drinking... Then she could be very impulsive. And that was her downfall. Once she actually strangled a girl on the street who had seduced one of her wealthy clients. She was locked away and thus had plenty of time to consider what a real courtesan is. I found her again in our next lives as one of the most sought-after prostitutes in the city of Seville. She was called Estrella, and she was surprisingly similar to the Venetian courtesan who had been her role model in her previous life...

I became thoroughly sick of that way of life. Men only 'loved' me for sex, but I desired something else. I had emptied the last drop from the cup of lust, but was still tortured by a strange and unquenchable thirst.

In the end I married an older man – the only man who really loved me. He cared for me with gentle, solicitous and considerate love, and was somewhat able to fill the gaping hole in my soul. During the peaceful, happy, passionless years we spent together strong emotional ties grew between us that would once again draw us together in our next lives. He reached the shore first in Marseille. He was called Nicholas Lamy... my crazy-hearted father.

❖

It was awkward to return to the present so suddenly after that long time travel. The present seemed just as dreamlike as those memories dragged out of the ashes of time. I sat hunched by one of the corridor windows for ages before I finally started to see again. Berthold and Emanuel were sweeping sparklingly fresh snow off the garden paths. Shambu, the naughty pup, Kama Pura's newest resident, was chasing the brush and jumping around in the powdery snow, rolling over, sneezing... yelping... The world all seemed so amazing, so perfect! The guys straightened up and looked towards the horizon where the rocky, snowy peaks of the distant mountains stood tall in this clear weather. Did they know that they had been together several hundred years ago, maybe looking out to the blue Himalayas the same way? And Shambu? Had he been with us too? Maybe he had been a mongoose at the time, protecting those living in the temple from snakes...

The first person I met was Gregor. Silently I hugged him to me, strongly, like an old friend I hadn't seen for a long time. A very, very long time... He said nothing, asked nothing. From the strength of my embrace he sensed the experiment had been a success, and that the secret had been uncovered. Finally I did say something, my voice slightly quavering after the long silence.

"Did you know all that?"

"Yes, I've known it for a long time."

"Why didn't you tell us that you know who we are, where we came from and what our task is?"

"It's better if everyone finds out the secrets to their own pasts when the time comes, when they are mature enough. Until then no one really believes it, or they tend to color the events with their own imagination... But I did mention it to you the first time we met. Remember?" he added smiling.

"I remember but at the time I thought you were just joking..."

"You see? That's what I was talking about."

"Yes, but it's hard to judge whether you're joking or being serious."

"I'm telling the most serious truths when I seem to be joking."

"Exactly. Like the Master."

"Yes, like the Master. You know, he and I are one," he said, and it seemed as though he was simply joking again.

"And what happened to the others?"

"Some of them left the path completely. They weren't given the chance to meet us again. There are others I've met with but are not yet ready for me to bring them here. Probably they will be amongst us again soon."

"I've met a person who was there with us then: Antonin Gautier. He lives in Marseille at the moment. Recently he's started to be interested in Tantra. He has amazing abilities, and guess what the most interesting thing is. It's as though the nostalgia for that spiritual community still lives in his spirit. In Marseille he tried to establish an artistic community, but unfortunately he wasn't mature enough, spiritually. He didn't have enough knowledge so he didn't succeed. Of course the people weren't mature enough either... they were too arty."

"Yes, artists form an interesting category of people. Artistic spirits perceive invisible and intangible aspects of Reality more easily than others. They are capable of feeling and sensing things and depths inaccessible to others. They have excellent talents for spiritual practice but they still find it the most difficult to open to spirituality. They find it hard to accept the discipline necessary on the spiritual path – and difficult to accept guidance from another person, from a master. They feel their freedom is threatened, along with their personality and individuality. Those who manage to rise above their attachment to their individuality and open towards universality are able to achieve outstanding results not only on the spiritual way but also in the arts."

"I hope Antonin succeeds – and I hope he'll soon be with us."

"You can help him greatly... to find his way here."

"I've already started. But let's get back to the past for a moment. A few things are still unclear. So, not everyone here in the present Kaula was there in India."

"Yes, there are new ones too. I haven't tried to get all the former members back together. I just wanted to revive the spirit of the former community. Anyone can be a member of the Kaula if they are spiritually ready and have the right spiritual attitude."

"I see. And the Master? I didn't find him among my memories. But I feel that I have met him before."

"The Master was there too. But he didn't mean much for you then. You hadn't recognized him as a Master so you didn't retain any memories of him. Actually he only visited the community once while you were there – not long before the great ritual."

"And what happened to the community after I left the temple?"

"After the failure of the ritual people lost their trust in me and the teachings I represented. Many left and the community broke up."

"And all that happened because of me!" I started to feel guilty now for what I had done five hundred years earlier.

"No," he replied. "It was my fault and my fault only. The Master – who was also my master back then – had warned me that the people weren't ready for the ritual... But I disregarded his warning. I was fixed on holding the ceremony then and there. I knew your situation and I also knew that just one person could cause the whole ritual to fail if they were not in the right spiritual state. But I still tried it. That was a serious mistake. I hadn't realized either that the Master's warning was actually about me; I wasn't mature enough to lead such a ritual. It's really only now that I see how much I didn't know at the time, how unprepared I was. Yes, I've had to learn much since then. And most of all that I should always follow the Master's instructions – under all circumstances."

25 Chakra Puja

It was a Kaula meeting in February when Gregor solemnly announced that on the occasion of the Maha Shiva Ratri, we would be celebrating the ritual of the great ecstasy of love, the Chakra Puja. As he pronounced the words, waves of excitement spread subtly among all of us. That was the first time in the history of Kama Pura any word had been spoken about the possibility of carrying out this enigmatic ritual. Gregor had recently returned from Bucharest where he thoroughly discussed the details with the Master. The Master did not allow everybody to participate. Besides Gregor and Evelina ten couples had the permission to take part in the ritual. Gregor read up the list of names in a calm, resolute manner in the crossfire of sixty-one tense pairs of eyes. Laurianne grasped my hand and held her breath. After we heard our names she held me tight in relief.

In the second part of the meeting only we, the chosen ones, remained in the hall. As a consolation for the others Gregor had added that, were the ritual to be successful, it would be repeated, and more participants would be allowed. But for the first time only those Kaula members were considered by the Master who were well-prepared from every point of view.

Next, Gregor outlined the ritual step by step. We talked over every detail extensively, cleared up all issues that might arise and at the end swore secrecy concerning the magical elements of the ritual.

During the week long preparation we had to be apart from our lovers. We were not allowed to meet them until the start of the ritual. The girls stayed in Kama Pura, we, the men, set out for the mountains. Gregor took us to an astonishing place that had been used for initiation rituals by the priests of Zalmoxis in ancient times: the Great Sphinx of the Carpathians. A mystical atmosphere infused the surroundings even today.

A wild storm raged ceaselessly in the first three days. It swept through the barren rocky plateau with enormous force and covered the white desert with snow dunes of incessantly changing shapes and forms. The firmament, laden with darkly billowing clouds, faintly settled on the uplands. The murky daylight, chequered with snowflakes, was barely able to vanquish the long, black nights. It was impossible to leave the chalet.

We sat in the room all day long and practiced yoga. Interestingly, nature's shrieking and squalling apocalyptic symphony did not bother my exercises one bit. In fact, it was even easier to find that mysterious silence lurking behind the turmoil of clamour and noise: the perfect standstill that cradles all motion.

On the fourth day the elements became silent. The storm glided away together with its snow-laden clouds leaving a clear, deep-blue sky behind. Sparkling sunlight spread over the frozen waves of snow, its blinding whiteness broken only by the emerging flat-headed mushroom stones, and the sphinx in its cloak of silence, that had been guarding the austere horsts and curvilinear glacier valleys with wise dignity for millions of years.

The scenery was breathtaking, the moment unforgettable. The observing mind could easily enter the state of penetrating contemplation and then the deepest meditation. Gregor had chosen the perfect place for our preparation. The surroundings emanated strong yang energy, and even without our conscious knowledge, connected us with the hidden spheres of a cosmic masculinity. If we accept that exceptionally blessed places do exist on Earth, where the divine energy that nourishes spiritual development is more intense than anywhere else, then the Sphinx of the Carpathians is one of these rare areas, along with the plateaus of Tibet or the mysterious valleys of the Himalayas.

Due to the extraordinary atmosphere of the area and, of course, to the intensive spiritual practices, we returned a week later to Kama Pura completely transformed and reborn. We brought with ourselves the power of the fearsome tempest, the majestic silence of the sparkling snow-ocean, and the timeless wisdom of the Sphinx.

In our absence the girls prepared the shrine of Shiva. They placed a platform adorned with flowers in the centre of the hall for the couple who would be leading the ritual. All around there were settees shaped as eight-petal lotus flowers, each with a wooden tray holding accessories for the ritual. The magical space was delineated by a golden thread forming a perfect circle with 108 candles waiting to be lit. Vases filled with splendid flowers hung on each of the four main columns that represented the four cardinal directions of the space.

First only we men entered the sanctuary. According to Gregor's instructions the girls arranged the physical space – it was the men's job to establish the subtle, magical space.

We carried out everything in elevated spirits, in a joyful and tranquil manner, in silence. We all knew exactly what to do. Gregor rang a bell to signal each phase of the preparation. After we were all ready and had lit all the one hundred and eight candles and the incense, Gregor rang the bell three times. The sign for the girls.

Evelina was the first to enter. Her body was covered with a fine, silvery veil that floated stunningly. Only her arms and shoulders were left uncovered. Before stepping inside the magical circle she stopped for a second and closed her eyes. On her face, bearing oriental marks, the light of transfiguration was shining. Fully conscious of her act, she stepped in, and started towards her partner with slow, gracefully erotic steps. An indescribable wonder, a true mystical awe flamed in Gregor's eyes as he helped his beloved, radiating a heavenly beauty, onto the podium. It was easy to recognize in them the divine couple. Shiva and Shakti, god and goddess, expressed themselves perfectly in their beings, now meta-morphosed by the magical power of transfiguration.

Then the other girls came in. Each wore a different veil – the specific colours of the feminine cosmic forces they embodied. They surrounded the central dais and started a glorious dance of invocation. They danced dressed in invisible spheres of energy. I watched them transfixed. Each showed a trait I had never seen in them before and had thought in-compatible with their identity – but in fact they were only incompatible with the limited picture I had formed about them.

Amrita, whom I had known with a fragile body and dreamy eyes, now made me shiver with the frightfully penetrating look, and ruthlessly beautiful smile of Kali, the goddess of Time, death and ceaseless change. Éva's tigress body – always ready to burst – was now covered by a veil that evoked the deep calm of a blue sky. Her slow and generous movements summoned the great cosmic power of the infinite space, the birth-giving mother of the visible and invisible worlds, Bhuvaneshvari, and her all-embracing love. Antonia's warmly inviting body was now engaged in a tempestuous dance evoking Chhinnamasta's power. Her shining eyes were spreading sparkles, and her impetuously swinging arms hurled lightning bolts of a divine brilliance able to destroy all illusions. I saw my lionhearted love, the uncrowned queen of Power and Will, appear in the form of the merciful Tara, wearing a simple white veil. Tara's compassionate and all-forgiving love reflected on her angelic face, and in her eyes Tara's silently calling starry gaze was shining.

All girls' dances were breathtaking. Each in itself, but together they formed a kind of sublime unity, a perfect, unearthly harmony. They managed to evoke Universal Beauty, the transcendental essence of Nature's thousand-faced grace. The rainbow splendour of the iridescent veils, the jewels glittering in the candle light, hips gracefully swaying , undulating naked arms promising embraces, never to be forgotten, breasts peeking through the veils waiting to be stroked... all this combined into an embodiment of the female mystery. That ancient power, so unfathomable, so unreachable and inconceivable but so alluring, as it bears the promise of the ecstasy of beauty and unrestrained happiness. The power that makes the World go round, and enables Nature's yearly rebirth, that gives life to all the living and confers meaning to every life, every passing pleasure, sorrow and suffering, every battle and victory. My senses greedily drank in the splendid sight, and slowly the recognition crept to the bottom of my heart that beauty is nothing else but love become visible, love *made* visible.

The tinkling sound of the bell awoke me from my blissful daze. The girls had completed their dance and were walking towards their partners. Laurianne, both palms folded on her breasts, approached me with slow steps. Laurianne? No. Tara herself, goddess of divine compassion and mercy. I reached towards the belt of her lily-white dress with timid excitement and shaking hands, as though I was about to untie the silk thread of a precious gift. That is what it was, a true gift... the most sacred gift man can receive from Life.

After a few timeless moments, her stunning nudity unfolded before my eyes. A nudity so familiar – every inch of it imprinted in the memory of my skin – yet so mysterious and new, so alluring and soul-stirring; I had the feeling I was seeing her for the first time. She undressed me, and we sat down on the lotus flower settees facing each other. We performed the ritual of the five elements summoning and calling to life in our inner universe the hidden forces of the earth, water, fire, air and ether.

When finally our bodies, now turned into channels of cosmic energies, united, I felt my consciousness exploding into millions and millions of tiny drops of light. Each drop separately knew and loved the wonderful creature I had in front of me, who was more than a hot embracing body, more than human emotions. She was boundless divine love, encompassing all the tiny light-seeds of my consciousness that were filling the unlimited space. I felt this was the perfect fulfilment, the utmost aim from where there is nowhere else to go, the end of the road. But I was wrong. The miracle continued as our bodies – the most limited part of our being – set in motion. I experienced in surprise that the completeness I considered as perfect developed yet further, enriched with new colours and more and more subtle shades. I turned my attention back to the marvellous mechanism that even in its limited nature is able to connect with the absolute and the endless: my body that even in its material and mortal condition can host the immaterial and the immortal. The transcendent consciousness of my wholeness did not cease to exist when I turned my attention towards the material world. It was like a double consciousness: I was transcendent and immanent at the same time and lived both conditions of existence with great joy. My senses launched into the infinite I ecstatically drank in all things that were around and inside me. I was exalted to breathe in the intoxicating scent of incense and candles, the maddening fragrance of the love-making bodies, to drink the sweet breath from the wet lips of my Laurianne. I watched in beatitude and wonder the gently undulating movements of the couples melted into each other in the ecstasy of love.

The scope of what I could sense expanded more than ever before. I clearly saw, heard and felt everything happening inside the magic circle of the candles. I could hear the slightest friction of the farthest bodies as distinctly as I heard my own lover's sighs of pleasure. On my skin I felt the scorching nakedness not only of her body, but that of all the women present. It was only then I realized I had stepped through the threshold of all physical sensation. Even when I closed my eyes I was still able to see everything. Eyes open or eyes closed it was all the same. It was an extraordinary way of looking. Wherever I focused my attention I could see everything from all sides and angles, as if my observing eyes were present in every point of space at the same time...

It was an entrancing feeling. Miraculous. Scents, tastes, sounds, touches melted into a perfect unity. Just like harmonies of a heavenly symphony. Each sensation was enthralling by itself but in their simultaneity could elevate the soul to celestial heights. My consciousness expanded to cosmic dimensions again and I felt boundless. Nights and days alternated to the rhythm of my heartbeat, and the tiniest atoms of my body became stars of the cosmic space with electron-planets revolving around them. I was infinite Space and eternal Time – and everything beyond them. I experienced the state of pure and lucid existence that is sheer ecstasy and immeasurable happiness. That was the first time I felt anything like that, and I was astonished to see that this divine joy had the same taste as fulfilled love. The veil dropped from a great secret. I understood that love is the greatest and most valuable gift we have received from the Creator; and through consummated love, man can truly become alike to God. The man who the Omnipotent created in his own image. Not the thought was new – my mind knew all these long before – but the sensation and the experience. It was fresh and indescribable, intangible yet so alive and so very real. In the light of this immense feeling all everyday problems, all the things we fight and suffer for with such proud gravity seemed so absurd, so unreal.

Immense gratitude flooded through me for all that I had been allowed to live, to feel. But the next beat of my cosmic consciousness was compassion. I realized that for most people the reality consists only of the struggles, little joys and annoying inconveniences of everyday life. They do not even dream about the existence of this other reality, the true reality – at most, there may be silent hunches lurking in the bottom of their souls sending silent messages about it. This idea saddened me. Because of this human feeling, my cosmic consciousness withdrew into its human limitations. The difference is that now I was heavy with a new desire: to share my experience with others, with those who still wriggle in the net of ignorance, sentenced to suffering by their own self-imposed ideas of helplessness. I almost felt the pain caused by the suffering in the world, like great Christian saints must have felt. Then I remembered the Master's words speaking about the difference between saints and wise men. He said: "Saints suffer together with the people, wise men teach them how to put an end to their suffering". I did not want to be a saint, I wanted to become a wise man, just like the Master, who taught so many people how to be happy.

That was the moment I realized that the spirit of the Master had been with us the whole time. He protected us and guided us throughout the ritual. The universal state of consciousness, experienced not only by me, but all who had the chance to be there, was also his gift. These thoughts conceptualized in me only after my mind returned to its normal condition. I was again aware of where I was. My love was still sitting in my lap, her hands and thighs embracing me. She stayed motionless, only her chest was trembling from the emotions breaking forth from the depths. Tears glittered on her transfigured face.

I looked around. All the others were still embracing; Éva and Berthold were looking deep into each other's eyes; Emanuel laid his head and black locks of hair on Antonia's breasts and was holding her tight; Natalia sat in her sweetheart's lap, her head leaning slightly back, large tears streaming from her closed eyes. He was looking at her, his eyes shining with adoration. Gregor and Evelina were no longer embracing but looking around smiling.

Laurianne was the first to move. She squeezed my hand, stood up slowly and made for the centre of the circle. First she embraced Gregor, then Evelina. A little later Amrita joined them. Then I saw Emanuel walking towards the centre, followed by Antonia, Berthold, Éva, and all the others. I was the last. I wanted not just to feel but to see too the celebration of happiness becoming consummate. As if we wanted to preserve the unity acquired in the realm of spirit, taking it to the material world. We had but one means to do it: our body, and one way to attain it: to embrace.

26. "As above, so below..."

A dry, icy wind swept along the street, stirring up a suffocating cloud of dust, whipping the rubbish freed from the blanket of snow into a wild dance. Blackened leaves, newspapers with flapping wings and squashed plastic cups like startled birds whooshed into the air only to land again a few meters away.

A dark-skinned boy was sitting on the worn steps of a high-rise, his back hunched. An old man at the age of ten. Tatty pumps on his feet, no socks, drowned in a huge shabby pullover. Only his bony fingers were poking out of the ragged sleeves, gripping a smoking cigar butt. Bold eyes looked me up and down as he inhaled the grey poison with defiant enjoyment.

People in tatty old clothes were passing by: builders with lime on their caps; hard-faced, prematurely aged gypsy women; staggering men with dishevelled hair; an irritated young woman dragging a whining child; an old tramp with a yellowed-grey beard. All looked at me with mistrust and a suspicious curiosity. They realized from a mile off that I was a stranger to these parts, a residential district on the edge of the city inhabited by people squeezed out to the periphery of both settlement and society – mainly gypsies.

The sounds betraying a horrific argument could be heard from a window. A male voice swearing vehemently; a screeching woman's voice suffocated in hysterical sobbing; the heartbreaking cries of a baby. I stopped for a moment under the window. I listened, my heart constricted, my stomach churning whilst my imagination painted vivid pictures of the terrible family scene. I heard a violent crash, and then some dull thuds before terrifying silence... broken by the baby's uneven cries a few minutes later.

Horrified I walked on.

Since I'd moved into the ivory tower of Kama Pura I had forgotten that this kind of life exists on earth. Or at least I had tried not to think about it. Now, faced with it again, I shuddered. A few hours earlier I'd been playing with the girls in the exotic plant paradise of the Shakti Loka. My skin retained the memory of the bath water, the scent of the fine oils and the pleasant tingle of the sensual massage. Now I was going along that potholed street saturated with the heavy stink of onions frying and rotting sauerkraut, walking at the foot of towering concrete boxes, drying sheets flying like flags above my head, and my privileged life in Kama Pura was making me feel uncomfortable. Somehow I felt responsible for these people to whom

Life had been so tight-fisted when handing out joy. They had to fight a daily battle for their survival, unravelling their lightless lives from Destiny's net with apathetic indifference. People, who in their embitterment and helplessness make each other's lives even bitterer, even more unbearable...

Actually I had come here to awaken the feeling of compassion in myself. We were preparing for the ritual of the Maha Shiva Ratri day and each of us girls had drawn a straw to decide what cosmic powers we were to embody during the ceremony. I had received Tara, cosmic power of divine mercy and compassion. That had really set me thinking. Particularly since Evelina said she had made the magical integration for the drawing of lots so everyone would receive the cosmic power from which she had the most to learn, and whose specific energy and attributes she most needed to awaken in herself...Close self-examination revealed compassion was definitely not among my main qualities. Instinctively I had always valued and admired those people who were strong, courageous, determined and ready for action. I was looking down on the weak, the coward, the compromiser. I judged everyone who was unable to take control of their own lives or step out of suffering, debauchery and poverty. I thought all this stemmed merely from weakness and negligence, and that everyone had the chance to change their lives. I had never considered that not everyone has the same degree of personal freedom, nor had taken into account what a significant role karmic debt has on our lives... That might have been the reason Tara chose me. And inspired me to come here so I could better empathize with those Fate had ordered difficult life circum-stances in this incarnation.

A grubby-faced kid stretched out his even grubbier hands towards me. A pleading and coaxing smile on his face. I reached into my pocket and dropped all the change I found into the waiting palm. He ran off without saying thank you. The next second another five were leaping up around me. I had no idea where they could have sprung from so suddenly. They begged in whining voices, imploring me to give them some too. I took some bank notes out of my purse. They snatched them from my hand immediately, then from each other too. They grabbed each other, fought terribly, hitting and kicking. They even tore two of the notes to shreds. The third was scrunched up and stuffed into a mouth before being swallowed.

Disappointment flooded through me. I would have liked to help some-body. I clutched my money to me with the thought that I would divide it between the truly needy. I was well aware I wasn't going to change all the suffering of humanity. I wasn't even going to be able to save this hovel from want. But I still hoped I could at least provide some people with a little joy. Although my first attempts had drowned in disgraceful failure, I didn't give up. I searched for more needy people. A shabbily-dressed, middle-aged woman was standing at the bus stop with a wide-eyed boy who was clinging to her skirts. He was in a threadbare tracksuit he'd long since outgrown. I was sure some financial aid would be welcome. I approached them and proffered my offering, a decent amount. First the woman went red before she practically screamed at me that she was no beggar and that, even if their clothes were not as new as mine, they would rather die of starvation than accept alms from someone.

I stood abashed and felt terribly ashamed. The people around me were staring at me as though they'd caught me stealing... if not something worse! I stuttered an apology and tried to leave with dignity, but as fast as possible.

My God, it was so hard to help these people! Some were capable of poking out the other's eye in greed. Others pushed away an outstretched hand out of ridiculous pride! Suddenly I saw the whole thing as totally pointless. My throat went dry, and I felt drained. As if I were paying for my failed attempts with my own energy. I asked Tara for help.

I wandered around aimlessly for a while until a place with BAR written above it caught my interest. I stepped in cautiously. It was a smoky, smelly pub with four or five tables, and a couple of men who looked like regulars. Every eye fixed upon me. I was too embarrassed to turn tail and escape, so I went up to the bar and asked for a glass of mineral water. I thought I'd just drink it quickly and then disappear. But in the meantime a man of about fifty caught my eye. I didn't know why, he was no different from the others. I studied him closely. His cheekbones stood out on his stubbly, sagging face. Large bags swept under his eyes. He must have been a good-looking man once; the lines describing his high forehead and noble arch of his eyebrows were testament to that. A bottle of gin stood in front of him. Not much was missing, but the man looked determined to finish it. A deep sadness filled his eyes. Something moved inside me. Did I feel sorry for him? Maybe... Suddenly I moved next to him and asked if I could sit at his table. He gestured I could with poorly disguised confusion. I saw a gleam of happiness but also that he felt extremely awkward. He didn't dare look at me, keeping his eyes down, as though he had something to hide.

I drew him into conversation. I asked about all sorts. Whatever popped into my mind: his life, work, family... Slowly he loosened up and started to tell his story. He lived alone, his family had left him, and he'd been kicked out of the school where he'd worked as a history teacher – all because of the alcohol, of course. He spoke about his wife and two children with bitter nostalgia. He said he wasn't even allowed to see them anymore, that they called him a good for nothing, and were 'right too' because his life was 'worth nothing' and everything 'was over anyway'.

I was genuinely sorry for him and would have loved to help. But I had no idea what I could do for him. I just sat and listened... and I sensed he was happy to get it all off his chest. I was secretly pleased to see he'd forgotten about the bottle. He said he'd read a lot at one time and written poems. When we started to speak about books I saw just how much his mood changed. I tried to get him to talk about his positive experiences, hoping I'd be able to rekindle some hope for life in him. I didn't want to go into the destructive effects of alcohol – he already knew about them all too well and hated it just as much as he was a slave to it. I chose to speak of the beauty and pleasures of life; about people having the power to change their own lives; about being less helpless against the power of Fate than we think; about the chance for change at any time, being better and forgiving ourselves for our past mistakes; about being able to put right our faults – if we genuinely regretted them...

As he listened with increasing interest I felt my words had left an impression on him. Maybe not my words so much as the energy they radiated. An energy that was not my own. I was merely the surprised witness of its manifestation.

I glanced at my watch and nearly cried out in amazement – I'd been there for three hours! I'd been smoked for three hours in this stinky dive. It was as though time had stopped, but I had to leave. I invited him to a smart restaurant for lunch the next day. I felt something had started that had to be continued. He was speechless in his surprise, his face shone with true pleasure.

The next day at noon he was waiting for me outside the restaurant. It was my turn to be surprised. Shaved and with brushed hair, wearing an ironed suit and white shirt, he looked rested and totally different from the previous day. He announced with pleasure that he hadn't drunk anything since we'd met and that he'd even left the open bottle there on the table. He produced a bunch of garden flowers from behind his back, blushing slightly as he gave them to me. I don't think I had ever been so happy to receive flowers.

We continued our conversation at lunch. I started about my life. I couldn't speak about Kama Pura, but I told him about my student years, about the man who'd nearly become my husband, my Indian adventures, dance and love. I also said I had a partner I loved very much. I told him about Tantra and my sexual experiences. And I saw his amazement not only at what I told him but also at my naturalness and openness.

We walked for a good while in the park after lunch. He was in excellent spirits and was already talking about his plans. He wanted to start a new life. He wasn't going to drink anymore and, if he couldn't be together with his former family, then he would try and start a new family. He also confided in me that there was a woman he'd liked for some time but, because of his destructive addiction, he'd never approached her. But everything would be different. He asked my advice about how to captivate this woman... I was delighted to assist. I reassured him that if he followed my advice he would definitely be successful.

Before we parted he kissed my hand politely and thanked me cheerfully for my company, saying he felt as though he'd been reborn...

I didn't weave illusions. I knew the rebirth of alcoholics is usually short-lived, but somewhere deep in my soul I still trusted that our encounter had been fruitful. Because I felt it was not Laurianne who intervened but Tara, the power of divine compassion and providence. She was capable of any miracle. And I realized that you can help people. Just not everyone and not at any time. But if the desire to help is genuine, then life will always bring to you people you can really help.

That was Tara's lesson for me. I felt ready for the ritual.

❖

Stepping into the Shiva sanctuary was like entering a magical space, a different world. A parallel world in which the form of things resembled the usual, but their substance was somehow other. It was more ethereal and surrounded by a mysterious floating light. I stood amazed for a moment. Although we girls had prepared the room for the ritual, it was so changed. I glanced around. One hundred and eight small candle flames were guarding the golden thread that marked the magical space; the intoxicating scent of delicate incense filled the shimmering air. Tiny points of light shone on the vaulted sky-blue ceiling like mysterious stars suggesting immeasurable distances or like miraculous light beings, heralds of the heavenly light gathered for the celebration of Cosmic Love. The pictures, statues and reliefs around the walls emitted an enigmatic luminescence as though they were made of transparent crystal and had secret light sources concealed under the surface. And the men! I had thought I knew them all so well. After a week apart they looked completely transformed. Sitting there in a perfect circle, their motionless bodies like pyramids emitting the stability of cliffs. Their faces radiated the light of an inner sun. I had never before experienced this stunning manifestation of male energy.

Enchanted, and slightly excited, I stepped close to the line of the magic circle. The second I entered that small universe marked by the candles, an unusual tingling ran through my body as though a subtle electric current had been switched on in me. Filling me with a pleasant sensation, it gave me enormous dynamism. Suddenly I felt that here, within the light circle, the boundaries of the material world dissolved and the laws of physics lost their power. I felt I could fly or move objects, even people, with the power of thought. The seductive temptation of omnipotence flashed through me for a moment, and I sensed the danger this power represents on the spiritual path. But I was also aware that at that moment my only task was to transform this enormous energy, transfigure it into its purest and most elevated form: all-embracing love.

With one single thought concentrated into a shining mantra sound and slow movements I began my dance of invocation. Intent male looks flew towards me from every direction like flaming arrows, igniting a secret fire in me. A kind of fire that flames and illuminates, but doesn't burn.

My body moved almost imperceptibly. The real dance came from somewhere inside. It was the dance of my energies flooding from the invisible sphere of my being directed by my focused consciousness with crystal clarity. The luminous power lines of my astral body met with other energy currents ignited by the dance of the girls in the invisible energy realm. I felt this miraculous shared energy dance become ever more in rhythm to the beating of God's heart, an active part of the Universe's mysterious circulation. In this universal energy current I maintained the awareness of being myself. When I finally walked up to my Balder I was both the compassionate Tara and the in-love Laurianne. But this Laurianne was not only a sensual lover now, but also a caring mother, attentive sibling, generous friend and initiatory woman imbued with divine powers. All in one person. I felt the pressure of some ancient desire, to melt into the man standing before me who, strangely, was now simultaneously my lover, my father, my brother, my friend and my child. I desired to sink into him, to melt with him, to feel in my own being that enigmatic something that that made him *him*. That made him disturbingly different from *me*, and irresistibly attractive too...

When the moment came and his arms embraced me, my body receiving his, I felt the invisible parts of us were also finding each other, fusing together, and permeating the other. As we dissolved like milk and water mixing I felt that what he had been up till that point I was now too. I was both he and me for a while. I experienced the mythical androgynous state. I was woman – mysterious, like the moon draped in a veil of cloud; enigmatic like the dark depths of the seas; tender as a velvet petal; strong as lightning born of summer clouds. But I was also man – I felt the radiating power of the shining sun in me; the life force of vigorous trees reaching for the sky, the transcendental harmony of the music of the spheres, the all-attracting and all-uniting power of an upward whirling spiral.

The movements of our bodies fed this miraculous something with renewed waves of delight, this wonderful feeling of unity that kept expanding its boundaries until we enfolded all the other bodies around us, dancing the mysterious rhythm of love's ecstasy. The waves of joy conceived in my body rippled out without obstruction to the others' bodies, and the intoxicating elation of my twenty-one companions was reflected in me a thousand fold. As the feeling in me grew to unbearable proportions a powerful new desire was born: to share it, pour it forth, give it to someone else, to everyone... I was experiencing the most profound mystery of the desire to give. Maybe the Divine existence before the Creation had been a similar state. I felt I was capable of creating new universes from my fathomless love. I could care for my creations as the Divine Mother does, to nurture these beings, to protect them and look after their lives. To punish them, as a warning, my heart aching, when they go astray. To teach them the great secrets of Life with cryptic whispers; to give news of the existence of the invisible reality with the attractive magic of visible beauty; to ignite the leading fires of transitory pleasures for them on the concealed way that leads to the realm of timeless happiness. The intuition of the inexpressible and ineffable secrets of the Creation vibrated in me and for a few moments I felt myself become part of the miraculous Divine Existence. And during these few moments staggering revelations emerged in me. I understood that sexual desire and spiritual aspiration are one and the same energy; that every sigh of delight is a step towards the Creator; that it is God's loving closeness that we seek in every embrace. I understood that every human quest is a quest for the Divine. No matter whether we are looking for pleasures, for love, for wealth, for power or for happiness.

Because the desire for power is none other than the memory of our divine omnipotence. The search for delights stems from the unconscious resonance with the ceaseless divine bliss. The thirst for knowledge is the calling of divine omniscience; life instinct: the hidden faith in divine immortality; the longing to love and be loved: the reflection of the divine unity in us; the desire for freedom: the omnipresent God dwelling in us...

Now I understood the deepest essence of Tantra – this wonderful spiritual path, the way of the great Yes which judges nothing, denies nothing, renounces nothing and is attached to nothing. It accepts all with wisdom, understanding and joy. The journey that teaches us to accept all impulses – the ones bursting from our ancient human nature as well as those rooted in our present character, temperament and habits that reflect the level of our spiritual maturity. To accept, transform, refine and transfigure all these impulses and change their direction from transitory values and everyday ambitions to the Universal, to the Divine, to eternal values: the true goal.

Now I deeply understood the meaning of all that the Master had been emphasizing over the years with such resolute tenacity. I finally under-stood why it was so important to be a real woman for those born in a woman's body, and to be a real man for those incarnated as men. I understood why we need to heighten the tension between the two polarities, why we need to take sexual desire to its extreme... I felt infinite gratitude to the Master through whom I had been able to experience all this and discover Kama Pura, the real Kama Pura: the Isle of Delights that is within us! That special station on the spiritual way where the soul can provide itself with the most valuable nourishment for the last and most difficult stretch of the journey.

For the stage where practical methods are no longer of any use, and all intellectual knowledge becomes worthless. Where the only power taking us forward is the infinite desire to unite our hearts with the heart of God, and where there is only one aid we can count on: divine Grace.

I felt the Master's presence. The Master's true essence, the vast energy sphere that had been with us throughout the ritual, watching out for us and directing us. I sensed the Master's *spirit*, that had nothing more to do with the *body* I identified him with than I shared with the veil that my love had freed me from…

The Master's presence seemed so obvious that I instinctively opened my eyes to see him in his body. But all I saw was his exquisite and penetrating eyes illuminating from a portrait of him. His spirit though had filled the magical space and his power, the effect of which I already knew so well, was radiating from the centre of the circle. From where Gregor was sitting. It was as though the Master was present through Gregor's body.

It was the end of the ritual. The couples were embracing, motionless. Gregor was looking around smiling, happy, satisfied. We caught each other's eyes for a flash, and an unusual tingling ran through my body – it was like looking at the Master!

I felt an irresistible desire to hold him in my arms. I went over to him. His hug radiated the Master's all-permeating love that attracted everyone towards the centre like a magnet until we were moulded into one enormous hug… all twenty-two of us.

It was deeply moving to recognize just how strongly the body desires the union the moment souls unite. "As above, so below." The union was now complete. We realized it on all levels. From Spirit to Matter.

Yes, we were finally one. After five hundred years! We had needed five hundred years to prepare for this… It was five centuries ago that the Kaula, the idea of a spiritual community based on the unity of hearts, had been born in one of the Master's yet immature disciples. The secret threads woven between us so long ago still linked us together.

They pulled us together once again from the remote distances of space and time to unite in this wonderful spiritual oasis. And the Great Ritual of Love's Ecstasy that we had wanted to realize on a Maha Shiva Ratri five hundred years earlier, was to be completed only now. On this God-blessed day of 12th March 2002. The very day India was celebrating Maha Shiva Ratri… and the Master the fiftieth birthday of his present life on earth…

27. Together

"Do you remember the moment when we met the Master after the ritual?"

"Yes. He hugged us both to him like a worried father would his children returning from a long journey. You had tears in your eyes and asked, 'Master, was that Enlightenment?'"

"And he replied, 'That was *an* enlightenment. But not the final spiritual liberation. For a moment you experienced the state of cosmic consciousness of your oneness with the Divine. But you still have a lot to work until you reach the immutable and complete revelation of your Divine Self. And you have to be more awake than ever. There have been many who reached enlightenment, but then slid back again and the fog of oblivion settled on their mind.' That seemed so unbelievable I cried out, 'My God, how on earth can someone forget a state like that?'

'On Earth you can' he continued, 'Before you reach final liberation you will always be inclined to forget. Our smaller self, the ego, can regain control of the wheel at any time and at that stage the ego hides in a particularly refined disguise that is difficult to recognize. Shadows of spiritual conceit might be cast upon this divine state of consciousness. The ego will treat the experience as its own realization, its own possession, starting to be proud of it. So the experience of enlightenment begins to dim, fading into a distant, foggy memory. The snake of doubt slithers between our thoughts insidiously, unnoticeably. Was it really true? Or was it only my imagination playing tricks on me?'"

"When I asked what we should do to preserve this state, he said: 'Relive it over and over again. As often and as intensively as possible. This is the secret way to overpower Time, this is the way you can turn your past into your present, and consciously create your future. Let your every meeting in love be like this, at least. A true cosmic union. Never feel satisfied with less because then you will regress.'"

"Hearing the Master's words you sighed in a happy relief and said, 'that means our journey together has not come to an end!'"

"Yes, and I remember the Master's subtle smile when he replied, 'Your journey together has just come to a beginning. Now you have finally met and recognized one another, and you remedied the mistakes you once made out of ignorance and lack of experience. Now you can continue walking your spiritual paths together as a tantric couple until you achieve the glorious state of androgyny. From there it is only a step to the complete and ultimate Liberation.'"

"Yes, those were his exact words. I felt such happiness that I could travel along the path with you!"

"You'll see what a wonderful and exciting journey it will be."

"Come, my love, play your music. I want to dance for you."

Lightning Source UK Ltd.
Milton Keynes UK
UKOW05f1933291216
290998UK00001B/176/P